Mourning Child

Letters From The Grave

J. K. Grueber

MYSTIC RIDGE PUBLISHING, LLC

Mystic Ridge Publishing, LLC

Mysticridgepublishing.com

ISBN: 978-1-965796-14-6 (Ebook)

ISBN: 978-1-965796-15-3 (Paperback)

ISBN: 978-1-965796-16-0 (Hardcover)

Cover design by: J. K. Grueber, Bruce Sanderson, Anne Graff, Andrew Grueber, and William Grueber.

Contributing cover photo and editor: Bruce Sanderson, Sanderson-Decello Design, LLC.

Printed in the United States of America.

Dedicated

To all of those who have mourned a loss.

In 1969, psychiatrist Elisabeth Kübler-Ross introduced the five stages of grief as a means of understanding and navigating the emotional terrain of loss. The stages—**denial, anger, bargaining, depression, and acceptance**—can be mild or overwhelming with every one of us suffering in our own way.

In this novel, the fictional main character, Kip Patterson understands the stages from an early age, but even he finds himself in an emotional tailspin when tragedy strikes.

If you, or someone you know is struggling with this emotional minefield, know that you are not alone and help is only a phone call away. Be sure and reach out to grief counselors, hotlines, or support groups in your area.

By J. K. Grueber

The Envy Series:
COLORS OF ENVY: A Paranormal Romance Mystery
FACES OF ENVY: A Paranormal Romance Mystery
ECHOES OF ENVY: A Paranormal Romance Mystery

The MacDade Brothers Mysteries:
EXPOSED IN SHADOWS: He Who Plays.
A Paranormal Mystery Rekindling Lost Love
EXPOSED In The CROSSHAIRS: He Who Rides
A MacDade Brothers Paranormal Mystery
EXPOSED By The RIVERSIDE: He Who Lives
A MacDade Brothers Paranormal Mystery

The Vampire Tales:
Cursed At Conception: The Vampire's Henchman
Damned By Death: The Vampire's Hammer

Prologue

The instant the elevator doors opened, the screech resounded off the paisley-papered walls, ricocheting at a siren pitch. Pain! Wicked pain! Lean muscles lurching off his thin bones, Kip Patterson shoved the metal cart into the hall, his gray eyes darting in either direction. The West Wing. No one dawdled in the halls, neither in wheelchairs nor on walkers. On other floors, ambulatory residents would point him in one direction or another. Here, not even a nurse hustled toward the faint bleep of a call signal. The corridor was empty; the siren wailed above an undertow of moaning and whimpering from the open doors in either direction.

By instinct, abandoning his cart, Kip launched toward the deep end of the hallway, toward the resident's lounge, although few West Wing residents ever occupied the room. Maybe he recognized the pitch, the tone, or something more profound, ethereal, that led him. With a single thought to help the evening charge nurse with the distressed elder, he raced down the hall and spun into the open doorway of Mrs. Ramsey's suite. Skidding, his soles squealing on the shiny floor, he caught his balance on the door jamb.

The smell slammed him, a noxious blend of bowel and urine, then all things at once.

The ding-dong of the nurses' call button emanated from the control dangling near the single recliner. A puddle of black bowel smeared across the floor, flowing from the immense elderly woman presently clinging to the side of the raised hospital bed. Alone in the room, her keening wail echoed off the close walls. Her slippers peddled below her swollen ankles, skidding as if attempting to find balance on a treadmill. She wore a gown, but the fluids soaked the pastel flowers, slicing a stain from the center of her broad back to its hem. Under the bright fluorescents, her gray-streaked black hair bobbed against the pristine white sheets, keeping time with her cries. She hadn't soiled the bed—hadn't fallen off the bed. The russet stream marked her trail from the recliner near the window, where the last vestiges of daylight mixed with the overhead lights.

Immersed in pale gray fog, Mrs. Ramsey clung to the bed within the mist, and Kip knew, as he always knew, the elder wasn't dying—not today. Clearly, he identified the aura encasing her and drew a breath of relief—barely.

Sliding, losing her tenuous hold on the bed, she appeared to melt, drawn toward the walker lying haphazardly in the spreading wretched puddle.

Without a thought, Kip launched forward, breaching the astral shroud and ducking his arms under the flabby limbs. "There now. There. I have you," he heaved and doubted his words an instant later. Three hundred pounds of loose muscle sank against him, and he braced for impact as his load doubled and tripled. She'd relinquished her hold on the rail. Her arthritic fingers grappled with the linens as she slid, by gravity, by slick floor. His rubber soles skidded, and as he halted her descent, the fire shot from his center, snatching his breath, choking and suffocating him. As if skewered, he suffered the flames shooting through his system—suddenly not sure she would survive. If this was her pain—

Her full weight rammed against him. The last of his balance expired as a single thought raged—cushion her fall!

Not losing his hold on the immense body, he skidded in a last-ditch effort to avoid the vile puddle, unwittingly peddling them both away from the bed. Her catheter had either broken or overflowed. Already soaked before he struck the floor, his breath exploded with the fires razing his lean frame. Whether his pain or hers, no longer mattered. Her cries cracked to huffed sobs and broken apologies while struggling to climb off him.

Lungs collapsing, Kip heaved for breath under her weight, fleeting regret over his successful weight loss over the past seven months. On his thirteenth birthday, he'd determined to lose the 'baby fat' that most of the residents were quick to pinch or pat. For just this moment, he wished he were either still short and plump or as musclebound as some of the linebackers in Randall High. He was neither. At close to five feet five, he'd become as lean as a lynx, and under Mrs. Ramson's 300+ lbs., he felt like a pancake—a pancake on fire on a griddle.

Struggling like a wicked comedy routine, he managed to slide from under the once delightful older woman, battling his need to fold against the spikes racing through him. At the edges of his darkening mind, he heard the repetitive ping of the nurse's call signal, silently praying someone would answer that call. Mrs. Ramsey had called for help; the monitor had already pinged when he arrived. On this Wing, someone should have answered that call in seconds.

Heaving reassurances in breaths, Kip read the shame and horror on her rounded crimson face, in her hazy gray eyes. "It's all right, lassie," he huffed with the Irish lilt he'd adopted through old Irish McGuire. His voice soothing in fits and starts, he added his scant weight and will to Mrs. Ramson's struggling effort, manipulating her first to her knees. "Here then—just grab onto this bar, lassie—we'll have you abed soon," he promised in soft huffs.

"A-ah-uh, Kip-pen—you should-na be—oh nooo—" she strained, every breath as pained as his as she woke to the stench and mess surrounding her.

"Aye, let's we just—take it slow." But he'd love to hurry! Already, the edges of his sight had turned black, and his senses reeled with the pain. His pain, he knew, even before he accepted the bulk of her weight and began lifting her onto the bed. What had begun as spikes and skewered sparks turned into hot pokers of fire lancing from his center to his skull, shooting white lights through his vision. No matter the horror of his revelation, certain he was dying now, he eased the elder onto the clean sheets, fleeting sorrow at her physical ruin, over and above the pain of her growing tumor and failing health. If he could repair her dignity, bathe her, and clothe her, he surely would try, but his mother would likely shoot him ... or at least fire him from his current orderly post.

He needed to find a nurse! But first, he needed to find his balance, swallow the pain, douse the fires. Holding onto the bar, his blond head sank; his curls brushed against the newly soiled linen. The swollen hand landed on his crown. Her huffed apologies and fears penetrated his spinning skull.

"What—!" The shriek lurched his collapsing muscles, halting the start of his knees buckling. "What the devil are you doing in here!" the charge nurse shrieked again as she flew into the room, grabbing his shoulder. "What are you doing!"

Trying to stand up! He'd scream if he could.

With the tangy scent of onions blowing over his shoulder, he struggled for a clear breath while battling against his buckling knees. And suddenly, he recalled the hour—the lunch hour that had drawn him to the fourth floor with his serving cart of soups and puddings designated for the half-dozen residents who could still eat. Lunch hour . Janet Cross had either deserted the floor to visit the cafeteria downstairs or ... or she'd ignored the call signal to finish her lunch. And suddenly, Kip's thirteen-year-old temper exploded, lending him strength to rise and find the boxy face, the wide, angry eyes. "Where the hell were you?" he demanded.

"That's not your business!"

With the danger to Mrs. Ramsey past, the disaster thwarted, Kip tabulated the details at light speed, from the puddle of fluids near the recliner, to the room's call control pad dangling off the arm of the chair and resting in the fluids, to the catheter bag still dripping off the bed. The bag had overflowed, and Mrs. Ramson had tried calling for help before ever attempting to reach her bed. She'd begun her journey sitting in the recliner, where she shouldn't have rested long enough to overflow her catheter bag.

Looking into the narrow, enflamed dark eyes, Kip knew that she'd ignored the call—deliberately ignored it. In a lower pitch, one not often heard off his soft lips, he asked again, "Where the hell were you?"

"I—" She started then squared her shoulders, pinching her masculine features; something happened in her eyes. "Your mother's going to hear about this! And if Mrs. Ramson suffered for this—" Her eyes sailed downward, sizing up his soiled clothes, maybe judging the disastrous conditions in the room. "I should make you clean—"

"If I find out—you ignored Mrs. Ramson's signal—you'd better hope my mother doesn't hear about it—"

"Don't you come in here threatening me, mister!"

Suddenly, his stomach churned, and his head spun faster. Unless he left this room, this ward, someone would likely find him curled up on one of the shiny floors. And the good doctor Frances would likely see a reason to strap him to a bed and dissect him.

He probably shouldn't have thought that last. The image of a dead fish filleted on a shiny table, and the smell of formaldehyde chased him from the room as effectively as a single word and laughter called after him. 'Undertaker!'

Barely able to contain the eruption, Kip ran clumsily from the room, turning toward the lounge and the nearest public restroom. He reached the room in time—barely. His insides exploded into the porcelain bowl as he caught himself on one knee and he sure didn't like the red tint splashing into the pale blue water. At the edges of his vision, at the fringe of his wavering sight, a gray haze lingered as clear as the swirl below him.

Internal damage. A hernia. Either could kill him. And if he looked in the mirror, he'd likely see a gray curtain draped about his shoulders. Shuddering, spooked, he fumbled with the commode's lever and flushed the toilet, settling on his shins and hips, sinking against the wall as he collapsed into a fold. If he just rested for a little while … just a little while.

Part One

Homecoming

Chapter 1

Standing at the head of the gathering, accepting and resenting that honor, Kip Patterson listened to the unfamiliar voice, chanting all too familiar words. A tribute to death, a testament to life. The words flowed over the physical remains of a woman Kip had respected, if not admired, from a distance. Behind him, cloth rustled, soles shuffled on the marble floor, and an occasional muffled cough or sniff spread contagiously to create a constant background static. Those sounds, too, were familiar. The crunch of a solemn crowd packed into a comparably small room, a familiar room, a room from his past.

Déjà vu in reverse, Kip considered. Absently, his gaze drifted past mounds of flowers. He'd stood inside this mausoleum once, if not a hundred times, in the past. In brass wall sconces, electric candles glowed somberly against the marbleized squares, illuminating brass plaques inscribed with generations of family names. He might have read all the names carved on the plaques. Might have stood, committing the legends to memory for as familiar as the sights appeared to him. Overhead, the cathedral ceiling, a masterpiece of narrow tongue-and-groove strips in the pre-turn-of-the-century design, shone with the patina of glass. Original, perhaps, but not authentic. The mausoleum was barely twenty years old, built in the early sixties. By design, the building remained symmetrical with the ancient headstones and Gothic black pillars at the entrance.

Misty Haven Cemetery—Whistlebrook Nursing Home. By style, by essence, the landmarks coexisted as Kip's childhood haunt.

The twitch in his mustache evoked nothing of humor as his abstract gaze returned to the everlasting vessel prostrate before him. His attention caught, held on the gold ribbon scrolled across a spread of red poinsettias. *Beloved Mother.* Even to his inner ear, those words sounded hollow and foreign, as if he'd finally found a language for which he possessed no quick grasp. Ironic, the words scrolled in English and basic cursive script. He certainly should understand those words. Simple, basic words.

Beloved Mother.

Had she arranged for that spread personally? Or had Bill Bickerman, her right-hand man, or the *good doctor* Frances ordered the flowers? Marilyn had certainly left nothing to chance. From what Kip recalled of the past three days, his mother had arranged every detail, as much a stickler in death as in life.

Well, why not? She'd been alive when planning this auspicious occasion. It wouldn't surprise him to learn she'd posted an ad in the Randall Trib seeking a stand-in son to replace him in case he had business elsewhere. Clearly, he pictured her sitting primly in her winged-back office chair, conducting auditions as efficiently as she ran interviews.

Another twitch affected his mustached lips, but nothing of genuine amusement touched his gray eyes or busy mind. Undecided between annoyance and anger, or simple admiration for the lady's countenance, Kip stood in regimental balance. Uncontrollably, his stomach protested the cloying floral perfumes as he stared at the crimson petals in perfect contrast to the emerald casket. She must have planned the Christmas décor, anticipating the season of her departure.

His attention snagged on the glistening brass, and an almost overwhelming urge to throw the latches and yank open the casket gripped him. He hadn't seen his mother, not once laid eyes upon her since his arrival, and that thought bothered him more than he cared to consider. How dare she deny him that honor and right? To see her one last time?

She'd known she was dying. Eight months ago, she'd known she wouldn't last another full year, but apparently, that detail had slipped her mind four months ago when they'd met at the airport. Or had she truly believed it wouldn't matter to him one way or another? Damn it, he should have known. He should have seen...

With an iron resolve, Kip halted that thought, steeling his nerve and concentrating in time to hear Fr. Jordan's words.

"In the name of the Father, and of the Son, and of the Holy Spirit. Amen."

"Amen," Kip mouthed silently, if only to justify his single contribution to this ordeal. Whether adding the Catholic service represented a blessing or a final mockery of their relationship, Kip neither knew nor cared. Enlisting a priest seemed appropriate, and on that decision, he'd stood resolute.

"This concludes our interment services," a deep, hauntingly familiar voice intruded on the moment of silence. "Mr. Patterson has asked me to invite all of you to attend a luncheon being held at Whistlebrook in Marilyn's honor."

"Mr. Patterson?"

Jolting at the hand touching his elbow, Kip glanced at the intent brown eyes. Fr. Jordan. But for an instant, the face belonged to a younger man, a bearded fellow with a spark of mischief to enthrall one lonely child.

'New hat?' the young priest asked, tapping the brim of the Brook's Bros. with just enough force to knock the crown to Kip's nose.

Automated, Kip tipped his abstracted gaze, catching briefly on the gold inscription 'Beloved Mother.' *His Mother.*

"You have my deepest sympathies," Fr. Jordan spoke in a gentle cadence inherent to his profession.

"Thank you," Kip answered and released one hand from his hat brim, clasping the proffered hand firmly. "Beautiful service," he managed awkwardly, uncertain of the protocol. Fifteen years—fifteen years had passed since he'd last attended a funeral, and some memories were better left buried. "Thank you, sir."

Bodies shifted around them, voices subdued, sniffing. Before Jordan could offer further solace, another hand landed on Kip's shoulder. Fitzpatrick, the younger Fitzpatrick. Déjà vu in reverse.

Robert, eldest son and heir apparent to Fitzpatrick's Funeral Home, wore a grim smile, undoubtedly perfected in some elective mortician's class. Grim Smile 101. But he appeared sincere, eliciting only sorrow as he enlisted body language to steer Kip from the casket. "We'll drive you to Whistlebrook," the mortician spoke in a reserved tone while insinuating himself between Kip and the brass poles. "My father and I plan to attend the reception."

In an odd instant, Kip froze, his attention riveted past Fitzpatrick's lean shoulder, landing on the emerald casing. This was it—the last time he would see that ominous box. Gripped in wicked tension, Kip suffered an unbearable urge to snap the clasps and yank open the lid. Pandora's box.

Marilyn's box!

An internal shudder sailed from his curly blond head to his shined-black heels, but as Kip turned toward the coffin, an arm slid about his elbow, tugging his shoulder. Abstracted, his attention dropped and snagged on the little woman shuffling against him. Rounded and flushed, almost glossier red than the crimson lipstick on her quivering lips, the woman's upturned face appeared wrecked. Blood-streaked brown eyes lifted, searching him and Kip braced as if doused in a tumbler of ice water as the revelation slammed him. Edna Feeney ... Nan Feeney.

He'd known this little woman his entire life, but her appearance had thrown him. He'd never seen her outside the Home, outside her element.

Rather than the usual food-stained white apron and black hairnet, a sheer black scarf covered her mound of puffy auburn hair, and at close range, Kip spotted the silver strands in the curl above her creased brow. The Yin to Marilyn's Yang, Edna had never embraced a fad, neither brow-plucking nor hairstyle, and the fashion industry had never made a nickel on her wardrobe. Even on this most auspicious occasion, she wore a sensible, teal-colored wool coat over a simple black skirt and blazer. Costume pearl clip-on earrings and a colorful beaded necklace accented her ensemble of black flats and a practical brown handbag.

Disoriented, Kip's attention flashed past the scarf, landing, locking on the emerald vessel. Already, Fitzpatrick's assistants had begun removing the bouquets and flower arrangements from the pedestals around the casket. The service and rituals had ended. A 3'x8' hole awaited—*impossible!* Marilyn Patterson could not rest inside that blasted box! Four months ago, she'd joined him at a restaurant near the airport, late as usual, but her colors ... *damn it!*

She was gone. Her remains rested inside that casket.

According to the elder John Fitzpatrick, Marilyn had demanded a closed casket, refusing even to consider allowing a troop of strangers to ogle her remains. Despite the elder mortician's reassurance and a sense of Marilyn's vanity, however, Kip knew she'd considered only one stranger when arranging her final ride, and the revelation struck a wicked blow.

As much anger as pain flashed through his mind as he accepted the press of bodies turning him, directing him toward the entrance. Slipping his arm free of Edna's grasp, he glimpsed her pained eyes as he rested his arm more comfortably about her shoulder. At his shoulder blade, another hand rode, nudging him, keeping him moving as if sensing his need to pivot. Vaguely familiar and unfamiliar faces swam around him. Some of his mother's closet friends and associates, like Edna, hovered close to him, forming a gauntlet. Déjà vu in reverse. He'd seen these same listless glazed eyes, the tragic solemn expressions, the sorrowful shine of tears as if choreographed for a stage production. A tragedy. He'd seen all this before, had experienced the same detachment as a spectator.

Readily, the memories assaulted, more wicked than the wind whipping over the hillside and spiraling white powder across the salted stone walk. All the tiny details swept through Kip's mind, from hand gestures to his mother's arm, lifting, embracing a bereaved relative's shoulder, steering the sobbing loved one to a waiting limousine. Fitzpatrick, or another of his ilk, paced the stricken survivors through the rituals from the first viewing to the internment. A priest, pastor, or reverend always hovered close at hand with soft consoling words and reassurances of life everlasting.

Vacantly, Kip accepted dozens of murmured words, arm squeezes, and fleeting touches on his black sleeves. Donning his hat, a memento from the past, he tipped the brim low to offset the wind, recalling a time when a slight breeze on the crest of this hill had sent him chasing after his hat. The hat fit him now. Only a hearty gust of wind would render his head bare.

So many funerals. So damned many deaths. Uncontrollably, Kip shuddered, cursing his thought as he assisted Edna into the rear compartment of the first limousine in the long line. Momentarily, he stood, fanning his shaded gaze over the hillside, collecting impressions, remembering ... orienting. Snow swirled around tall stone monuments, the wind undaunted. Tall pines and snow-capped hedges lent the oldest cemetery of Randall the aesthetic attraction of a golf course.

Across the lane on the snow-swept rise against a backdrop of pines, two suited men stood in a position to survey the entire procession. Despite the hedge and tall emerald pines at their backs, they remained conspicuous, and Kip's attention snagged with a sudden thought of officials. By instinct, his senses keened, watching. One, sporting a pale gray coat, lifted a camera and panned the bodies hustling toward cars along the lane. Officials posing as paparazzi? For an instant, Kip wholly doubted the probability of genuine photographers and reporters.

Reality.

Marilyn Patterson had reached celebrity status in Randall. A woman of means, a lady ahead of her time with the foresight and fortitude to preempt the women's lib movement of the 60s. Somehow, however, her status didn't justify the photographers capturing this event for posterity or the reporters trailing after the State Senator and a half dozen other familiar, famous faces in the dispersing crowd.

In his annoyance, Kip rousted from his ambivalence, suddenly closer to his true nature than at any time in the past two days. Catching Fitzpatrick's sleeve, Kip dipped his head in time to avoid the panning camera and met the slightly older man's mourning gaze. His pale eyes direct and chilly, shaded beneath the hat brim, Kip stated, "Get rid of the photographers, sir, as well as the reporters if you can. This is a private reception."

Fitzpatrick's gaze darted, and anger flashed across his thin lips as he spotted the twosome on the hillside. The father, not the son, this aging mortician had dealt with his share of difficult circumstances. As if chiseled in steel, his jaw stiffened, and his voice lowered an octave. "I'll take care of it, young sir. Rest assured."

Satisfied, Kip started into the car but froze as his attention snagged. Too swiftly that face had pivoted, too smoothly ducked below a wide, swooping black hat brim! His heart slammed a nasty beat as the woman turned, flowing into the procession, filing toward the line of cars. She was lost—lost in the swarm of dark-clad bodies—*the lady in black!*

Lifelike, the image slammed Kip ... The mists swirling between headstones, as unsettling in memory as in life, fifteen years earlier. He'd only imagined her, then, surely. But how his imagination had run wild in those crazy seconds. Impatient and listless, he'd stood outside the crowd, awaiting his mother, anxious for the drive home. Then he'd seen her. The lady in black. She stood within the mist beyond the crypt, an apparition with a black veil swaying from the brim of a hat, concealing her facial features entirely. He shuddered, now, as he had then. She'd stared at him from behind that veil. He'd felt it. A vision of ill omen ... *and death had followed.*

Under his breath, Kip uttered a curse at his probable insanity and ducked into the shadowed compartment. The woman he'd just seen was neither an apparition nor an ill omen. With his flashing glimpse, he'd identified a fine, slender build and classy style. A New-York-style. She probably worked for the National Enquirer.

Barely restraining a second curse, Kip settled into the seat alongside Edna.

Still sniffing, she wiped her cheeks and eyes with an embroidered handkerchief. And that, too, remained familiar. At a base level, Kip grasped her grief and understood the deep hollow pain she'd suffer in the days or weeks to come. He had no idea how to console her, any more than he knew how to handle the turmoil wrecking his equilibrium. This once, he truly had no control over the events or circumstances around him, and that wasn't a condition he intended to embrace.

The sooner he concluded this affair and boarded a plane to a far more agreeable climate, the better.

His thoughts drifting, Kip gazed through the tinted glass, preferring not to watch the crowd scattering. A mantle of angry gray clouds suspended above the towering pines—the promise of more snow was too blasted obvious. And as much as he'd once loved a decent snowfall, the mere thought tipped his precarious balance toward anger.

He should have stayed in California. If he'd been thinking clearly three mornings past, he might have hired a stand-in son to attend this event. God knows, few people would have noticed or known the difference. An imposter—an intruder. He was an intruder here, little more than excess cargo occupying space in a limo reserved for friends and family.

That revelation appealed to him no more now than it did fifteen or twenty years earlier. Oliver Twist had held nothing over Kippen James Patterson, he considered with a rueful smile.

Without a glance, Kip knew when Bill Bickerman and Dr. Mark Frances entered the shadowy compartment, their presence only confirming and qualifying his dark thoughts. He honestly didn't belong here, not in this limo, not in their company. They belonged. Edna Feeney—second in command at Whistlebrook despite what titles any others wore—had lived in the Home forever, a friend and ally, as close as a sister to Marilyn. And Mark Frances, physician, friend... Hell, probably, her lover, to stand through thick and thin throughout the years. Bickerman had arrived later, but if the past three days were any indication, the man had gained Marilyn's favor and reciprocated in full. They belonged—

"Kip?" the deep, strained voice intruded.

Jolted slightly, Kip found Mark Frances studying him grimly and wondered if he was truly as transparent as he felt.

"How are you holding up?"

Once, a very long time ago, the 'good doctor' Frances had been intimidating, if not outright terrifying. With a physique befitting a lumberjack standing well over six feet, the good doctor had always commanded attention. The years hadn't changed him tremendously. He still wore a beard and mustache, and his stark blue eyes possessed a tendency to see far more than one intended. Errant strands of gray highlighted his beard and temples, sweeping through the neat mahogany waves and lending credence to his sophistication. Presently, shadows lingered under his eyes, contradicting the hint of laugh lines webbed at the corners.

As if time stood still at Whistlebrook, the faces, Mark, Edna—and a handful of others—remained unchanged.

"Are you alright?" Frances asked more carefully.

"Fine," Kip answered evenly and suffered an odd, distant memory. "Kipper," he said absently. The *good doctor* had called him 'Kipper.' "Like a herring," Kip recalled the doctor professing, and remembered despising that nickname. Although he'd never mustered the courage to admit that detail. He was neither shy nor a man easily intimidated any longer. "I hated that moniker," he commented, likely verifying his mental capacity. Or incapacity, as Mark's faint grin and glance at Edna suggested.

"Suppose it's too late to apologize if it offended you," Dr. Frances said lightly, sinking more comfortably into the opposite seat as the limousine rolled forward.

"Suppose it is," Kip agreed and turned his focus through the tinted glass. Tombstones stood like dominoes, awaiting a good wind to fall. Passing around the edge of the hill on the ridge road that overlooked a forest valley, the oldest section of Misty Haven came into view. At least two Gothic stone crypts clung to the hillside, braced against the ever-present wind that channeled off the river through ravines and slopes. Some of the smaller slabs and simple masonry crosses listed precariously, as if defying gravity to remain upright. Halfway down the hill, a small court surrounded by short, clipped hedges paid homage to a grand statue of St. John who stood erect, arms spread, palms dropped open, bestowing a blessing. Weathered stone steps descended the hill to reach the sanctuary, where masonry benches offered a quiet retreat and welcome respite from the steep hillside... *Someday, he would venture down those steps.*

Barely, Kip suffered the sway of nostalgia when he spotted the mini excavator balanced on the hillside. Only two slight rows of headstones separated the lane from a mound of overturned dirt. A gaping black wound in the snowy landscape designated Marilyn Patterson's final resting place.

His gaze held on the construction site as it passed, but his thoughts veered, recalling more involved projects, the smell of diesel fumes and hot oil, the crunch and grind of gears, and explosions of stone. Religiously, Kip visited his new acquisitions at least once in the early stages, despite his firm adherence to anonymity. One more pair of dusty blue jeans, dirty t-shirt, and hard hat generally went unnoticed with the size of the crews that Morning Sun Enterprises employed. More than once, Kip had satisfied his dark amusement to spend a day taking orders from a harried foreman of Neanderthal build and disposition. Demolition sites had always stood high on his list of entertainment. Far more exhilarating than a night at the opera. And slightly more satisfying than sex, although he wouldn't likely admit that to his latest roommate. Morgan, like dozens of others—long, blond, and athletic—believed that her performance rated as the eighth natural wonder. Unfortunately, she couldn't hold a candle to a dozen carefully placed explosives shattering tons of iron, metal, glass, and steel into a heap of smoking debris.

Braced against the chilly wind, Kelly Mulden watched the tall, handsome man escorting a small, unpretentious woman from the mausoleum to the nearest limousine. Kip Patterson. Kelly would have recognized him even if she'd glimpsed him in a stadium full of strangers. She wasn't a child or some twittering dove to flutter and faint at the slight of a handsome man, but just for an instant, glimpsing his shaded face beneath the brim of that classy hat, her knees shuddered.

Expecting him, anticipating a glimpse of him, she hadn't truly prepared for the effect of seeing him. Hadn't once considered the gut-gripping shock of the instant. What had she expected? To find a wide-eyed, curly-haired little boy? God knows, that was the image she'd carried with her for the past fifteen years. The image of a boy, the most handsome boy she'd ever encountered ... *and he'd stood in her house, in her living room.*

"Are you all right, hon?"

Grateful for the intrusion, Kelly sent a wayward balance to her mother, catching Colleen's eyes before turning. "Fine, mom," Kelly answered, belatedly aware of the cold nipping at her ankles and calves, relieved to be climbing into the Lincoln. If ever she felt like a hypocrite, never more than now. If she possessed any good sense, she'd ask her father to drop her off at home, but it was too late for second thoughts, even if she suffered a few.

Her gaze adrift through the tinted glass, Kelly's attention caught on two uniformed police officers advancing on two men a short distance away. One man stooped, stuffing a camera into an oversized leather bag on the snowy lawn. Photographers. And reporters, she added with a memory flash of a fellow dogging a State Senator whom she hadn't readily recognized.

'Senator..? A few words?' the reporter had shouted before a Randall Officer had intervened.

At least she wasn't as bad as those fellows. Neither a need to gawk nor a desire to capitalize on this event had brought her racing across three hundred miles. Unfortunately, that detail offered no comfort or relief.

False pretenses. A hypocrite. Kelly had never met Marilyn Patterson in life.

"He still looks lost," Colleen said in the front seat, breaking into Kelly's thoughts.

Even without clear sight with the car seat between them, Kelly knew the expression to accompany that distraught tone. Petite and built trim, no one ever mistook Colleen's heritage. Twinkling hazel eyes, softly freckled round cheeks and pixie nose, a tint of strawberry to her blond shoulder-length hair, Colleen had inherited the 'best of the Irish,' as Jarred Mulden was often quick to announce. When Colleen laughed, which was often, her eyes sparkled and cheeks flushed, and when she grieved or worried, her face reflected the sadness and sobriety to dull the sunlight on a clear summer day.

Jarred Mulden, from whom Kelly had inherited her black Irish traits, was nearly the opposite. With the gift of the Irish, he could spit in the face of adversity, rarely displaying a shred of ill temper, forever the counterbalance to Colleen's flights of fancy. A rock in a swirling tide.

This wasn't the exception. Kelly glimpsed his blue eyes, the only trait she hadn't inherited, as he glanced sideways at her mother. With a quirk in his lips and a combination of peculiar curiosity and concern, he commented, "I'm guessing here, but you're referring to Kip, right?"

"No. That other fellow who lost his mother," Colleen said dryly. "Who else would I mean, for heaven's sakes, Jarred?"

"Forgive me, dear. I'm just having a hard time figuring out how you can tell."

"I can tell," Colleen said solemnly.

"Woman's intuition. That fabled of all mysteries," her father sighed, and his eyes flashed to the rearview mirror, capturing Kelly's gaze for an instant.

"Mother's intuition," Colleen corrected.

The line of cars had started moving. Jarred touched the gas, choosing a safer subject. "Think it's going to snow again. We might have a white Christmas after all."

"I wonder if he'll stay at the Home."

"Colleen—"

"This is an awful time of year to lose a loved one," Colleen continued distractedly, her gaze apparently turned out the side window. "Especially a mother."

Depressed suddenly, absorbing the words, Kelly gazed through the glass. At any time of the year, a loss could be painful, but her mother was right—Christmas was the worst. Abruptly, Kelly felt like crying. For Marilyn Patterson. For Kip. For herself, with a thought that she might one day face this same sorrow. Her parents weren't old in her eyes. She'd never thought of them as old, but her father could retire in two years with a full pension. Already gray highlights sprinkled his dark hair, and new laugh lines fanned his temples. Colleen, too, had aged subtly, although she could still pass for thirty. Under a full sun, silver streaks glinted in her hair, a detail Colleen seemed to find more delightful than distasteful. Mortality. One day, they might both be gone.

Kelly would have her brothers and sisters-in-law.

Kip had no one.

Kelly's heart gripped with sorrow. No brothers or sisters, no father or grandparents, uncles or aunts. Kelly had read the obituary that Colleen had clipped from the Randall Trib. Marilyn Patterson ... survived by son, Kippen James Patterson. As if to compensate for the lack of familial wealth, the lengthy, well-written obit had read like a tribute to an immortal, citing a list of accomplishments from civic membership to political achievements. Without a doubt, Marilyn Patterson had led a hectic, successful life, only beginning with her sole proprietorship of the largest nursing home in the area, an alleged 'family-owned' establishment.

Family. Mother and son.

Would Kip stay at the Home? Would he live there now? Remain in Randall?

"Wonder if JD will make it in," Jarred said offhandedly.

Distracted, Kelly glimpsed her father's pensive eyes in the rearview mirror, although he watched the procession ahead.

"He said he'd try. I'm sure if he can get a flight, he'll be here."

Ever the optimist, Kelly considered. She wished she possessed her mother's faith. Where her next-older brother was concerned, however, she'd learned not to hold her breath. Ever since his divorce, if not before, he'd become a stranger. No one blamed him. No one blamed Laura either, for that matter. The Muldens still treated Laura like a member of the family, and Laura reciprocated, allowing them the pleasure of their grandsons' company. Neither JD nor Laura had ever admitted what came between them, but Kelly thought she knew. JD had changed. He wasn't the same boy—the same big brother who'd gone to Vietnam.

"Don't guess you'd want to skip this reception, would you?" Jarred asked as he followed the stream of cars turning toward Randall, hence Whistlebrook.

"Unless you really think we should? No, I'd rather we don't," Colleen said dismally.

For JD, Kelly knew abruptly. Perhaps on a subconscious level, her mother attended this affair to represent JD, knowing in advance that he wouldn't come. JD wasn't the same boy who'd befriended Kip Patterson shortly after they'd moved to Randall a lifetime ago. He wasn't the same fun-loving big brother who'd always sided with the underdog, not the guy everyone could depend on. A good friend, a loyal son. Colleen might defend JD forever, but on a base level, she knew he wasn't the son she'd born, any more than Kip Patterson was the same child whom they'd known so briefly.

For the first time since leaving her apartment in Baltimore, Kelly regretted her impulsive decision to return home three days ahead of schedule. She should have waited and ridden with Richard on Saturday.

Absently, Kelly fingered the diamond engagement ring on her finger, studying the prisms to catch the shallow light. She loved Richard Whitman. She loved him enough to accept his proposal and watch him slip the diamond ring onto her finger. He was handsome, charming, and witty in his own way. Intelligent and reliable. Solid. He hailed from a decent family, the middle son of a wealthy southern family. In his own right, he'd be rich after he finished his internship. Money, however, never factored into her attraction, not to Richard or the long line of other suitors in her past. She wasn't destitute.

Survived quite well, in fact, between her dance studio and several sound investments.

What was she doing in Randall? What in God's name was she thinking when tossing clothes into a suitcase and rushing to her car?

Chapter 2

At a glance, Kip recognized the black cast iron gate as the limo slowed for the turn. Forever, those gates stood open on galvanized hinges. Not in his lifetime had those dual gates served a function other than decorative mementos of a glorious bygone era. In an elaborate scroll, the black threads twined to form a tremendous 'W' on either panel, and perhaps these gates, attached to gothic black stone pillars, formed the coalition of Misty Haven and Whistlebrook. God knows, the original structure of the Home spawned from the same era, undoubtedly, a country estate predating the Civil War, if not the Constitution.

Two days prior, when Kip had arrived, the sprawling landscape had been brown, caught in that dormant phase between fall and winter when the earth surrendered and died. Kip couldn't recall exactly when the snow had prevailed and triumphed. Reminding him of a funeral shroud, a white canvas lay upon the descending slope. Like cheesecloth, the flakes clung to the black trunks of oaks that arched over the paved lane. With white-capped branches sagging, tall pines littered the hillside, and he remembered the paths presently concealed beneath the shroud. Endless, the shaded walkways threaded over the estate in a network of comfortable footpaths.

A winter wonderland,. but a lot colder than he remembered. Already, he shivered inside his long coat despite the heat blasting into the limo's rear compartment. Absently, he wondered if the constant breeze or the atmosphere created the chill.

Whistlebrook Nursing Home. His home.

He hadn't warmed up since stepping through the front doors.

His thoughts shifted, drifting toward the past, remembering the snowfalls and a short wooden sled. A long, winding stretch of unmarked snow trailed into and through the pines on the descending hillside. Alone, he navigated that treacherous path. Already, the wind chilled his cheeks, stinging. Determination steeled his nerves as he sprawled on the shiny wooden slats. American Flyer. In bold red, the words scrolled on the varnished boards. As if breaking through cobwebs, the memory scrolled ... himself prostrate on the boards, a short version of the Michelin Man covering the wood, sinking the runners into the fresh snow. Gloved hands clasped the crossbar on either side; he thrust off with his toes and blasted off. On the steepest hill on Whistlebrook, that sled reached demonic speeds with the fresh powder burning and stinging his cheeks, blinding him.

A twitch of a grin touched his mustached lips as he remembered his oversight of a lifetime past. Too late, he'd identified the cyclone fence that separated Whistlebrook from the forest valley, but that, too, had become a private game. Only once, he'd miscalculated his speed and jack-knifed 'Hornet' slightly too late to avoid a collision.

If not for Nan Feeney's insistence that he 'bundle up' in a snowsuit thick enough to toast him in the Arctic, he wouldn't have walked away from that spill.

Alone, Kip remembered picking himself up and peeling off his gloves to wipe clumps of snow from his cheeks. Only in his mind, he'd imagined the laughter of young voices joining him on the magnificent hillside, cheering him for his daredevil ride. Alone, he'd trudged up the hillside, dragging his trusty American Flyer. *'Once more, then we're going in, Hornet. Getting awfully cold out here.'*

The door opened beside him, snatching the memory from the foreground, but the sense of abandon lingered as Kip slid and stepped from the limo. Momentarily startled and disoriented, he scanned the trail of late-model sedans and aging compact cars spilling into the plowed parking lot. In slow motion, he followed the tree line, unconsciously pulling his coat closer to ward off the chill.

Cars continued turning into the main entrance, and for a moment, Kip considered counting the vehicles. *Bad luck.* Allegedly, it was bad luck to count the cars in a funeral procession, but how could there be any worse luck than riding in a funeral procession? Unless, of course, one happens to be riding *prone* within a funeral procession. That would certainly be a stroke of worse luck..

'*A good turnout,*' a soft, whiskey voice echoed in his head, and Kip agreed. There seemed to be no end to the parade. Surely, half of Randall had *turned out* to pay respect to Marilyn Patterson, the matriarch of Whistlebrook Nursing Home.

Absently, Kip cupped a flame to a cigarette, vaguely aware of the elder Mr. Fitzpatrick striding around the front of the limousine, aware of Mrs. Feeney climbing from the car with young Robert's help. Fitzpatrick. This elder John Fitzpatrick had known about Marilyn's heart condition. He was one of a half dozen who might have enlightened Kip weeks, if not months ago, when she'd begun making these arrangements. Kip's eyes turned a smoky gray as he looked toward the Home.

With stately elegance, the original structure, undoubtedly, of European descent, had maintained its dignity through dozens of transitional phases, incorporating the architectural changes of several generations. Three full floors high with a length to transcend a city block, the original mansion rested on a broad, flat plateau, a part of the natural landscape. Higher than its roofs, countless ancient oaks and elms shaded the windows of the upper levels. In early American style, an expansive covered porch, white-columned and spindle-railed, spanned half the facade and wrapped partway around the receiving end of the Home. Three wide steps and a ramp for the walking-impaired led to the main doors. From where he stood, Kip identified the doves within the original leaded glass sidelights to either side of the more modern glass doors.

Two other front entrances existed beyond the end of the porch to his left, entrances that might have accommodated servants in the early years. Concealed behind tall hedges and arched stone walls, the entries provided employee access, with narrow cement walks leading to the sectional parking lots beneath the oaks that shielded the Home from the valley winds.

At a glance, Kip noted the cars filling the visitor lot, flooding into the employee lots. If ever so many vehicles crowded the lot, the memory eluded him, although he remembered a dozen or more funerals that had brought a respectable crowd. A funeral.

Always.

Pulling his collar up to ward off the sudden chill, Kip glimpsed the strangers climbing from cars, some already starting toward the entrance.

Abruptly, he wanted no part of this affair. *Proper etiquette, bedamned!* He'd attended enough funerals and wakes to last him a lifetime. More than enough to pardon himself, now, without regret.

At the start of a hand linking about his arm, Kip collected himself more fully, glimpsed Edna's glassy eyes, and likewise the lumberjack physician spying him in grim speculation. Both appeared to await him to begin the procession toward the doors. Far be it from him to disappoint them, despite his sudden thought of becoming the Master of Ceremonies in an extremely grim parade.

Holding one of the glass doors for Edna, the first wave of kitchen aromas slammed him, filling his chilled nostrils and lungs, gripping his stomach with a near-buckling cramp. *Nothing had changed! Not one damned thing had changed!* A mere glimpse of a serving cart wheeling through the lobby confirmed Kip's decision to skip this affair. He'd satisfied his obligation. Not even his mother would expect him to sit down and indulge in another dinner for the dead after all these years.

Touching Edna's shoulder in courtly fashion, Kip drew her sorrowful eyes. "Excuse me, will you, luv. I'll be along in a moment," he lied smoothly. Then, acknowledging Dr. Frances with a slight nod, Kip veered right toward the French doors that led into the executive wing of the Home. With little more than a glance, Kip passed the antique reception desk stationed outside the door, managing only a glance and nod at the morose woman of like vintage as he passed through the door, currently wearing a 'closed' welcome sign.

At one time, the entire wing had served as a grand ballroom. But that ambience had faded long before a Patterson had claimed the home. Partitioned into sections, the administration wing comprised an executive office, assistant administrator's office, secretarial pool, conference and waiting rooms, several storage cells, and last, but not least, the matriarch's private chambers and a semi-private restroom. Slightly wider than the French doors, the main corridor stretched over thirty feet, bypassing three doors before reaching a junction of connecting halls. Within that strategic maze of junctions, unsuspecting visitors cooled their heels until the Queen of Whistlebrook granted an audience.

God knows, she'd snagged her only son in that loop. Fleeting, he recalled sitting in the compact private waiting room, hoping for a moment with his mother. Hours, decades later, he'd discovered her exodus through a second, more private exit into the rear hall.

Shying from the memory, Kip veered left into a newly carpeted corridor. For a moment, he imagined himself in any number of modern offices. Tasteful scenic prints in simple gold frames accented the long length of beige walls.

'What do you think, darling? Like it?' A breezy voice swept through his muddled mind.

Two years ago. At least two years ago, Kip had stepped through the French doors off the main hall and nearly tripped over his own feet in his shock. Over two years ago, Marilyn had renovated the corridor, along with her private domain, a suite he'd shared with her throughout the first fourteen years of his life.

Not quite fourteen, Kip corrected with a slight edge as he drew up short outside the oak door, reading the bold, gold plate designating PRIVATE. Two months shy of fourteen years, he'd dwelt behind this solid door. Fifteen years and one month ago, Marilyn had made it perfectly clear—she didn't give a damn about what he thought or what he felt.

By the time she squeezed him into her schedule and asked for his opinion about those renovations two years ago, Kip had recovered enough to comment, *'In need of a tax write-off, are you?'*

'In need of a change,' she'd answered shortly.

Guilt was a natural phase of the grief process, but Kip felt nothing as he pushed through the private door, his soles sinking comfortably into a thick brown carpet.

Absently, his gaze fanned over the modern sofa, recliner, and matching chair. On heavy cherry-wood shelves, accenting a collection of leather-bound books, an array of colorful figurines stood in a multitude of dance poses, from Victorian partners in ball gowns and wigs, to prima donnas in rippled lace. They occupied every available space, each one granted its spotlight, catching the subdued light of a single lamp that burned forever in Kip's memory.

By far, the most impressive dancer stood within a glass dome on the console television, and like a miller to light, the Wallendorf drew Kip. The prima donna had stood on a dust-layered shelf, surrounded by other dusty statues of questionable heritage. England ... a little shop outside of London. A splendid blonde had hung on Kip's arm, doubting his good sense and giggling. *'I thought we were hunting for a hat?'*

Christmas, he remembered, though he'd said nothing in response. Instead, he'd paid the ageing junk dealer twice the price, and still not near the collector's value.

'Most people dicker down, *not* up, *luv. I really* must *educate you on the fine art of antiquing.'*

His fingertips resting on the glass dome, Kip remembered cleaning the statue, packaging her in mounds of newspaper and wood shavings, and tucking a single sheet of hotel stationery on top of the pile. *'Merry Christmas, Mother,'* and the customary, *Love, Kip.'*

Her letters had arrived in similar shorthand with the natural cadence of a telegram. *'Hello.* (stop) *Haven't heard from you lately.* (stop) *Still seeing that lovely girl?* (stop) *Marriage?* (stop) *Love, Mom.* (stop) And Kip imagined her tossing an envelope to Carolyn McAnthony, her executive secretary, while breezing from her office. *'Find my son's address, will you? And drop that in the mail. Thanks, so much.'*

Always an afterthought. *Oh my goodness. I have a son somewhere. Now, where is he? Oh, he'll turn up…*

Beneath the dome, the delicate upturned face evoked an image of lofty reproach, a near chiding pose. So few letters. So few visits. And it was way too late to suffer regrets. Kip had learned a very long time ago about the finality of death, the futility of regret or remorse. If mourning could be considered an art form, he'd become a master long before retiring his talent.

An image of white stationery swam within his mind's eye. *A black, silky cover fell open in his mind—*

The album.

"Damn it," Kip uttered and withdrew his fingers from the dome. Dropping his brimmed hat on the console, he turned and moved without a conscious thought, catching the doorknob and pushing through his bedroom door.

Not once in the past two days. not once in the past fifteen *years* had he opened this door. As if catapulted through time, he froze, positive of a hallucination. He'd pulled this door closed behind him a lifetime ago and never opened it again. And he felt suddenly as if he'd just lifted the lid off Pandora's box. A shiver slid down his rigid spine.

Not one thing had moved or changed. His favorite Afghan, checked black and white, lay on the single bed as if he'd made it only this morning. His books, his all-time favorite classics from 'Sherlock Holmes' to 'The Swiss

Family Robinson' to 'Moby Dick' ... a half dozen hardbacks stood between brass-horse bookends on his desk. The walls, the ceiling, and the chest of drawers—all remained frozen in time, buried beneath hundreds upon hundreds of age-yellow faces and still-life images cut from magazines and pasted on every surface. Strings of colored beads hung across the closet door that abutted his camouflaged headboard. There hadn't been enough space for a solid door. Colorful strands of plastic beads had become a fad, and a cheap indulgence his mother had granted only after he finished nailing the strings to the doorframe and presented her with the result. Pushing aside the strands, Kip stood gazing at the plastic-covered shelves. In slow motion, he pulled away the plastic, somehow not surprised. In neat, pristine rows, hats of all shapes, sizes, and colors stood in meticulous stacks as he'd stacked them after removing a dozen of his favorites a lifetime ago.

Unconsciously, Kip lifted a tweed cap from in front of him, fingering the old material as the beige color blurred in his vision. His mother had never condoned excessive clutter. If something couldn't fit on a shelf, it had no right to exist in her domain, and every inch of Whistlebrook comprised her domain.

He hadn't fit—

"Thought I'd—"

With his start, Kip lost his grip on the cap and shot his abstracted gaze toward the intruder in a half turn. The good doctor Frances filled most of the open doorway. And for a split second, reading the man's troubled, startled gaze, Kip remembered his intimidation, as surely as he recalled his outrage when anyone invaded his private space. Another ... another face swirled in his mind, younger, sturdy, arrogant. JD Mulden.

"—find you here," Mark Frances finished in an apologetic voice. "I didn't mean to startle you."

He should be only grateful for the interruption! Kip stooped, recovering the tweed from the narrow floor space. Coming here to be alone with his grief? Was the past still so well preserved in his mind that he should seek his private refuge to feel safe against remorse? After every funeral, he'd migrated here to be alone, as he'd always been alone before that fall of '72. Thirteen going on eighty to his way of thinking. A little clumsily, Kip rose and returned the hat to the shelf.

"Mind if we talk for a moment?"

Frances had removed his overcoat, but he still wore his tailored black suit. He leaned casually against the door jamb, as if he'd rested there for quite some time.

Annoyed with himself for neither hearing nor sensing the intrusion, Kip met Mark's gaze directly. "About?"

"Obviously, we could cover a multitude of subjects, but at the moment, I'm most interested in your plans for the next hour or so."

"Meaning?"

Sorrow continued to haunt Mark's blue eyes, but his gaze held steady. "The words you spoke to Edna," Mark answered hesitantly. "I've heard them before."

His *words*? Kip barely considered becoming more annoyed with the apparent game when the memory surfaced full-blown. His commencement ceremony ... Dr. Mark Frances and Marilyn had stood on the lawn. A single picture, the very same picture that stood next to the Wallendorf in the next room. In the photo, Kip's arm rested over his mother's shoulder, his gaze averted as if distracted at the last moment. His mother's arm circled his waist, her pale blue eyes laughing.

'I have to return my gown,' Kip had said while moving from the pose as Mark Frances had tried snapping another shot. *'There's a reception in the gym. I'll join you in a minute.'*

"It occurred to me that those were the last words anyone heard from you for more than three years. Personally, I didn't see you again for better than five," Mark said in a low, reflective tone. A shadow of a troubled smile touched his bearded lips. "Is there even a slight chance that you might be planning to leave without saying goodbye?" he asked directly.

"I don't imagine it's any of your business if I were," Kip answered evenly. "Nor should it be your concern, doctor."

"You're probably right, it's not my business," Mark conceded without moving from his lean. One immense hand hooked by a thumb at his hip pocket, his black jacket held back at his wrist where white silk cuffs and a gold watchband glinted from the folds of ebony. He looked like a model posing in a J.C. Penny's catalogue; his faint bearded grin was set for a pensive effect. "Has it occurred to you that despite your long absences, Kip, you still have friends here? People who value your friendship and worry about you. People who might like to keep in touch regardless of what the future holds for Whistlebrook."

Almost amused, Kip realized this was the first time anyone had mentioned the fate of Whistlebrook directly. As sole surviving heir, he stood to inherit this monstrosity, a revelation he'd struggled unsuccessfully to ignore over the past two days. Eventually, he'd need to hear Marilyn Patterson's Last Will and Testament, a document held in trust by the Home's legal firm. His decisions, then, would undoubtedly affect the Home's future.

"Frankly, Kip, I'm one of those people," Frances continued in a quiet, reflective tone. "As much as I know you keep most people at a distance, I've known you long enough to consider you a friend, and I'd hope you feel the same."

True, Kip had known the good doctor Frances for over two-thirds of his life, but he could say the same about J.F.K. or the do-gooder George Washington, neither of whom he'd consider a friend. If ever friendship ranked high on his list, that day had passed.

"Kip," Frances said in a soft, compelling tone, his blue eyes intent. "I know you've always had a unique way of handling a loss," he said quietly. His focus drifted, canvasing the room, his smile more haunted as he continued, "I knew I'd find you in here. This room was always your sanctuary—the one place you could come where you felt safe. No putting on smiles or airs. You could let your guard down here for a while and allow yourself to feel all the hurt and frustrations. The losses. Some patterns are hard to forget, and old habits are more difficult to break, but I don't believe it'll work this time," he said solemnly. His gaze had stabilized, more sober and faintly desperate. "Despite the differences that came between you and your mother, you loved her, and it's going to hit—"

"Is there a point to this insight?" Kip interrupted.

Faltering, Frances studied him more critically. Only seconds passed before he answered, "Dinner's being served, and you probably haven't eaten much since Monday." Calculated and direct, just enough hint of emotion to sound slightly miffed, if not genuinely angry, Frances added, "Regardless of how you feel, you have a certain obligation to appear in your mother's honor."

At least Frances hadn't mentioned an emotional obligation to seek solace from the gathering. Annoyed that Frances would slam him with 'civic duty,' Kip studied the steady gaze curiously. The doctor's curt tone betrayed nothing of ulterior motives, although several likely existed. "I believe I should resent that remark, doctor. You seem to imply I've somehow failed in my obligations thus far."

"Let's skip the theatrics, Kip," Frances said candidly. "I know you left here an extremely hurt and angry young man, and I don't doubt you've harbored resentments over the years. I also know you're not as superficial as you behave. You are hurt, you are angry, and you're probably ten times more devastated than the rest of us, even if you're not willing to admit it even to yourself. I know how difficult this is going to be—"

"Do you really?" Kip asked, his tone suddenly void of emotion, his gray eyes darker with his sudden anger.

Halted, Frances looked at him, perhaps, seeing for the first time what several executives saw too late across a negotiating table. The doctor recovered smoothly, swiftly, a hint of sorrow in his grim smile. "Yes," he answered. "I do, really, Kip."

Reality! Damn it!

Dr. Mark Frances was probably one of a select group of people in Whistlebrook who knew that Kip Patterson wasn't the fop he portrayed. Unlike Bickerman, who hovered, condescending to Kip as if speaking to a misfit child, Frances had undoubtedly seen to the details with sincere intention to support a friend in a crisis. More than once over the past two days, Frances had succeeded, offering a word here, a gesture there. Over a thousand miles of phone cable, Mark Frances had intruded on Edna's blubbering announcement to offer simply, *'She didn't suffer, Kip.'*

Just slipped away during the night—

"Kip," Frances interrupted quietly. "Why don't we join the gathering? Doubtful anyone will begin eating until you arrive, and if you need it, I'll find something to help settle your stomach."

Annoyed instantly, Kip cast the doctor a sharp glance and realized the physician not only knew his apparent digression but deliberately used that statement to draw him from his daze. "Thanks so much, doctor," he said flippantly. "But I've sworn off sedation."

"Probably haven't had a physical in years either, have you?" Frances taunted.

"I assure you, sir, I'm in fine health."

Frances lifted a brow while darting his gaze down and up, mocking inspection and speculation.

Uncontrollably, Kip suffered a fleeting discomfort, annoyed when he noted the doctor's flash of perception.

With a visible effort, Frances tried to jest. "You do appear fit. You must spend a lot of time on the beach. Or do you prefer simulated sunlight and health spas?"

"Depends entirely on the mood," Kip said dryly and started toward Frances, wanting, needing to be out of this room. Far too many distant memories pulsed beneath the surface, memories he'd buried a long time ago for his mental health. "Suppose we should join the ensemble. Proper etiquette and all that poppycock."

Dr. Frances remained frozen, blocking the doorway. A faint amusement touched his eyes, not betraying his sobriety or grief. "Despite the circumstances, Kip, I meant to tell you. It is good to see you." His large palm came between them, offered with his shallow grin. "This old place was never the same after you left. It was as if you took a large part of its spirit with you."

"I have no doubts," Kip said dryly, accepting the handshake. "I took a lot of ghosts with me."

Their gazes held for several seconds before Mark nodded. "Yes, I believe you did," he uttered and turned, stepping aside. His hand touched Kip's shoulder blade briefly, then fell away as they crossed the living room.

As an afterthought, Kip paused at the door, slipped off his long coat, and dropped it onto the recliner where he'd slept for the past two nights. Maybe he'd postpone his flight, haunt a motel with a bottle of 100 proof and drink himself into a sound sleep. God knows, he hadn't slept well since lifting that phone three nights ago. Had he thought ahead, he might have taken pause and checked into a hotel near the airport before driving to Whistlebrook. Time had been a factor, however, and the merry-go-round hadn't slowed down since he'd stepped off the plane. Tonight. Tonight, he could afford to jump off the treadmill and offer his mother a proper adieu.

Did he truly want to be alone, though? To grieve?

Just the thought of sitting alone in a hotel room, drinking himself into oblivion, was depressing. Perhaps he should have accepted Morgan's offer to accompany him. He could have checked her into a hotel—

No. Bringing Morgan would have been a mistake. Conceivably, she might believe he felt something other than a physiological attraction, and nothing could be further from the truth. If he wanted company tonight, he could indeed find someone willing to accommodate him.

Kelly had never set foot inside Whistlebrook Nursing Home. She'd passed the gates a thousand times if once, but she'd never driven down the long, maple-lined lane or set foot through the double-pane glass doors. Uncomfortably, she strode alongside her mother, not entirely immune to heads turning or the fellow who hustled up the steps ahead of her. He reached the doors and held one panel open, offering a quick, anxious smile, and barely refrained from bowing butler-style as she passed. At another time, at another function, she might have accepted the flattery, but under the circumstances, she wasn't altogether comfortable with the attention. She managed a faint smile as she entered and nearly halted in her sudden surprise.

Rather than a nursing home lobby, she'd stepped into a tremendous foyer, perhaps one found at the entrance to a Victorian mansion, if not a castle. In undeniable elegance, a wide, carpeted staircase descended from the second floor directly across from the main doors. Even through the crowd shuffling and drifting toward a set of open French doors to the left, she spotted the tremendous knoll posts offset from the bottom step. Wide oak banisters and hand-turned spindles rose to a second-floor balcony where several doors and a brief span of hallway remained visible from any angle. From the second-floor ceiling, a tremendous chandelier, undoubtedly converted to support electric candles after Edison's debut, cast crystal prisms on the papered walls that rose to the ceiling.

A documentary, some silly documentary about the houses of the rich and famous. Kelly had seen that style of mahogany beams and panels that spanned the ceiling. Jacobean style. Circa 1800s, without a doubt. Underfoot, wisely protected by a plastic carpet runner, an immense oriental carpet, predominantly blue with touches of crimson, centered the room. In perfect symmetry, slag, Tiffany-style lamps and parlor settees graced the perimeter walls. A particularly pretty set filled a warren just to the right of the doors and the sight of an antique desk and silver-haired receptionist barely altered the museum-quality atmosphere.

A nursing home—not a palace. Almost relieved, Kelly glimpsed the gold embossed signs listing Home hours and apparent regulations, along with a bulletin board beyond the desk and a set of smoke-glass doors to her immediate right. 'Administration,' the etched glass professed in bold script, and beneath the words, a single 'Closed' sign hung.

At her shoulder, in a conspiratorial whisper, her father asked, "Think those lamps are genuine Tiffany?"

Kelly passed him a fleeting glance, noting her father appeared likewise impressed, and apparently a first-time visitor too. "Doubt it," she whispered in return as they fell into the crowd, passing through the open doors. Within moments, however, she reconsidered.

As disorienting as the lobby, this reception room carried all the elegance and style of a classy restaurant, from the French latticed windows spaced at intervals on the outside walls to the large, round, linen-draped tables spread across the pristine hardwood floor. Hovering around a single long table just inside the room, several apron-clad women busily arranged industrial-sized pans and cookers. Several stacks of heavy china plates stood on a separate table. Kelly's attention caught on an immense Baby Grand piano—possibly an original—dwarfed against the inside wall toward the rear.

Finding a table toward the back of the room near the piano, Kelly slipped off her coat, anticipating another of her father's comments, if only by the spark in his eyes as he leaned to whisper.

"Think they'll charge by the plate?"

Kelly stifled a smile along with her impulse to slap him, whispering, "You better behave. If mom hears you, you're done for."

He mocked horror but glanced at Colleen with a slight smile while stepping toward her to take her coat. "If you ladies will excuse me," he said in his inherently deep voice, affecting the sophistication he often concealed.

Kelly heard her mother's discreet humph and glimpsed her eyes roll as they both settled into chairs. Already, linen napkins, silverware, and glasses stood in perfect order at every damask-cushioned chair. At a glance, Kelly located the beverage table situated toward the front corner of the room. An industrial-sized coffeemaker with several spouts, along with plastic racks of cups and two immense containers providing cold beverages, added to the restaurant ambience, as disorienting as the fusion of voices.

No one sobbed now, but Kelly noted the flushed faces, grim smiles. How many of these people had truly known and loved Marilyn Patterson? Were they here out of genuine sorrow? Or obligation? Had they donned appropriate masks of grief and dismay to fit the occasion? Or did they genuinely feel the loss of this woman whose life accomplishments read like a directory of noteworthy ambitions? Her thoughts turning, Kelly heard the nearby comments and tuned in to the nearest snatches of conversation.

"I figured him for older..."

"He'll probably sell..."

"It doesn't seem possible..."

"This place will never be the same without her..."

"Wonder where he's been all these years? I sure as hell never met him."

Unconsciously, Kelly panned her gaze, searching for the 'him' in question. She recognized the older woman from the limo, fussing over the long table, talking with one of the aproned women. Neither of the other two men from the limo, nor Kip, stood anywhere within the crowd milling near the entrance. Her heart gripped with a thought of Kip possibly breaking down somewhere inside the Home, needing those two gentlemen's assistance to pull himself together. She should have asked for a ride home. Meeting him, coming face to face with him, under these circumstances, after all these years? Even if she'd meant to be here for him, to comfort him, she had no idea what she'd say, or even how to explain her presence.

Kelly hadn't admitted her reason for her early arrival, not to either of her parents; instead, she'd merely implied that she'd cleared her schedule earlier than anticipated. Some things a mother need not be told. Colleen, if no one else, knew exactly why her wayward daughter had come home early, but with a mother's intuition, Colleen hadn't broached the subject aloud, nor even alluded to the possibility. That Colleen knew, however, played heavily on Kelly's mind. A betrayal of sorts. She was engaged. She had no right to sit in this room, no reason for braving near blizzard conditions to attend this funeral. She'd met Kip Patterson exactly once and seen him only a dozen times a lifetime ago. Doubtful he'd even noticed her then; doubtful he'd remember her now.

An almost overwhelming urge to grab her coat and run stole over her.

Chapter 3

Keeping pace with Dr. Frances, Kip strode through the executive wing and passed through the French doors into the main lobby. The crowd had thinned at the entrance to the Oak Room. A monotonous lull of voices suggested a sizeable crowd. Momentarily, Kip's gaze landed on a pair of shapely legs and sped his attention upward, dismissing the young woman before she caught him noticing. Her legs remained her ace.

With Mark's touch on his elbow, Kip faltered a step and glanced in the direction Mark indicated. In the cove alongside the steps, Bickerman stood, sequestered with a stately gentleman. Between Bill's jutting jaw and sloped shoulders, the fellow put Kip in mind of a mole, which accounted for his instant annoyance as he veered toward the cove. For guys like Bickerman, the fashion industry had created football-padded shoulder insets, but Bill apparently preferred department-store-rack jackets, imitation silk ties, and cotton shirts as well. Administrator, second in command. Kip noted the strain of a white shirt at the man's slightly sagging middle. Desk job material. His eyes, quick and small, contradicted the mole image, more mouse-like and feral. And Kip had never adopted any fondness for rodents.

Dismissing Bill, ignoring him, Kip focused on the elder man. In perfect contrast to Bickerman, this character wore a tailored charcoal suit, pale chambray shirt, and a silk tie touched with wine-colored swirls. Formal without ostentation, a sleek, loose wave fell over his high, intelligent forehead. Salt and pepper brows punctuated his direct gaze; a like-colored mustache accented his chiseled features and firm jaw. A young sixty or a well-preserved eighty, Kip wagered before his memory kicked into high gear.

"Found him, did you, doctor?" Bill said offhandedly and clasped Kip's shoulder as if to present him forward into the attorney's arms. "Kip, I don't know if you've ever met Att. Madison. Senior partner of Madison, Cummings and Wade, the Home's legal firm. John, Kip Patterson."

Bickerman could have skipped this introduction. Madison darted a glance at the administrator, apparently sharing the thought. "Mr. Madison," Kip said while clasping the firm hand. "I suppose I can't say it's good to see you again."

"Under the circumstances, no," Madison said in a smooth, cultured voice. An honest sorrow affected his pale blue eyes. "My deepest sympathies."

"Thank you, sir."

Apologizing with his expression, Madison continued, "I realize this is an incredibly difficult time, Kip, but I just mentioned to Mr. Bickerman. There are several legal issues I'll need to discuss with you ... personally. If you could call my office at your earliest convenience? Possibly, we could schedule a meeting in the next day or two?"

Personally? Had Madison added the word routinely? Or had he applied a touch of emphasis on that word for Kip's or Bill's benefit? Looking into the pale blue eyes, his own abstracted. How much had his mother confided in this elder senior partner? Enough, apparently, for Madison to know Kip could enlist his personal attorneys to handle this affair as he'd planned. "Imperative, is it?"

Bickerman gripped Kip's elbow again while intruding. "I know this is the last thing you want to think about right now, Kip, but the sooner you meet with John, the better chance we'll have of keeping the Home running smoothly. If you like, I'll have Carolyn give John's office a call and arrange a meeting for tomorrow. I know you're probably eager to get back to California and all, but we have a lot of people depending on us."

Glancing down at the pudgy fingers denting his sleeve, Kip lifted his gaze to Bill's darting eyes and decided on the instant. He would need to change his travel plans after all. If for no other reason, he might enjoy sticking around long enough to unnerve this pompous ass, but on a far deeper level, Kip's thoughts turned. *Wrong. An inflection, a tone, a pitch,* something wrong, something niggling at the edges of his mind. "Do you really think so, Bill?" Kip asked offhandedly, allowing a hint of concern to affect his voice.

"Do I uh…? Think so, what?" he asked.

"People, Bill," Kip said with a slightly worried note. "Depending on us, and all that shit?"

Bill cast Madison a helpless glance, as if seeking support. Or offering confirmation? His tone softened, addressing a dim-witted child. "A great many people, Kip."

Interesting. Either Marilyn hadn't confided in Bickerman as well as he believed, or he was one hell of an actor. In every conversation, in every word, the idiot seemed to carry an unspoken question of genetics, as if the fellow doubted the integrity of Kip hailing from Marilyn's exceptional gene pool.

"Tomorrow then," Kip said smugly and looked at the attorney, who studied him more critically than a moment ago. Undoubtedly, the man knew something beyond the widespread in-house rumors. "Tomorrow then, sir. I'll let Bill handle the details. The sooner the better. As he said, we don't want to let anyone down if they're counting on us." With all the pizzazz of an absentminded professor, Kip drew his gaze away and fleeted a glance toward Mark Frances, long enough to notice the physician hadn't appreciated his performance. "You did say they won't start without me. We have to get in there." As an afterthought, he glanced at Madison with a breezy, "You will join us, won't you, sir?"

"In a moment," Madison said absently.

Nodding, Kip completed his turn, moving at the doctor's side toward the Oak Room.

Under his breath, Frances commented, "You missed your calling, Kip. You could win an Oscar."

Obviously, he'd need to temper his dramatics in the good doctor's presence. Either Frances had become Marilyn's confidant, or he relied on his memory to doubt the multitude of rumors. Doubtful Marilyn had ever boasted about her son, and truthfully, she might not have known a great deal to tell even if she was inclined toward bragging. Self-employed, independently wealthy, jetsetter.

The dancers, Kip considered in a fleeting instant. His mother had never once asked why he'd begun sending her ballet dancers, and that discrepancy had disturbed him more than a time or two.

Kip barely stepped through the Oak Room doors when heads turned, and the nearest conversations faltered. Had he known he'd be inundated again, he might have taken drastic measures to avoid this affair. But it was too late to bow out gracefully.

Detached, Kip accepted another round of condolences that only began with the burly state senator, Adam Blackwell, who suggested they get together sometime soon. Undoubtedly, to discuss a campaign contribution. Blackwell's counterpart in the political arena, Mike Fischer, vied for equal time, while his pageant-winning wife, Lorain, smiled a little too sweetly, monopolizing Kip's hand in a light grip. Randall's mayor, Carl Simon, and his portly wife, Peg, who flushed when Kip returned a chaste kiss on her round pink cheek, weren't to be outdone. Back-to-back, the offbeat pair offered condolences and extended social invitations.

Behind Kip's listless smiles and gazes lurked the mind of a cynic, one belabored with a niggling thought. How many of these alleged friends meant to pay their respects, and how many had arrived only to gain points with the heir apparent to Whistlebrook? From politicians to physicians to local and not-so-local businessmen, only the faces and phrases changed.

"Such a dear..." "We'll miss her..." "We're so sorry..."

When Carolyn McAnthony edged into the group, blue eyes misty and her lovely face haunted with sincere dread, Kip offered his undivided attention. She'd only begun her career at the home the summer before his departure. An office gofer, he recalled, a first or second-year college student. With no trouble at all, the tall, shapely blond had flaunted her long, slender legs beneath trendy mini-skirts, driving one introverted thirteen-year-old half crazy. For weeks, he'd remained in a frenzy of raw nerves before he controlled his hormones long enough to manage a smile in her presence. Talking had come later. About six or seven years later, Kip realized in a lame moment. By the time he'd reopened communications with Whistlebrook, Carolyn had secured a degree, risen to senior secretary, and taken vows of loyalty to Samuel McAnthony. Kip had been crushed.

When she offered, Kip accepted her embrace, returning one nearly as firm. Halfheartedly, he wondered if she was responsible for his ongoing attraction to blonds. With the scent of her perfume, he held her a little longer, and to hell with Sam, who stood at her back. Where Edna Feeney had lagged, Carolyn had picked up the slack, forever bridging the shaky fault-line between himself and Marilyn Patterson.

Parting, Kip glimpsed her wiping discreetly at tears while he turned, offering his attention and hand to her husband. Only once in passing, several years earlier, Kip had met Sam McAnthony, but Kip knew him well enough. Leave nothing to chance. If nothing else, Marilyn had taught him that much.

Sam dressed and acted the part of a Princeton grad, his silk tie knotted in a perfect double Windsor, his suit tailored and impeccably creased. He wore his pale brown hair cut and styled to an acceptable business length, not too long to appear liberal, nor too short to portray conservative. His only redeeming quality was his open adoration of his wife. A fact he evinced with a hand on her back and a fleeting, concerned glance before accepting Kip's handshake.

"Glad you could make it, Sam," Kip said mechanically.

"My condolences, Kip," McAnthony said gravely, his handshake firm, his gaze intent. "I have to leave in a couple minutes, but if there's anything I can do for you, feel free to call or just mention it to Carolyn."

Was there a hidden message, a discreet admission of sorts? Or was this simply another lame invitation, an obligatory response like so many others extended over the past two days? Doubtful, McAnthony knew enough about Morning Sun Enterprises to understand whom he addressed. More than likely, Sam offered his financial expertise and assistance regarding the rumors Carolyn might have carried to him concerning Kip's inheritance. Whistlebrook was worth a fortune, and its sole beneficiary ... *a moron?* "I may just take you up on that offer, Sam. Thank you," Kip managed before more bodies pressed about him.

Unwittingly, the crowd had shuffled him toward the head of the buffet line that extended the width of the Oak Room. Just the concoction of smells, from steaming pans of lasagna to broiling pans heaped with chicken and sausage, was enough to pitch his stomach in angry protest. Either he should have carried through with his decision to leave, or he should have come equipped with a pain reliever. God knows, he hadn't expected the violent episodes he'd suffered before limiting his intake to a cup of coffee. Fifteen years, for God's sake. Fifteen years, and he still couldn't stomach the sight or smell of food after a funeral. Genuine dread passed through his gray eyes and mind as he scanned the long table. No way could he reach the other end and salvage his dignity.

Apparently, his distress hadn't gone unnoticed. Edna touched his elbow on one side.

In a glance, Kip read her concern and understanding in her soft brown eyes.

At his opposite side, Mark Frances leaned, whispering discreetly, "Are you going to make it? Or would you rather just go sit down?"

Grand! Flashing a faintly hostile glance at Mark, Kip leaned just as discreetly, whispering with a faintly bitter edge. "Rather belated, this concern of yours."

Mark suffered a slight flinching smile, the concern not entirely lifted. "You don't look well. Possibly, you should just enlist Fr. Jordan to say grace."

Rather belated, this transference of duty as well, Kip considered. Until now, his only contribution to this entire ordeal had involved his firm request for a Catholic priest to conduct the services. Pre-mortem, his mother had suggested a minister of generic license. Understanding why she might have neglected or rejected Catholicism at her end, knowing damn full well she'd been baptized into the faith, bedamned if he would allow a minister to commit her remains on some rampant journey into the stratosphere. Collecting his thoughts, aware of his genuine lapse and not appreciating the intensity of Mark's gaze in its wake, Kip firmed his gaze, leaning again to whisper discreetly, "If you require another blessing, sir? By all means, enlist Fr. Jordan, but I suggest you do so quickly."

Frances agreed hurriedly and stepped away to find Fr. Jordan.

More grateful than he would admit, Kip returned the heavy industrial plate to the first stack. As Fr. Jordan called for silence, he bowed his head to receive the blessing.

Only once in his life, he'd ridden on a roller coaster. Only two or three years ago. He'd been considering the acquisition of an amusement park, diversifying and capitalizing on the entertainment industry. One ride on that roller coaster had altered his plans when entering the negotiations. Exit amusement park. Enter shopping mall. And he suffered the same sway and pitch now.

Too soon, Fr. Jordan concluded his blessing, and Edna delivered another plate into Kip's hand, uttering, "You need to try eating a little bit, sweetie."

Forcing his hands still, Kip lifted several sprigs of raw broccoli, celery sticks, and carrots to his plate, not thrilled when one of the kitchen assistants hoisted an immense square of lasagna from the pan. His focus shifted as his stomach cramped. He might have missed the woman's aim if not for Edna catching his forearm, directing the plate. With a faintly amused glance, Kip read her tense gaze and shrugged. "Obviously, still a problem," he commented quietly.

Patting his arm gently, she suggested, "Why don't you take that, sweetie, and go sit down?"

In a slight glance down the filled table, he nodded as he turned, and nearly collided with Bill Bickerman, who clasped his elbow.

Caught between a smile and a grimace, Bill started, "We have a table—" His gaze dropped to Kip's near-empty plate, his mouth twisted in a classic grimace. Rising, his dark eyes epitomized concern. "Heck, kid, you need to eat more than that. Let's get you—"

"Excuse me," Kip interrupted while glancing at the hand on his elbow up to Bickerman. For the past two days, Bickerman had insinuated himself into conversations and initiated dominant physical contact like a parent reprimanding an unruly child. In a steady stream, Bill had demonstrated his superior knowledge of the Home and Marilyn Patterson and reiterated his authority while feigning paternal concern. Unless Marilyn had slipped off the edge toward the end, it was doubtful she'd ever disillusioned Bickerman into believing her wayward son needed constant supervision. Kip could only conclude Bickerman considered number-one-and-only son a threat, however ineffectual, and intended to establish his reign posthaste. Judging by his character, or lack thereof, Kip suspected the insecurities lingering behind his feigned concern.

What redeeming qualities had Marilyn noticed to keep this fellow as her right hand? Obviously, Bickerman possessed a talent for subterfuge, if nothing else. Only his eyes betrayed his contempt in fleeting glimpses. His only other apparent talent lay in his ability to annoy a certain wayward son.

Without losing his grasp or his expression of concern, Bill stepped back and indicated the center table, wisely forfeiting another mention of food. "What's your pleasure, Kip? Coffee, tea? A soda?"

Glancing vacantly at Bill, Kip caught several people watching this interplay before locating the coffeepot stationed in an alcove of windows beyond the buffet table. Maybe coffee wasn't a bad idea. God knows, he felt slightly off balance, like a sleepwalker rather than a thinking, functioning adult. Was it any wonder the idiot called him 'kid' and Edna Feeney still called him 'sweetie' as if he were a toddler? Sliding the plate between a set of silverware, he turned and nearly ran into Bill.

"I'll get it, Kip. Just tell me what you want."

"At the moment, I'd appreciate a clear path to the coffeepot," Kip commented in an inherently soft voice, not to be mistaken for humor.

Bickerman was swiftly becoming an irritant, and with the stubby fingers locking again on Kip's elbow, tension slid down his spine. On a good day, uninvited physical contact could be a problem even without the implication of restraint—and this wasn't a good day.

What the hell had Marilyn seen in this character to place him second in command?

Unconsciously, Kip lifted a mug from the industrial plastic rack. His focus trailed through the old, beveled glass, across the snowy lawn, remembering. Remembering voices, faces. Memories, so damned many memories. For the past two days, in every dormant moment, the images and sounds of the Home had assailed his mind. He needed to put them away, all of them, close the book on them.

Kip Patterson was definitely not the boy whose image had haunted Kelly for more than half her lifetime—not the cute curly-haired boy who'd slammed into the front door, propelled against the maple wood beneath the massive paws of their golden retriever. In a flashing instant, Kelly remembered his gray eyes wide with fright as Max had plastered him with a wet tongue. Even anticipating the changes after glimpsing him at the cemetery, Kelly hadn't fully prepared for the full impact. He was not cute—he was heart-halting handsome from the shock of sun-streaked blond hair to the quirk in his pale brown mustache to the flash of his pale blue, nearly gray eyes.

Across the heads and shoulders, between dark cloth and pale faces, Kelly had watched him, taking the full measure of this stranger in slow degrees. She would have recognized him, would have known him anywhere, but the reason eluded her. Only an echo of the boy haunted the man's features. He wasn't the gaunt, pale-faced child who'd seemed so shy and uncertain a lifetime ago. Tall, built solid, his physique enhanced within a tailored black suit, he carried himself with confidence and arrogance that overwhelmed even the more impressive characters in this crowd, including the senator who didn't lack charisma.

Watching him, stopped now in silhouette against the window, Kelly suffered a weird anticipation, vaguely aware of her pulse hiking, her heart aching. Rather than a smile, that soft quirk in his mustache evoked sadness;

his eyes, even across this distance, reflected the gray afternoon light. His eyes. Swamped in long dark lashes, the color of his eyes … she would know him anywhere. And those eyes were the reason. Gray. Never in her life, not before, not since, had Kelly met another with eyes more gray than blue. Very nearly the color of polished steel, she realized, wondering if his present posture offered a trick of the light. God, he was handsome, more handsome than she'd imagined, and for just an instant, she wished she'd found him short, fat, and entirely disgusting. She could have walked away. As superficial as that admission sounded even in her mind, she could have walked away if her first true love had appeared tarnished and warped by time.

Not good, Kell, she nearly uttered aloud, oblivious of the voices around her as well as the bodies rising to take their place in the buffet line. She was engaged—happily, wholeheartedly—engaged to be married to a man she most assuredly loved. This fellow, this stranger from the past? A fool's fantasy. A childhood fling. Her first case of puppy love. She wasn't a child now. Not an eleven-year-old to fall head over heels in love with an older boy. Three years had seemed like an insurmountable age difference to her scant eleven years, and how she'd hated JD for mentioning all those double dates. Even then, Kelly had tabulated the years, had calculated how many years would need to pass before he might consider her old enough to become interested.

Sixteen, she remembered as her gaze misted with reflection. At sweet sixteen, Kip was supposed to ride onto the Muldens' front lawn on a white horse and carry her away in a shower of balloons. No further would her eleven-year-old mind calculate, and she'd thought then, she would forgive him for being so much older.

He would be close to thirty, now, and he'd never ridden into Randall—in a car, much less on a white horse—before she'd left for college. For the first time in fifteen years, Kelly knew where to find him, and—if only to herself—she could admit her desire just to see him, to be here for him. And that thought had confirmed her decision to come home early.

Damn him! Just damn him for not wearing a ring on his left hand, for not at least dragging a woman on his arm, for not having a dozen children trailing after him. For not looking like a *toad!*

"Oh my goodness," Colleen whispered.

Distractedly, Kelly's attention turned and riveted, watching the tall, dark stranger sidestepping through the buffet line. *Wonders never cease.*

"Penny for your thoughts."

Momentarily lost, caught within an image from the past sounding far too real, Kip tilted his blind gaze. Hazel eyes, barely a spark of humor apparent, a dark mustache and beard, both neatly trimmed around a faint grin, rather long, sleek, dark waves ... Fr. Richard? The face came from the past as surely as those words echoed from the past.

'Penny for your thoughts.' The voice had resounded and intruded, bouncing off the collage-covered walls at a pitch to jolt his every taut muscle. Kip had strangled sobs, too startled to breathe ... not Fr. Richard.

Doubting, Kip dropped his focus, scanning the sturdy shoulders and solid trim build within a tailored pinstriped suit. Familiar, this bold, balanced pose, the square shoulders, and rugged, handsome features. The past. Everything in Whistlebrook hailed from the past. Faces and images swam beneath a murky surface, refusing to either remain buried or bob into crystal clarity.

He should have hired a goddamn stand-in and skipped this entire ordeal! He'd stayed here too damned long already! Too long trapped inside the ancient walls, too many faces and impressions, too many glimpses! And this shaggy face, haunted with as much concern as sorrow, was yet another enigma. The eyes, intelligent hazel eyes, quick with perceptions and wisdom in a face far too young. No Zen master, this. A prodigious student. Perhaps one with an impressive calmness and a talent for observation.

Only seconds passed, but the stranger made no move to close the respectable gap between them, as if he understood the dynamics of personal space and intentionally awaited an invitation to enter. Confident, this fellow, and patient enough to await the recognition he apparently expected to strike at any second.

"It's been a long time," the enigma spoke in a deep voice, presently subdued and hauntingly familiar.

Tense from head to heel, Kip studied the face, noting the disheartened twitch at the corner of the mustached lips. As if a wall crumbled inside his head, the face transformed. Younger, barely a hint of a mustache shaded the upper lip, always tipped in a smile. Even when JD Mulden raged, he'd smiled, although he'd affected more of a snarl. Between his hazel eyes, capable of reaching a hue close to emerald, and his rugged face open to endless expression, the integrity and intensity of his emotions had always shone on the surface. More subdued, more patient, this man who'd replaced the child of yesteryear. But the years seemed to fall away, rolling backward at light speed.

The bearded lips twitched, and hazel eyes strained toward amusement.

Kip felt his expression breaking. A genuinely bewildered smile crept onto his lips only half a second before reality struck. This wasn't a chance meeting at a restaurant or a gas station. Not one of a million other places where Kip had suffered a memory to believe he spotted Mulden in a crowd of strangers. Not a party.

Mom's dead!

Hot coffee plopped over the rim of the heavy china cup, stinging Kip's fingers as surely as the tears stung his eyes. Not in a millennium had he considered Marilyn Patterson his 'Mom.' Abruptly awake to tremors coursing through his veins, Kip set the cup down clumsily and found a stack of napkins through a blur. "Damn."

A powerful grip caught his shoulder, and in a stopped instant, Kip found JD Mulden's hazel eyes turned to glass. In slow motion, Mulden's gaze slid through the window. Blinking away tears, JD echoed, "Damn."

In another instant, the years blew away, and to hell with appearances! They started a handshake, started smiles, but more tears threatened. And JD Mulden was the only person in this room who'd arrived with the single intention of consoling Kip Patterson. This once, the embrace was neither semi-formal, cordial, nor an obligation. Good God, he felt like he was thirteen, going on fourteen again! For just a brief moment, he wasn't alone in the room, not alone with his grief or detached from it.

Parting, Kip swallowed a lump in his throat and tried blinking away the sting, realized the futility, and wiped discreetly at his eyes before focusing on JD. How many times had he considered looking up Mulden, always hoping their paths would cross just once more, but not like this, not under these circumstances. Not with a funeral shroud over his head, death hovering in the wings. He felt sick, sick and nearly as confused and vulnerable as he had when he'd first met Mulden. Too many memories threatened to break the surface. Too many emotions lingered that he couldn't allow himself to feel.

Time, there would be time later, when he was away from here, distanced in body, as well as mind.

"Almost didn't recognize you, man," JD said with a grin. "What? You don't wear hats anymore?"

"Not indoors," Kip answered, suddenly feeling awkward, as if he should know what to say. How to say it. What is there to say after fifteen years? *So, how've you been? What have you been up to?* Banal amenities reserved for dinner parties and inconsequential acquaintances. Mulden deserved better. Required more. But this once, Kip was at a loss. Thirteen. Insecure. Unsure of how much to confide or how to trust. *'…I'm enrolled in a seminary school.'*

'Bullshit! That's bullshit! You're kidding, right? This is your warped fucking idea of a joke—'

"I uh … I'm really sorry about your mother, Kip," JD said quietly. "I'd have been here sooner, but I just found out last night. How you holding up, man?"

Shaking his momentary daze, Kip shrugged, bouncing a glance off Mulden's sober gaze. As a teenager, JD had never been truly sober. Or had he? *Oh, sure, he had. Twice—damn it! Stop it! Put it away!* Kip collected his thoughts to hear an echo of a distant female voice coaching, *Poise!*

Glancing over several curious faces, Kip realized he stood blocking the coffeepot, and a line had formed. "Coffee?" he asked JD, while collecting his cup and refilling what he'd spilled. Again, his hand shook, and several drops sailed over the rim. *Damn it! This wasn't supposed to happen!*

"Maybe I'd better pour it, huh?" JD offered. "And I probably oughta offer to carry yours to a table if you're serious about drinking it."

"Damned spout's leaking," Kip commented flippantly, and managed to fill a second cup, handing it to JD while pulling himself together. With an effort, he fell into his role, catching Mulden's curiously bemused gaze. "Cream and sugar, you'll need master solo. Obviously, I won't make it as a waiter." His timing was off. He could feel it, hear it, and see it in Mulden's more complex gaze. *How to play the fool with a man who apparently knew better?* Then, too, fifteen years had passed. Things changed. People changed. Mulden was as much a stranger as every other face in this crowd.

As Mulden accepted the offer and added cream, Kip glanced at the table where he'd left his plate. Edna, Mark, Fr. Jordan, Bickerman, and Carolyn McAnthony occupied the table now. Apparently, Sam had departed. At the empty chair, a loaded plate waited. Annoyed, Kip caught Edna watching him. She darted a weak smile toward Bill, who leaned in conversation with Fr. Jordan. Poise, Kip remembered as another stranger offered a condolence instead of a 'pardon me' while reaching past him to collect a cup from the tray.

In a split second, Kip flashed a thought and signaled Mulden to start them moving toward the reserved table. "You remember Mrs. Feeney?"

"How could I forget?" JD said, though he appeared slightly curious as he glimpsed Kip.

Coming behind Bickerman's chair, ushering JD ahead of him, Kip noticed Edna eyeing Mulden, no doubt scouring her memory. With his first honest amusement, Kip watched her recognition dawn as he began, "You remember JD?"

Pushing quickly off her chair, more tears erupted in her eyes. "Why... Of course, honey! Just look at you!"

Stifling a chuckle, JD leaned to hug her and brushed a kiss on her cheek. "Still my favorite gourmet," he told her, back-to-back with, "My sympathies, ma'am."

Only JD Mulden could combine those two lines and sound sincere on both counts. Perhaps Mulden hadn't changed tremendously, still as smooth and confident as ever.

"Lordy, I thought by now, you'd weigh 300 lbs. with the way you put away food. Just look at you," Edna spoke with an echo of her old self, her eyes dancing down Mulden in genuine delight. At least at this moment, the grief had lifted from her rheumy eyes.

"I don't eat *quite* as much as I used to, and I get plenty of exercise," Mulden confided. "You're looking good."

"Do sit down, JD," Kip suggested while pulling out the empty chair behind the filled plate.

"Looks like someone's sitting there," Mulden said with a curious grin.

"Actually, I thought I was, but apparently, I've misplaced my plate," Kip commented with an errant glance at the surrounding tables. "I'm sure I'll locate—"

"Kip," Bickerman interrupted as expected. "That's your plate. That little bit you had on there—"

Making the mistake of glancing at the plate, Kip's gaze halted. The lasagna had listed to one side, spilling red sauce in a puddle. Strings of melted mozzarella and white chunks of Ricotta swam into a mound of yellowed potato salad. Rigatoni noodles and sauce crowded a breast of chicken. A scoop of coleslaw swam in the dredges, adding white paste to the entire wretched tapestry. Even on his best day, the sight of that disaster would test Kip's mettle. He suffered the rise at the lowest level, uttering in a breath, "Good God, what an atrocity." Not quite recovering, he found Mulden watching him with a faintly curious grin. "As I said, please," he nearly stammered. "Sit. Bon appétit."

"Kip," Bill spoke while pushing from his chair. His smile and grimace clashed as he bounced a wary glance off JD, his wheels turning to identify this apparently well-known stranger.

What? Someone you don't know, Bill? Kip asked silently and might have inclined toward amusement if he felt less like vomiting on Bill's wretched polyester suit.

"Buddy, you really need to get something in your stomach," Bill said in a paternal tone. "I'm sure your friend would prefer to help himself at the buffet and join us when he's finished—"

"No. Actually, this looks pretty good," JD said and caught Kip's gaze. "You want me to get you a couple celery sticks or some pudding before I sit down?"

Oh, Mulden hadn't changed at all, still in tune and just as quick to grasp a situation. Kip glanced toward the door, calculating the distance to the restroom. Unfortunately, his attention snagged on the buffet table. Too late, he realized his mistake. At the sight of an obese woman flopping an oversized slice of lasagna next to a stuffed sandwich, Kip's stomach wrenched with enough force to send a wince through his eyes. Bringing his gaze to Mulden, Kip swayed with the start of tunnel vision, his stomach rolling. "N-o," he collected himself, barely. Touching Mulden's elbow in a signal to sit, he managed, "Excuse me a moment. I'll be right back."

Edna knew; her eyes flashed speculation. And JD probably knew. Mark, too, by his swift glance as Kip sidestepped around Mulden. With as much elegance as he could muster, Kip cut a path through the strangers in the buffet line, accepting condolences swiftly. In the main lobby, he quickened his pace, passing into the administrative wing and breaking into a trot. Barely in time, he passed through the restroom door and caught a hand on the porcelain tank. A single gulp of coffee and a pre-funeral cup of tea splashed into the commode. When only dry heaves remained, he sidled unsteadily to the first of four sinks and leaned on his forearms, splashing cold water on his face and gasping for breath against the acidic burn in his throat.

Nothing's changed—My God, nothing's changed, he chanted silently while finding a starched white towel and holding it against his face. His stomach still cramped, threatening to rip skyward. Lightheaded, he slid down the ceramic wall, resting on his haunches, burying his face in the towel on his raised knees.

Nothing's changed. So many funerals. Oh God, so many funerals. A sob tightened in his throat, thickening, threatening to break loose, *and this wasn't supposed to happen! Not again after all these years!*

Uncontrollably, he remembered...

Thirteen,

At thirteen, his stomach had begun to rebel. He'd raced to the nearest john and sat in that quasi-public restroom, dry-heaving, tasting vomit and wishing he'd eaten something to throw up to relieve the wicked cramps. Ignorance and innocence had passed. He'd known more about death and final journeys than he'd ever needed to learn. No longer could he hover graveside, listening calmly to a benediction, feeling only sadness and wishing an old one well on his way. He was thirteen, almost fourteen, awakening to the opposite sex, thinking about life after high school, and he'd given himself a hernia while rescuing an obese elder woman from a dangerous fall, a lethal fall. The East Wing. Ramsey. Her name came to him. He'd stepped out of the elevator, pushing a cart, always pushing a cart by then. *The sound. That sound. A keening wail—*

Chapter 4

"Ya know," JD's voice echoed.

Kip jolted; his breath caught within the towel.

More carefully, quietly, Mulden continued, "You were sitting a lot like that the first time we met." In the pause, slick soles skidded on ceramic tile, shifting. Cloth skidded on the wall, descending. "First day in a new school," Mulden continued at closer range. "Some guy comes running in the john at lunchtime and loses his cookies? I can tell you—I had some reservations about buying my lunch."

The memory evaporated. Grateful for the interruption, Kip caught the implication and amusement, his thoughts swaying, collecting. His breath started again, a little easier. Drying his face, he lowered the towel and tipped his head against the wall, reading Mulden's sober concern. "Didn't bother you for long," Kip remembered. "As I recall, you seriously altered the school's supply of cheeseburgers at least once."

"Not before I checked with the hospital for any regular cases of food poisoning," Mulden commented, a haunted amusement lighting his hazel eyes.

"It takes eight to ten hours for most symptoms of salmonella to manifest," Kip commented helpfully.

"Yeah? You probably knew that back then, too," Mulden said with a humph. "I didn't have your brain power. It just looked suspicious as hell to me."

"You're still full of shit," Kip decided, realizing abruptly. "It really is good to see you, JD"

"Same here. Just wish the circumstances were different."

Kip nodded; his focus wandered with his dread. "Me too."

"Ya know, I used to check in here every once in a while," Mulden reflected quietly. "I spoke to your mom a few times to find out where you were. Seems to me you disappeared for a while," he paused, maybe thinking, hoping for a comment.

Nearly three years, Kip answered silently, offering nothing.

"So ... Where are you living now? Around here?"

"L.A. most recently," Kip answered, looking over. "You?"

"Colorado. Aspen, most recently." Mulden smirked before seeming to remember why they were here. His expression dimmed; his focus trailed as his voice adopted an apologetic note. "My folks still live around here. They tried reaching me when they heard about your mom. I've been on patrol for the past week. One helluva snowstorm blew in last Friday."

"You're in a ski patrol?"

Shrugging, JD commented, "A ranger. At least that's what I am at the moment. I was in the service for a while. Air Force. I just sort of bounce from one career to the next. How about you? What are you up to now?"

Nothing he would admit to. His thoughts drifted along with his gaze. Mulden a ranger? Not surprising.

'You can't spend your whole life reading. So, what do you want to do? Hunting, fishing, boating? Tennis? Racquetball? We could lift weights...'

"Hey? Earth to Kip. Do you read me? Over?"

"You're not on patrol," Kip stated and pushed off the floor, rising in a single easy motion. Too many memories. Too much tension. His stomach still hurt, but he could probably manage a little longer. Folding the towel, Kip considered hanging it on the rack. This wasn't his bathroom in the privacy of his apartment. He tossed the soiled towel in the industrial bin against the wall and motioned Mulden toward the door.

In the hall, JD asked, "So, are you going to answer me or keep me in suspense? It doesn't look like you became a priest."

Amused, Kip glanced over while ushering Mulden around the corner. "Obviously, I'm not wearing a white collar or toting a Bible."

"Obviously," JD smirked. "But then, I never figured you'd become a priest, so that doesn't come as a major shock. So?"

With a flashing annoyance, Kip ran into Mulden's gaze. "I forgot what a persistent son of a bitch you were," he commented lightly.

Taken aback, JD's curiosity lingered behind speculation. "You're still a smart ass."

Talking helped. Vomiting helped. More relaxed, Kip ushered JD into the Oak Room. Bickerman no longer sat at the head table. Kip spotted him hovering over John Madison and two other well-dressed gentlemen at a table across the crowded hall. Mark Frances and Carolyn were engaged in conversation. Mrs. Feeney spoke over her shoulder to another elder woman, probably a member of the Ladies Auxiliary. A line of people still ambled at the buffet table. Kip motioned to JD, suggesting, "Help yourself to another plate. I'm nearly certain there's something edible in that spread, and I probably should mingle for a moment."

JD's gaze shifted with a thought. "I probably should find...? There they are."

Kip followed Mulden's gaze across the rows of tables and faces, landing on the handsome couple in time to see the middle-aged man lowering his hand from a brief wave. In a split second, Kip remembered seeing them both recently. Last night. Both had come through the line in Fitzpatrick's.

"Damn," he uttered aloud, annoyed with himself for not recognizing them earlier. From his father, JD had inherited his rugged handsomeness and capable build, along with his dark, wavy hair. Fair-skinned and light-haired, his mother wore her strawberry blond hair neatly styled to enhance her slender face. He should have remembered them. Damn it!

Too many names had assailed him, along with faces, while Bickerman stood boasting about his supreme knowledge of Marilyn Patterson's friends and acquaintances. The Muldens hadn't rated high on Bill's list. He'd shuffled them past and cast them aside like spectators with general admission tickets.

Deciding abruptly, Kip veered into the center row, his focus catching on the young woman seated next to Mrs. Mulden. Good God! She was magnificent! Deep green eyes, long lashes, a truly awesome scatter of wild walnut curls and waves framing her delicate features, which reminded him instantly of the porcelain faces in his mother's collection. If her figure below the table matched what her head and shoulders promised, she was, indeed, a woman to stir his imagination, and quicken his heartbeat with the swirl of wondrous color spreading from her image. If ever he'd seen such vibrant colors in an aura, none like these. Yellows, greens, blues, glorious reds to evoke passion—

First, address the Muldens, he remembered with an effort and sidled through the last two chairs, halting alongside Jarred Mulden's chair. "Mr. Mulden," Kip said formally, proffering his palm and bouncing a concentrated focus, careful not to look past JD's mother. "Mrs. Mulden. I appreciate you both coming last evening." Without pause, he tipped his focus to Jarred Mulden. "Truly sorry we didn't have a chance to speak then."

"Understandable, Kip," Jarred said while clasping a second hand over their locked palm. "You have our sympathies."

"Thank you, sir," he said sincerely, slipping his hand free, taking a step to touch Colleen Mulden's hand. He parted his lips, intending to speak, but stopped, suddenly, looking into the younger woman's soft hazel eyes at close range. A vision of flushed cheeks, a nervous smile, a ponytail flashed through his mind, along with a sudden revelation that these were JD's eyes filled with a heady blend of restrained anticipation and honest sorrow. She'd been a pretty little thing, ten or eleven to his manly thirteen, rounded and happy.

"My God," he uttered as he drank in the slender contours of her face. *Truly magnificent!* Only a dusting of color and liner enhanced her almond-shaped eyes, and her slender cheeks carried a natural pink blush, likely from the chill outside. Finding voice, he managed, "You're JD's little sister ... Kelly, isn't it?"

Her hand came into his, which he couldn't recall offering. His thumb descended of its own accord to touch upon the slender fingers as if trapping a butterfly by its wings.

Respectably restrained, a soft smile haunted the natural curve of her full, glossy lips, the color subdued. Her eyes, looking into his, into him, conveyed a sympathy as soft as her touch. "You have an incredible memory, Mr. Patterson," she said cordially, perhaps recalling, as he was, that they had only met once.

"Please, just Kip, Miss Mulden," he managed smoothly, struggling to compose himself. Rarely, very rarely, he suffered an immediate desire to know, to be known.

"Kelly," she offered with a fleeting smile. An aura of dismay returned as she added, "I'm really sorry about your mother, Kip."

Odd, for a moment, he'd forgotten why they were here. Why she was here. Visions of an immense golden retriever staggering him, slapping his face with a wet tongue, and drenching him accompanied the echo of young voices transcending time. He'd never come face-to-face with a dog, let alone the golden monster to slam him against the Muldens' front door. His grin wavered as he collected himself to the reality of droning voices in real time.

"Thank you," he offered absently, stepping back from Kelly, only to jolt slightly when a chubby claw snared his hand.

Twisted on his chair, the stout man looked up with a round, blood-pressure-flamed face.

Reality. Just another face in the crowd of quasi mourners.

"Don't know if you remember me, Mr. Patterson. We met yesterday afternoon. Sam Haliday, Haliday's Linen Service. We've been supplying the Home here for a lot of years. Your mother always treated us right, and vice versa. You get a chance, sir, you give me a call, and we'll go over those contracts we have. Get you squared away."

What needed to be squared away? And was there any point in telling this rotund man to speak to Bickerman if a problem existed? Knowing he probably appeared momentarily dazed—as he was told, he always appeared dazed when thinking—Kip slid his hand from the grip. "I'll do that, sir," he commented absently.

A not too discreet voice whispered, "He looks so lost."

"I didn't even know she *had* a son."

"Handsome boy," another whispered.

"Kip? Are you alright?"

Absently, he found Colleen Mulden studying him. Her hand rested on his, which had caught the back of her chair. Nodding, he concentrated, collecting his thoughts. Honestly? He wasn't one bit fine. He'd rather be mountain climbing in the Alps than standing in this wretched lounge. "Fine, thanks," he answered.

"You look—"

"Kip," Bickerman interrupted Mr. Mulden's words; his hand flopped onto Kip's shoulder. "There's someone over here I'd like you to meet. He's an old friend of your mother's—"

Unleashing a momentary rage in his gray eyes, Kip focused on Bickerman. The man's friendly hand retracted as if bitten, as his smile turned to an honest grimace. If this weren't a crowded room, if this weren't a reception in honor of Marilyn Patterson, Bill Bickerman would be picking his teeth off the floor and swallowing bits of jawbone. Enough was enough.

"You feeling alright, buddy?" Bickerman asked in a voice to attract several glances. "Maybe we ought to go get a breath of fresh air. I know this isn't easy, buddy, but we'll get you through it."

Enough—is—enough. With a natural eloquence, Kip caught Bill's shoulder in a friendly grip and leaned. Bickerman indulged him, leaning to receive the discreet whisper. In a low, careful tone, Kip commented, "If you grab me like that again, Bill, I swear to the Almighty Holy Father, I'll break your fucking wrist—" Bill recoiled; Kip firmed his grip, welding him to the floor. "I appreciate your enthusiasm, but tone it down or we'll have a problem."

Bill looked at him without a trace of a smile or a grimace. His dark eyes emitted genuine contempt, the first sincere expression over the past two days. A split second later, Bickerman smiled his slick, condescending smile, the smile of a man making concessions under extreme conditions. "No problem, buddy. How about I introduce you to this gentleman? Then you could return to your friends?"

Masking his contempt, Kip looked into the dark eyes, sensing the intimidation as surely as the tension within the administrator's shoulder. "Lead the way, Bill," Kip said in a benign tone, remembering appearances and proper etiquette as he glanced between the Muldens. His gaze lingered on Kelly a second longer as he offered, "Hope to speak to you again. Truly glad you came. If you'll excuse me...?"

Following Bickerman through the tables, Kip stopped nearly a dozen times, accepting strangers who inevitably needed to touch his hand or sleeve as they professed sympathy or offered help. Neither reporters nor photographers had gained entry, but it remained an odd collection. From Whistlebrook staff—those off duty, others obviously taking their breaks coming and going in brief intervals—to the children and grandchildren of residents, both living and deceased, to an upscale crowd of businessmen and women. Legal, financial, political...

One elder gentleman stopped Kip and spoke at length about how Marilyn Patterson had taken care of his father and how she'd made the old man's life comfortable for over a dozen years. Only as the fellow mentioned 'the Prince of Whistlebrook,' Kip's attention riveted. He hadn't heard those words in years. Not in nearly fifteen years, he realized, and listened as this aging man continued, mentioning 'bagpipes' and 'a full Veteran's funeral' which the Prince had arranged at his own expense.

McGuire! This was Irish McGuire's son. Like the Muldens, this man hadn't merely come to honor Marilyn Patterson. For a moment longer, Kip held the firm handshake. Sean McGuire had come to console and thank the 'Prince of Whistlebrook' who'd given a life-worn old man a reason to live and his dignity in death.

Sean McGuire hadn't been the first person to mention the past, a past Kip had buried and mourned when he'd departed a lifetime ago. In a maelstrom, bits and pieces of his childhood swirled, fusing with the present reality of ambulatory residents joining the reception of civic groups and auxiliaries.

One woman mentioned having their meetings, "In this very room," and "Will we still be permitted to use your facilities?"

"You'll need to take that up with Mr. Bickerman," Kip had answered, though he couldn't recall when he'd spoken those words.

"Kip, I'd like you to meet Denton McDaniels. Mr. McDaniels, Kip Patterson."

"Sir," Kip said absently, automated as he grasped the older man's palm. For an old man, McDaniels had a firm grip, but then, clearing his focus, Kip reconsidered the man's age. White-haired, yes, but his lined face with a half-mast grin and a penetrating pale blue gaze seemed to counter his age. A premature gray, Kip realized while noting the stately elegance in his tailored suit and appreciating the flash of a Rolex and gold rings. His mother's old friend had class, along with a faint English accent.

"Pleasure to meet you again, lad. You have my condolences."

"Thank you, sir," he answered, automated as he tried drawing the arrogant features from the past. Too many faces. His mind ceased to respond. "You knew my mother well, then?" he asked vacantly, locked into the concentrated gaze. He should know this face; he had seen this man before.

The half grin wavered with his nod, and he parted his lips to speak.

A shaky, raised voice drew Kip's attention to the wall where a line of frail elderly residents rested in wheelchairs with aides hovering over them. Several ambulatory residents had joined the gathering, most of them visibly sequestered in a corner to the far right of the room. *Out of sight, out of mind, by whose arrangement?* The others, those confined to wheelchairs, lined the wall like used cars in a new car lot. Within ten seconds, Kip understood the elderly man's agitation and recognized his discomfort to be on exhibition. Parkinson's Disease, Kip diagnosed. The gnarled fingers trembled and lost grip of the spoon. Red gelatin splattered the tray, and Kip needed only a second more to sense a disaster unfolding. In a chair next to the old man, an equally frail woman attempted to move her tray—

The tray flipped before an aide could grasp it. A second hardy dose of red gelatin splattered the old gentleman's chair, and a mini module of chaos erupted as aides' and elders' voices collided.

Two nurses' aides tried sidling around the chairs. The elder man had already picked a glob of gelatin off his trousers. Without reservations, he slam-dunked the glob onto one of the aide's white shoes.

Bickerman arrived on the scene then, demanding, "That's enough, now! Mrs. Chelsey! Mr. Louten! Calm down—"

"You hold on there, sonny!" Louten demanded in a trembling hoarse voice. "Look at this mess!" For emphasis, Louten fingered a chunk of lasagna off his plate and lost his hold, depositing the glob at Bill's feet, possibly assaulting his shoes for as quickly as Bill stepped back.

Stifling a grin, Kip excused himself from McDaniels, passing through the tables as he noted another old woman alongside Mrs. Chelsey. Gray—a pale gray halo glowed at the edges of her white hair, and for an instant, Kip's step slowed, missing a stride.

No. Only that thought gripped him as the shiver started at the nape of his neck. Tense, he forced his concentration, willing himself to see only her reddening round cheeks. She would burst into tears at any moment. Her rheumy eyes watered, widening like a confused child spying on the others.

"Mr. Louten, you *promised* to be nice," the young aide pleaded, and might have broken through his outrage. She held Louten's attention for an instant before Bickerman intruded.

"Miss Singer! I suggest you take Mr. Louten upstairs and let him calm down. Miss Black, see that Mrs. Chelsey gets back to her room."

Spindly, ashen fingers lifted to cover the red cheeks and eyes, the white head bowed, and the gray mist rippled within the atmosphere at her quaking shoulders.

Feeling the woman's confusion and Louten's shame, Kip closed the distance as Mr. Louten protested Bill's directive and Miss Singer hurried to scoot behind his chair, eager to obey.

"I haven't finished here," Louten's voice quavered as another aide clasped his tray to lift it away.

Without missing a stride, Kip caught the tray, startling the young male aide, halting him. "I'll take that," Kip said simply, and as the fellow removed his grip, Kip returned the tray to the arms of Louten's chair, then met Miss Singer's worried gaze. "The tables in this room accommodate wheelchairs, Miss. I suggest you ask Mr. Louten where he'd prefer to sit and see that he's seated properly." Not skipping a beat, Kip half turned to find tears streaming down the second woman's face; the other woman hid behind her gray-gloved hands, apparently humiliated. With an iron resolve, he refused to accept the gray shroud haloing the huddled shoulders, refused to acknowledge what every sense told him at this moment, but like a lighthouse beacon in a fog, he knew. This little woman wasn't long for this world.

Odd how swiftly the old ways returned. Sidling, stooping, Kip clasped one of the reedy hands and lifted his free hand, brushing the tears off the flushed cheeks of the woman nearest him. "There now. Nothing to fret about, lass," he said with a theatrical Irish lilt.

"Look what I've done," she sobbed, flashing her pale blue eyes toward Mr. Louten's chair. Her fingers fluttered in Kip's grip. "I just m-meant t-to help."

"Aye, lass, and there's not a thing you've done, we can't remedy with a napkin," Kip said gently, and his attention drew to the next woman. His heart ached suddenly, gripped with sorrow. Uncontrollably, he touched the spindly arm, jolting internally with the chill breaching her blouse sleeve. She wore blue, the color of her eyes. Needle spikes tingled his fingertips. *No. Damn it! Not possible! Not after all these years!* "There's no need for all this worry over spilt milk, to be sure."

How he'd loved them. All of them. Their idiosyncrasies, their sophistication, their frailties, their strengths, and weaknesses. And oh, too, how he'd missed them in every quiet moment. Within his room at St. John's, he'd cried a river of tears, missing their stories, their faces. Missing his only true friends and family. Different faces, different names, but each one filled with life and love.

And how he grieved for them, his heart aching even now as he touched this wasting elder, knowing, feeling her pain. Looking over to her, he knew—could *feel* the medication battling the fires razing her thin flesh, but how long would those help? How much would they help when the end drew near?

"Oh! Oh, you. You're him," the little woman nearest him stammered. Her pale blue eyes cleared, her free hand lifted, wiping her tears more anxiously.

"Kip," Bickerman said in a low voice. "I think you'd better let me handle this."

"Elsa," the woman spoke, turning her wide eyes toward the second woman who peeked from between her fingers. "Elsa, it's the Prince. The Prince is *here!*"

Startled at the words, not at all certain of either his hearing or his sanity, Kip flashed a glance toward the frail little woman who'd initiated the chaos. Her brittle fingers parted to peer at him through murky brown eyes. Her trembling hand came to his sleeve, collecting a handful of black cloth within her stick fingers. Her waxy eyes danced off him to Mrs. Chelsey, then back. *The Prince?* Had he truly heard those words, or was this yet another grandiose delusion brought on by a flood of nostalgia and the first signs of chronic fatigue? The Prince of Whistlebrook had been a story, a grand story told by Irish McGuire a million memories ago. *Surely that tale hadn't transcended the years.*

"Oh, he *is* the Prince," Mrs. Chelsey uttered in a soft, now shaken voice, the voice of a little girl in awe of a magic land where kings and queens rule, and princes ride on gallant white stallions. A little peasant girl—

In a struggle for reality and a battle against the floating in his mind, Kip turned his palm, offering a handshake, "I'm Kip Patterson, Mrs. Chelsey."

"You're the Prince of Whistlebrook," the little woman clutching his sleeve professed.

Feeling oddly threatened, Kip glimpsed this second woman's hand reaching for him and turned his palm to receive her fluttering digits. "Might I have the pleasure of your name, ma'am?"

As if suddenly nervous or embarrassed, her liver-spotted hand trembled in his palm, and she blushed across the prominent ridge of her thin cheeks. Around her tight, white, wiry curls, the gray halo swirled, threatening to engulf her. "Elsa Taylor, of the Richmond Taylors," she said in a drug-thickened slur, her voice quivering and cracking.

Whatever the hell the 'Richmond Taylors' meant, Kip nodded, fighting a raging battle against an urge to kiss the back of her hand like a knight greeting a lady.

For God's sake! I'm almost thirty years old! Not five! Not ten! I'm not falling into a fantasy world! Dear God, in a nearly silent, crowded room full of spectators! Poise! Damn you!

Chapter 5

Pushing from his stoop, Kip leaned, brushing a kiss on Elsa Taylor's cheek, then followed suit with Mrs. Chelsey. Both women still held his hands. The aides in his immediate view stared openly, as much shock as intimidation fleeting in their eyes as he glanced between them.

The short, bone-thin young woman behind Mrs. Taylor appeared positively terrified, but he couldn't even recall seeing her, much less meeting her before now. He might have passed her last evening when perusing the Home's upper floors, but surely, he hadn't said or done anything to make her flinch under his gaze. Of all the reactions he'd ever created in women, terror was certainly unique. Faintly curious, Kip retracted his hands from the elders' grips, glancing between the old women and Mr. Louten. Deciding on Mrs. Chelsey, he asked, "Would you care for another tray, now, ma'am?"

She nodded, blushing shyly, "Please."

"Kip," Bickerman interrupted discreetly, wisely keeping his hands to himself. "I think they'd be more comfortable in the cafeteria."

Kip looked to Mrs. Chelsey's escort, the young man from whom Kip had swiped Mr. Louten's tray. The boy appeared only curious. "You will see that Mrs. Chelsey has another tray, sir," he said evenly and glanced down the line to the other half dozen aides who stood poised and stunned, their expressions likewise reflected on the elders in their charge. His gaze fixed more firmly, landing on each of the elders as he commented, "I appreciate all of you coming. Thank you." Scanning the aides, he stated, "Find places at the tables, and unless they request to leave, I suggest you assist them here."

"Yes, sir," several voices uttered, while others flashed glances at Bickerman, seeking either direction or confirmation.

"Prince?"

Kip glanced too readily at Mr. Louten, glimpsing Bickerman's angry gaze. With an effort, Kip focused on the wrinkled, gaunt face and outstretched jittery hand. Definitely Parkinson's Disease, Kip confirmed as he sidestepped and clasped the fluttering palm.

"Rob Louten," the old man growled while trying to strengthen his grip on Kip's palm.

"Kip Patterson, sir."

"Damn shame about your mother," the old voice quaked in its solemn oath. "We're going to miss her. She was a proper lady. It won't be the same without her."

If he'd been 'the Prince,' she'd truly been 'the Queen,' an adored Queen. Kip nodded, finding no words to either comfort the elder man's remorse or express his own. Sliding free of the grasp, he attempted an elegant departure, far too aware of the spectators and quiet conversations bursting in his wake as he navigated the perimeter of the Oak Room. To duck out now would portray either weakness or shame, neither of which Kip suffered despite the queer glances he received on route to his reserved table.

Someone had cleared the space between JD and Edna. A coffee cup and an ashtray awaited him. As Kip slid into the empty chair, he lifted his cigarettes from his jacket while catching faintly curious glances and subtle smiles from Mark and Edna.

"You haven't lost your touch," Mark commented.

What touch was that? His ability to fall hopelessly lost in the elderly's dementia? To regress on an instant's notice? *To know* when one of his loved ones would pass away in the next day or week? Without comment, Kip caught a flame to his cigarette, running into Mark's appreciative smile.

"I seem to recall you always had a rather remarkable talent for calming the agitated or distressed," Mark considered in reflection. "I'd often thought if we could bottle your talent, we could do away with synthetic drugs entirely."

"Would have been counterproductive for you, it seems to me," Kip commented, holding the good doctor's gaze. "I'd often wondered if you held stock in Johnson and Johnson."

Frances smiled with an intent gaze. "Haven't forgiven me for that either, have you?"

"On the contrary," Kip countered. "It was a long time ago and, as I recall, you didn't have any options." If not for sedation, Kip remembered, he might have died during recovery. The details swept away as swiftly as they erupted. Listlessly, he turned his coffee cup, remembering his mother in no definite form or incident. Hard to believe. Still hard to believe. She'd always been so filled with life, so full of energy. Even four months ago...

He'd stopped on one of his spontaneous visits, as most of his visits were spontaneous. A layover in Pittsburgh, he'd admitted from a payphone at the airport, omitting the fact that he'd scheduled the five-hour layover with her in mind. Just a layover, and would she meet him for dinner?

'Let me check.' Long pause, then the usual breathless, *'Oh darling, I have a meeting tonight. Could we make it tomorrow? Say lunch?'*

Meetings. Appointments. *'Maybe another time, then. I'm only in for a couple hours.'*

'Oh? Well then heavens, darling, I suppose I can miss this one meeting.'

He should have known, then, Kip realized belatedly. He should have suspected something was wrong when she'd missed her meeting to join him for dinner. God knows, he visited on other occasions and spent his hours flirting with Carolyn or pestering Edna, leaving without ever seeing the Queen of Whistlebrook. Yes, he should have known, then, but he'd been too damned surprised to consider any ulterior motives.

Dinner, he remembered absently. They shared a rushed dinner as most of the moments with his mother were rushed. She arrived at the restaurant late. Something had come up at the Home. *Something always came up.* With a half dozen pre-dinner cocktails in his system, he'd barely restrained his annoyance as she'd rambled incessantly about residents, politics, employee problems. Not death, not a mention, not an indication. How could he have missed the signs? How could the aura have eluded—

"Hey?"

With the jab of an elbow, Kip jolted from his reflection and glanced to find Mulden studying him. "A problem?"

"You alright?"

"Fine," he answered, not understanding JD's quirky grin.

"Nothing like rolling back time," JD mused. "You were always fine. And the way you said it, you dared someone to dispute you."

"We didn't know each other very well, did we?" Kip considered.

"Well enough," Mulden answered, sobering slightly.

Looking sidelong into the hazel gaze, Kip considered, "Seems to me, you weren't here long before I left. We didn't spend more than three or four days together in Randall High."

"Exactly two full days," Mulden verified. "And I think two half days."

"You have an excellent memory," Kip commented, not certain whether to be impressed or annoyed considering his recent affliction of memory loss and overload.

"Actually, I couldn't tell you the last vice-president," JD said. "But that was the screwiest five weeks of my life. You made one hell of an impression."

"Irish called you a scoundrel," Kip remembered with a vacant grin.

"Seems to me, I got several nicknames around here," JD smiled as he glanced past Kip to Edna and winked. "*Renegade* comes to mind."

Kip nodded, no longer listening. His focus drifted past JD, finding the alcove windows despite the bodies collected around the coffeepot. *'You bring that scoundrel around to see this old coot,'* An old man's voice trailed into his mind.

'I promised him, JD—'

His memory vanished. His attention caught between the sight of snow falling beyond the glass and a truly magnificent woman leaning to fill a coffee cup. Kelly Mulden's lower half matched her upper half. Small waist, rounded hips in a form-fitted emerald jacket and skirt. A glimpse of long, slender legs winked from a slight slit in the skirt. Cascading over her shoulders, her dark hair spilled halfway down her back, scattered in wild curls and waves to prism the light.

My, my, my—

"Whatever you're thinking—stop," JD intruded shortly. A grin snagged his bearded lips; honest amusement danced in his eyes. "She's engaged."

Kip barely glanced at JD before looking toward Kelly in time to see her turn. Their gazes touched. A tainted, compelling smile haunted her lips; her eyes caught, locked and held momentarily. With a faint quivering grin, she acknowledged his slight appreciative nod before collecting gracefully and continuing her turn as if she hadn't paused. "A dancer?" he wondered while catching JD's gaze returning from his sister.

Mulden feigned surprise. "I'm not going to ask how you figured that out. But I *am* serious. She really is engaged."

"Happily?"

JD huffed in mocked exasperation. "That would be my guess. The wedding's set for April."

"What a shame," Kip commented, watching her return to her table. Their gazes touched again as she slipped into her chair. He'd sworn off married women a decade earlier. *But engaged?* "You married, JD?" Kip asked absently.

"I uh," his voice drifted a moment. Kip focused in time to see Mulden's gaze return from Kelly's direction. A more sober curiosity held in JD's hazel eyes. "I was for a while," he finished. "Long enough to have two sons. Seven and nine. You?"

"No," he answered and lifted his coffee, running into Mark's curious gaze while gulping several lukewarm swallows. What was Frances thinking? *Seeing?*

"You were engaged for a while, weren't you?" the doctor asked. "Seems to me your mother mentioned something to that effect."

"I'm sure she did," Kip commented evasively, letting his focus scan the faces beyond the doctor. *'When are you going to find a nice girl and settle down?'* she'd asked him as they'd walked from the restaurant.

'When I'm a candidate for the East Wing, mother.'

Odd, how people glanced away as his focus touched them. Even Bickerman, Kip noticed with faint amusement. The administrator looked like a deer caught in a headlight beam for a half second before he bolted his attention to a stout associate.

"You really look tired, sweetie," Mrs. Feeney spoke discreetly. "Are you alright?"

His focus found one of the nurse's aides in the crowd, one not on duty apparently. She wore a black dress with an indiscreet neckline, a lot of dark make-up enhancing her eyes, and a seductive grin as she met his gaze. She reminded him of someone, possibly someone on another continent, if not in another life. His focus continued to drift. Only once, possibly on one of his first return visits, Kip had accepted the seduction of an employee. Word had traveled swiftly to Marilyn Patterson, and she hadn't taken a subtle stand. Vaguely, he recalled her saying something about 'bordellos' and 'harems.'

Staff members were off limits.

What about your auxiliary buddies, mom? His focus found another pair of eyes, slightly less enhanced. The sad smile was almost identical. *'I'll comfort you,'* her expression promised.

Not today, babe, he answered silently, and his gaze wandered, snagging momentarily on Kelly Mulden, watching her smile at something her mother said. No open laughter. The young woman possessed too much class for laughter in this crowd, but her eyes sparked and twinkled as if she might laugh easily and often. By God, she was one fine looking woman. Before she caught him staring, his gaze continued traveling listlessly.

Gratefully, he spotted someone—at last—donning a coat. The sooner everyone ate and departed, the sooner he could get the hell out of here, away from the *goddamned Memories! Away from the grief! Away from the goddamn specter of death!* And death was here. He could feel it. *See* it when his gaze drifted toward the far corner.

Riveted, Kip gazed toward the ancient faces, panning the silver heads and gaunt features. Mrs. Taylor of the Richmond Taylors.

As clearly as he saw her white hair bobbing in silhouette against the deep shine of oak panels, he witnessed the smoky gray outline, a mere shadow as if caught in a double exposed print, and he felt his own color draining. A prickle lifted at the nape of his neck. A chill spread off his shoulders. She was dying. By the color, her illness advanced. How much time did she have? How much time did any of them have? His gaze trailed, abstracted. The hazy outline shrouded several other images and his blood chilled, his heart ached—

"Are you planning to stick around here for a while, Kip?" Mulden interrupted.

Bringing his murky gaze from the image, Kip shivered internally as he focused on Mulden. "A day or two, I'd imagine."

"You uh ... you probably have things to do later, huh?"

Hesitating, recovering, Kip wondered, "How long will you be in town?"

"Haven't decided," he answered with a vague grin and an estranged sobriety that he covered by lifting his coffee. "I have some vacation time coming and I haven't been home in a while." He shrugged and caught Kip's gaze, smirking. "Just as soon not go back to that mountain just yet, anyway. I'm really not that great on skis."

Probably a lie. If nothing else, Kip remembered JD's athletic talent and love for almost all sports. Apparently, Mulden had become a little less arrogant or confident with age. The fellow had never boasted, never needed to, but he'd never denied his capabilities in the past.

"Why don't I give you a call tomorrow?" JD suggested. "Maybe we could get together. Go out for a drink. Hear there's a pretty decent lounge over in Clarion."

Kip nodded indifferently. "Don't imagine you'd invite your sister to join us, would you?" *Might make an extended stay worthwhile.*

Mulden bounced a glance off the ceiling as if besieging God's divine intervention. "Definitely no white collar or Bible, right?"

With a faint grin, Kip noted JD glancing at Fr. Jordan seated past Edna. Mulden's expression wavered with the eyes of a man who'd just tried eating his shoes. "No, I suppose not," Kip commented, bailing him from the awkward moment. "And it wouldn't be a good idea to bring your sister." On that note, he decided—*to hell with proper etiquette.* He'd remained long enough. Bickerman could entertain this crowd. "Feel free to call," he commented, then leaned, resting a hand on Edna's shoulder. Drawing her startled gaze, Kip whispered, "I'm leaving. Extend my apologies when necessary."

Her hand came over his at her shoulder; her eyes emitted a deep, familiar shine of concern. "Sweetie, I know this is hard, but you shouldn't be alone right now."

A warning? A genuine fear? Sliding his hand free, Kip pushed from his chair, whispering, "I won't be." With a natural ease, he brushed a kiss on her cheek then lifted his attention, offering the proper amenities to those at the table, again thanking Fr. Jordan for a beautiful service before making good his escape.

Stopping in the private suite, Kip picked up the smaller of his two leather bags, donned his coat and hat and made his way to a fire exit at the side of the Home. With little effort, he avoided both departing visitors and kitchen staff and found his rental where he'd left it in a corner of the rear private lot. He found the keys above the visor, shaking his head at how easily he'd adapted to Whistlebrook and its false sense of security. In any of a dozen cities he frequented, leaving the keys in a new car would be considered insanity and God knows, if a thief wanted the rental, the cameras at the stone pillared entrance wouldn't have provided a deterrent.

Rolling through the stone pillars, swinging onto the highway, the car skidded, and for several crazy seconds, Kip fought the wheel, cursing the car, the snow, and his insanity. By the time he wheeled the front end into the proper lane, he'd cleared the gates without denting a fender. Halfheartedly, he wondered if the gate camera had monitored and recorded his momentary distress. With thick flakes splattering his windshield and snow laced across the wet blacktop, perhaps he was a little crazy. Only a thought of all those soulful eyes and smiles, the haunting sense of despair and death, altered an immediate plan to pick any of a hundred cleared driveways and turn around.

Time now, time to put the grief process in motion. Rapid motion, he considered as he gripped the steering wheel, cursing the snow, the cold, and Marilyn Patterson. All with equal fervor.

"I never even learned to drive in this shit!" Kip snapped.

Chapter 6

Only slightly less estranged than the introduction with Kip, Kelly sat across from her brother in the front seat of JD's rented Dodge. More than once since hugging him inside the dining room, she'd sensed his distraction, noting the tension belying his ever-moving eyes. Watching him tilt his scattered waves and catch a flame to a cigarette, she realized how incredibly distant they'd become.

"What's it been...? Nearly a year?" Kelly asked and caught his fleeting gaze, seeing a stranger in place of the brother she'd known so well.

"Probably at least that," he said offhandedly and pulled from the parking space, timing his departure to coincide with their parents' Lincoln pulling out ahead. "Did I mention, you're looking good?"

"No," she said offhandedly. "But thanks, though I'm not sure I can say the same for you," she continued and glimpsed his lifted brow, haunted grin.

"That's what I love about you. Honest to a fault," JD said offhandedly.

"You look tired," she said lightly, taking advantage of the opportunity to watch him as he watched the road. With the snow already trying to cover the lane, as well as the highway, he remained seriously preoccupied, but not enough to account for the tension beneath his beard or in his eyes.

"Long flight, and a lousy reunion," he said distractedly.

"What made you decide to come?" she asked.

His gaze flashed toward her, less hurt than curious. "That's a pretty dumb question, Kell."

Considering the multitude of family events he'd missed, like Thanksgiving dinner, his son's birthday party, their little brother's graduation, she wondered how he could fault her question. "Really?"

His gaze flashed again. His brow furrowed, and his brows knitted. A glimpse of white teeth enhanced the curious smirk he'd worn as a boy. "Yeah, really. Any reason you're giving me the third degree? Or is it just on principle?"

"I really didn't think I'd see you here, JD," she admitted. "But I'm glad you came." And if she pushed too hard, he'd be gone the instant they reached their parents' house. "And I apologize if it sounds like the third degree," she added.

Not relaxed, he flashed another glance and dragged smoke from his cigarette as he cast his gaze toward the highway. "Where's your fiancé?" he asked offhandedly.

"He's coming in on Saturday," she answered.

"Things all right between you two? No cold feet yet?"

Considering her mental kibitzing for the past several hours, Kelly wasn't quick to answer. "Not as far as I know."

"Richard, right? Whitmark—Whitman," he corrected and fleeted a more playful smile. "What's he like? Does he treat you well?"

"Now, *that's* a pretty dumb question," she emphasized. "Do you really think I'd be engaged to a man who treated me like shit? Or wasn't absolutely perfect in every way?"

"You're sure about this guy, Kell? You really love him?"

Typical big brother, she considered. Perhaps he wasn't quite so different in every way. If he faked his concern or interest, nothing in his expression betrayed him. His eyes remained sober while his lips twitched into one of his more pensive smiles. Was it any wonder he and Kip had become fast friends? Except, they were more alike now than as children. Meeting Kip at the table, catching his gray eyes more than a time or two in the aftermath, she'd sensed the tension in him, as surely as his confidence behind his handsome smiles. Not naive by a long shot, she'd recognized the interest in those repeated glimpses.

"I noted, you're not answering," JD said carefully. "You love him, right?"

"Yes," she said offhandedly, believing it at this moment, regardless of her distraction. Whatever this attraction—or infatuation—with Kip, it would pass. Seeing him, meeting him again after all these years, had been good regardless of her initial fears and reservations. Belatedly, she was glad she'd come.

Unaccountably, a smile quivered on her lips as she remembered his surprise, very nearly shock when he'd met her eyes over her mother's head. Why she found that moment vastly satisfying—and just a little exciting—she dared not ponder too deeply. Fleeting, she remembered the heat of his thumb trapping her fingers in his palm.

An odd thing to remember, but the gentleness of his touch, the strange tingle in her fingers...? How such a slight gesture could create a flutter in the pit of her stomach. And the mere memory rekindled the reaction.

Damn it. Not good! A carryover from her childhood. Infatuation.

This would pass.

Richard would come on Saturday, and in four months, they'd begin their life together. They'd already agreed to remain in Baltimore. When he finished his internship, he'd apply for a permanent staff position and eventually open a private practice, a general medical practitioner. A thing of the past, he often remarked, but his father was a general MD in Charleston. Eventually, they'd start a family. They'd already agreed on at least two children, an event that would demand expanding her dance studio to include at least one more instructor. Her career, Richard had assured her, was as important as his, but she wondered about that profession. Dancing and medicine were at opposite ends of the stratosphere. And while her love of dance placed her career at the top, she wasn't an idiot. Medicine involved life and death situations; dance was art, a luxury that she'd turned into a profitable business. No one would suffer if she closed her studio. No one would die if she made a mistake.

Would Richard change after the wedding? Would he suddenly expect her to close her studio and run his household, become the mother of his children, a doctor's wife? Presently, their arrangement worked. With his grueling hours at the hospital, she spent a great deal of time alone, but he'd assured her, promising once he established himself, they'd have more time, plenty of time.

Damn it, she'd worked through these doubts. Put them to rest months ago when Richard had asked her to marry him. Or had she? Obviously, some questions lingered, but only time would provide the answers. She believed him, believed in him. When they were together, the world felt right, peaceful. She trusted him.

To the engine decelerating, Kelly woke to the silence in the car, as well as the silence lingering between her and JD. Nearly cursing her preoccupation aloud, she looked over to find him likewise preoccupied. He hadn't minded the silence, might not have noticed it. For one heart-wrenching moment, Kelly wished she could turn back time, wished she could reach over and slug him for some big-brother taunt or trick. JD had always been wild, unpredictable, and laughing. He was one of those rare boys who'd never needed to fake a macho image. Never strutted around pretending he was the cat's meow. Girls had dropped at his feet; boys had revolved around him in a constant stream, idolizing him, but he'd never taken advantage of his charisma.

Having him as a big brother had been a pain in the butt sometimes, but more often, it was a blessing. By the time Kelly entered Randall High, despite his scant year and a half in that esteemed institution, his reputation had paved the way for instant friendships and fame. If she'd been a boy, God pity her. The coaches might have railroaded her into every blasted sport on the curriculum. Instead, she'd landed on the cheerleading squad and won the leading role in the school play for two years running. Not to mention, she'd become Homecoming Queen and Prom Queen in her senior year ... and he'd returned from Nam that summer.

Changed.

Her thoughts carried her from the car, and for a moment, she stood scanning the split-level house, her childhood home. Before the summer of her eleventh year, they'd moved a lot. This house, though, had become home. Here she'd grown up, learned about life and boys, and sorrows. Losing Gram had been a sorrow. Her grandmother had lived here with them in those first three years. Cancer had snatched her away, and for an instant, Kelly felt like crying again, maybe for her grandmother, maybe for her childhood. Maybe for JD, who came around the front of the car to join her, his eyes curious and tense. For the boy he'd been, for the childhood forever gone.

"Better let me help you," JD intruded, offering his arm with a glance at the snowy pavement and her shoes. "If memory serves, high heels and snow don't jive."

Shaking off the depression, she accepted his arm, aware of the estrangement between them, appreciating his arm when she slipped. Collecting her balance, tossing him a smile, she kept hold of his arm as she ascended the steps and followed her parents' footprints in the thin layer of snow. "How long are you staying, JD?" she asked as they reached the covered porch.

"Probably just a day or two," he said with a fleeting smile and wink. "Long enough to meet Mr. Perfect, if only to lay some ground rules."

"Be gentle or I'll have to hurt you," she teased as JD clasped the door with his harrumph, stepping aside, the perfect gentleman.

"If he can't take the heat, Kell, he'd better stay out of the oven."

"It's *kitchen*, JD and—"

"We'll see, huh?" he smiled wryly, then chuckled and followed her into the living room. "I promise not to turn the heat too high. Better?"

Had she, on some base level, held onto as much faith as her mother? Could she have known or anticipated finding JD here? For whatever had spurred her into immediate action, Kelly could be only grateful. She'd missed him and, without a doubt, she'd wanted JD to meet Richard before walking down the aisle with him.

The house was quiet, surprisingly quiet. Generally, the chaos of a house full of Muldens would begin the moment she arrived home, but perhaps her parents, like her, intended to keep JD around for a while. The phone calls that would have drawn brothers, sisters-in-law, nieces and nephews, sons, remained on hold. Rather like walking a tightrope, neither of her parents even suggested placing those calls. Instead, they parted briefly to change into casual clothes.

In her room, Kelly tugged a sweater and jeans from the top of her suitcase, waking to her urgency as she yanked the jeans to her hips. Stopped, sitting on her childhood bed, one sock in hand, the other already on her foot, Kelly listened for sounds from the other rooms. Almost reluctantly, JD had asked if he still had a bed upstairs, and until that moment, Kelly hadn't realized how truly estranged he might feel, how unwelcome in his own home. He hadn't lived here long, less than eighteen months. He'd turned seventeen in this house and departed at eighteen. Shortly after returning from Nam, maybe less than a year later, he'd married Laura, his high school sweetheart from that brief stint in Randall High, and moved out again. His room remained. A guestroom. And his sons had probably slept in his bed more often than he ever had. She needed to hurry. A fleeting thought of the Spiderman quilt on the bed and the children's toys in that room jolted her into motion. Those mementoes of his sons might drive him directly from that room, through the front door, to the nearest bar. Family. Something had happened to her brother, a severance of bonds, a destruction of responsibility to others and to himself.

Her brother, the middle son of a clan of seven, was as alone and isolated as Kip Patterson.

Unless she hurried, she might not beat him to the front door, and God knows when she would see him again. Doubtful, he'd even arrive at her wedding.

The guestroom door stood open, his suitcase flopped open on the quilt, his suit lying haphazardly over the end of the bed. He hadn't unpacked, but he hadn't departed with his luggage either. Kelly found him in the kitchen, along with her father, who'd begun making a pot of coffee. Colleen wasn't far behind, and within a few glorious moments, they sat at the kitchen table, chatting as if time had turned back. Noticeably, the conversation steered clear of delicate subjects. JD asked about his boys, Jamie and Justin, conveniently evading any question of Laura and not, Kelly noted, saying whether he intended to spend time with his sons, not in the next day, much less over Christmas.

Key word—pressure. Neither of their parents applied pressure, but then, they never had. In carefully orchestrated subtleties, Colleen alluded to the hope of JD spending time with his sons, as surely as Jarred offered lighthearted anecdotes about Jamie's football season, undoubtedly hoping to trigger distant memories. Jarred had always been there for all of them, but especially JD.

Their father had never missed an important game. He'd stood as flushed and excited as all others in the stands when JD had struck a home run in Pony League or tackled the opposing team's linebacker and prevented a winning touchdown. Life. Old days. If James David Mulden noted their parents' attempting to bind the tattered threads of family ties, he showed no signs of dismay. Instead, he resorted to his old standby, offering a humph or chuckle, steering the conversation toward safer territory. Offhandedly, he tossed jibes in Kelly's direction that she fielded and fired back with no problem at all.

One does not stomp a remiss son or brother into the ground the moment one sees him. One makes the moment last, hoping eventually, a time would come for mending fences. Even occasional phone calls would be an improvement over the past five years, and toward that end, Kelly accepted whatever direction JD chose. He was tense. Despite his smiles and banter, tension belied his eyes. In almost constant motion, his gaze darted from the clock to the refrigerator when its motor ignited, to the back door when the neighbor's dog started barking. No pressure. He looked like a man on the edge, acted like a man unsure of his surroundings, and seeking to acclimate within a strange new world.

Ten years ago, he'd returned from that foreign world, a stranger. In twenty-twenty hindsight, Kelly remembered the hurt and anger born of confusion. She hadn't understood the changes then; she understood them now and loved him more, although if she admitted that, undoubtedly, he'd flee. Vietnam wasn't a subject he would broach, nor one that any of them would mention. Someday, perhaps, she'd find the courage and confidence to tell him simply, *Welcome home. I'm glad you're alive.*

Now, she could only be grateful for his presence, and in paradox, hated herself for the fleeting thought that Mrs. Patterson couldn't have picked a better time to pass away. God, help her, as horrible as that sounded within her own mind, Kelly knew it was true. She wouldn't have wished it. She would have preferred that a joyous celebration had brought them together. Not for an instant would she have hoped to meet Kip or talk to JD under such morbid circumstances, but she couldn't shake the thought of something good prevailing over tragedy.

As if Kelly needed a reminder, JD chose a brief lull to mention calling Kip and ask if he might use the den. When he returned less than five minutes later, he offered nothing of whatever conversation had passed between them, but the subject steered in that direction with a bit of help from Colleen.

"How did he seem to you, JD?" she asked with a natural concern. "Do you think he'll be all right?"

"Wish I knew, ma," he said offhandedly, sounding young and troubled as he lighted yet another cigarette from a near-empty pack. "He said something to the effect that we really didn't know each other that well, and he was right," JD said simply, apparently suffering doubts about his own presence. "I'd imagine he'll handle it. He's not a kid anymore."

None of them were, Kelly might have admitted, but the rumble of a high-pro engine entering the driveway stifled her thought. Within moments, their youngest brother, Mike, burst through the back door, and chaos erupted, quickly countering Kelly's thought of children. And that was the beginning.

Belatedly, she recalled her mother mentioning her arrival to Shelly, her older brother Jack's wife. Without fail, on those bi-monthly weekends when

Kelly visited Randall, her brothers, their wives, her nieces, and nephews inundated their parents' homestead, and this wasn't the exception.

Before long, Colleen hustled in the kitchen, preparing a feast for a dozen, and with JD's unexpected presence, the crowd grew slightly more rowdy than usual. Mike, typical Mulden, started the wrestling match and dragged the elder brothers into a donnybrook in the living room, the likes of which would have seen them all tossed from an Irish pub. Over her shoulder, Colleen called the simple, very familiar words, "Watch my lamps!"

Ughs, chuckles, curses, and *ka-booms* rocked the house before someone landed in a deadlock, and silence prevailed. Sidling into the living room entrance, Kelly leaned watching, somehow not surprised to find JD had gained the upper hand, pinning their younger brother as well as Jack. Comically, he rested with a brother's head locked under each arm, his legs tangled in a quagmire of blue jeans. His hazel eyes sparkling, he managed a glance and a shrug in her direction.

"Comfy?" Kelly asked.

"Quite," he said smugly. "Wouldn't want to light me a cigarette, huh? I think I may be here a while, and I sorta have my hands full—"

"You son-of-a—" Jack huffed and heaved, starting the battle in renewed vigor.

"Oops!" JD laughed and tumbled.

Shaking her head, Kelly returned to the counter and her potatoes, glimpsing her mother's twinkling blue eyes. Without a doubt, Colleen had touched heaven. "Boys will be boys, right?" Kelly commented in mock disgust.

"Forever," Colleen agreed and started laughing.

Very briefly, dinner calmed the lions, and conversations flowed, ranging from 'What's new in the field of architecture,' and 'How's life in the Rockies?' Jack was more than happy to discuss his latest project, an office complex he was erecting on the outskirts of Pittsburgh. Shelly, his wife and confidant, filled in the blanks when his enthusiasm overlooked details.

The phone rang amid the lively discourse, and seated closest to the kitchen, Kelly rose naturally, preempting the inevitable gazes that would elect her if she hadn't volunteered. Richard should call soon, which might account for her position near the wall phone. On the second ring, she lifted the receiver, glancing at the clock above the stove and a little startled to realize the late hour. Nearly nine, already. "Hello, Mulden residence."

"What a joy to hear your voice."

Richard? This certainly didn't sound like Richard. Low and lyrical, this soft, deep voice. "Uhhh, who are you looking for?"

"Now, there's certainly a loaded question, love. Who were you expecting?"

That voice! She knew that voice! Her heart skipped a beat, and she clamped her jaw before speaking the name that might escape far more breathlessly than intended. Kip Patterson. God. A lifetime ago, she would have hocked her soul to answer this telephone and hear that voice. A funeral. His mother. Fifteen years. He was probably returning JD's phone call, though that would be a first. All too swiftly, Kelly recalled how often JD had sputtered angry oaths when deciding to drive to the Home rather than await a phone call. "Are you—"

"Not fair, I suppose. I'm asking to have my heart broken. Engaged, or so I've heard. Happily so, or was your brother declaring a blatant lie?"

He sounded strange, Drunk? No slur in his voice indicated intoxication. "Are you alright?" she asked quietly, unconsciously lowering her voice.

"Ahh, the lady doubts," he said in a deeper voice. "Is your fiancé with you at the moment?"

"No," she answered, only more curious.

"Curious, aren't you?"

"About?"

"Is JD about?"

Cursing the effect of that question, the slight drop of her heart, she held steady. "Yes, he is. If you'll hold on—"

"Don't," he cut in shortly. "Don't get him for me. In fact, I'd prefer you not mention to whom you're speaking, if that's possible. Is that possible?"

"Yes," she answered, wondering if he held onto a single thought for more than a second, wondering why her heart slapped a quicker beat. Unconsciously, glancing toward the living room entrance as if to confirm her statement, her focus shifted toward the kitchen window. "And now I am curious," she admitted with a slight quiver of a smile. *If not JD...?*

"Ah, a wavelength connected," he said, and she nearly heard the smirk in his voice. "I've found myself in serious need of a friendly voice, a rather sensuous, extremely sexy voice, and it occurred to me, you have just such a quality. Do apologize if I've caught you at a bad time, but—"

His words continued, but for a moment, Kelly had no idea what he was saying. Perhaps, she'd lost contact with reality. In the next, she realized he'd switched to another language. Definitely not English. French? Italian? In a pause, she admitted, "I have no idea what you just said."

"Loosely translated, I needed to hear a lovely song. Your voice is that song, and if this is a bad time, it's far too late to worry about it. Did I mention at all that you are possibly the most lovely lady I've seen in some time?"

Not good, Kell! Her heart missed another beat. "Thank you."

"Suppose such a droll compliment deserves such a simple response. How many men have you slain with that walk, darling? Five or five hundred?"

"Excuse me?" she asked with a smile.

"Hmm, much better," he said, sounding delighted. "The element of surprise. Keep them guessing, but I'd still like an answer. Broken necks? Broken legs? Mishaps, like sending some poor bloke off a pier, turning him right when he should have veered left? How many casualties to your credit?"

She stifled a laugh. "None that I'm aware of."

"Bzzz. Wrong answer. You've certainly slain one. I'm nearly certain I died and went to heaven, however briefly. Women with your talent should wear signs, luv. Something simple like—Hazardous Material. Ah, or better still—Lethal Weapon. My, my, my, but this is a strange conversation. If you hung up, I wouldn't blame you. By now, I'm certain you consider me a maniac. I should point out, however, this is not an obscene phone call. Have you hung up?"

Kelly stifled another laugh. "No. I'm still here."

"And a pity that, luv. I'd much rather you were here."

In that simple line, her heart gripped, but it wasn't the suggestion in his words. His tone. He was alone, and despite the running dialogue, he was depressed. "Where are you?" she asked quietly.

"Better left a mystery, luv. If you offer to join me, there's no telling where the evening would end," he hesitated, and continued with a note of disgust. "Well, that's a bald-faced lie. I know where the evening would end, and I'm far too good at getting what I want. A phone call's the safest alternative."

"For whom?" she asked.

"You, luv. I'm not wearing a ring. Well, I am, but not on that critical of all fingers. Much better this way. Were you here, I'd have to kiss you from your head to your toes, and you'd hate me in the morning."

The image those words conjured was enough to tighten her grip on the receiver and hike her pulse a notch. *What would it be like…? No!* That wasn't an image she dared speculate. "I see," she said, and nearly cursed the honesty in that single line. She did see. All too clearly, she imagined that rakish twitch in his mustached lips, the heated spark in his gray eyes.

"Doubtful, but I refuse to argue with a woman of such substance. Learned the futility long ago. Now then, I suppose, this song's ended, and I truly shouldn't have phoned. Just seemed like the thing to do."

"I'm glad you did," she said, and again cursed her words, her urgency, sensing he was about to hang up. "I make a good listener, and this isn't a bad time."

"Depends on which end of the phone line you're on, luv. Just the melody you're playing is having a serious effect. Sorry to have disturbed you. I'll sign off now, but rest assured, whatever face I find tonight, yours will be the one I see. Thank you."

Double-time, her heart hammered in her chest, her senses riveted as the click and silence pressed against her ear. Kip Patterson. He hadn't called for JD. In a fugue, Kelly dropped the receiver in its prongs, vaguely aware of her hand still gripping the receiver. How could this be? How could this perfect stranger stir her blood with a word, a glance? Good God, she was engaged to be married!

But Richard...? Had she ever reacted to Richard as she'd just reacted to this stranger from the past? A few lousy words, just the offhanded mention of kisses and intimacy, the suggestion in his words, the deep, soft rhythm of his voice brushing against her ear, touching her. How? Why? Could she still, on some subconscious level, carry a spark of longing and ... love? She'd driven to Randall for him, to be here for him when she believed he'd need a friend. Had she romanced those childish whims and wishes so long that she'd honestly feel a friendship for him or had she come here hoping to hear exactly the kind of words he'd just spoken?

The equivalent of love accolades?

Troubled, torn, she lifted her hand, shifted to turn. The telephone blasted at her ear, slicing her thoughts. Whether she hoped to hear his voice again or merely reacted with a start, she yanked the receiver to her ear and heaved, "Hello?"

The caller hesitated, then, with a faint southern accent, "Have I reached the Mulden residence?"

Richard! This *was* Richard. Her heart pounded a leaden beat, and Kelly suddenly felt the heat in her cheeks. A raw, gut-wrenching guilt gripped her, as if she'd already betrayed him. "Richard?"

"Kelly?" he sounded doubtful.

"Of course, silly," she said while trying to sound natural, trying to catch her breath.

"Is everything all right, darling? You sounded anxious? Upset?" he asked quietly.

In the background, voices and hospital sounds echoed in a familiar cadence. The hospital doctor's lounge. His home away from home, as he professed.

No sounds had echoed in the background when Kip called. God! Richard! She needed to concentrate and regain her balance. How the blazes had that stranger knocked her for a loop in ten seconds flat? Surprise. The element of surprise. If she weren't slightly off balance, she'd be more surprised. "Fine. Everything's fine, Richard," she managed and willed herself to believe it. Concentrating, she thought of Richard's lean, handsome face, his soft lips, and short, sweeping brown hair trimmed close to his ears. He stood a solid six feet despite his lean build. With the hectic, long hours spent at the hospital, he wore a perpetual, pale, haunted appearance, but that would change. He was handsome, kind, and decent. A gentleman in every way. "How's every little thing?" she asked, hoping to keep it light, knowing those words would set his mind at ease.

"Aside from wishing I were there with you, every little thing's fine."

"It's only two days, honey," she said smoothly, more in tune with his weariness, more attentive. She should have waited for him and ridden with him on Saturday. She would have driven while he slept. "Have you had any sleep at all?"

"Sleep? What's that?" he asked, trying to sound funny, but he'd used the line several times in response to her concern. He just sounded tired, as tired as the jest. "How was your day? Did you and your mother go Christmas shopping?"

Belatedly, she realized she hadn't mentioned the funeral, had merely mentioned her intentions to leave early and spend a little more time with her family. She could have come four days earlier. Should she have told him? Was that oversight a lie? A betrayal of sorts? Damn it! She was accustomed to living alone, never answering to anyone. Sharing the simple things—joys or pains—seemed suddenly a problem. "We didn't go shopping," she said, and decided abruptly that she wanted no secrets between them. Whatever this infatuation with Kip, it would pass. "Actually, I went with my parents to a funeral. An old friend of the family—actually, my brother's old friend—lost his mother."

"Oh, I'm sorry," he said with the proper amount of solemnity. "That's a miserable way to spend a day. No wonder you sound upset. Did you know her well?"

"Not at all," she answered honestly. "Truthfully, I didn't know him that well either. JD came in, though," she continued on safer ground and heard Richard's hesitation, understanding his mild surprise. She'd mentioned JD just often enough for Richard to know her brother had become something of a sore spot with the family. "Hopefully, he'll be here when you arrive on Saturday. I'd really like you to meet him, but I'd better warn you. He can be a bit much, and he'll probably grill you."

"Sounds delightful," he said with a distracted note, in tune with the mechanical voices in the background. The echo of a hospital intercom had caught his attention. "I can't wait," he said absently.

"Sounds busy there."

"We've had a lot of accidents ... broken bones. A lot of abrasions and contusions. A lot of needlework," he said offhandedly.

'Broken necks... Broken legs.' The words slid through Kelly's mind in a deep, flowing rhythm that brought a smile to mind. But she wasn't smiling now. When Richard spoke those words, he meant people. Life and death. Kip had been teasing, taunting. How could such similar words evoke such different emotions?

"Damn it," Richard uttered. "I have to go, Kell. I'll try to call again if it's not too late when I get another break. Love you," he said, almost as an afterthought.

"Love you too," she responded mechanically, but he was already gone. Anxiously, he addressed one of his cohorts before the phone clattered into silence. A doctor's girlfriend. A doctor's wife. She'd better get used to emergencies. And truthfully, until this moment, she thought she had. A hundred other words careened inside her head, wanting a release. She wanted to talk about JD. Wanted Richard to understand. To realize the genuine shock of JD's arrival. The joy? 'Sounds delightful. Can't wait.' Sounded more like something one would say about a scheduled dentist's appointment.

Too critical! She was being ultra-critical. But after the lighthearted—heated exchange with Kip Patterson, a man who'd just lost his mother? Suddenly, she had a lot to think about. A great deal to think about.

With the symphony of Kelly Mulden's voice playing in his ear, Kip spun the tumbler in his grip, spinning the glass on the shined bar top in front of him. Watching the amber liquid swirl within the glass, he brought the lovely face to focus in his mind's eye. Overlapping, he remembered the wide innocent hazel eyes, the dark shiny locks jutting haphazardly to frame her rounded cheeks. No longer round, those lovely cheeks. Like that blasted Wallendorf poised on his mother's console, a bisque finish showcased her aquiline neck and slender, sculpted cheeks. If not a dancer, she could be a model. He'd dated enough to know. Morgan was just the latest in a long line of that breed.

Kelly Mulden.

He hadn't lied. When placing that damned call, he'd intended to invite Kelly to join him, and to hell with the consequences. If anything could drag his mood from the pits, that young lady qualified, and the image of JD Mulden—the boy, not the man—had countered his selfish thought in time to avoid calamity.

Subdued, the lighting and the softly playing music added to his melancholy. A dozen other wayward travelers, likely stranded with the delayed flights, rested belly up to the bar or occupied tables in the half-moon floor space. Rather than words, voices underscored the classical melody piping from random speakers at the corners of the room. Like most hotel bars, this one wasn't designed for a crowd nor fashioned after a honkytonk or corner bar, more like an airport lounge where the patrons might dally an hour between flights.

No dance floor. If Kelly had joined him, they might have braved the elements—

His attention snagged on the tumble of brunette waves at the end of the bar, and for an instant, he imagined Kelly looking back at him. His focus cleared on the instant as the ruby lips curved, and the head tipped in speculation. Blue eyes studied him, and, in reflection, Kip recalled the lady taking an interest when he'd first entered the lounge. His natural instincts had kicked in, mirroring her interest and appreciating her slender legs below a conservative, business casual skirt. Despite the deeper shadows, the slit in the skirt revealed shapely, slim calves and thighs, and even unbuttoned, the fitted jacket suggested an impressive figure. If she were available...

A ring glittered on her finger. On her right hand. A simple gold necklace shimmered between the folds of the navy jacket, drawing his attention to her cleavage, carefully visible between the open buttons of her pale blue blouse. Slowly, he lifted his focus to find her studying him more intently, and the shimmer of intense crimson, like a halo of blood shrouding her dark waves, eliminated any doubts.

With a slight tip of his head and twitch in his mustache, he offered a silent request and received a slight nod of acceptance and invitation. Collecting his glass and the stack of bills he'd left on the bar to keep his tumbler full, he slipped off the high leather stool and passed two gentlemen engaged in a grumbling match. The music transitioned into a Christmas tune, souring Kip's mood slightly despite his smirk as he indicated the empty chair beside her. "Mind if I join you?"

"I'd be disappointed if you didn't," she purred as her eyes glittered with mischief.

Nothing shy or backward about this lady, and with those words, she set the stage. Sliding onto the stool, Kip sent the bartender a signal for refills before offering his hand and the standard KJ monicker that had become his legal name since the age of eighteen. Outside of Whistlebrook, no one called him Kip or Kippen. But he hadn't minded hearing it spoken in Kelly Mulden's silky voice. Like the taste of a fine smooth whiskey, the syllables had slid into him, striking an odd chord, and unless he wanted to sleep alone this evening, he'd better strike Miss-happily-engaged-Mulden from his mind.

With a serious effort, he collected his thoughts along with his companion's first name as they engaged in the age-old dance of small talk and banal trivia. Three drinks later, uncertain if he'd offered the suggestion or merely accepted her invitation, Kip secured another bottle of Jack and escorted Ginny from the bar, through the brief hall to the nearest elevator. Only five short flights, but long enough. The doors barely closed before she launched against him, and they landed in a lip lock to determine the wild pace ahead.

Only by luck—and determination—he found his room key in his suit pocket, dispatched the door, and staggered them into the brief anteroom. Jackets landed in a heap, and buttons magically flew apart. Body parts collided as teeth and tongue tore at white lace and nimble, manicured fingers raked the zipper away, sinking into a raging heat. Where his hands failed, hers assisted, and when her fingers fumbled, his engaged. Again, only luck carried them to the bed, where they landed with a force that slammed the headboard against the wall and rattled the impressionist picture frame.

A cure for mourning. He'd finally found a cure for mourning, and with that thought, his thoughts sailed away on a low, deep laugh to carry his paramour into ever greater excitement.

Chapter 7

Vaguely, Kip recalled telling Mrs. Feeney he wouldn't be alone, and when he woke to a low rumbling drone of a jet engine vibrating the windowpanes, he knew he hadn't lied. Climbing from a tangle of blankets, he paused long enough to rub sleep from his eyes. Subtle indicators lingered in the room, if not within his stiff muscles. A half-dozen lipstick-smudged butts rested in the ashtray on the nightstand. Two glasses stood on a table in front of the beige drawn drapes. A bottle of Scotch and another of bourbon reflected on the dresser mirror, along with a single soda mix and an ice bucket. He'd obviously shared someone's company, and as he stood in the shower, letting a spray of cold water revive him, he remembered flashes of an attractive brunette with huge breasts and immense eyes.

Kelly.

Kelly Mulden. JD Mulden's sister?

He'd called her from this hotel room. But he'd refrained from inviting her to join him, although even in his sluggish awareness, he knew he'd have enjoyed her company. Something about that young woman pressed his buttons, but he suffered no illusions. Blonds were more his style. His digression toward dark-haired females would pass.

He couldn't even recall his companion's name, nor any clear physical traits beyond her versatility and ample breasts. Vicky? Valerie? Viola? "Damn," he sputtered under the spray, annoyed with his indifference. Not a blond. That much he recalled.

By the time he dried and began dressing, he remembered entering the hotel lounge, listening to the generic Christmas carols, and indulging in a couple of drinks before hitting on the brunette. Morgan had always reminded him of a Vegas showgirl, the type to sashay about with feathers on her butt and excessive makeup to add an alabaster finish. Last night's consort had worn utilitarian vogue—a conservative sweater, hip-hugging skirt with a slit just thigh-high enough to catch the eye. An executive, visiting Pittsburgh on business. Something Freudian about that, he was nearly certain and dared not venture too many thoughts to confirm his diagnosis.

Brunette, willing, and obviously able.

Who picked up whom, he wondered as he collected his cigarettes from the table. His attention caught on a sheet of hotel stationery under his lighter.

Good Morning, Mourning Prince...

His thought shattered; his attention riveted. Mourning Prince? For Chrissake! Had he told some stranger...? He might have admitted he was in mourning in the course of the evening, but prince? Shaking his head, he lifted the stationery, focusing.

Glad I could comfort you in your time of need. Sorry I had to leave. Early appointment. I'll be finished around five. My flight leaves at midnight. Room 1012 if you're awake and interested. Leaving my card. If you ever get to Chicago, be sure to call.

Lady in Waiting, Ginnie

His mind took another violent leap until he lifted her card. Virginia Vandell—President. Vandell's Marketing, Inc. Marketing what, he wondered absently, shrugging. If ever he needed to remember, and she'd told him, the information would surface. Mind like a steel trap, Marsh Baxel had told him often enough.

With his thought, Kip halfheartedly considered calling Baxel, donning his watch. By now, Marsh should have compiled the latest figures on Corbin Company. 8:30 a.m.? His attention riveted. Holding down the date button, he gazed at it momentarily, doubting its accuracy. 12-16?

He'd received Edna and Mark Frances' call on the 12th—California time around one a.m. He arrived in Pittsburgh by midafternoon on the 12th. Buried his mother on the 14th. He'd walked out of the Oak Room two days ago?

Maybe he should call Baxel again. By now, people were probably wondering if he'd hung himself or walked off a cliff in his grief. Vaguely,

Kip recalled threatening the hotel clerk—and manager—with bodily harm if anyone happened upon his name in the hotel's register. Even when placing calls before hitting the bottle, Kip hadn't divulged his location.

Glimpsing his reflection above the ice bucket, he found himself smirking. Honest amusement crept into his gaze. Sleep had helped. Virginia had helped. *Certainly, found a cure for mourning this time, didn't you?* "Keep it up, asshole," he uttered aloud. "They'll put you in a rubber room and toss the key for sure."

Great! Back to talking out loud in an empty room. Thanks, Mom, I really needed a full-blown backflip.

Annoyed, Kip collected his discarded suit parts from the floor and chairs, stuffed them and whatever other belongings he found into his leather bag, and scanned the room once more. Decidedly, he lifted the bottles—both half empty—and stuffed those into the bag. Whistlebrook had a decent wine cellar, but it was doubtful his mother kept any whiskey on hand. At least sleep had countered the hangover. He suffered only a mild thump at his temple. Likely the onset of starvation, a situation he could remedy in the restaurant downstairs.

Leaving his suitcase by the door, he made his way to the lobby, where a crowd of fellow guests loitered, apparently bemoaning the weather. A glance at the glass doors enlightened him and confirmed his decision to dine in. What made him look, a sixth sense or something slightly more tangible, Kip wasn't sure. In a less conspicuous second glance, Kip spotted a suited gentleman seated near the entrance door and caught the furtive eye movement off the morning paper. At a second glance, Kip confirmed his suspicion. He'd seen the fellow before. Possibly in the lounge on the night of his arrival? Probably in the lounge. He'd gone nowhere else since arriving at the motel, and before that? His mother's funeral.

Collecting the Pittsburgh Press from a rack near the restaurant entrance, Kip ignored the hostess sign and seated himself in a position to watch the door. At times, his paranoia confounded him, but then, he'd made enemies over the years. If some of them ever discovered the name and face behind Morning Sun Enterprises, life could become slightly more exciting, and that possibility always existed.

Halfheartedly scanning the paper, scanning the stock exchange with little more than a casual glance, he paused long enough to order a sizeable breakfast. Obviously, his appetite had returned. When his order arrived, he sparred words with the little redhead who flirted just a tad, then set upon the stack of pancakes as if he hadn't eaten in months rather than days.

Making a dent in the meal, Kip thought of Nan Feeney and her gourmet-style cooking. He'd compared her to some of the best chefs in the world on other occasions, but the mere thought of her shifted his thoughts to Whistlebrook. As much as he preferred to put Randall and the Home behind him, he couldn't quite close the book on that affair. Madison's word, '...personal.' Bickerman's ignorance. If anyone should know the status of one wayward son, that administrator should have a clue. And something far deeper niggled at his mind.

To return, however, to walk willingly into that haven for the damned? Could he really manage that with a clear head? A mind not lost in the shock and torment of a funeral? Not since leaving the Home fifteen years ago had Kip attended a funeral, and he'd vowed then that he would attend only two—Marilyn Patterson's and his own. One without a choice, the other out of familial obligation. No others. *Ever*. If he returned and another elderly person passed

A shiver slid down his spine as if ice water poured off his scalp.

So many deaths. So many funerals. How could he? Why would he?

He had no choice. Something ... something unfinished. Unsettling. Something other than obligation. Damn it. Marilyn's Will. He had an obligation to hear her last requests, and by Madison's subtle implication, Kip sensed something slightly off kilter.

Whatever his differences, whatever his pet peeves with Marilyn Patterson in life, he couldn't simply walk away from her in death. He hadn't walked away from the Home fifteen years ago. Twelve years ago, perhaps, but not fifteen. She'd given him no choice, no option. Like all else in his life before the age of seventeen, she'd controlled his fate as easily as she'd controlled Whistlebrook.

He should despise her. On a base level, Kip knew he should despise her, but he wasn't a child. More true, he should be grateful. He'd indeed found a productive, profitable vent for the hostilities lingering from those early years.

Somewhere between emptying his plate and picking up his suitcase in his room, Kip reached the decision to return to Whistlebrook. The fellow with the newspaper had departed, but another man, dressed nearly in the same ensemble of dark jacket and tie, white shirt and creased trousers, lent Kip pause.

Stereotypical officials—he'd run across enough of those over the years to recognize the type.

After paying his bill in cash and enlisting the valet to retrieve his car, Kip stood near the doors, watching an incredibly sedate snowfall beyond the glass. In slow motion, the tiny flakes floated, gathering in harmless pretense on a layer of dirty snow outside the window. The parking lot pavement wore a quagmire of dirty slush, lending thought to the trip ahead. The Expressway might be clear, but the roads in Randall would be a mess.

His gaze panning across the murky gray sky, he felt the vibration of another plane beyond the white haze. No delays today, apparently, despite the snow. He should call the rental agency to pick up the Regal here, call a cab, and return to the airport. If he bought a standby ticket, he could catch a departing flight in a reasonable time. With the weather, the airlines may have a surplus of cancellations. The world was filled with neurotics looking for omens to fuel their phobias and just as many fanatics who'd believe God sent snow to alter their flight plans. Likely to spare them a final journey in a great ball of flames. Iced wings, poor visibility, a salt truck on the runway, any number of extenuating circumstances existed to end in tragedy.

Under his breath, Kip uttered a curse. Death, always, death. He might have left Whistlebrook a lifetime ago, but Whistlebrook had never left him. Exchanging physical death for a more abstract rendition in a corporate setting had changed its colors, not its stripes.

He should phone Brad Sinclair.

Automated, Kip checked his watch, calculating the hour with the four-hour time zone difference before uttering another curse. Currently, he stood in the same time zone. Sinclair would be in his New York office. If Kip placed the call now, by the time he landed in LAX, Sinclair would have spoken to Madison, and the wheels could already be turning. Whistlebrook could land on the open market before the first of February. No one on God's green earth could spin the wheels of the legal system as fast as Sinclair and his band of merry men and women. Sinclair, Bartlem, and Meech could rip a contract to shreds more quickly and efficiently than any mechanical shredder patented to date. Hell, with a little nudge, Sinclair could probably hand Kip the entire package gift-wrapped for his thirtieth birthday on the fifteenth—

'Personally.'

A fleeting image of Madison's concentrated gaze halted his idling thoughts. Kip's attention split between the Buick arriving outside the glass and the thought of other anomalies, something undefined prickling his psyche and lifting short hairs under his collar.

Omens, phobias, Kip considered absently as he hoisted the leather strap to his shoulder. A bellhop hurried to assist, but Kip flagged him away and pushed through the first set of glass doors, holding the second door for an elderly woman who struggled with a suitcase large enough to accommodate a set of encyclopedias. Gratitude flashed in her wise eyes; a strained smile touched her lined lips. A hazy blue-gray aura of fatigue haloed her scarf-covered head.

An omen, damn it!

"Allow me, madame," he offered his hand to accept the case.

With a flash of embarrassment mixed with relief, she handed him her bag, huffing, "I can't imagine how I packed so much."

Delivering the case through the second door, Kip spotted and flagged the bellhop, a youngster with a cocky swagger and collegiate haircut. Pulling out his wallet, Kip leafed a hundred and handed it to the boy while fixing him in a chilled gaze. "See that the lady doesn't lift this case again, not arriving or departing, and have room service deliver a complimentary breakfast—"

"Young man, really, that's not necessary—"

Kip's chilly gaze fell to her, warming on the instant. "I think it is, gram," he interrupted smoothly, leaned, and brushed a kiss on her startled cheek, flashing her a smile and wink. "Be comfortable and enjoy your stay." Fleeting a glance off the startled bellhop to the luggage, Kip asserted his demand and stood only long enough to see the boy tripping over himself to lift the bag. With another fleeting wink to the bewildered elder, Kip passed through the glass doors. His smile vanished before the chilled air touched his lungs.

Omens. Phobias. He needed to return to Whistlebrook. Why he believed he could slip away, he couldn't imagine.

Tipping the valet, Kip threw his bag onto the passenger seat and climbed into the driver's position, pausing only long enough to wonder if he possessed a death wish. Snow, wet roads, airport traffic?

Within a half hour, Kip verified his earlier thought of Randall's hazardous conditions, not relaxing behind the steering wheel until he pulled onto Whistlebrook's plowed lane. More than once, between the expressway and stone pillars, he'd wheeled into a slide, twice finding himself stopped against a mound of dirty snow that hid the curb of a sidewalk. Twice, he changed his route, calling on distant memories to avoid the steepest hills and find the most traveled lanes. If he needed to drive again, he'd either rent a four-wheel drive vehicle or confiscate the security pickup that caught his eye as he rounded the back lane. With its snowplow attached, the Ford appeared more than capable of navigating the treacherous roads.

For a moment, Kip rested within the warmth of the Regal, catching his breath, stilling his rattled nerves as he scanned the back lawns. Again, he looked at the pickup, trying to decide what struck him odd. The new vehicle was quite a jump from the garden tractor that Mr. Culver and his assistants had once driven to plow the lanes, entrances, and parking lots. Sidewalks, too, Kip remembered as he drew from his thoughts and climbed from the car. The garden tractor was probably still in use. He caught an echo of a small engine somewhere on the grounds and imagined the old man issuing orders to one of his younger assistants.

Culver wasn't that old, Kip countered. All these people who'd become fixtures at the Home...

Odd how they all looked the same when they'd seemed so old to him while growing up. Perhaps not as old as the residents, but old compared to him. To find them still in their prime and him looking at them through the eyes of an adult felt truly strange. Strange, indeed. He was nearly the same age as Mrs. Feeney when she'd set his place at the breakfast nook for the last time. Not much younger than Frank Culver when the fellow had offered to run a security check on JD Mulden's New York license plates.

Unconsciously, Kip stopped at the iron handrail and drew a last drag of smoke and chilled air. Old habits die hard. His focus trailed along the wet salted tarmac, rising to scan the three cement docks built into alcoves within each of the weathered additions. With infinite care and craft, the modern necessities blended with the natural elegance. His gaze lifted, sensing shadowy faces behind the glass, lingering momentarily on a rounded tower that rose from a lower roof near the far end of the Home.

'Spring Chicken,' a raspy voice echoed inside his mind.

His attention fell away, sliding toward the white lawn, passing blind through the carriage house and four-bay garage. Through frosted branches, he identified the cut of the brook traveling in bends and twists down a gentle slope. Maintenance hadn't bothered clearing the paved paths on the hillside. An occasional cast-iron bench marked the trail. Flagstone islands, dormant bushes, and cast-iron tables designated patios where the residents might sit for hours, enjoying a warm summer breeze or a visit from a loved one.

But so few loved ones visited.

Memories. So damned many memories. In flash frames, Kip recalled walking those paths, sauntering along at the hip of an elder, or lounging on one of the benches listening to tales of old. God, how he'd loved their stories. Old Irish, that old coot could spin a yarn to give Hemingway a fair run for his money. Once ...

Kip remembered standing on the bridge, his gaze finding the mere hint of the cast-iron rails within the snowcaps. He and JD had stood on that bridge once, and undoubtedly, Irish had seen them from the tower window. Echoes. Damn, how the echoes slid through his mind. He'd wanted the past to remain past, wanted never to think or feel, or fret again.

"Damn it," Kip uttered, blowing an exhale of smoke and flicking his cigarette butt behind him as he strode up the steps to the kitchen entrance.

Of the dozen entrances into Whistlebrook, the kitchen door created an instant feeling of home. The storm door hinges no longer squealed. As he pushed open the inside door, a blast of cold air followed him and alerted the half dozen bustling employees within the kitchen. Momentarily startled, Kip stood, feeling like an intruder, as if he'd taken a wrong turn and entered the kitchen of a fine restaurant instead of a restroom. Industrial-sized burners and several ovens extended halfway across the outside wall. Freezers and refrigerators ran parallel on the inside wall. At a midway point, in a small alcove, a restaurant-style booth formed an inlet between the industrial bins and the wall. Between the floor-to-ceiling storage shelves and the industrial dishwasher, a solid oak swinging door separated the kitchen from the executive wing. Through the center of the expansive room, the long metal preparation counter appeared dwarfed by the sheer size of the room. Overhead, iron racks held every imaginable kitchen implement, from tremendous colanders to meat hooks.

Abruptly, metal crashed, jumpstarting his heart. A plastic plate clattered, smacked the ceramic tiles, and bounced across the checkered floor. Riveted, Kip watched the plate roll toward him, shot a glance at the stunned, vaguely familiar kitchen assistant several feet away, then landed his focus on Edna's stricken gaze.

In a split second, Edna jolted from her surprise. Relief washed over her drawn face as she pivoted from the sinks across the room and hurried toward him. "Oh, Thank God! We've been so worried! Are you alright?" Her hands clutched his forearms in a manic grip. Her soft brown eyes darted down and up, welling with tears as she threw propriety aside and wrapped her arms around him. "Oh, thank God," she heaved. "Thank God, you're home!"

Perhaps, hanging himself or hang gliding off a cliff—without the wings—hadn't been too far off the mark. Faintly amused, Kip returned Edna's embrace. "I assure you, I'm fine, mum, but—" He waited until she wiped her eyes to clear a flood while stepping back, smiling slightly as he continued, "I could use a cup of coffee."

"You need more than a cup of coffee," she said with an echo of reproach. "I'll have your breakfast in—"

"Really, mum. I just polished off the equivalent of a small sow. Just the coffee will do." With the flash of hurt and indignation in her eyes, Kip doubted he should have admitted his indulgence in a kitchen other than this.

"Let's just get that wet coat put up, now. And why don't you change out of those wet shoes? You're not used to this cold air anymore."

Back-flipping in time and faintly relieved with her quick recovery, Kip realized the futility of removing his own coat. No arguing with a woman, especially this woman. Letting her tug his long coat off his shoulders, he watched as she hung it on the rack nearest the large ovens. Half expecting to be scolded for tracking up the kitchen floor, Kip wiped his feet on the mat and verified her observation. He wore sopping shoes—and equally wet socks. Leaning against the door, he removed both. God knows, he had plenty of sensible leather shoes, and he could certainly afford a pair of boots. Canvas loafers had been a mistake.

Disgusted, Kip stooped, rummaged in his leather bag until finding a pair of clean socks at the bottom. With the socks in hand, he stood up, glimpsing a young male aide who averted his eyes a little too swiftly. Leaving his bag at the door, Kip strode barefoot across the floor, remembering abruptly how his mother had once caught him barefoot in here and taken time out from her busy schedule to lecture him as well as Nan Feeney about the sanitation codes and the practical application of the rules. Diseases could be contracted through the most mundane sources. Kitchen floors were the worst, according to Marilyn Patterson. From September to May, a pair of small brown slippers stood at the kitchen door.

Kip barely finished pulling on his socks and slid more completely into the breakfast booth when Bill Bickerman swept through the swinging door from the executive wing. Halted, Bill glanced off Edna's back to the assistant stacking trays at a metal bin, then found Kip with an instant conflict of relief and dread.

"Kip!" he heaved in forced enthusiasm. "Great God Almighty! That *was* your car coming in!" Continuing to the booth, Bill swung his girth onto the opposite bench, clasping the edge of the table as if he might spring forward. "God Almighty, where've you been? We've been going nuts around here trying to find you! We called your lady friend—Morgan, right? In California! We'll have to call her. She's probably frantic by now! Damn, kiddo, where the hell'd you go, anyway? We thought... Well ... never mind what we thought. You're alright, right? That's the main thing."

Looking at Bill while catching a flame to his cigarette, Kip couldn't help but wonder if Bickerman might be amphetamine dependent. Or had the assistant taken lessons from Marilyn Patterson on how to fit twenty minutes of dialogue into twenty seconds? Like Marilyn, Kip suspected, Bill would slide from the booth and fly away if given a dozen or so silent seconds. God knows, Marilyn had never sat long, and she'd never cared for her son's ability to let silence linger indefinitely. Patience was a virtue, silence a tool. *Prophecy, by Kip Patterson.* Kip smirked, still watching Bill, noting the man's growing discomfort.

Leaning across the table, Bill clasped Kip's forearm, enhancing his concern. "Are you okay? Really, kid? You still look wiped out. I mean, I know how tough this all is. It's been a shock to all of us." Under bright fluorescent light, the lines strained about Bill's dark eyes, aging him considerably. His lips thinned to appear stressed. "Your mom, She was one special woman. We all loved her—"

"Are you gay, Bill?" Kip interrupted while shifting his gaze from Bill's hand to his suddenly stricken face.

Bill yanked his hand back as outrage raced into his sprinting eyes. "For Christ's sake!" Bill huffed, sending a heated glance toward Edna Feeney and her assistant. A tray skidded, clattering around the corner of the booth, and Kip suffered a fleeting thought of the teenager standing within earshot. Bill's gaze returned with genuine anger. "I think that was uncalled for," he stated crisply. "I know you're not thinking clearly, but that's no reason to be insulting."

"It certainly wouldn't disturb me if you were, Bill," Kip commented without lifting his voice or wavering his smirk. "Providing you refrain from touching me when you speak to me."

"I'm well aware of the fact that we've never gotten along very well," Bill stated in a struggle for civility and discretion. "I'm sure it's partly because of jealousy, Kip. You probably resent me for being close to your mother, but for her sake, and the sake of this facility, I think we should try to get along—"

"I don't have a problem with you, Bill. Do you have a problem with me?" Kip asked evenly, watching anger lance the dark eyes. Too well, he knew Bickerman despised him. Jealousy perhaps? Blood being thicker than water and all that rubbish? Or was it more basic, the fear of losing his position in Marilyn's absence? Undoubtedly, the administrator felt threatened.

"I've bent over backward trying to make this easier on you." Bill strained to remain calm as he continued, "I promised your mother I'd help you through this. I know you've never dealt well with death. No one," he emphasized. "Wants to see you go off the deep end, here, Kip. Already, you disappear for two days, not a word to anyone. You turn up looking like a strung-out teenager, asking if I'm gay—"

"Do I really?" Kip asked with a shadowy amusement.

"Do you—*what*—really?"

"Look like a strung-out teenager?" Kip supplied, sincerely curious, still amused behind his abstracted gaze.

"Yes! As a matter of fact, you do. You're white as a sheet. Your eyes are glassy. It doesn't look like you've combed your hair in two days—" Bill stopped abruptly, retracting his hostility, forcing an almost impressive calm. "Look, I'm sorry, Kip. Really. But I promised your mom that I'd look out for you if anything ever happened to her. She knew this would be hard on you, you being alone now and all...

"The thing is, buddy, there are some things I can't take care of for you. I know Mr. Madison has things he needs to discuss with you. He needs your signature on a couple of documents. Probably just formalities, but we can't put it off too long. I can buy you a few days until you're feeling a little better, but shit, kid, you can't go running off and getting lost. Like it or not, you have a responsibility here."

"Oh, I see," Kip commented, glancing at Edna as she arrived with his coffee. An almost alien contempt flashed in her glance toward Bill. Like a mother cat protecting her young, Kip considered while feigning to appear wounded as he caught her immediately soft smile.

"What ... do you see?"

Returning his distracted gaze to Bill, Kip answered, "You believe I'm an *irresponsible* strung-out teenager." Maintaining his surface calm, Kip held Bill's nearly black gaze. How much did Bill Bickerman truly know about Marilyn Patterson's wayward son? A look here, a glance there, a catch in a condescending note? Were those the anomalies Kip had sensed?

Did it matter?

"Look, it's no big surprise that you've wanted nothing to do with the Home," Bill said haltingly, striving for understanding as if he were a kindergarten teacher addressing a daft student. "It's supplied you with a comfortable lifestyle for a lot of years, and it will continue to do so. You'll be taken care of, Kip. Like I said, there are just some formalities. Once those are out of the way, you can return to doing your own thing. If you want, I'll go along with you when you meet with John Madison."

"How long have you been here, Bill?"

Stopped, Bill considered before answering, "Ten years this coming May."

"Really? I thought longer," Kip commented while adding a dollop of cream to his coffee. Ten years was long enough for Bill to know Marilyn's son didn't rely on Whistlebrook for financial security. Either the man faked his ignorance, or Marilyn truly hadn't confided in Bill as entirely as he seemed to believe. "Tell me. Are you Catholic, Bill?" Kip asked offhandedly, fleeting a benign glance.

"No."

"Atheist?" Kip wondered, raising a brow as he sipped his coffee.

"Protestant," Bill answered, annoyed. "Why do you ask?"

Swallowing, Kip shrugged, glimpsing Edna turning from the counter across the room, advancing with an insulated coffeepot in hand. Edna, on the other hand, undoubtedly knew a great deal about one Kip Patterson's enterprising spirit. Offhandedly, Kip glanced at Bill, "Why don't you get a cup of coffee?"

Again, Kip caught Edna's contempt in a fleeting glance as she slipped the pot to his side of the table. She'd always been his mother's confidant, as well as a second mother to him. Apparently, she still loved him even if she didn't entirely approve of him, his lifestyle, or theatrics. Undoubtedly, she considered him a disappointment in many regards. Flashing Edna a smile, Kip appreciated her softer smile and warm gaze. "Thanks, mum."

"You're welcome, dear. Can I get you anything else?"

"Fine, thanks," he said.

Obviously annoyed, Bill spoke as she turned. "Edna, I could use a cup of coffee."

Kip imagined her biting her lip as she had when Marilyn Patterson aggravated her. With impressive control, Edna never publicly confronted the lady of the Home. Out of mutual respect, the two women had only tangled in private, and on those rare occasions, Kip knew he'd usually been at the heart of it. Edna had always stood in his corner. Not that it helped.

'Irresponsible strung-out teenager.' Bill wasn't the first person to make that observation. Presently, however, Kip's condition might be attributed to those hair-raising episodes on the highway. God knows, he'd deliberately, successfully, avoided snow and cold weather for the past dozen years ... partially owing to his lousy driving skills.

"Why did you ask how long I've been here?" Bill asked.

"Did I?" Kip asked absently.

Bill hesitated. "Yes, if you're asking me if you asked me. For Christ's sake, Kip, are you *on* something?"

"Oh," Kip commented and dragged off his cigarette, still watching Bill without a hint of amusement on the surface. Did Bickerman fully believe the great Marilyn Patterson had created such a moron?

"Oh, what?"

With his exhale, Kip commented, "Now, I'm a *stoned*, irresponsible, strung-out teenager."

"Why don't I make an appointment with Dr. Carmine? He's scheduled to drop by this evening. I think you need to talk to someone," Bill said while sliding from the bench.

"Bill?" Kip waited for Bill's gaze. "Your coffee's coming."

Bill stood up, looking at Mrs. Feeney. "I'd like to speak to you for a moment."

Kip caught her annoyed glance as she set the cup down. Obviously, Nan and Bill weren't the best of friends, a detail Kip had sensed days ago without delving too deeply into the mechanics or atmosphere in Whistlebrook. Scooting to sit with his back against the wall, deciding to stick around until Edna returned, Kip watched the precision of the staff in the post-breakfast rush.

He should have waited for breakfast. Despite his estrangement from the Home, the bonds still existed, regardless of how one-sided those bonds might be to him. Edna was his second mother, or his only mother, more often than not in those early years. No one could make eggs over-easy like Edna. Unfortunately, Kip hadn't suffered so many bouts of nausea in the past dozen years as he'd suffered in the past week.

Not since leaving here fifteen years ago, Kip considered absently, his thoughts drifting. Hernia ... or funerals? One or the other, a combination of both, had been responsible, but God knows, those memories were hazy. His whole life had crashed and burned in three short weeks. That much he remembered. Home, schools, lifelong friendships, new friendships. Hell, even his love life.

Carolyn hadn't held his undivided attention. Vacantly, he scanned the kitchen, not truly seeing the aides hustling about. Another young woman had worked here around that same time. Black hair, heavy cosmetics, blue eyes. He'd nearly run into her a dozen or more times when coming through the swinging door or rounding a corner. Eventually, she'd invaded his refuge, too. She'd barged into his room, uninvited. To escort him to Dr. Frances's examination room.

Christ, he'd hated doctors! Good, bad, or indifferent, Kip had avoided all of them.

His gaze drifted to the laundry-room door across the room and the memory swirled to the surface. They'd trapped him in that room. Penned him like a damn mouse. The floral scents of laundry soap and dryer sheets surfaced in his mind. He'd only officially begun working two months earlier. Something had happened at school, though. His mother had put him on light duty, enlisting him to mop the little room. Right, and the door had just accidentally locked with him on the inside. She hadn't known about his hernia ... but the school nurse had taken his vital signs, looking for signs of drug abuse.

Drugs.

Perhaps he'd always, unwittingly, fit the profile of a *user*. Between his unruly blond waves and his blank gray eyes, he supposed he could pass for a junky.

On dual planes, Kip considered Bill's observations while recalling his panic yesteryear when finding that door locked. He'd never suffered claustrophobia before that moment, but the panic threatened to explode his heart. Years. Fifteen years later, and Kip finally found the humor in that wretched event. At the time, he'd known only terror, knowing damn full well his mother meant to collect him when the *good doctor* Frances arrived.

Compared to his fear of the 'good doctor,' that twelve-foot drop from the single window in the laundry room to the ground below had seemed like a breeze, and all these years later, he accepted the age-old wisdom, 'It's not the fall, it's the sudden stop that gets you.' If his condition hadn't been serious before his great escape, he'd certainly taken a turn for the worse in its wake. And belatedly, Kip recognized the irony of that entire affair.

By the time Franny collected him from his bedroom, he'd needed her help to find his shoes. But she'd dawdled a while. And nearly repaired his fear of doctors while she examined him. A hazy image of a red, high gloss fingernail trailing down the center of his bare chest held him in a momentary grip. If he'd known then what he knew now, they might never have reached that examination room—

His attention riveted as Edna strode through the swinging doors. Without a doubt, Bickerman had given her orders to keep track of the wayward son until Dr. Carmine, the resident psychologist, arrived. Her eyes conveyed concern as she reached the table, her voice careful. "How's your coffee, dear?"

"Things haven't changed tremendously, have they, mum?"

She eyed him critically. "What do you mean, sweetie?"

"Let me guess. You're instructed to report my directional moves to Bill and if I should say...? Don my coat and take my leave? You're to notify him immediately."

"Bill's not the most pleasant man sometimes, but he is a decent administrator," she conceded with a resigned sigh. "He and your mother were close, and I think he's concerned—as we're all concerned."

"Was I always so fragile, mum?" Kip asked absently despite his concentration.

A sad, gentle smile touched her lips and eyes. "The Prince of Whistlebrook," she said fondly. "Irish McGuire gave you that title—a fitting title. The old place never truly recovered when the prince left us." Her eyes misted, moistening as she studied him; sorrow etched in every soft line of her rounded cheeks. "I think that sending you away was the most difficult decision your mother ever made. She so loved you, Kip. I think more than you'll ever realize."

"Oh, I'm convinced," he said with a sincerity to betray his sarcasm. "I've always believed, if you love someone, deep six them early on. It certainly saves time." He winked and smiled as he began sliding from the booth.

Edna caught his arm, looking into him with penetrating concern. "Will you keep the appointment with Dr. Carmine, sweetie?"

"For you, luv? Anything," he lied with a smile. God knows, he probably needed to see a shrink, present circumstances withstanding, but he would certainly not choose one from the ranks and files of Whistlebrook. Somehow, he'd never embraced an alcoholic's philosophy about dog hair and being bitten. In canine idioms, he preferred 'let sleeping dogs lie.'

Leaning, Kip brushed a kiss on Edna's cheek and glanced toward his suitcase. Nothing he needed immediately, he decided. "Is Carolyn in the office?"

"I believe so."

"Don't bother reporting in, mum. I'm sure Bill will blow by while I'm flirting with her." Again winking, he collected the warming pot and his cup, sidestepped past Edna, and strode into the administrative wing.

Considering the need for a pair of shoes, Kip veered into the PRIVATE suite. Rather than pick up his wet shoes, he strode into the bedroom and lifted a hat from the second shelf.

Should never have taken my favorite hats, he considered absently.

Systematically, he'd lost all save three of the dozen he'd taken to St. John's Academy. The prefect, a broad-faced Brother Adam, hadn't cared for an atheist whose knowledge of Catholic burial rites had superseded his own. Nor had the fellow cared for an atheist who only took off his hat to eat, attend mass, or class. Brother Adam's opinion hadn't altered even after the atheist's official Baptism.

Chapter 8

Wearing an old blue and white baseball hat, a flannel shirt, faded jeans, and stocking feet, Kip strode into the secretarial pool. Across the room, Carolyn glanced up from a document she held for her younger assistant's view. In a double-take, her attention froze, her words halted in mid-sentence. She eyed him from head to toe without closing her soft pink lips.

In a similar appraisal, Kip admired her long, slender anatomy, not entirely concealed in a dark, flowery skirt and navy-blue jacket. In deference to Marilyn's passing, Carolyn wore dark colors, and shadows lingered under her lovely eyes. Rather than her fluffed neon blond waves, her hair swept back and up in a Victorian style to define her high cheeks and slender neckline. Like a face on an antique cameo, her haunted, dull brown aura enhanced the image.

Misery loves company. *And wasn't he just full of clichés today?*

Kip glanced off her startled blue eyes to her young assistant, Angie-something, then back to Carolyn as he continued forward. Far more critically, she studied him.

Without a doubt, Bickerman had passed the word. *Watch the prince, he's losing it, or lost it.* Though Bickerman had probably said 'the kid.' Carolyn wore the wary doubt of a woman prepared to call security, and she honestly should know better.

What the hell was going on here?

Halting, Kip glanced to the open folder hovering in Carolyn's hands, then looked at her dumbstruck assistant. She was a pretty little thing. Unmistakably Italian, she wore her long raven hair tied back to slim her still-rounded cheeks. Nineteen or twenty, Kip guessed, and apparently new to Whistlebrook, which meant she could have been hired at any time in the past six to nine months. He hadn't visited the Home since... Hell, not since a fly-by late last spring, early summer. "Angie, isn't it?"

She nodded slowly, warily, and another familiar spooked shine lent Kip pause. Maintaining a harmless smile, he sidled around Carolyn as he commented, "Please, don't let me interrupt." With a natural ease, he settled on the corner of her desk. Bouncing a glance between them, he motioned with his hands in universal sign language. *Carry on. Don't let me stop you.*

Carolyn handed the file to Angie, distractedly. "You have the general idea. Take care of what you can." Turning to Kip, she asked, "What can I do for you?"

"Well, now that you ask, there is something," he commented, turning with her, remaining sidesaddle on her desk as she swept into the swivel chair. "Could you get Att. Madison on the horn for me?"

Removing a small stack of notes from under a snow dome paperweight, she handed the pile across the desk. "You might want to check those first."

In rapid succession, Kip flipped through the switchboard notes. JD Mulden, Morgan Lamont, Father Jordan ... each repeated several times at different times over the past twenty-four hours. More than a dozen names apparently offering condolences. Another half dozen names carried familiar foreign exchanges. "Damn," he uttered and sent Carolyn a faintly desperate grin. "It seems I'll need the use of a telephone for about an hour."

She flashed a distressed glance toward the executive offices. "I'm sure you could use Mr. Bickerman's office."

Instantly, her implication disturbed him. Kip dropped a vacant gaze to the notes. Bickerman in his mother's office? Why should that bother him? God knows, someone needed to occupy the executive office at least for a short time, and the queen had hand-selected and groomed Bickerman for that position.

"Kip," Carolyn interrupted, standing, leaning, and touching his arm. Her gaze carried sympathy as well as an apology. "I'm sorry, hon. Why don't I just go speak to Bill? I'm sure you'd be more comfortable—"

"Actually," he interrupted lightheartedly. "I'd be more comfortable in the suite. Ring Att. Madison and transfer the call to that extension." Sliding off the desk, he strode from the office, tossing Angie a wink before passing into the hall.

No. Bickerman, in his mother's office, shouldn't affect him. What had he expected? That he'd someday become reigning lord and master? He'd made his position clear to his mother a very long time ago. As if he'd ever taken a stand against her. Passive-aggressive tactics. He'd merely disappeared from the day of his high school graduation until after his twentieth birthday, and two years later, he'd visited rather than sent a postcard with 'Alive and Well. Love, Kip.'

Jolted on the first ring, Kip focused on the notes in his hand, then pushed off the door where he'd leaned. In three strides, he settled into the recliner and lifted the receiver on the second ring, "Yes?"

"Kip, I have Att. Madison. Hold on, I'll connect you."

A familiar cultured voice slid through the line, "John Madison, here."

"Hello, Counselor," Kip stated in an empty tone. "I'd imagine we have an appointment to schedule? Is this afternoon convenient for you?" The sooner the better, damn it! He had his life, and hanging out in a damned nursing home wasn't his idea of a vacation!

"If you need a little more time, we could schedule for Monday."

"You're booked for this afternoon?"

"Nothing pressing but—"

"Why don't you come here?" Kip suggested, considering the snow. "Around one?"

Madison hesitated. "I'll see you then."

"Very good, sir," Kip answered and dropped the receiver into its cradle. Wading through the notes, he shuffled them into priority sequence, lit a cigarette, then lifted the receiver and punched the first number. Priority, he considered vacantly, wondering why he rated Morgan fourth in line. A soft voice slid into his ear with a lyrical, "Hello."

A flash of hazel eyes riveted his attention. "Even your voice dances."

"Uhhh..."

He couldn't afford this fantasy. Far more naturally, he commented, "I hope this is JD's little sister and not his mother."

"Kip!"

"Kelly?" *God, he loved the sound of her voice.*

"Yes?"

"We're certainly making progress," he mused. "And possibly I should speak to JD before I say anything incredibly stupid."

"If he wasn't standing here trying to grab the phone, I'd risk it! JD!"

"Hello!" JD stated. "Where the hell are you?"

"Good morning," Kip said lightly. "Sleep well?"

"Shit," Mulden stated, recovering. "Right. Good morning, and *no*, I didn't sleep well. A friend of mine disappeared off the face of the earth for a little while."

"You worry far too much, JD. You worried. I mourned. Wonderful friendship we had for five weeks. Enter déjà vu. Free this evening?"

"What did you have in mind?"

"I seem to recall a suggestion for drinks. I'll buy if you drive. Around six?"

"Six works."

"See you then," Kip commented and pressed the disconnect button, waited for the dial tone, and placed the second call. *Friends ... priests ... business associates ... lovers...* Had his mother systematized in a similar order? He could imagine her list. *Residents ... residents' families..* "Father Jordan, please." *Staff ... medical practitioners.* "Father? Kip Patterson. You were trying to reach me?" *Funeral directors ... community services.*

"I wondered if we might have a chance to talk. I heard you mention you might be leaving soon."

Auxiliaries ... linen services. "Tomorrow. One o'clock?" *Caretakers ... lawn services.*

"Sounds fine, son. How are you?"

"Fine. See you then."

Click. Dial tone. Next number. *Priests ... utilities ... janitors ... son.* "Marsh. How's tricks?"

"My deepest condolences."

"Was that why you called?" Kip asked with a subtle warning in a descending tone.

"You called the Corbin Company to the letter. What do you want done? It's on the move."

"Sell, Marsh. Dump it all. Anything else?" Kip asked, casting his gaze.

"Christ, Kip. Any idea what that will do?"

"Next question."

"This can't be a good time for business. Are you sure you don't want to think about that move? In a couple of days—"

"—I could find another broker," Kip finished.

A brief pause settled on the line. "Consider it sold. Should I call you there?"

"Relay through Morgan. I'll return your call."

"She sounded distressed."

"Obviously," Kip said absently as a vision of Elsa Taylor popped into his mind's eye. Elsa Taylor, of the Richmond Taylors. So eloquent and sophisticated. Was his mother still running the Home by the old protocols? Did he really want to know? With less than a heartbeat pause, he decided, "Do me a favor, Marsh. See what you can find out about an Elsa Taylor. Richmond, possibly Virginia. Old money. Sizeable dowry. Taylor could be a maiden name. She's in her eighties. My guess, a widow." Not much to go on, but Marsh was like a bloodhound once he caught a scent of green. *God help you, Mother, if you're still playing that anonymity game. I don't need that sort of complication in my life.*

"Anything else?" Marsh asked cautiously, breaking the pause.

"Keep in touch," Kip said and disconnected the call while turning his attention to Morgan. Apparently, she was 'distressed,' or she wouldn't have given Marsh Baxel Whistlebrook's number. "Damn it," Kip uttered and dialed the California number to his apartment. Glancing at his watch before the second ring, he understood the sluggish 'hello' before her brain cells electrified with a second sharp, "Hello!"

"Forgot the time change, babe. So, sorry. How's the hibiscus?"

"How's the...? I don't know why I like you," she stated. "Not even 7 a.m.! You drive me *crazy*! I've been getting calls day and night from *lunatics*! Foreign-Fucking-Lunatics—"

"Worry lines leave permanent wrinkles. Are you aware of that?"

"Tell it to my analyst! Who—by the way—would *love* to get her hands on *you*!"

"Are they pretty?"

"Are *who* pretty? The hibiscus—"

"Her hands?" he asked absently.

"You're *impossible*!" Morgan huffed. "And No! Her hands worried too much thirty years ago! Now—" Her voice lowered with a breath. "How *are* you, my certifiable lover?"

"How should I be?" he asked vacantly. "Alive. Well. Terribly horny."

"Then you're depressed."

"Actually, no. Not at the moment," he said honestly. "Are you feeling better?"

"Am I...? You really are insane, Kip. I think you spend far too much time in the sun," she played. "But, yes, I'm feeling better. Now tell me, honestly, are you alright? The call—that Bickerman clown sounded dreadfully worried when you flew. I trust she helped?"

"I should resent that question, shouldn't I?" Kip asked vacantly.

"You sound down, honey.

The Prince of Whistlebrook. His focus landed on the Wallendorf Prima Donna within her glass tomb. Absently, he panned a gaze over the compact suite, hearing the tick of a clock, the distant sounds from the office and kitchen combined. Three stacks of business journals and magazines stood in neat piles, evenly spaced on the squat table in front of him. Marilyn Patterson's subscriptions ran along the same vein as his own. Had she begun choosing her reading material with him in mind? He could recall spending that first night, Monday night, flipping through one magazine after another just to keep his mind from wandering. *The Prince of Whistlebrook.* He uttered, "The Queen's dead."

"What, Honey?"

Morgan. Christ, he still held the phone to his ear. A subconscious desire to confide in her? At the mere thought, he startled himself. He hadn't shared a pain or triumph with another living soul, not in fifteen years, and he had no desire to change at this late date!

"Nothing," Kip said firmly and flashed a thought of her insinuation, as well as her infidelity. "Enjoy your company, but do have the maid service in before I arrive, will you? E.T.A. Sunday, all goes well," he touched the disconnect button, holding it down as he leaned his head back and closed his eyes against a sudden sting. The weight of the receiver dragged his hand down. This wasn't supposed to happen, this sudden grip of revelation. *The Queen is dead.* The queen only dies in Fairy Tales, damn it, and there was always a plot. How could the great Marilyn Patterson be alive one day and gone the next? She was fine four months ago, Goddamn it. How could he have missed the signs? He'd grown up with death.

Forever the shadow of death hovered about the Home and it was still here. He smelled it. Tasted its bitter scent on every breath. Like icy fingers, he suffered its clammy touch at his nerve endings. If he listened closely, he'd hear it whispering through hallways, snaking down stairwells and elevator shafts, rattling windowpanes like an internal wind seeking escape.

Opening his eyes, he focused on the closed door to his mother's bedroom. Not once in twenty-five years had he passed through that door into the Queen's chambers, but death had passed through it, finding the queen and taking her quickly. Like a black knight on a chessboard, death had stolen the queen, and no king had ever existed. He should have known, damn it. Death had never surprised him.

But that wasn't exactly true.

Fifteen years ago. Death had blindsided him fifteen years ago. The fall of '72, he remembered absently. Up until then, he'd always known when an elder neared his or her time. One after another—six in less than two weeks. He remembered feeling sick, remembered thinking it was the hernia, but people were dying. His friends. His family. Dying. And he remembered loathing the sight of his black suit. He'd hated hanging it in the laundry room, knowing it would return cleaned and pressed to wear again, soon.

"Undertaker," he uttered aloud, no longer feeling the pain, but remembering. Until his freshman year in Randall, he'd worn the nickname, 'Kip the Blimp.' In calculated determination, he'd begun shedding pounds, burning away all the cute 'baby fat' that provided ample padding for the elders to pinch. On his thirteenth birthday, January of '72, he'd begun his crusade against excess and by the end of the school year, his nickname had changed.

Undertaker.

Damn it. He'd felt like an undertaker, or worse. The Grim Reaper. Not until that sojourn, so many deaths, and he hadn't ... he *truly* hadn't known. Before those deaths, before his life had crashed, he'd always sensed death. Felt it, seen it, known and prepared. He'd said his farewells and comforted those he could as the gray shroud had darkened around them. Months, sometimes he'd known months in advance when an illness turned, but he'd lost that ability. Suddenly, people were dying without warning—

No. A lie. A coincidence. He'd grown up, matured, stopped listening to the whispers of death and seeing the gray ... and that was a worse lie. Even now, when he walked through the halls of the East Wing, he knew by the shades of gray who would live long and who would soon depart. A shiver slid through him as he recalled his walk only four evenings past. Several were close to their final journey.

How in God's name had he missed the signs four months ago? How was it even possible that his mother had suffered a terminal illness, and he hadn't glimpsed some sign, hadn't felt the chilly prickle at the nape of his neck? If he'd remained sober while waiting for her in that restaurant at the airport, would he have seen this event on the horizon?

Maiobi, his teacher, his mentor in the commune so long ago, had taught him to accept what his eyes foresaw, had convinced him to believe what he'd never found the courage to admit aloud years earlier. Forces existed, gifts beyond the realm of art and music, sculpture and dance. His talent lay far left of field, but Kip had stopped denying it years ago. When fatal illnesses afflicted, he knew it, just as a doctor might glimpse a patient and sense a deeper problem, or a policeman might rely on gut instinct to catch a criminal. His relationship with death had become intimate, a second nature, a natural phenomenon that never failed him.

Life and death. The images swam in Kip's mind as he rested, gazing at his mother's door. Life and death. Death hung above his head, he remembered, now. Death was the poster of a wrinkled old man. The face of an old man ... a proclamation against 'Euthanasia.' He remembered pasting it on the ceiling directly above his pillow. In perfect contrast, life projected from a one-foot square on his desk. Meticulously, he'd cut the pictures from a photography magazine and arranged the still-life images to decorate his room. One of the residents had been a professional photographer.

Listening to the idle rambling of that old man as the fellow had drifted into senility had honed his photography skills and appreciation. So much knowledge ... zoom lenses, shutter speeds, light meters, chemical solutions, and timing. For a time, Kip remembered his fascination with cameras, had even considered setting up a darkroom in the basement—

"Damnit," Kip uttered, jolting and collecting himself in the chair, finding more than a dozen notes still in his fisted hand. Phone calls to make. Damned nostalgia! Damned the silence within this room that cracked open a vault of memories. Silence was not quiet. Silence was a bomb detonating inside his mind, shattering conscious thought and activity. "Phone calls."

Turning his focus to the following note, he read the name, not at all comfortable with his subconscious decision to rank Denton McDaniels ahead of other, more familiar names and faces. He couldn't even consciously recall when the name had landed in his subconscious. Regardless, Kip dialed the given number and waited through a half dozen rings. As he was about to disconnect, the line engaged.

"McDaniels residence," a faintly English voice answered.

"Mr. Denton McDaniels, please?"

"One moment."

In the silence, Kip read the long-distance number. He didn't readily recall the area code, which likely ruled out a half dozen major cities in the U.S. By the accent, it might be one of the New England states. He should have checked the phone directory—

"You've reached Denton McDaniels," a faintly familiar, distinctly English voice broke the silence.

"Kip Patterson. I'm returning your call." *And wracking my brain to remember your face or our introduction. Recently. Had to be. Why the pause?* Had McDaniels hung up? Silence is a tool. Waiting, Kip listened to the pause. If the dial tone erupted, he could hang up. Odd, he hoped to hear the dial tone. Something about this dead silence against his ear sent tension rolling through his limbs.

"How are you, lad?"

Another condolence. *Damn it!* No wonder the silence had affected him. "Fine, thank you."

"You were rather preoccupied when we met. I wondered if you'd return my call."

Abruptly, the memory exploded—a white-haired gentleman, premature gray, a stately elegance, and exceptionally well dressed. "An old friend of my mother's, as I recall," Kip said without conveying his relief. If he stayed here too long, he might lose his friggen mind.

"Tell me, lad. Did your mother ever mention my name to you?"

"She may have in passing," he answered indifferently.

Again, the pause, an irritating silence lingered for several seconds. "Your mother was a remarkable woman."

An old friend with a need to reminisce? Kip waited through another pause, wanting to interrupt, refusing himself that luxury. Had he at long last found someone as capable of utilizing prolonged silences as himself?

"You now have my number, young Prince of Whistlebrook. Should you need anything, don't hesitate to call. Do take care, lad."

Prince of Whistlebrook. "Thank you, again, sir, and if there's any way I can be of service to you, feel free to contact me."

"Adieu, Kippen."

Holding the disconnect button down, Kip gazed at the note in his hand, committing the number to memory despite his annoyance. Prince of Whistlebrook. McDaniels had apparently sat near enough to that scene in the Oak Room to overhear the title, 'Prince of Whistlebrook.' That title certainly had more flair than *Undertaker*.

Kippen? Not just 'Kip' and McDaniels had spoken the words softly, nearly a whisper, as if he hadn't meant to be overheard.

Another dozen calls to make. Kip set the McDaniels note aside and dialed another, longer number from memory. Overseas calls took longer to place. As he waited through the connections, he again considered the annoying conversation with McDaniels and made a mental note to satisfy his curiosity sometime soon. An area code, a name, and a couple of phone calls would tell him whatever he needed to know about his mother's 'old friend.'

'She might have in passing,' Kip had lied, as much for his benefit as to appease the gentleman's fear that Marilyn Patterson had forgotten him. Closer to the truth, Kip might have answered, 'Not even in passing, but don't feel bad, sir, she and I stopped passing years ago. I know very few of her current friends and associates, much less one of her old flames—'

"*Wie gehts?*"

"*Gute, Herr Kern*," Kip spoke into the line, holding the receiver closer to his ear to hear the faint voice while adapting to the dialect and switching his thoughts.

Watching JD as he landed the receiver on the jutting prongs, Kelly read as much relief as tension within his twitching lips. She understood his relief. On the pretense of awaiting a call from Richard—a little white lie she refused to contemplate—Kelly had reached the phone a measly ten seconds ahead of JD. Why her brother had mentioned Kip's disappearance yesterday afternoon, she hadn't decided, but his concern had become contagious.

As JD turned and caught her watching him, his expression animated into a more natural smile. "His telephone manners haven't changed much, but I guess I should be grateful. At least he returned my call."

"He didn't say where he was, did he?"

A flash of something akin to anger flitted through JD's tense eyes before he softened his expression toward natural concern. "Kell, do me a favor," he said and flashed a glance toward the living room where their mother and siblings chatted. His attention returned, tense. "Don't complicate your life by getting involved with Kip."

Not sure whether to be hurt or merely curious, she studied her brother's expression. Those words sounded like a warning, a misplaced warning. She hadn't even alluded to the possibility of becoming involved, hadn't mentioned the phone call the evening before last, hadn't mentioned Kip at all beyond the natural concern for a man facing a difficult time. "I don't think I appreciate the implication, JD. And I'm pretty sure I don't understand it. What makes you think I'd even consider getting involved with Kip?"

"Come on, sis," he said offhandedly, attempting to smile, keeping his voice low. "I wasn't blind. I know you had a serious crush on him—"

"For God's sake, JD. That was fifteen years ago," she said with a start of temper.

"Yeah, it was. And we're not kids anymore," he said carefully. "I might not know him too well, but I know his type, Kell. Trust me, he's not the same shy kid we knew way back when, and I don't want to see you get hurt."

"That's cute," she said as she studied his more uncomfortable gaze. "You're saying we've grown up and considering me a child in the same breath. And it still doesn't explain this, JD. I barely talked to him for two seconds the other day."

"He's a good-looking guy and you're too damned pretty for your own good," he said in a lower pitch, a hint of annoyance. "And I'm really not blind. I saw the way you looked at him, and believe me, honey, he's the type to notice. If he thinks you're interested, he won't think twice about taking advantage of the situation, and you will get hurt."

"I don't know what bothers me more," she said honestly. "That you'd think I'm a naïve child, or that you're saying this about a man you once considered a friend? What happened to you, JD? When did you become so cynical and forget what it meant to be a friend?" The instant the words escaped, Kelly regretted them, and her brother's stopped, abstracted gaze only enhanced her dread. "I'm sorry," she said. "But this just doesn't—"

"Forget it," JD stated bluntly. "Forget I said anything. You're probably right. I'm reading more into a situation than I should, and it's really not my business one way or the other."

Gratefully, Colleen entered the kitchen, drawing their attention to her faintly curious, instantly alert gaze. "Was that Kip?"

"Yeah," JD said and turned away from Kelly, as well as their mother, heading toward the coffeepot on the counter across the room. "He's apparently back at the Home," he said offhandedly.

"How was he? Was he alright?" Colleen asked.

"He sounded alright," JD answered and reached toward the pot, changed his mind, and sidestepped to the sink. Emptying his coffee cup, he drew a cup of water instead.

In the pause, Kelly glimpsed her mother's worried eyes, her troubled glance. JD had called the Home a half dozen times between Wednesday night and this morning. By no surprise, his concern had carried to all of them, but more than once, she'd heard the indifference in his tone.

More than once since that phone call, Kelly had reviewed the funeral and reception in her mind. Only once—only once she'd witnessed Kip respond spontaneously, almost clumsily, and draw another man into an embrace. And she'd been watching. She'd seen the shine in their eyes and glimpsed Kip wipe his eyes as they'd parted. Friends. Until JD's arrival, Kip had appeared distant, accepting handshakes and comments as if he were a stranger or estranged. No old school chums had hovered about him, no females from whom he might have sought comfort in a crisis. A little lost, he'd stood through conversations, as indifferent and distracted, as out of place as he'd once appeared when standing in her living room a lifetime ago.

Distracted, Kelly strode from the kitchen, barely acknowledging Shelly with a glance and smile before striding up the steps to be alone with her thoughts. Until JD had arrived in Randall High, Kip had worn the nickname 'Undertaker,' an awful label to ostracize him. JD had turned that name around, although Kelly had never learned the details. By the time JD finished with the boys who'd given Kip a hard time, they'd spoken that nickname with a touch of respect, if not wariness. By what rumors JD had transformed that derogation into a revered title, Kelly had no clue, but she recalled the number of boys—JD's eventual friends—who'd wished the "Undertaker" had stuck around.

A loner, Kelly considered as she flopped down on her bed, pillowing her head on her hands, thinking, remembering. Kip Patterson had been a loner, then, and he was a loner, now. No close friends had accompanied him to the funeral. If he had friends, none had deemed to share his grief or pay their respect in person, to be here for him. What kind of man was he, now?

Recalling the deep rhythm of his voice, Kelly started a smile, then considered JD's warning, his words. Had she sent more signals than she had meant to send? God knows, Kip hadn't even acknowledged that conversation when phoning moments ago. Not a word, not a tone, not a single indication that he'd placed that call and spoken the equivalent of poetry in her ear. Had he responded to her subtle signals the night before last, called to share the evening with her, then, for whatever reason, changed his mind? Perhaps, out of respect for JD's friendship?

What kind of friendship was that? Her brother had flown halfway across the country, allegedly, but he certainly didn't appear too thrilled to renew that friendship. An obligation, then? Had JD felt obligated, perhaps, driven by some disenfranchised obligation to the past, to be here for Kip?

Too many curiosities, too many questions, but one certainty remained. Kelly still felt something for Kip Patterson, and apparently, the past wasn't as far away as she'd believed. If nothing else, she needed only consider the past two lousy nights of insomnia and the images created in his low, rhythmic voice. What to do about this situation remained the single most crucial question. Should she ignore her brother's warning and explore this infatuation? Or should she ignore the infatuation and commit herself to becoming the wife of Dr. Richard Whitman?

Until seeing Kip, she'd believed that childhood obsession was a child's fantasy. A heavy case of puppy love. Her first true love. But at twenty-six, she wasn't a child, nor prone to fantasies. She'd dated her share of decent men. Even considered accepting a marriage proposal once before Richard—twice if she counted the whirlwind romance in her college days. Had she, on some primal level, held off and remained the wide-eyed child waiting, hoping, Kip Patterson would ride into her life on a white horse? God knows, no others, not even Richard had ever stirred her blood as swiftly as Kip had kindled a flame. Was it fair to Richard? Was it fair to herself to marry any man when she might still love another?

With that simple benediction striking lightning in her mind, Kelly bolted upright. Was that true? Was she truly in love with Kip Patterson even after all these years? She didn't know him, hadn't known him then, knew him less, now. Hell, she had no idea who he was, where he lived, or how he lived. She knew absolutely nothing about him beyond the fact that he was as handsome as the devil and a loner, even now.

JD's warning slid through her mind, an ominous forecast, 'You'll end up hurt.'

Oddly enough, it sounded like the same premonition, the exact dire prediction to follow her to New York nine years earlier. Despite the silent warnings and sniggering, despite the odds that a small-town girl could make good in the Big Apple, she'd attended Juilliard and landed a slot on Broadway. Maybe she'd never reached superstar proportions. But she'd never set her goals that high. Ever since kindergarten, when taking her first dance lesson, she'd dreamed of opening a dance studio. Broadway had provided a stepping stone, proving the naysayers wrong and providing a financial edge to follow through with her long-range goal. A year ago, her dreams had become a reality, and at twenty-six, she employed four instructors and boasted a hundred full-time students. Financially, she could afford to do whatever she felt like doing.

And presently, she felt like chasing another dream and exploring the unknown.

Kip Patterson.

Part Two

Conspiracy

Chapter 9

To the intrusive clatter of steel and china, the distant squeal of metal carts, Kip's attention was riveted, as familiar as the slide of a typewriter roll or hum of a copy machine. The sounds of his childhood, a cross-section of activity, the heartbeat of Whistlebrook. Forever, he'd lived, caught between the kitchen and the administrative office. Only in the darkest hours, silence had crept into his private rooms, his home within the Home, but genuine silence had never prevailed.

Mashing his cigarette in a crystal ashtray, Kip pushed off the recliner and moved into the hall. If the heart had ever stopped beating, Whistlebrook would have died.

Driven by nostalgia, Kip followed the sounds to the kitchen, lured by the banquet of aromas transcending the hallway. Nan Feeney, a constant in the kitchen, never stopped cooking, as much a fixture in the kitchen as the industrial ovens, dishwasher, and long preparation tables. Her assistants changed. Some moved into other positions within the Home, some just moved on. Marilyn Patterson had started every new aide in the kitchen, and only now Kip understood her reason. Keeping a new employee within her immediate realm, she monitored their progress and work ethic. Without a doubt, Edna had helped judge an aide's qualifications and became a deciding factor in prolonged employment.

Entering the kitchen in time to see Edna instructing a young blond on the proper placement of dishes within the industrial washer, he realized nothing had changed. Amazing woman, this Edna Feeney who'd become his mother in Marilyn Patterson's shadow. Three times a day, she prepared a banquet for sixty-plus residents, balancing diets between keeping refrigerators and shelves stocked, ovens on high, all eight coil burners glowing red.

Two kettles of soup simmered incessantly at lunch hour, along with a third kettle of beef or chicken bouillon. Reaching the stove undetected, Kip satisfied his curiosity. Indeed, soup kettles, the first, chicken, the second, a heavy vegetable, probably beef. Not beef. Fridays would demand a vegetable stock base, no meat for the Catholics at Whistlebrook who adhered to the old rites of their faith. In another pot, remnants of macaroni and cheese clung to the base and sides. Certainly, cheese, always cheese on Fridays. Cheese soup, cheese sandwiches, several of which rested on plates under plastic wrap on the counter. For a nominal fee, the staff could enjoy their meals prepared in this kitchen. On Two West, in the hub of the patient wings, a smaller kitchen existed where the staff could dine on prefab-service meals.

Vaguely, Kip recalled when his mother installed the vending machines and food services on the second floor. At least twenty years now. He couldn't have been more than seven or eight, but he recalled his mother's stern rules regarding that service. No prefab or frozen foods for the residents. Marilyn's clients paid for home-cooked meals, and by God, at Whistlebrook, they got what they paid for. But the employees needed a place to buy a quick burger or greasy fries. At seven or eight years old, Kip remembered developing a fascination with the perfectly shaped burgers. For a time, the burgers had become the staple of his diet until his mother discovered his unhealthy habit. No artificial foods for the son of Marilyn Patterson, not when Nan Feeney provided a balanced meal. When the two matrons joined forces, he'd never stood a chance.

Unconsciously, Kip stood stirring the chicken soup, watching the broth and noodles swirl. With the touch on his arm, he moved in a start, hooked the ladle handle on the rim of the pot, and met Edna's smile with a faint grin. "Smells fantastic," he said as he backed from the stove, feeling like a child again, one about to be scolded for standing too close to danger. "You haven't lost your talent."

"Why don't I just fix you a bowl, sweetie?" she said, while lifting one of the sandwich plates to him.

Breakfast had stayed put, and either he'd answered a subliminal call or his appetite had returned in full. Could his early programming have survived after all these years and triggered an automated response to seek the kitchen in the half-hour pause between departing and returning trays at noon? With a glance at the clock, Kip knew the post-lunch rush would begin soon. Already, the creak and squeal of another trundle cart echoed through the service hall. Lifting the two halves off the plate, Kip flopped one atop the other, winked at Edna, then moved down the counter, lifting a cup from the top plastic rack. One-handed, he filled his cup and the time registered. 1:05. Att. Madison should have arrived by now.

Balancing the sandwich on his steaming cup, Kip pushed through the swinging door and started up the carpeted hall, halfheartedly thinking he should have picked up his shoes in the kitchen. Too late. A dozen steps ahead, Bill Bickerman rounded the corner, leading John Madison from the main entrance. Both men halted and stared openly. What was there to do?

Feeling oddly like a man caught with his fly open, Kip paused and took stock. Stocking feet, a striped railroad cap, and his mouth open about to take a bite off the point of a sandwich. With a mental shrug, Kip finished the bite, faintly amused as he continued past the PRIVATE door. Hopefully, Madison would consider him suffering the temporary effects of grief. At thirty, Kip doubted he could qualify as eccentric. Smiling faintly, he glanced at Madison's startled gaze and motioned toward the secretarial office with both hands. Hard to talk with a mouthful of melted cheese.

"Kip," Bickerman spoke carefully. "I'm sure you can take a moment to finish your lunch." He glanced discreetly at Kip's stocking feet with a silent suggestion. "I'll show John into the office."

His mother's office—now Bickerman's office. Kip swallowed, glanced down at Madison's briefcase, and decided abruptly. "You have everything with you?"

Madison nodded, not comfortable. "If you need a moment—"

"Have you had lunch?"

"Before I came," he answered hesitantly, his expression reeking of doubt and concern.

How much had Bill told him? Kip barely wondered before he countered the thought. What Marilyn might have told her attorney mattered far more. "Certainly you have pens and notepads," Kip commented while glancing again at the case, then Bickerman. "You'll bring Att. Madison a cup of coffee, won't you?" Without pause, he glanced at Madison. "Cream? Sugar?"

"A little sugar."

"Fine. Come with me." While turning, Kip caught Madison's fleeting glance at Bill. *A conspiracy? Were they comrades?*

"Kip—" Bill said haltingly. "We'd be more comfortable—"

"Have Mrs. Feeney fill another warming pot, will you, Bill?" Kip said with a glance and again motioned Madison to follow. Taking another bite, Kip started up the hall. By the time he halted at his PRIVATE door, Madison studied him with a lawyer's instinct for deception. Swallowing, Kip tossed him a grin and motioned toward the knob. "Could you get that? I despise steamed bread. It turns soggy. Can't stomach it when it hits that slimy stage."

Reluctantly, Madison opened and held the door.

"Thanks a bunch," Kip said loftily. "And do excuse the mess in here," Kip commented while entering. His larger suitcase, with clothes piled on top, stood in front of the chair, canted at a corner to the recliner. With a stocking foot, he shoved the case toward his mother's bedroom door, then motioned Madison into the chair while sitting down in the recliner. Setting his coffee near the phone on the end table, Kip freed one hand, leaned, and pulled the magazine-laden coffee table in front of them. Lifting one end of the squat table, he sent the magazines skidding off the far end, landing them near his suitcase in a scattered heap. "Workspace," he said offhandedly, glancing at Madison as he settled back on the chair. He took another bite of his sandwich while kicking out the footrest to support his heels.

Madison lifted his gaze from the fallen magazines, his pale blue eyes intent beneath his salt-and-pepper brows. Definitely a man searching for discrepancies and flaws, likely struggling with his preconceived notions. His briefcase remained closed on his lap. "Son, do you understand the importance of what we're about to discuss?"

Nodding, swallowing, Kip held Madison's gaze. "It concerns my future, I'd imagine, so," Kip said with a touch of flippant indignation.

"As heir apparent to your mother's estate, there are extensive legalities you'll need to be made aware of. Your mother left an extensive Will, over which I became executor. In the event your mother survived me, that responsibility would have passed to the next senior partner of my firm—"

"Background isn't necessary. You're here, apparent executor and attorney of record. I'd imagine you have my mother's Will in your briefcase. As single heir apparent, I'm granted private privilege to hear her bequeaths," Kip paused, letting Madison introvert the sudden change. Playing court jester for Bickerman and others of his ilk was an entertaining interlude;

however, unless Kip intended for this ordeal to last indefinitely, he and Madison needed to reach an understanding. Dropping the act entirely, his tone dropping to a low, quiet timbre, Kip continued, "Despite what Bill obviously told you, I am not an *irresponsible, strung-out, dope-afflicted* teenager. I prefer not to enter my mother's—or Bill's—office. If you'd be more comfortable, I'd be delighted to don a suit, tie, and shoes and comb my hair. The latter won't help, however. I've always had too damn many curls, and greasy tonics are offensive." He bit off his sandwich without lifting his platinum gaze from Madison.

Doubts and perceptions flashed through the attorney's pale blue eyes. A twitch crept into his salted mustache. Withholding a comment, he turned his attention to opening his case and began rifling through the contents as the knock interrupted.

"It's open," Kip said in a slightly elevated voice.

Bill started in, paused, bounced startled glances between them, then continued inside, carrying a cafeteria tray. Two cups, cream and sugar bowls, and an insulated pot stood on the tray. Stooping at the short table, Bill set the tray down and lifted the pot, glancing at Madison. "I could have a folding table brought in if it will help, John."

"This is fine," Madison said offhandedly, preoccupied with his search.

Bill added sugar to one cup, stirred, then lifted the second black coffee. Standing up, he glanced between the two remaining chairs. As he settled into the nearest chair, he noticed Kip's gaze. "You look a little more relaxed. Carolyn mentioned you picked up your messages. You should have come into the office. I know I left you stranded this morning, but I had about a hundred calls to return. Reminds me, we're invited to a luncheon in your mother's honor Sunday evening. I took the liberty of accepting for you, but ... well, we can discuss this later," his gaze shot to Madison. "You're probably ready to get started."

Kip glanced at Madison's closed briefcase, then at Bill. "Thanks for delivering the coffee, Bill. I'm sure you have something to do."

"I freed up a block of time," Bill said paternally. "There's probably a lot of things I can explain a little easier—"

"Excuse us," Kip interrupted without betraying his annoyance.

Bill cast Madison a desperate glance, then tried again. "Kip, I think in the interest of the Home, I should stay and help clarify—"

"Excuse us," Kip repeated, his gaze unwavering.

"Damn it, buddy—"

"Bill," Madison interrupted calmly. "I could have you paged if we need any clarifications."

Reluctantly, Bill held his ground a moment more, sending Kip a shadowed, peeved glance before resigning. "I'll be in the office."

When the door closed in his wake, Kip shook a cigarette from the pack in his hand, caught it between his lips, and found Madison's studied gaze over the spurting flame.

"Bill means well," Madison said after a moment. "He's been an asset to your mother, and I dare say, he's a little lost without her."

Studying the attorney's shadowed eyes and drawn features, seeing the man's gaze list toward the Wallendorf with as much fondness as grim reflection, Kip suffered a sudden insight. With an exhale of smoke, he asked, "Do you like her collection?"

Madison bulked a split second and glanced about the room as if seeing it for the first time. An apparent deception. "It's a handsome collection."

"Did you ever sleep with her?"

Madison's gaze returned sharply, his cheeks suddenly taut, his eyes startled and offended. "I don't believe that's relevant, young man."

"I'm sure it's not," Kip said absently, and his focus trailed toward the Wallendorf. Had he known her at all? This wasn't Madison's first visit to this room, and Bill was no stranger here. Her private sanctuary. His own. Years ago, aside from him, his mother and Nan, no others entered this suite.

"Yes," Madison stated almost too sharply; his gaze steady when Kip looked to him. "Your mother and I had a brief affair several years ago. Our romance ended; however, we remained friends, and my love for her has never changed. Does that satisfy your curiosity?"

"About you, obviously," Kip answered evenly, omitting 'for the moment.' Madison apparently possessed enough character and confidence to withstand the possible wrath of an offended heir. By his forthright manner, he'd elevated the affair from debauchery to a respectable *affaire de coeur*. A man of integrity, then. "Possibly we should begin."

With natural ease, Madison turned his attention to the business at hand, his voice relaxed. "As you know by now, your mother was ill for quite some time. She knew as much as eight months ago that she didn't have long to live," he paused, looking up from the papers, his gaze intent. "I never understood what came between you, but I know you shared a rather ambivalent relationship. That she loved you, I have no reservations, nor should you."

How often had he heard that recently? "Please, waive your opening statement," Kip interrupted calmly despite a niggling alarm. "Relevancy?"

Madison paused, looking at his papers, back. "Actually, it is relevant. I doubt—considering the nature of your mother's provisions—that she understood you any better than you understood her. After meeting you, I understand that far more than I did before."

Provisions? As in clauses and stipulations? Should he be at all surprised? His mother obviously knew him.

"Seven months ago, your mother came to me to begin liquidating her assets," he said lightly and caught Kip's gaze. "Were you aware of her diversity?"

"Stocks, bonds, IRAs, real estate properties, and trust funds," Kip nodded, concealing his annoyance as well as his rising alarm. Liquidation. Seven months ago? Apparently, she'd learned of her son's periodic interest in Whistlebrook's financial status, which, in itself, should have remained impossible, and all too obviously, she hadn't expected to live another full year. Seven months. She'd begun liquidating shortly after the close of the fiscal year. Controlling his anger, Kip finished evenly, "I'd imagine I know most of her assets."

Madison nodded, looking closely. "At the moment, you are an extremely wealthy young man, Kip. There are several long-term trusts in your name, along with several savings accounts for your immediate access. She said something to me once, I didn't understand—"

"Mr. Madison," Kip interrupted without affect. "Read the Will."

Madison hesitated, then lifted the folder beside him. "When I drew up the original document, you'd barely started kindergarten," he said lightly and looked over. "Frankly, the bottom line never changed. You are the prime beneficiary of all Marilyn Patterson's worldly goods; however,..? Why don't I read the document?"

Grand idea! Why didn't I think of that?

In silence, Kip listened as John Madison mouthed the final requests of Marilyn Patterson. Formalities, Bill Bickerman had said, a few signatures, and oh, how right that asshole was. As in life, in death, Marilyn had overseen everything. Liquidating her assets to allow him 'pin money,' a term she'd used when sending him a hundred dollars a month at school. She'd given him five hundred upon graduation. With roughly thirty-three hundred dollars in his pocket, Kip had lifted one of his leather bags, climbed into a cab, and walked away from her, from college scholarships, from Whistlebrook.

Pin money. Roughly 2.5 million in 'pin money,' John Madison commented at one point. Of course, as in all things, Marilyn Patterson held final control. She designated a quarter million dollars to be released every five years. With the nature of the trusts, the money would perpetuate into infinity, regardless of how long the beneficiary chose to live. She'd allotted another quarter million for various charities and medical research foundations. In various increments of ten thousand, Edna Feeney, Frank Culver, Carolyn McAnthony, and several other employees with more than ten years of loyalty to Whistlebrook received supplemental bonuses to their retirement funds.

No mention of Bill Bickerman or the *good doctor* Frances, Kip realized absently.

"This last clause, and by far the most complicated, as you probably realize, concerns Whistlebrook, your mother's primary investment," Madison said lightly and began reading again.

Complicated? Oh no, not complicated at all. Quite simple, in fact. His mother intended for Whistlebrook to perpetuate in her absence, and she'd, at long last, validated her indifference to her only son. If he wanted the Home, he could have it, but to hell with him either way. *Postmortem checkmate.* He could own Whistlebrook, but he could neither interfere with it … *nor destroy it?*

Apparently, she knew how he'd amassed his fortune. Listlessly, his gaze fanned toward the Wallendorf as John's deep voice resonated in the close quarters. Clearly, she'd received the message loud and clear. Marie van Alt a.k.a. Marilyn Patterson. Maria Van Alt's School of Dance.

A dark, angry shine slid into his murky gaze. She'd never once bothered to ask him for specifics, or even verification about how he discovered her love of dance.

Kip's thought clicked to the phone call earlier—McDaniels, New England accent, indeed. Kip should have remembered that area code.

Boston, Massachusetts. Undoubtedly, the home of a very old friend who'd kept in touch over the years and informed Marilyn when her former dance studio crumbled under an iron ball, along with about a dozen other buildings spanning an entire city block.

Making another mental note to investigate McDaniels, Kip turned his full attention to the clauses, unconsciously internalizing the details and identifying a dozen loopholes to rip the Will to shreds.

Absentia ownership versus immediate sale. That was her bottom line. He could hold onto Whistlebrook indefinitely, as long as he remained content to simply review the financial statements quarterly and accept the profits. Retroactively, should he in some way interfere with the management or profit margin on the Home, Madison, Cummings, and Wade would be notified to establish the immediate sale under Marilyn's stipulations. Checks and balances. The law firm retained control for a duration of ten years. About the same amount of time it could take an average heir to contest the Will. In the meantime, he couldn't even dismiss a janitor without Bickerman's final word, and the son of a bitch had known it.

Clever lady, Kip mused. After all these years, she apparently decided to have it out with him, and this was justice, if not a splendid irony. Financially, she could never have won a battle against him if he'd ever truly contemplated owning and destroying Whistlebrook.

Therein lay the irony. He'd never harbored any desire to either own or destroy Whistlebrook. It was her Home, her domain, her life, her legacy.

"Kip," Madison said after several moments of silence. "Your mother loved this Home and the people who've lived here, and this goes back to what I said earlier. I don't think she understood you, so she's given you options—"

"Take it or leave it," he said smoothly.

"I think that oversimplifies, Kip."

"Do you really?"

"She wants you happy," Madison said in an odd voice, drawing Kip's focus to his steady gaze. "In her way, I believe the options she's given you are based on that single premise. She mentioned to me once—"

"You've read the Will. Obviously, there are papers I need to sign," Kip interrupted sedately. The sooner he signed and departed, the sooner he could return to his chosen path, and God help those poor bastards at Corbin Co. Kip suffered an acute desire to destroy something, if not Whistlebrook.

"You intend to sign away Whistlebrook," Madison either asked or decided, his tone lingering in a paradox.

"Does that seem odd to you, counselor?"

"Yes, I think it does," he stated intently. "I should think you'd want to give this a little thought."

"Don't you find it odd that she'd go to the time and trouble of negotiating with state and federal authorities—in the event of her passing—down to the least detail? She's accounted for employees, vendors, God, even gardeners, to keep me from fucking up her life's pleasure," he stated calmly. "In her own subtle way—as subtle as a steamroller—I believe she's made it perfectly clear which option she preferred I take. And far be it from me to disappoint her, postmortem."

"That she went to the trouble does seem odd to me," Madison stated. "But for a reason you might not have considered."

Chapter 10

For several silent moments, Madison continued to study Kip, then dropped his attention to his briefcase. In slow motion, he opened his case, extracted a business-length white envelope, closed the case, and looked over again. Nothing of his expression betrayed his thoughts. If not an attorney, he would have made one helluva card shark. "You know, young man, I hoped your mother was wrong. Obviously, I was wrong on both counts. She did know you." He paused, flopping the envelope absently on his leather case, counting off a few beats, possibly ten, before continuing. "At your mother's request, this Will was read to you—the prime beneficiary—in private. You honestly don't realize how much she loved you, Kip, and apparently, she understood at least that much about you.

"In the event that you intended to sign over Whistlebrook immediately, I was to give you this." He leaned, handing the envelope over the end table.

Suffering an instant of doubt, Kip leaned and accepted the envelope. Scrolled across the center in Marilyn's script, a tight, meticulous script with each line emphasized, he read his name, and a chill slid down his spine. Whatever this was, he preferred not to know.

Madison began collecting the papers around him. "At your mother's request," he continued with a casual glance. "You have three days to consider her options and reach a decision. At the end of that time, we'll schedule a formal reading of your mother's Last Will and Testament at my office. I'll notify the various beneficiaries mentioned."

"If I'd requested time to consider her options or chose to accept Whistlebrook in absentia, what action were you to take, counselor?"

Hesitating, Madison leaned back, looking over with a studied gaze. "Are you changing your decision?"

His mother had always enjoyed her reign, but she'd never played games. What was this about? "Possibly, I *should* think on this. It feels odd," he offered indifferently, honestly. Something truly felt amiss at this moment.

"How long would you need?" Madison asked while sliding a folder into his briefcase.

"A couple days. A week," Kip shrugged, watching Madison, who appeared to adhere to a rehearsed script as surely as a barrister in a B-rated flick. "How much time do I have before I need to make a decision?"

"We'll meet, Monday—informally—before the formal reading," Madison said smoothly, his gaze intent. "If you're still undecided, we'll reschedule the reading."

"Should I assume that in the event my decision stands to relinquish Whistlebrook, you're to strongly suggest that I reconsider or simply allot more time?"

Madison remained impassive despite his studied gaze. "I'm not to sway your decision one way or another. If I've led you to believe otherwise, I apologize."

Not unlike his admission to the affair, Att. John Madison maintained a steady gaze and refrained from recovering the envelope. Doubtful, he was a man to neglect details. What was this about then? A new form of manipulation? Another of those power plays for which his mother reigned supreme?

Madison started to push from his chair. "I'll—"

"Relax, counselor," Kip stated and motioned to the coffeepot while turning the envelope. "Even good sex can be accomplished in ten minutes if one knows how to climax quickly." Ignoring Madison's stopped reaction, Kip ripped the end of the envelope, blew it open, and extracted the folded pages.

Shaking a cigarette from the pack on the end table with one hand, he flicked open the business fold, rested the open pages on his raised knees, and began reading while lighting the butt:

Hello Darling,

If you're reading this, I have obviously taken my final journey. You always called it that. Remember? Ever since you were small and first heard the song, Gather by the River. So much death in our lives. I never realized how badly I hurt you. Not until that day in your room when you spoke to Mark Frances. You were so much smarter than I could ever hope to be. Truly brilliant, and I feared for you with your brilliance. Believe me when I tell you now, I never meant to hurt you. I thought I was protecting you. I only realized when you vanished how badly I had hurt you. First, by teaching you to accept death as a part of life. Then, by sending you away. I couldn't stop them from dying, darling, and I couldn't bear the thought of losing you mentally or physically.

I wanted you to understand that, Darling, but I never knew how to sit and talk to you. I know this is no excuse, but I honestly never understood children. I never had a brother or sister. My mother died when I was very young, and my father was very old. I suppose that explains why I kept Whistlebrook.

Darling, if you're reading this, you've accepted my option. As much as Whistlebrook means to me, you mean more, and I won't beg you to change your mind. I know you loved the Home—an ambivalent love. Equal parts hate. I understand that better than you know, my darling. I, too, loved and hated our life here. So much pain and death. I often think I should have given you up for adoption and given you a better life, a mother and a father. 20/20 hindsight, darling. I couldn't bear to give you up. How I loved to stand and watch you sleep, and how I envied Edna's instincts. She was so much younger than I, but so much better at being a mother. I think now, you became her son, too. The son God took from her when He took her husband. Edna and I—we were a great pair. Her, a widow at twenty-three. I, an unwed mother at thirty-five. Ask her about our first interview, darling. It's a wonderfully silly story.

How the years have flown, and how I regret not knowing you as a mother should. The regrets of age. All my life, I've listened to our elders rambling about how they could have done things differently. I told myself, I'd have no regrets, live each day to its fullest, but alas, I'm facing death, and see what I never stopped to see. I never knew how to show you I loved you, until now, perhaps. Freeing you of Whistlebrook was all I could think to do for you. Perhaps you will put it behind you now.

I've asked John not to let you sign the papers until the Will is formally read, only because once you've signed, you'll be expected to depart. In effect, darling, I've bought you three days to collect our personal effects. Please, darling, take

*my dancers with you when you leave, and don't forget your hats. They're
as you left them.*

P.S. Don't mourn for me, darling.
God favors small children and old fools.

My Love Always!
Mom

Unconsciously, Kip wiped a sting from his eyes, and a faint grin
twitched his mustache. Not a power play. Just an odd glimpse of her final
thoughts and several stunning facts. Like—who the hell was Ronald E.
Patterson if she was an *unwed* mother?

Madison's hand clasped Kip's shoulder. His eyes no longer carried the
concentration of an attorney. "I'll see you Monday—"

"How long have you known my mother?" Kip asked as he looked up,
dry-eyed.

Shifting his gaze in reflection, gazing toward the Walendorf, Madison
answered. "Close to twenty-five years. She was a remarkable woman."

"Did she ever speak to you about her past? Her life?"

Again, he considered. "Not that I readily recall."

Three days, Kip considered absently, to collect personal effects?
His mother had written this while slipping into senility or dementia
consistent with a heart condition. He read the date on the first page.
September. Damn it. Probably around the time of his last visit, she'd
written this ditty like a piece of cake without the frosting! On impulse,
Kip caught the top of the pages and sent them flying off his lap. Watching
them float to the center of the floor, he felt Madison watching him.

"Are you alright, Kip?"

No. He was not all right. After thirty years, Mrs. Patterson
becomes a Miss, and the name on one Kippen James Patterson's birth
certificate—under Father—turns to dust. Three days to remove 'our
personal effects... dancers and hats ... expected to depart ... not going to
ask you to change your mind... Once you sign—'

Kip looked up at Madison. "After I sign those papers, transfer
ownership, am I expected to depart immediately? No returning, even for
my bags?"

"The paperwork is in order, but I sincerely doubt anything would happen that fast under the circumstances."

Kip tipped his head, more curious about Madison and those words. 'Bought you three days … expected to depart.' *Hostile takeover?* Paranoia! His focus drifted momentarily, calling an odd thought to mind. Bill Bickerman. Under both options, Marilyn had provided for Bickerman, his position secured as chief administrator. As assistant administrator, how much did Bill know about the second option? Formalities—signatures? Kip looked up to Madison. "Counselor, sit down, will you? And pull out those sheets concerning the employee contingencies if you will."

Madison hesitated, then decided to humor him, probably for Marilyn Patterson's sake. "You have questions, Kip?"

"A few," he answered and lifted the telephone, pushing the button to reach Marilyn's office. As expected, Bill responded with a sharp, "Yes?"

"Careful, you don't know the question yet."

"Kip?"

"Sure, and it is. Come on over, righto," Kip dropped the receiver on its cradle and leaned over to accept the papers Madison held. Sitting back with the pages in hand, Kip read the list of contingencies.

His mother had, in fact, taken care of Bill Bickerman. Under the new administration, he would become Chief of Staff, as well as a long-term beneficiary along with several other employees throughout the Home. The head nurses in all four wings, one of Culver's security men. Funny, she'd neglected to mention Dr. Frances anywhere in the contract. She'd secured food services for five years. Doctors Sheffield and Carmine were accounted for along with a half-dozen other physicians and therapists. Kip glanced over to Madison. "The other sheet—under my ownership?" Again, he read, barely shifting his glance to accept the page. Holding both sheets side-by-side, he glanced back and forth, assimilating details while asking, "Did my mother ever mention my occupation to you?"

"No, I can't say that she did."

"Good friends, were you?" he asked, still reading.

"Yes, we were."

"Good."

"What is your occupation, Kip?"

"Demolitions, by trade," he answered and met Madison's startled gaze abruptly. "But you won't find that on paper, and should you feel a need to repeat it, you'll mourn the death of your agency. Do you understand what I'm saying to you?"

"It sounds distinctly as if I'm being threatened," Madison said with a steadfast gaze.

"I'd prefer you consider it a friendly warning, sir," Kip said evenly, his focus unwavering even as the knock intruded, and he called, "It's open, Bill."

Madison withdrew his focus, glancing at Bill, then leaning to pour himself a refill from the insulated pot.

"You have some questions?"

Kip nodded, motioning both sheets and giving Bill a dumbfounded gaze. "I haven't a clue what this shit means," he said absently, watching Bill's sharp gaze trying to focus on the fluttering pages. "You said formalities? Signatures? Maybe you can tell me what my mother intended me to do. Did she say anything to you about what position I should take?"

Bill stooped down alongside the recliner, steadying his balance on the armrest. "She talked to me about changes," he said while looking over Kip's arm at the papers and up with a strained grin. "As I understood it, you're becoming something of an absentee owner. In simple terms, the Home runs as it's always run. I'll pretty much handle the administrative end."

"What am I expected to do?" Kip asked, absently glancing over the top sheet of contingencies in the event of his 'absentee ownership.' The second option concerning the contingencies associated with an immediate sale rested on the bottom.

"Basically, what you've been doing, Kip. The accountants will transfer profits into a separate account for you."

"So, if I sign this, I just collect the money?"

"That probably about sums it up, but I'm sure John can explain if you have any other responsibilities."

Bill apparently had no knowledge of the second option that could ultimately transfer Whistlebrook into alien hands. Not that it should concern Bill. Either way, his future remained secure. *Damn it.* Kip gazed down at the sheets, shrugging. "Sounds simple enough."

Bill addressed Madison in an all-business tone. "I'd imagine there are a lot of contracts. Insurances, vendors, services and the like. We have several exclusive physicians as consultants and agreements with a couple of schools for internships. Did you already cover all of that?"

"To an extent," Madison answered indifferently.

Toward Kip, Bill commented, "That's my strong suit. I helped your mother negotiate those arrangements, and we were going over the other aspects." His eyes shadowed with uncanny sympathy. "She wanted this to be simple. She knew how tough it would be for you."

Nodding, Kip leaned his head back. His focus wandered absently before settling on one of the figurines. "She loved her dancers," he commented.

Bill nodded. "Especially the Wallendorf," he said lightly. "That was her favorite, I think, but she loved them all. That's the only one she never took to her office—" His gaze returned to Kip with an unnatural smile. "Every time you sent one, she'd take it to her office and show it off for about six months. The Wallendorf never left this room. That was hers and hers alone to enjoy. You sent it from England, huh, buddy?"

Unconsciously, Kip nodded. He'd found it on a shelf of filthy, worthless statues and bought it for a song. *Did you really love it that much?*

"Did you have any other questions? Something I could clarify, John?"

Without losing his absent focus on the statue, Kip found himself caught between nostalgia and an annoying revelation that he'd fallen too readily into reflection. Damn it, his mother did know he managed to survive without her money, just as she knew his talent for reading contracts and handling negotiations. And something felt terribly wrong about this scenario. In fact, he caught a distinct odor of death—corporate death. *But who? And why?* Bill Bickerman certainly stood to gain either way this blew. But why had she overlooked Frances in both contingencies? The *good doctor*, her long-time friend, a man nearly canned fifteen years ago for calling her a 'spiteful bitch' after she'd attacked his ego as a skilled practitioner.

Had she held a grudge?

"We'll call you again if we need you, Bill. Thank you," Madison commented.

"I'll be in my office," Bill said easily and pushed to his feet, touching Kip's shoulder before departing.

"Are you alright?"

"I shouldn't be, should I?" Kip asked, looking over to Madison's critical gaze.

"Under the circumstances, no."

"Why do you *truly* believe my mother gave me the option to be rid of Whistlebrook?"

"Truthfully," Madison hesitated. "I couldn't tell you."

"Freudian slip? Couldn't? Or won't?" he asked smoothly.

"Couldn't," Madison stated, his gaze level. "But with your occupation in mind and after the performance I just witnessed, it raises an interesting question."

"Elaborate."

"You don't trust what you've read on those pages. Which, frankly, disturbs me more than I care to consider since I helped your mother negotiate them."

A note off key, a flash of something troubling in the pale blue eyes. "Who approached whom for the deal?" Kip asked, watching Madison.

"Your mother came to me."

"Redundant. Did she contact the state or vice versa before coming to you?"

"She came to me. We approached several different sources before finding a buyer."

"I'd scarcely consider it a sale, Counselor. Did she ever mention the Wallendorf to you?"

Madison adjusted swiftly, glancing to the figurine then back. "Enough to know Bill's accuracy. It was her favorite."

Leaning, Kip slid the pages into Madison's briefcase. "Call me with the time on Monday."

Putting the papers away, Madison collected his case, hesitating. "Without breaching the trust your mother placed in me, I'd like you to know that should you decide to claim Whistlebrook, I believe it would be a pleasure to work with you."

Kip met his gaze. "My favorite sport is squash, Mr. Madison. What's yours?"

"Golf," Madison said flatly.

Kip smirked a grin, appreciating Madison's perception. "I tried that once. Always landed in left field."

Rising, Madison commented, "I believe you're mixing too many metaphors."

"Do you like Scotch?"

Halted, Madison looked at him carefully, no doubt, searching for another metaphor. "Yes, if we're discussing liquid, but I'm more partial to brandy."

Pushing the footrest down, Kip leaned, collecting the fallen pages of his mother's letter, folding them as he stood up and gestured to the door. Tucking the pages into his back pocket, he followed Madison into the hall, motioning toward the kitchen. In silence, he directed Madison into the private booth, then continued into the bustle of a half dozen aides moving in an impressive symphony, setting trays at the long counter, filling bowls and plates, capping the dishes in plastic lids. Passing a wink to Edna, who hovered like a ship's Captain at the helm, overseeing and assisting her underlings in precision, Kip crossed the room to his leather bag. Stooped, he recovered the bottle of scotch. On route to the booth, he veered and collected two juice glasses from one of the metal cabinets. Without uttering a word or offering Madison a glance, Kip poured two doubles, set the bottle aside, and lifted one of the glasses, only then looking at the attorney, waiting.

Curious, Madison lifted his glass as if awaiting a toast.

Kip touched his glass to Madison's. 'To Marilyn Patterson,' Kip said silently while looking into the man's curious gaze, his own shaded abstract gray. In rapid swallows, he downed the hot liquid and checked his watch while setting the glass on the table. 4:30. Was it any wonder he'd stepped between hustling aides and metal carts? Unconsciously, he glanced over the activity, only now aware of the sharp averted gazes and uncanny silence. Edna eyed him a little too critically while trying to ladle soup into bowls at the stove. Several drops splattered the floor. Turning his focus to Madison, Kip offered his hand, and Madison returned the clasp, still curious. Sliding his palm free, Kip open-palmed a wave and turned, passing through the administration door.

Returning to the PRIVATE suite, Kip engaged the lock for the first time and leaned against the door. Unconsciously, his gaze trailed over the compact room. Forever, the lamp burned in the corner above the phone, simulating light in place of a window. Personal comfort had always come second or third to the demands and consideration of others. Not one of the three rooms in this suite possessed a window to the outside world. Sanctuary. Isolation. In odd reflection, Kip remembered, he'd never minded hiding in the closets and storage rooms at St. Johns—he'd felt right at home.

Three days, and yet another irony. Fifteen years ago, Marilyn had allotted him three days to adjust to her decision and resign to the arrangements. Three days to offer 'fare-thee-well' to his friends and family.

'...Three days to collect our personal effects...'

Options. Options or ultimatums? Keep Whistlebrook with Bickerman at the helm, or complete the final negotiations and let the Home become a public health care facility?

The first option was no option at all. She wasn't fool enough to believe he'd even consider 'absentee ownership.' Regardless of his indifference to Whistlebrook, he wasn't a man to consent to an arrangement wherein he held no control.

The second option, then, represented her actual desire to see the Home perpetuate, and therein lay the paradox. If she fully believed him capable of destroying her life's efforts, to the extent that she'd spent several of her last months contriving a swift means to her desire, why would she fail to consider how easily he might contest her will? On one hand, she obviously considered him a monster, one with a grudge; on the other, she believed he'd merely accept her wishes and relinquish the Home. Enough so, that she'd written him a personal note lacking any hint of gratitude over his decision.

All wrong, something felt all wrong, like a familiar song sung in the wrong key. The words belonged to his mother, the manipulation, undoubtedly of her contrivance, but the tone ... the tone was all wrong. *Options* had never entered Marilyn's vocabulary, a lesson he'd learned and applied when cutting the umbilical cord, a little over twelve years ago. Marilyn's way, or no way. To believe her words—freeing you of Whistlebrook—as a sign of her love was akin to believing in Santa Claus. If she'd truly loved him or trusted him—or felt anything other than a subtle resentment toward him—she might have just dumped the entire albatross around his neck and consented to whatever decision he made in its regard. Giving him options, either of which she might have known he wouldn't accept without a fight, served only to negate her profession of love.

Shaking his head absently, Kip pushed off the door and stepped toward the middle of the room. When all else fails, meditate, he mused as he sat down, fully intending to spend the next hour or more unwinding the knots threatening to snap his muscles. The buzz of the in-house line stopped him before he reached the lotus position. Muttering a curse, he moved onto his knee and lifted the receiver. "Penny for your thoughts."

Hesitation, then a faintly amused voice. "Make it a quarter and I'll tell all," Carolyn played. "Before that, however, you have a visitor. A Miss Kelly Mulden."

His heart skipped a beat at the name, and he nearly cursed as Carolyn continued.

"She's been waiting a while, hon. I told her you were indisposed, but she insisted on waiting—"

"Send her down the hall," he said while rising off his knee.

Chapter 11

Big mistake, possibly the worst, Kelly considered as she accepted the direction to leave the small, cramped lounge that she'd occupied for the past hour. Undoubtedly, the attractive blond manning the secretarial pool harbored a wealth of questions that she'd refrained from asking, which might attest to how often Kip Paterson entertained strange females. Just one more among the many, a thought that nearly reversed Kelly's course in the hall. A dozen times already, she'd almost set course for the nearest mall and made good on her excuse to her mother. Damned Catholic upbringing. She might need to shop before heading home after lying about her intended destination.

One way or the other, she needed to work out this infatuation. For herself and for Richard.

Pleasant and surprisingly modern, the hallway wore the aesthetic attraction of a doctor's office with pale beige walls and impressionist prints evenly spaced between several shiny mahogany doors. An even blend of old and new, the hall might more resemble a hotel corridor, but noisier with the distinctive sounds of a kitchen enhancing with every step. Maybe she'd missed a turn, or a door. She barely considered turning around when a door opened halfway down the corridor. Unwittingly, Kelly gripped her purse strap with her sudden anxiety. He emerged only a half step and paused, and Kelly's heart slammed a wicked beat. No illusion. Nor fantasy. His gray eyes fleeted, appraising her from head to toe with the tip of his head, a kink twitching his mustache. Wearing blue jeans, a predominantly blue flannel shirt, and a baseball cap, he appeared younger than two days ago, and his stocking feet only added to the image. He needed only a wad of chewing gum to look like a wide-eyed boy eager for his first time at bat. But his eyes betrayed him long before Kelly's attention darted off the quirked grin in his mustached lips. Curiosity, doubt, anticipation? Anything might have offered more reassurance than the casual confidence in his pose and smile.

Abruptly, far more nervous, Kelly continued her stride with a firm resolve. Just an offer of friendship, a tentative offering at best. Despite her tumultuous emotions, she wanted nothing more than to get to know him as she might have gotten to know him ten or fifteen years ago. Until she spoke to him, until she knew what sort of man he was, she couldn't fully exorcize the uncanny effect he seemed uniquely capable of creating. "Hi," she said simply.

"Low," he said with the twitch of a smile and reached through the opening. Shoving the door inward behind him, he canted his head as she stopped. "Enter at your own risk."

Good God, that was a loaded offer and tilting her head to look into his gray eyes, she suffered a momentary doubt. He was definitely tall—taller than Richard by at least three inches—and she suddenly felt extremely short despite her 5'6" height. Thank God, she hadn't worn a dress, had deliberately chosen a bulky sweater and somewhat loose-fitting jeans. No sexual suggestions or implications. But looking into his eyes, she knew the futility of her intentions. He'd just stripped her in his mind. "Sounds like a warning," Kelly said simply, maintaining her balance.

"Very bright young woman," he said with a slightly deeper smile. "And I probably should apologize, but I won't. I vaguely recall a phone conversation."

"That's not why I came," she said, meaning the result he'd mentioned in that brief chat, and he knew it. Throwing caution to the wind, she accepted the invitation and stepped into the room, anticipating an office. Abruptly, certain of a mistake, she scanned the living room ambience, complete with blankets piled on the corner of a sofa and a bed pillow haphazardly topping the stack. Not much on housekeeping. She glimpsed a clutter of magazines on the floor and a disheveled suitcase at the far end of the room. The door snapped shut behind her, and her muscles gripped in a quick jolt. She turned smoothly to find him watching her with a strange, nearly indifferent gaze. The distance she'd witnessed two days ago had returned. The haunted essence of his eyes heightened in the lamplight. "How are you, Kip?" she asked simply.

"Fine. You?" he asked quietly, the pitch of his voice identical to the tone lingering in her ear.

"Concerned," she answered, starkly aware of the distance between them, the estrangement. She might have coveted a million fantasies, but he stood before her in the flesh, oblivious to the relationship she'd romanced for years. She was his old friend's kid sister. A stranger, then. A stranger, now. "I've been a little concerned since you called the other night. It sounded like you needed more than a song."

His eyes sparked with a subtle amusement. "Very perceptive, but I settled for the song at least for a little while." His indifference had broken. He flashed a glance toward the armchair at her back and motioned with his hand. "Care to sit?"

She accepted the offer and settled into the chair.

He moved with a natural grace, slipping into the recliner, already reaching for his cigarettes on the stand at his side. His gaze returned with a glint of curiosity. "I have to admit this is a pleasant surprise. Can I get you a cup of coffee, tea? A soda?"

"No, thanks," she said lightly. "I'm fine."

"I couldn't agree more," he said with a twitch of a smile, a fleeting glance. "Very fine, in fact."

"Kip," she said smoothly, vaguely uncomfortable with the tempo of this conversation thus far. "Whatever you're thinking, I'd prefer you don't."

"Perceptive," he confirmed as he leaned back more comfortably in the chair and tipped his head. His eyes never wavered from her while he caught a flame to his cigarette.

Handsome men had never made her nervous, not the shine in their eyes, not their smiles, but in the pregnant pause, Kelly's muscles knotted, the tension palpable between them. "I realized after we spoke, we never really knew each other," she began with an effort. It was a speech she'd rehearsed but found mundane and foolish under the circumstances. Despite all rhyme and reason, she felt as if she knew him, felt as if they'd been friends forever, and he seemed not at all surprised by her presence despite his comment. Did women he hardly knew truly make a habit of popping in on him after a single introduction and a phone call? Or did he consider her a friend simply through his relationship with JD? Something like osmosis? "Anyway, I was concerned. You sounded like you could use a friend."

"Your brother doesn't know you're here, does he?" he asked smoothly.

"No, he doesn't," she admitted. "But it's not his business."

"I'm sure he'd say differently," he commented with a bemused smile. "And I'm far more certain, he wouldn't approve. You are engaged, luv, and I don't do well with platonic relationships, male or female."

In that single line, he rejected her offer of friendship and implied the possibility of a physical relationship. Rather than offense, Kelly wondered at the simplicity in those words, the indifference in his eyes. How much more did he remind her of JD now? A loner. Alone. "Perhaps, you haven't met the right kind of people. Male or female," she said, and wondered at her intuition even as she noted his slight surprise. "Where do you live now?" she asked.

"The west coast," he answered.

"Any place in particular? Or do you claim the entire shoreline and live on a bench?" she asked and noted the slightest indication of a dimple at the corner of his mustache. Damn, that subtle, almost genuine smile was far more handsome than his smirk.

"On a bench, under a cardboard box, under a pier," he shrugged. "Wherever my hat hangs, I call home."

"Nice hat," she said with a glimpse toward the cap and read his amusement. "Hats were something of a trademark for you as I recall."

"Now you see my dilemma," he said with a mocked sobriety. "I have an awful memory. Make a habit of leaving hats lying about in the strangest places. Hard to remember where I call home."

"That does sound like a dilemma," she said, enjoying the spark in his gray eyes, the play of light at his shoulder.

"Whatever became of the little girl with the pigtails?" he asked.

"She grew up, went to New York, and eventually became a dance instructor in Baltimore," she answered. "What happened to the boy who nearly went through our front door with the help of an overzealous retriever?"

"He never recovered from his fear of four-legged critters, goes spastic at the sight of a schnauzer, and has suffered numerous neuroses relative to that single traumatic experience. Despite which, he grew up."

"That's dreadful."

Mocking astound, he commented, "More dreadful if he'd remained a child."

"To think," Kelly hesitated, donning a frown. "The damage I did with the slip of a hand. How *ever* will I make amends to that poor boy?"

"You ... *deliberately* sicced that monster on me?" he asked as if genuinely stunned.

Kelly smiled, dropping her dreading pose. "Not exactly," she admitted. "Truthfully, I tried holding Max, but—" she sighed. "Such was not to be. He got away." Which probably had something to do with her instant surprise and lightning bolt of love. But Kelly withheld that detail, if not her smile.

Skeptically, Kip eyed her. "Why is it that I don't find that smile reassuring or particularly honest?"

She stifled a laugh. "I'm sorry," she said almost honestly. "I was just thinking about how you looked that day."

"Uh-huh, and you have a ghastly sense of humor, Miss Mulden, I can tell," he said, but his eyes betrayed his mocked affront. "Doubtful it would have been so amusing if I'd had a coronary on your doorstep."

Coronary. At the word, his humor vanished despite the lingering smile, and Kelly understood. She wasn't as adept at concealing her emotions. Too much like her mother in that respect. For a moment, he'd forgotten about his mother, but that word had brought the reality home. Kelly's smile faded. She ached for him, feeling the grief behind his eyes, behind his smile. If ever she wanted to comfort another, never more than now. Unfortunately, she knew the futility. He wouldn't understand it, and in his arrogance, might expect an explanation, and she had none to offer.

Rather than dwell on it, she asked, "How long will you stay in Randall?"

"Probably only until Monday or Tuesday. How about you?"

"Through Christmas," she answered, thinking about Richard, thinking about the changes she might make in her life. Christmas was an awful time to break an engagement, but how long could she delay? Just the thought of her interest in the man sitting across from her convinced Kelly of the necessity. If she could betray Richard's trust, doubt her love for him at the mere sight of another man, she couldn't justify marrying him.

Distracted, Kelly found Kip gazing somewhat listlessly toward the television and it occurred to her, her misery couldn't compare with his. Losing his mother with Christmas a mere week away? Her mother was right. Christmas was the worst time to suffer a loss. "Were you close to your mother?" she asked gently and nearly bit her tongue as his eyes riveted, less distracted than tense, possibly angry before he turned curious.

"No," he answered in a carefully controlled tone. "Not for several years if at all," he continued and glanced about the room. His gaze returned, peculiar. "You've been in this room for at least ten minutes, I'm surprised you didn't mention the dancers, considering your profession. Do you like her collection?"

Kelly had noticed, without taking an interest. Fanning her gaze about the room, she glimpsed the various figurines, several of exceptional color and beauty, others exquisite by the sheer simplicity of the poses. She found his gaze, and he appeared more curiously intent. "It's a lovely collection. Did she like to dance?"

"As I've heard, she was outstanding," he said indifferently. "We never discussed it."

"Do you like to dance?" she asked with a slight smile and nearly cursed her direction as she noted his eyes change once again, his smirk slightly more catty.

"Darling, I love to dance," he said, and he was not referring to the Rhumba.

"I'm beginning to think you have a one-tracked mind, Mr. Patterson."

"You may be absolutely right, Miss Mulden," he said with a twitch of a smirk. "But I seem to recall admitting just such a curse on the phone two nights ago. Alluded to it, in any event. And I notice you're not wearing a warning sign, other than that rock. Truthfully, luv, I'm not sure if that tiny distraction will pose as a serious deterrent for very long."

"You're either the most confident man I've ever met, or the most candid," she said and watched him snub his cigarette butt without more than a glance. Not a word, he uttered not a word, just held her gaze as he pushed off the recliner and closed the distance between them. Tense, heartbeat hammering, Kelly suffered a quick prickling tingle as his hand brushed against her cheek. Without warning or invitation, he dipped his head and touched her lips. Far too stunned to pull away even if she wanted to, her hand betrayed her, lifting, landing against his cheek as he set off a powerhouse of sensations against her lips, her tongue, her teeth. At her neck, his thumb caressed, warm and gentle, rolling wave after relaxing wave through her tense system.

Slowly, he lifted, and she looked into his dark gray eyes, nearly the color of steel, and something in those eyes frightened her abruptly.

Never—absolutely never—had she reacted to a man so swiftly, so completely, knowing at this moment, she would consent, gladly, to whatever those eyes promised and to hell with consequences, to hell with matrimony, with engagements. To hell with the world. Whatever this strange attraction, he was dangerous, and the open desire firing his eyes was contagious.

"Have you decided?" he asked quietly, his thumb brushing in a hypnotic motion against her cheek, smoothing over her quivering lips.

"Decided?" she asked a little breathlessly and watched, stunned, to see the heat vanish from his eyes. The platinum gray returned as a slight smirk slid into his lips.

"Confident or candid?" he asked.

Upon a time, a question like that following a kiss like that might have crushed her or, at the least, flushed color through her cheeks. It was cruel and deliberately callous, dismissing those seconds of weird, incredible bliss to prove his talent at seduction. Undoubtedly, he'd mastered the art. Calmly, she commented, "Both. With apparent justification."

If expressions were accurate, he questioned her placid reaction. "Nice of you to notice," he said while sliding his thumb over her cheek, lifting tingles that she refused to notice. His eyes sparking with something akin to intrigue, he smiled slowly.

"Perhaps, you should wear the sign, Kip. Something nice and subtle like, Danger—this product may be addicting."

"I do try to be careful," he said with a slightly mischievous twinkle. "Some people, I've found, are far more susceptible, while others have a natural tolerance... Undoubtedly, building an immunity from over-exposure to other products of similar design."

The smart alec. He was suggesting, not too subtly, that she'd been around, simply because she hadn't just fainted under his spell. She shook her head, sliding her hand over his and clasping his fingers as she eased his hand from her cheek. Keeping his hand, she smiled slightly. "Keep one guessing, right?" she mused and squeezed his hand lightly while rising in front of him, forcing him to his full height, causing him to step back without releasing his hand. "If you ever find yourself in need of a friend, or just someone to talk to, Kip, call me. Either here or in Baltimore. My number's listed there under K. Mulden." Rising on her toes, she brushed a kiss on his cheek, noting the haunted quality in his eyes. "Take care of yourself, honey."

In a far deeper voice, he commented, "You do the same, fine lady." Keeping her hand, he walked her to the door, pulling it open. Halting her, he leaned, brushed a kiss on her cheek, and winked. "Keep dancing to your own beat, Kelly. It's a lovely tune."

Only as she strode up the hall, she realized. He hadn't offered a similar option. Not his phone number, nor even a hint of where he lived on the West Coast. She knew almost as much about him now as she had when arriving. But that wasn't exactly true. She knew she could never pursue a relationship with him. A confirmed bachelor, devout playboy. Without any apparent regrets or reservations, he'd evidenced his lifestyle and tossed the ball into her court. If she wanted to satisfy her curiosity and whim, they'd land in bed, and in his candid discourse, one detail held firm. Sex and emotional contact were at opposite ends of the stratosphere.

Chapter 12

Like a thousand times before, Kip strode through the swinging door and reacted instantly. Catching skidding plates in either direction, he froze at the sound of a startled gasp and scratching glass. Within crosscurrents of déjà vu, annoyance, and amusement, he looked into the stricken eyes of a young man—overlaid by a pair of dark eyes enhanced in thick cosmetics, and dark hair contained in a fishnet. Another face from the past. In a split second, Kip collected his thoughts, focusing on the young man in front of him. Noting the start of a quiver in the boy's mustache-fuzzed lips, Kip lost his annoyance, appraising the sharp-angled features and slightly long, dusty brown hair within a halo of faint rainbow colors. "Do you make a habit of running into people?"

Visibly straining to control his amusement, the teenager concentrated on repositioning the stack of dishes in his arms as he stammered, "Uh … no, man. Not uh—"

"Dropping things?" Kip asked, appreciating the swirl of his pleasant aura.

In a frozen instant, the brown eyes shot up, flashing annoyance, doubt, and intimidation. No more than seventeen or eighteen, he recovered swiftly, leveling his voice. "Not uh—"

"Your name?"

In a flashing dread, the boy realized the probability of losing his job for nearly running over the new owner. "Jason King," he answered with an impressive recovery, his brown eyes only slightly wary.

"Oh?" King. Whistlebrook had always needed a king. Was that this young man's redeeming quality in Marilyn's eyes?

"I'm really sorry, sir."

"High school graduate, are you?"

"Senior this year."

With an honest appreciation for the resilience of youth, Kip smiled faintly as he motioned to the metal cabinet and strode ahead to the rack, sliding plates onto a shelf. Again, déjà vu st. He and JD had both held plates caught from the stack Franny had nearly lost when they'd blasted through the swinging door.

College. Marriage . Kip shook his head slightly against the haunting echo of Marilyn Patterson's voice. With an effort, he shoved the thought aside and found King alongside him. Concentrating on the boy's curiosity, Kip asked, "Football?"

With a mild intimidation and more curious gaze, King nodded, "Halfback. Randall Varsity."

"That's a shame," Kip commented and glimpsed Mrs. Feeney ambling around the long table. A dinner tray in her hands, she offered one of her critical smiles, as if that should surprise him. How long had he stood idle, appearing dazed? Long enough for two other assistants to cast him nervous, worried glances.

"I thought you'd be coming in soon, Kip," Edna said lightly. "Hope you're hungry."

"This kitchen was never designed to accommodate that door," he said to Mrs. Feeney while glancing over the balanced tray—a double serving of baked fish, potatoes, and broccoli. Without pause, she carried the tray past him to the breakfast nook. "The table should be where the dishwasher stands and vice versa. Prepare another tray, double that amount, will you?"

Mrs. Feeney looked up at him. Instant perception and amusement danced in her soft eyes. "JD's coming?"

Kip nodded, noting Jason trying to decide whether he should wait to get the ax or return to the dishwasher for another load. "Do you enjoy working here?"

Dread passed through King's eyes as he nodded. "Haven't been here too long, but yeah," he said while glancing a little desperately at Mrs. Feeney.

"Kip, Jason's only been with us a week," she supplied and looked to King. "Go on and clean the trays, honey."

"Scholarship?" Kip interrupted, eyeing King.

"Uh ... no," he said hesitantly, anticipating either another question or 'you're fired.' Either way, he hadn't accepted Edna's offhanded dismissal.

"College?"

"Thinking about it. Haven't decided which one."

"Options?"

"Community, Penn State or Pitt."

"Major?"

"Undecided."

"Reject Community. Enroll in Penn State. Major in business. And give that door a wide berth for the next couple days." Kip started to turn.

"Why business?" King asked.

Kip caught the boy's instant regret, but King held his ground, not retracting the question. "Do you enjoy working here?" Kip asked again, watching the blue gaze start to waver. King barely started to repeat his earlier answer. Perception donned before the words escaped, and a smile quivered onto his parted lips. *More money in business.*

Not awaiting a reply, Kip continued his turn, winked to Edna Feeney, and slid into the booth, removing his English-cut cap by habit alone. Across the room, the back door swung inward, and time rolled backward as Kip watched JD enter. Mulden had been seventeen that year—a sturdy seventeen with an uncanny enthusiasm for life and a natural charisma. Always laughing, always clowning, and the most persistent person that an anti-social, introverted boy of fourteen had ever met. Across the room, an older JD Mulden advanced surreptitiously on Mrs. Feeney, who'd returned to the stove. Amused, Kip watched JD touch a finger to his bearded lips, silencing the pretty blond assistant alongside Edna. Still the clown. Still the prankster. Married, two sons, seven and nine, divorced—

A flashing thought of Kelly Mulden intruded, effectively distracting Kip. She was, without a doubt, the most sensual creature he'd met in some time, from the way she walked to the cant of her head and the depth of her hazel eyes. Pulling away from that kiss had cost him—

Mrs. Feeney's squeal intruded, and Kip jolted, amused when JD brushed a kiss on her cheek. Edna slapped his arm, but they both laughed. Nothing had changed. At least three spectators smiled curiously, falling under JD's spell on impact. These same people who eyed Kip with anxious intimidation needed only seconds to dub Mulden a friend. The 'court jester,' 'worldly sailor,' 'scoundrel,' Irish had professed. *A friend in every port,* Kip agreed silently. Their five weeks of camaraderie had been only one of dozens of sojourns in Mulden's life.

JD tossed a wool cap into the booth next to Kip's similarly styled cap, then swung into the opposite bench. "Do you know, I have almost two dozen hats? You're probably up to a couple thousand by now, huh?" he played.

"Excessive compulsive," Kip commented.

Mulden eyed him with a spark of amusement, sweeping his gaze downward and flickering his focus between their attire. More amusement lit his hazel eyes. "Do you get the feeling time stopped? Or is it just me?"

They both wore flannel shirts, blue jeans—JD wore army-issue boots and a black leather jacket. A wool scarf to match his hat hung between his open coat lapels, prepared for the Red Baron to toss over one shoulder.

"Proper dress code for catting, as I recall."

Mulden smiled, "We sure got accused of that when I came around."

Mrs. Feeney brought the second tray, sliding it in front of JD with a smile to broaden at Mulden's innocent, bewildered expression.

"I didn't really come for dinner," he played while sliding out of his jacket and winking to Kip. "But I guess I can't offend my favorite gourmet, can I?"

Kip glimpsed Jason King snatching curious glances while carrying another stack of dishes. *Don't feel bad, kid,* Kip told him silently, *I could never figure this one out either.* He and Mulden were complete opposites, but for a short time, they'd become inseparable friends. The only friend under sixty whom the Prince of Whistlebrook had ever claimed.

Slapping a pat of butter on one of three dinner rolls, JD paused, looking over, splitting his gaze between Kip's tray and his own. "Ah, come on. Déjà vu is one thing, but this is a little much. You're not gonna make me look like a glutton—again—after all these years, are you?"

"You ate enough for both of us," Kip commented vacantly.

Mulden studied him, more sober and concerned. "It's been a few days. You're still not eating?"

"Actually, I am," Kip decided and turned his attention to the meal despite a subtle protest in his stomach.

Between bites, JD spoke—as JD had always filled the silences—with a familiar persistence. "So, where'd you go?" he asked, not surprisingly. "You had that Bickerman character pretty cranked up... I talked to Mrs. Feeney;

she was a mess... I called a dozen hotels... Think they were about to issue an APB on you."

Some things had changed, perhaps. If anything, the Prince of Whistlebrook had become more private, more reserved, and far more adept at evasion. "Your sister has a lovely telephone voice... I think Bill's gay—"

Jason King dropped a handful of silverware and uttered a curse within the clatter, while stooping hurriedly, trying to concentrate on picking up his mess.

"Do you still lift weights...? No? That's a shame," Kip commented just as another explosion shattered the undertow of sounds.

Plastic trays bounced and skidded in all directions. Jason King stood, frozen. His stunned gaze dropped from his empty hands to the scattered trays, then lifted slowly to a shock-stopped Bill Bickerman. King's young face washed with an, *Oh, man, this isn't my day* expression.

"Young man! Get this *mess* cleaned up, and if you *value* your position in this facility, I suggest you learn to be more careful! Consider yourself on Report!"

King nodded, his dread fusing with frustration and a little anger, only until his gaze landed on Kip while stooping down. An almost embarrassed amusement flashed in his eyes. He covered it swiftly, pivoting on his heels to collect the trays.

"You *are* in here," Bill said as he stepped over a tray. Coming alongside the booth, he looked at Kip with a faltering, conflicting smile. "I stopped by the flat," he started, then seemed belatedly to notice their visitor. "Hello, Mulden, isn't it? JD?" Bill offered his hand to Mulden, enthusiastic despite his undercurrent of a private victory.

Mulden nodded, flashing amusement and curiosity.

"Kip didn't mention he was having you over for dinner. We could have had you served in the Oak Room," he said while looking to Kip with a condescending smile. "Suppose it's too late this time, but if you just say the word. Anyway, Kip, I'm glad I caught you. Do you remember our talk this morning?" He barely paused for a breath. "I talked to Dr. Carmine." Glancing at his watch, he continued, "He'll be here in about twenty minutes—give or take five. I really think you need to talk to him, buddy. He acquired Dr. Blake's old records, so he's familiar with your case—"

"Do you drink, Bill?" Kip interrupted.

Bill's smile wavered with his doubt. "No. Not regularly."

"Good," Kip commented and tipped his head to catch a flame to his cigarette.

"Kip, like I was saying. I think it's important you talk to—"

"Is it still snowing? Did you notice, Bill?" he asked with his exhale, looking up into Bill's tense eyes.

"No. It's not snowing. Do you remember the route to the conference rooms upstairs, buddy? There haven't been many changes up there. Carmine uses—"

"Do you like plants, Bill?" Kip asked, watching Bill's agitation.

"Come on, kiddo. Stick to the subject—"

"You don't, then?"

"Yes. Okay? I like plants. Now, are you—"

"Any particular type, Bill?"

"Mums, for Christ's sake!" Bill snapped, flashing a desperate glance to JD, who appeared more curious than helpful. "JD, maybe you can get him to understand this. I've made him an—"

"I would have thought something more masculine, Bill," Kip commented, still eyeing Bill within an abstract speculation. "Did you know some plants are bisexual? They contain both regenerative glands to multiply unto themselves."

"That's fascinating," Bill said in a dry tone and again concentrated on Mulden. "We have a doctor coming at seven. I think he's having a difficult time with all of this, JD. I'd like him to speak with Dr. Carmine, our staff psychologist, just to get him over spots."

"Sounds to me like he's giving you a lesson in horticulture," JD commented and looked to Kip with a smirk. "A hobby?"

"Man came antecedent to plants and animals, actually."

"By a millennium," JD agreed in a deep, serious tone.

"Man learns a great deal from plants," Kip commented and locked on Bill's stopped, critical gaze. "What time's that luncheon on Sunday?"

Bill's concentration divided; he needed a moment to recover. "Six o'clock."

"Odd time for lunch. Speak to John Madison before he left?"

Bickerman considered. "I ... about the luncheon? No."

"I didn't realize he'd been invited," Kip commented, wondering what Madison would have said before leaving.

"He *wasn't* invited that I know of," Bill said with rising exasperation. His cheeks flushed with strain. "Buddy, I know you're hurting, and you're trying to deal with this. But you don't have to handle it alone—"

With the hand landing on his shoulder, his patience snapped. In one motion, he clasped Bill's wrist, sliding and pivoting off the bench seat. Swiping a stocking foot behind Bill's scrambling legs, Kip eased him down almost gently and laid him flat out. With his knee resting on Bill's chest, Kip held the suited arm across the fellow's windpipe and looked down into Bickerman's wide, stricken eyes. "I've been extremely patient with you, Bill. I've accepted your sympathy. I've accepted guidance with appreciation. I've accepted your nature and taken into consideration that you're mourning the loss of my mother—"

"Ki-ip Pl-ease— " Bill gasped breaths, struggling to lift his arm as his manic dark eyes flashed about in search of— "He-lp!"

"I also warned you to stop touching me, and as for—"

"Kippen James!" Mrs. Feeney demanded, swooping down and grasping his forearm. "Sweetie, let him go!" she cried angrily while yanking his arm, trying to pull his hand from Bill's wrist.

"—the appointment with Dr. Carmine," Kip continued in a passive tone, his grip unmoving. "I suggest you visit him in my stead and discuss your apparent insatiable desire to fondle me. I don't appreciate it." As smoothly as he'd descended, Kip rose, releasing Bill's wrist and stepping over him as Bickerman folded, coughing and gagging, clutching his throat. In a quick scan, Kip noted the shocked faces. Mrs. Feeney turned her anxious attention to Bill. JD hadn't moved from the booth. He rested, leaning a little to peer over the table, shifting his attention up to Kip, down to Bill, again to Kip as a grin quivered on his bearded lips.

"Ready to roll?" Kip asked while leaning to pick up his hat.

JD picked up his cap and coat, sliding from the booth and looking at Bill, who'd scooted backwards a half dozen paces.

"Tha-at's assault!" Bickerman heaved, keeping one hand to his throat while accepting Mrs. Feeney's help to stand up. "Y-You made a big mistake, Kip! I know you're suffering! I know you're angry over your loss!" He backed toward the swinging door. "But you can't go around attacking people! If you refuse to see Dr. Carmine, I'll have to—to take action!"

Absently, Kip gazed at him while taking a mental inventory of Bill's possible recourse. Restraining orders, assault charges. *Bought you three days.*

"Bill," Kip said quietly. "In three days, I'll be gone from here. Refrain from fondling me, and we won't complicate our continued absentia-relationship, nor will we jeopardize Whistlebrook's reputation with a public scandal. Now, if you'll excuse me? I have a date with Memory Lane." Taking a step towards Mrs. Feeney, Kip noted Bill recoiling another step. Brushing a kiss on Edna's strained cheek, he winked and commented, "Don't wait up, Mum."

"Kip, you promised you'd keep the appointment," she started.

"I didn't make an appointment to keep," he said lightly.

A tiny spark of anger flashed through her eyes before a wash of concern doused the heat. Worriedly, she conceded with a weak smile and a take-care-of-him glance toward Mulden.

Dismissing his concern, Kip turned and started across the room on a collision course with a startled Jason King and the pretty blond. Both retreated in a hasty step, parting a path for him. Stopping in front of them, Kip eyed the young woman. "Connie, isn't it?" When she nodded warily, he offered his hand. More hesitant, she touched his palm. "Sorry to worry you, luv," he commented lightly, then held his hand to King. "We didn't formally meet. Kip Patterson."

"Nice to meet you, Mr. Patterson," King said with a hesitant grin.

"Try adhesive on your fingertips," Kip suggested and continued between them, reaching the door. Standing, he pulled on his tennis shoes as JD joined him. Lifting his long coat from the hook, he pulled it on, mirroring Mulden's amusement. Tennis shoes in snow, blue jeans, and cashmere? "I packed far too quickly," he mused.

"I dunno," JD mused, pulling open the door. "Seems to me, you always had a unique way of matching hats and coats to tennis shoes and blue jeans."

Realizing JD's accuracy, Kip commented, "Suppose old habits die hard."

"You're still pretty goddamn quick, too," JD commented as they stepped into a cold blast of wind coming across the snowy back lawns. "Pretty slick move."

"So, where are we going?"

"Me to know. You to find out," JD said and threw them back fifteen years...

How odd it felt to be sitting across from JD Mulden, two old friends sharing a drink across the corner of a varnished bar top. Absently, Kip scanned the patrons through a misty amber glow, not truly looking at faces, this once not searching for someone to warm his sheets. The lounge—as

JD had promised—was of a decent brand. Soft-cushioned stools, tables, and chairs, a dance floor on a raised platform with a half-decent disk jockey spinning sixties and seventies rock music. With a slow song just beginning, the dance floor had cleared momentarily, but couples ambled onto the platform, returning. The bar stood near enough to enjoy the sound from the speakers and allow an adequate view of the long legs on the platform, yet far enough away to enable comfortable conversation.

As if he'd shared the thought, JD leaned back on his stool and scanned the shadowy atmosphere. "Kelly was right. This place isn't bad."

"Does she come here often?"

Mulden smiled with his way of expressing 'should have kept my mouth shut.' Sobering slightly, he turned to lean on the padded edge of the bar. Absently toying with his beer glass, he searched Kip with an unusual intensity. "The introverted kid, I remember? He's gone."

"Age does that, I'd imagine," Kip answered, catching a flame to his cigarette, still holding JD's gaze, speaking with his exhale. "You mentioned children. Sons. Names?"

"Justin James—J.J., after yours truly—and Patrick John," Mulden answered with a glint of the proud but disheartened father. "Not married. No children. Anyone special in your life?" he asked as if he truly wanted the subject changed.

"Life's too short," Kip answered offhandedly.

"I married Laura," JD commented.

Studying Mulden's faint amusement, Kip taxed his memory banks to recall a pretty brunette as outgoing as Mulden. Abruptly, Kip understood JD's smirk. Laura and Jenna—oh, he hadn't thought of beautiful Jenna Scottsdale in a long time. Long blond hair, immense blue eyes, shy, but oh so much more knowledgeable.

"She and Jenna are still friends," JD commented lightly, his amusement alive within the shadows. "Boy, Jen had it bad for you. She went into a heavy depression when you left, but then," JD's eyes cleared and focused through a cloud of smoke. "A lot of us were pretty bummed out for quite a while. Things got pretty damned dull in Randall."

"Life goes on," Kip commented idly and spun the pretzel basket the bartender had set down in front of them. Pretzels, beer, peanuts. His focus caught the bartender's eyes. His gaze slid down her tuxedo-style jacket, black mini-skirt, and fishnet stockings on shapely legs. A grin tipped his mustache as he lifted his focus to her face. *Not bad. Not bad at all.*

"You know, I wrote to you about a dozen times. I never got my letters back, but I never found out if you got them either."

"I got them," Kip answered.

"Why didn't you ever answer one?"

Kip drew his attention from the bartender, watching the pretzel basket momentarily, remembering JD's letters. Like JD in person, his letters had carried an essence of life, and opening those letters had felt like opening a window in a tomb. "Too much light. It hurts the eyes."

"Excuse me?"

Kip looked over, seeing an older version of his only old friend and remembering, "I wrote letters. I never sent them. Death by cremation."

"Couldn't afford stamps?" JD asked in fake sarcasm.

"A mourning child doesn't write nice letters," Kip answered with a smile. "I went through a long period of mourning. The first stage is always shock and denial. Second stage—anger. Stage three—bargaining, and I used to bargain like hell, making all kinds of offers 'if only.' Then stage four—depression, where I'd linger for days. Eventually, I'd hit stage five. Acceptance. But I never truly passed stage four. After bargaining came only sadness, guilt, anger, and loneliness. All of which I perfected to an art form. With you, however, those phases amplified and lingered because you weren't dead." *And some of those letters had come from overseas.* All too well, Kip remembered worrying, fearing the letters would stop suddenly, hoping he'd never hear about his only friend's demise. He continued absently, "You wrote for thirty-three months, JD, and for thirty-three months, I lived my own private hell. End sad story. I couldn't maintain the pretense of corresponding with the dead."

"I wondered," JD said vacantly, toying with his beer before taking a swallow. When he looked over, his gaze carried distance and concern. "You never forgave your mom for sending you away, did you?"

Memory Lane could be a painful ride. "Actually, I ceased to think about it," he said lightly. "I've learned to reject resolution, idealization, and the recovery phases of the grief process by simply avoiding it altogether."

"You know, I talked to her a couple of times when I came home from the service. She had a private detective hunting for you, but honestly, I think she believed you did yourself in. The way I heard it, you did one helluva vanishing act."

"Never thought much about that either," Kip mused. "Excessive compulsive."

"You're not going to tell an old pal where you went, are you?"

"Some mysteries are better unsolved," Kip verified and lifted his beer, downing the last quarter. Setting the glass near the inner edge, he caught the bartender's eye with a slight nod, then glanced at JD's glass to include his refill.

"What are your plans now, Kip?" JD asked lightly. "Are you ... absentia," he said, answering his own question. "You're not sticking around Whistlebrook."

No comment necessary. Kip crushed out his cigarette, intent on the bartender's blue eyes bouncing between him and Mulden and back as she lifted their glasses. "Nice dress code," Kip commented, leaving little doubt about his appreciation. His focus trailed down her frilly blouse, form-fitted to enhance her endowments.

"My boyfriend likes it, too," she mused.

"Then he's semi-intelligent," Kip countered easily and lifted a pretzel from the basket, enjoying her smile and admiring her build as she turned. And semi-stupid for turning her loose in that getup.

"Are you planning on going back to L.A. on Monday?"

"Possibly," Kip answered without missing a beat in the conversation and looking over at JD's scrutiny. Mulden had become far more sober in his adulthood, and in the shadows, Kip sensed greater tension, wondering what had awakened Mulden to the dark side of life. The boy had never written too many details in those letters, but his writing had changed.

"Pretty tough being back here, huh?"

"You find that unnatural?"

"Nope," Mulden said with shadows haunting his gaze. "But I think you're putting on one hell of an act, Kip."

Interesting concept. Acting. "Acting, in what sense?"

"The off-the-wall comments. The word games. I haven't decided," JD said as if annoyed and bewildered by his inadequacy. Glancing at the bartender as she delivered their drinks, he offered "thanks," then returned his attention, leveling his gaze on Kip. In a flash of perception, he realized, "Something went really wrong along the way, didn't it? And the way you are—it's not an act, and it's not just losing your mother that has your wheels spinning."

"Does it seem odd?"

"What?"

"The way I am," he answered. Past JD's shoulder, a blond-haired woman of indeterminate age smiled toward him, leaving no doubt of her intended seduction.

"Did you go off the edge, Kip?" JD asked directly, his gaze intent and deeply curious. "Did you spend those three years...? Maybe in a hospital somewhere?"

Coming into focus without shifting his abstract gaze, Kip considered, "Odd, JD, I think you're implying I'm insane."

"I'm trying to figure out who you are," Mulden said honestly. "I flew close to two thousand miles to see an old friend because, for the first time in nearly fifteen years, I knew where to find him. and I don't know how to help you deal with the pain you're feeling. So why don't we talk, Kip?"

Lifting his cigarette pack off the bar, Kip shook one out and caught a flame. JD Mulden hadn't lied a lifetime ago. 'We're friends for life.'

"Come on, man, cut the shit," JD stated.

Suddenly annoyed, Kip focused exclusively. "What would you like to talk about, JD? That we haven't already covered?"

"For one, why do you put up with Bickerman?" he stated, his gaze intent. "I thought the other day, with the way he hovered around you... Is he a relative?"

"God forbid," Kip commented dryly.

"So, who the hell is he?" Mulden asked.

"My mother's assistant, second in command, soon to be chief administrator—hand-selected and groomed in her image, right down to his fucking toes—" *Damnit!* "Meaning no offense to your mother, but you truly are a son of a bitch," Kip decided abruptly and lifted his beer.

"Yeah. Tell me about it," Mulden grinned, his gaze unwavering. "So, the game you're playing with him—it is a game. And if he's bothering you so damned bad, why don't you throw his ass out? That's your home, Prince of Whistlebrook."

With an unnatural fury, Kip leveled his gaze on JD. His voice lowered an octave. "Don't you fucking call me that, JD."

"If the shoe fits, wear it," Mulden stated. "And that shoe *does* fit. Those people love you, Kip, and old Irish knew what the hell he was saying when he gave you that title."

An odd thought erupted, blowing away his rage. "What the hell is this, Mulden? What the hell difference does it make to you whether I take over the Home?"

"To me, no difference at all. Unless it affects you. I told you a helluva long time ago, we were friends. If that had changed, bearing in mind that you've spent fifteen years avoiding me, I wouldn't have come. As it is—Prince of Whistlebrook—I think it does make a difference to you. I think you've been pissed off for fifteen years because your mother sent you to live with a bunch of priests. Knowing you even a little bit, you probably *did* mourn for three years. After that, you were probably just smart enough and mad enough to give your mother a royal payback."

Leave it to JD Mulden to come so close to the truth. "You really are a son of a bitch."

"JD?" At the female voice, they both looked over as a short, dark-haired—cute—female sidled up to the corner of the bar between them. Surprise and laughter glowed in her eyes as she looked at JD. "JD Mulden?"

"Yeah?" JD's intensity wavered under his curiosity.

Kip sized her up in a glance and studied her flushed—artificially blushed—round cheeks and pixie nose. Her name bobbed to the surface. "Rachel Monacci."

JD looked at him. Rachel looked at him. Her eyes grew. "Undertaker!" she nearly shouted before swallowing her high-heeled shoe. Her cheeks flooded with a more natural flaming red. "Oh Gees! Sorry! Uhhh, wait! I know it was odd!" More embarrassed, her eyes laughed behind an intoxicated haze. "Different!"

Kip held out his hand, faintly amused. "It'll come to you."

Sizing him up as she gripped his hand, she forgot about trying to remember his odd name. Keeping his hand, she latched onto JD's hand on her other side. "I can't believe it! I haven't seen either of you guys in years! God! You have to come to our table! Oh—" An ornery glint sparked in her glassy eyes as she glanced between them. "Come on! She'll never believe this! See if she recognizes you."

Looking at JD, mirroring his 'let's play,' Kip slid off the stool, intentionally leaving his coat and money to mark their place at the bar. Why he followed, letting this woman drag him through the crowd, he couldn't decide. As he recalled, she'd once occupied a seat next to him in his Biology class and giggled as a dozen students teased him about sniffing formaldehyde. Christ, memory lane was a rough ride. Short legs, short skirts, short bouncy curls? She'd maintained her cheerleader build, but she wasn't of a style Kip generally noticed.

"Kip Patterson!" a far more promising brunette cried as she spun off a barstool and threw herself against him with the enthusiasm of a cheerleader. Darcy something, Kip vaguely remembered in the fleeting seconds as he accepted and returned an embrace reserved for long-lost lovers. Looking over her shoulder to Mulden's startled amusement, Kip parted his hands behind Darcy's back. She slid from him, trying hard to stifle an excited sparkle in her blue eyes. "You're looking good, Kip. I-I heard about your mother. I'm really sorry."

"Thank you," he said absently and glanced at JD

"Ahhh, JD," Darcy drawled, pouting. "Do you feel left out?"

"Not yet, but soon," he played and moved into an embrace. "How you doing, doll?"

"God! It's good to see you guys," Rachel said enthusiastically as she moved into the close circle. "You guys have to sit with us!"

You guys? Christ, he hadn't heard that in a while, but what the hell…? Looking to Darcy as she parted from JD, Kip slid his glass onto their table, asking, "Dance?" Even as he spoke the word, he thought of Kelly Mulden. Uncontrollably, his system heated, and his eyes darkened in the dull, smoky haze. Darcy couldn't compare with Kelly, but perhaps he'd learned something from JD long ago. *Any port in a storm*, and he could feel clouds brewing.

As he led Darcy to the dance floor, his gaze flashed by habit alone. For a split second, his attention snagged on a fellow who turned a little too swiftly to another raised table where a group of middle-aged couples stood shouting and laughing. What caught Kip's eye? The suit and tie, the glance, the odd-man-out position, putting four males to three females, hovered around the small table? Or the intensity of yellow within the hazy atmosphere surrounding this gentleman? Something out of kilter. Something odd. He'd seen that gentleman before, and abruptly, Kip remembered a man sitting in a hotel lobby, holding a newspaper. What the hell was this about? Had one of his enemies found him? Or was this a government tag team? They wore suits, plain suits. No high-dollar expense account for these gentlemen.

Damn it. Whose chain had he yanked recently to account for the Feds tailing him in his hometown? Did it matter? Despite his tactics, his methods were legal. If they wanted to fuck with him, they better have a damn good reason.

Darcy wasted no time plastering her long, slender anatomy against him, and Kip accepted the offer with a smile. With the friction already building between them, sparks ignited in her eyes. For a second, rather than blue eyes, the lovely olive eyes looked up at him with a promise so honest and pure, it made his heartbeat quicken and his muscles grip, and the kaleidoscopic halo around her brunette waves had held him rapt.

"You've changed!" Darcy nearly shouted in Kip's ear, drawing his attention.

Still, he needed an extra second to dismiss the persistent memory of Miss Mulden before dipping his head to taste the newest fare. Far too often, that lovely young woman seemed to be invading his psyche, and she was a distraction he could live without.

Chapter 13

"Stop!"

Stomping the brake, locking the back wheels on a patch of ice at the entrance, JD cried a curse as the Blazer started into a sidelong slide between snowcapped pillars. For several seconds, the Blazer continued skidding forward at an angle. Its rear bumper grazed the black stone as the front wheels squealed on wet pavement. "What!" JD demanded as the front bumper and one wheel rammed a mound of snow, pitching them both toward the dashboard.

Caught within an incredible wave of nostalgia and awe, Kip lifted one hand off the dashboard, fumbled, found the door handle, and shoved open the passenger door. Stumbling clumsily onto a mound of crusted snow jammed against the rocker panel, he caught himself from a slide and skidded around the door, barely remaining afoot to reach the front bumper. Stopped, Kip stood precariously balanced on the mound while scanning the vista before him.

Was it too many drinks or his imagination? Like candles in long slotted windows, the interior hall lights glowed faintly through dozens of slightly parted curtains, seeming to flicker, winking on and off between half-drawn blinds. Peaks and towers rose above barren branches, like a castle on an English glen against a backdrop of moonlit silver slopes. With the coach lamps along the lane and the glow of bright vapor lights from the parking lot, the alabaster parapets and porch columns carried an aura of a grand palace entrance, one filled with life rather than death.

"What ta hell's wrong?" JD interrupted anxiously, slipping and sliding like a clown in an ice capades before collecting his balance at the opposite fender.

"Awesome, isn't it?" Kip asked absently, still drawn toward the view. His senses floated with the vision, imagining himself as the prince for whom the lighted entrance waited, beckoning. "Truly awesome."

"Awesome," JD either agreed or questioned, his tone softening. "Did it occur to you that I just—nearly totaled my old man's truck—to get you this view? Or that it's about 10 degrees—without the God Blessed wind?"

Was it windy? Cold? "You didn't even dent a bumper," Kip said absently, floating within his admiration as a wave of sadness and pain swelled, threatening to choke him. His mother had loved this view. Here she was a queen, and how must she have loved turning through those pillars. Truly magnificent, this grand old palace, but oh, the burdens. Alone. Alone, she had carried the burden to keep this kingdom afloat, and in an odd epiphany, Kip knew he'd hated her for cutting him out of her life.

"Yea," a low voice drifted, halting Kip's thought. "It is awesome. Like a castle or something."

"Sh-ee was so a-alone," Kip uttered as tears gathered, stinging his eyes. "Damn it, she was so alone. And I-I'm sooo God-damned sorry," he breathed softly, sucking a swallow of icy air, swallowing a sob.

"Come on, man," a comfortable low voice accompanied the hand touching his cashmere sleeve. "I don't think she ever blamed you."

Oh God, the guilt! And there were cameras, now, cameras watching the gates. He remembered her telling him Whistlebrook was moving up, keeping pace. Computers and high tech, the wave of the future, and she'd pointed out the gate monitors, boasting how Whistlebrook was advancing with the new era. "Damn it," he uttered and stepped, skidding off the mound to reach JD's level. Mr. Culver nor any of his underlings at the monitor needed a bird's eye view of the prince breaking, no matter how badly Kip would like to turn and hold onto an old friend. The guilt was natural, a far too natural—familiar—aspect of grief, and he'd known it would come, felt it advancing, tugging at the corners of his frayed mind.

The grief had caught up to him in all of its glorious stages.

Stepping away from JD, Kip found solid pavement while rummaging in his deep coat pocket for his cigarettes. JD came beside him, knowing enough to remain silent. Tipping his head and cupping a flame to his cigarette, Kip swept the icy trail from his cheeks. Only now, the temperature registered with a chilled wind flowing from his favorite sledding slope. For a moment, Kip thought he heard the sobbing and sniveling inside the mausoleum. His mother's funeral . Not a weird dream, not a nightmare. Had he reached resolution stage already?

"It's getting cold. How about we get out of this wind, Kip?"

In an almost natural voice, Kip spoke while dropping his hands to pull his coat together. "I do believe, I need to walk, JD. Thanks for an interesting evening. I'll call you later today."

JD hesitated as if he considered arguing, then clasped Kip's back. "I don't know about you, but I had a great time. How you stayed single, I'll never know." Again, Mulden hesitated. "Be sure and call me."

Nodding and offering an open-hand wave, Kip started down the long lane.

"Hey," Mulden halted him. "Don't be too hard on yourself, Kip. I think your mother understood."

Again, Kip nodded and continued his stride. "Later, JD"

Marilyn probably had understood his resentment, his hatred, but no relief or comfort accompanied that revelation. Just once—if she'd talked to him just once about life rather than Whistlebrook, maybe things would have turned out differently. He remembered once, lying on the good doctor Frances's examination table, tense, anxious, and afraid to speak. Fearful that if he spoke, his mother would find a reason to leave his side. And she'd fled anyway, fled from his silence. And how he'd regretted not asking her something important. She'd been on edge, he remembered.

"Damn it," Kip uttered and dragged a smoky breath into his lungs. Yes, maybe things would have been different. Perhaps he would have returned for a visit rather than an occasional layover—any one of which he would have gladly prolonged. Not once had Marilyn ever asked him to stay, not even for a longer visit. She might have understood, but she'd never attempted to resolve their differences. Even when he came, she rarely spared a moment for him. Always meetings, problems, calls to make. A Home to run.

"Goddamn it, it was my home, too," he uttered sending a swell of smoke and mist about his shoulders. Once, he'd loved this palace. Even when he'd believed he hated it, he'd loved it. Never alone. She might have been alone, isolated by her position, but he'd never been alone. Always someone to talk to, confide in, someone with a story to tell, and how he loved to listen.

"Damn you," he uttered. *That's what you stole from me, Mother! And it hurt, Goddamn it, it hurt worse than dying!*

Several strides past the rear corner of the porch, Kip halted abruptly. At this hour, he doubted he'd gain access through the kitchen. He barely finished that thought when his attention landed and locked. For an instant, with the effects of too much alcohol still flowing through his veins, Kip judged the sight a hallucination. In the next instant, he identified the hearse backed into the furthest loading dock. Frozen, his chest tightening, his mind swimming, Kip stared at the too familiar sight. His muscles constricted despite the numbing flow of alcohol warming his blood. Uncontrollably, he stifled a breath of bracing wind.

Reality. He was back.

A hearse. God, how he hated to watch the hearses arrive. They came at any hour—day or night—but oh God, how he hated when they came at night. Fitzpatrick's colors were emerald and black, the most familiar color, but there were others. Laughlin's in silver and black. Edgar B Stone's, burgundy and black. And others. They came from other towns and counties, and occasionally, from different states where the resident had begun his life nearly a century past. But always they came, an ominous reminder of what lay ahead for everyone in Whistlebrook, the first step on a final journey.

In turmoil, Kip started forward, passing the inlet where a single bulb brightened the cement steps to the kitchen entrance. Only in his mind did he imagine the emerald and black wagon backed against the kitchen dock. Never in front. Marilyn Patterson would have departed on her final journey through a rear door.

Old John Fitzpatrick had come personally, Kip had heard, and Dr. Frances had written the death certificate.

Kip remembered seeing the certificate—the written script even less legible than usual. The good doctor had greeted him in the lobby, offering a cordial handshake. Halted, then, a great well of tears had turned the doctor's eyes to blue crystal; his face had strained beneath his dark mountaineer's beard. Even standing near equal height, Kip couldn't avoid Mark's strong embrace, nor the shattered illusion. Reality had slammed home in that instant.

'I'm sorry, Kip.'

'She's really…?' Reality had rocked his poise, and for several crazy seconds, Kip had held onto Mark Frances like a small child clinging to his father.

Other embraces followed. Kip had held Edna Feeney as she'd fallen apart in his arms—and Carolyn, and others—but none had affected him as completely as those seconds with Mark Frances.

Starting up the loading dock steps, Kip scanned the hearse, from its burgundy body to its black hood. The roofs were always black, perhaps a reflection of an era when executioners wore black hoods, the symbol of death. His icy palm slid along the iron rail, but his shoes froze suddenly, his grip tightened. In front of him, the modern glass door swung open under the back-stepping force of a man wearing a gray ski jacket and dark slacks. Edgar B. Stone, Kip verified as the man, his back holding the glass door, jockeyed the draped cart onto the landing. In gold embossed letters, Edgar B. Stone's Funeral Home scrolled across the velveteen cloak, emerging.

"Christ!" the man bolted, and the cart jostled sideways before the fellow grabbed the end. In the overhead fluorescent, the man stood frozen, still holding the door open behind him and gripping the side of the draped cart, his face drained in a frightened mask. "What the hell—? You trying to give me—? Who the hell—"

Kip started his step again as the fellow collected his breath and recognition.

With his growing fright and rage stifled, the man heaved, "Christ, Mr. Patterson! You scared the shit out of me!"

Kip pitched his cigarette off the dock, striding up the ramp as his focus slid over the burgundy cloth and rose to the now worried man. "Who?"

"Uhm—Victor A. Calfactor," he answered, taking a breath, starting the cart.

"Hold the door," Kip stated. The man halted. Moving closer to the covered cart, Kip leaned and lifted the cloth, folding it carefully off the upper end of the stretcher. A sheet, too. Kip hesitated then lifted it, folding it back. Why? Why did he need to see Victor A. Calfactor? He had no idea until he looked upon the ashen face under the fluorescent light. When he had walked through the halls—days or nights ago, reminiscing—he hadn't recorded names. Only faces. Always faces. And Victor A. Calfactor had been one of those faces. Victor had rested in the East Wing. Kip remembered standing in a doorway, listening to the irregular, labored breaths. He remembered the expression of pain etched within a thin plastic film of liver-spotted flesh. He remembered the desperate moaning, an uncontrollable sound escaping from the aging lungs, the last battle cry of a dying spirit, and the deep gray shroud misting above the bed had staggered Kip backward and sent him striding up the hall. His talent hadn't abandoned him. He'd known this fellow had entered the last phase of his earthly journey. And there were others on the East Wing who hovered on the brink of departure.

Blinking against tears, Kip cleared his eyes; his hand shifted to rest on the pasty scalp. A feel of cold plastic against his palm. Later, the flesh would adopt a waxy feel. But there was peace. Peace spread across the skeletal face and sunken lips. Victor was smiling, Kip noted, seeing beyond the discolored skin and sunken eyes. Victor Calfactor had found his peace, his happiness, and how Kip envied him. The feeling struck such an odd note, a weird chord. He truly envied this fellow for shedding that gray cloak, for earning the right to pass over.

Sighing, he offered his words silently. 'Farewell, old man, bon voyage, and enjoy your final journey. Pass swiftly and safely—and if you see my mother, tell her, I don't hate her.'

Kip's palm skimmed over the thin gray strands before he collected the sheet, folding it carefully to cover the face. More carefully, he draped the velvet cloth over the cart, then silently turned and passed through the open door.

Automated, he strode through the dimly lit corridors, bypassing therapy rooms, doctors' lounge, and in-house record and consulting offices, and a newly converted cancer treatment room. Marilyn had prided herself on that cancer treatment area, a service she'd negotiated through state hospital administrators. Residents' comfort came first and foremost, always. Transporting residents for their chemotherapy via ambulance—or that old van—had probably cost a hell of a lot less, but cost was never a factor. Residents' comfort. At Whistlebrook, the residents paid for comfort and care, paid a great deal, but they'd always received their money's worth from Marilyn Patterson. Rather than a two-hour trip of agony, the cancer afflicted—an amazingly great number within Whistlebrook—could take a brief elevator ride, undergo treatment, and return to their rooms before the latent effects advanced to make their lives a fetid hell.

Hearing the voices as he came upon the parlor-lobby via a swinging door, Kip halted within the shadow alcove alongside the steps.

"Well, then, where the hell could he have gone?" Bickerman demanded.

Unconsciously, Kip back-stepped and halted again, faintly amused. Undoubtedly, he'd reacted to a subconscious programming. God knows, he'd always hidden, though he couldn't recall from what or why. Those words had created a need to remain concealed. Someone hunting for him?

"I'm not sure, sir. I sent Mike to look outside," one of the security guards started.

"Why the hell didn't you call me when you saw him arrive?"

"I thought you were still on the phone."

"At this hour, for Christ's sake?" Bickerman drew a breath. "Just what I fucking need tonight. If they wrecked at the Goddamn gate, he's probably hurt and too fucking drunk to reach a door. Goddamn it! Go find him!"

"Yes, sir, Mr. Bickerman!"

"My luck, he's probably out there lying in a Goddamn snowbank freezing his royal ass off! I'll be in my Goddamn office. Call me when you find him!"

"You want us to bring him to your office when we find him?"

"No!" Bill snapped, then forced a strained calm. "And be careful when you find him. God knows, he's dangerous."

"Sir?"

"Just find him and ring my office. If he's hurt, take him to the exam room, and I'll have that intern—Dr. Nagel—sent down."

"Yes, sir, Mr. Bickerman."

Reaching behind him, Kip swung the door and strode out of the cove as if he hadn't slowed his pace to pass through the doors. Seeing both men across the room near the administration entrance, Kip stopped, feigning a startled expression, then continued toward them, swaggering just a little.

With an effort, Bickerman forced a bewildered smile despite a wary gleam in his eyes. "Damn, Buddy, are you all right?" he said while starting forward. Reconsidering, wisely, he halted. "Ted, here, just told me you had a problem at the entrance. I'll get Simon to send someone out there in the morning with more salt. Damn cold weather. Are you alright?" he asked while bouncing a critical scan from head to foot. "Shit, you look half frozen. Jack, get him a cup of coffee."

Ted eyed Kip warily while starting toward the courtesy table. "Yes, Sir."

Coffee sounded good. His fingers burned and tingled, rebelling against the warmth in his pockets. Kip glanced from the security guard to Bickerman's tense gaze. Two-faced came to mind as Bickerman tried to appear concerned.

"Are you okay?" Bickerman asked, growing anxious in the extended silence.

"Fine," Kip said bluntly. "Working rather late, aren't you?"

Bill hesitated, too many thoughts spinning in his dark eyes. "We had some problems tonight," he said decidedly, his smile wavering under a genuine weariness. "Nothing to worry about, though. I was just leaving."

"What happened?"

"Really, Kip, nothing for you to worry about," Bickerman said a little emphatically. "Just routine business. I'm glad to see you're all right. You had a good time with your buddy tonight, then? He seems like a decent guy. Well," his gaze shifted to Ted who arrived, handing Kip a cup of black coffee. "I'll see you in the morning, Ted. If anything else comes up, give me a ring."

"Yes, sir, Mr. Bickerman."

Bill pulled his coat together and started for the door.

"Anything to do with Stone's wagon out back, Bill?" Kip asked.

Bill halted, and his thin oval face flashed dread. Resigning, his smile faded. "I'm sorry you had to see that, Kip. I sort of waited as long as I could before calling Stone's to come over. That's probably the last thing you needed to see right now."

Honest concern? By God, it appeared genuine.

"We lost one of our residents tonight. He's been failing for some time." Bickerman glanced away, then sighed, his dark eyes haunted. "Buddy, that happens here. Unfortunately, it happened right now, but we can't pick and choose the time, and right now—as always—we have several terminally ill patients. I almost thought it would be best... I was going to suggest you stay at my house or a hotel. I guess I should have, but I didn't have the heart to mention it. You seemed to need to be around your mother's things. I thought it might help you get over the shock. Anyway, are you going to be all right? It's late and I need to be back early."

"Where do you live, Bill?"

"Just down the road a mile or so," he answered wearily.

"Be careful. The roads are icy," Kip commented and strode into the administration entrance. Making the turn into the long, carpeted corridor, he halted.

"Seems like he's all right," Ted said hesitantly. "I mean, he wasn't hurt—"

"He's stoned," Bickerman stated. "Call Mike in and have him watch the back halls. If Mr. Patterson decides to go for a walk, one of you stay with him."

"What if he doesn't want company, sir?"

"For Christ's sake, Ted, the man just lost his mother. Now, he gets hit with this? If he doesn't want company, I'm sure one of you can figure out how to stay with him without being seen."

"Do you...? I mean, what do you think he'll do? Should we—?"

"God knows, Ted. He's grieving. And as I recall hearing, he's never been too incredibly stable," Bickerman's voice grew distant. "Good night, Ted."

"You, too, sir."

Interesting, Kip considered while continuing silently down the hall. Without his cheap smiles, Bill Bickerman sounded like a genuinely concerned adult male of fifty, rather than a salesman in a plaid polyester suit. Even his crack about stability had sounded more concerned than sarcastic. Was this faceless Bickerman the person Marilyn had identified and groomed?

Within his PRIVATE suite, Kip slipped off his coat and kicked off his shoes. Momentarily, he stood sipping his coffee, listening to the stillness—never silence—contemplating the past few hours from dancing and kissing Darcy Robertson and Rachel Monacci to standing alongside Victor Calfactor to listening to Bickerman from the hallway. With his thoughts moving in circles, Kip glanced at the clock. He was wide awake at three in the morning, still running on California time, apparently, and not nearly as intoxicated as he'd been an hour earlier.

An overwhelming desire to see his mother's office without Bill Bickerman or anyone else hovering over his shoulder started him moving.

Coffee cup in hand, Kip moved into the hall, feeling oddly like a thief as he glanced toward the kitchen entrance. Mike-something would be hanging around back there, and Ted Dorson would be watching the parlor while monitoring the mini-television screen on the reception desk that doubled as a security desk after visiting hours. When Marilyn had mentioned her idea of hi-tech, he should have pointed out the inefficiency of placing a single camera at the gate. Cameras at every entrance would have been far more effective. Door alarms were obviously non-existent or useless. Kip had traveled from one end of the Home to the other without once considering his illegal entry or suffering the consequences of the same.

Stopped at the corner where he'd eavesdropped on Bill, Kip realized his foolishness. Whistlebrook was his Home—at least for the next three days—and he had no reason to sneak about like a thief. Uttering a curse, Kip started forward. Obviously, Ted rested at the desk, out of sight. A radio echoed at a soft volume, a newspaper or magazine page crackled, turning, verifying his thought.

Undetected, Kip strode through the shadowed secretarial office and into the alcove of the executive's waiting room. Bill's office door stood to the right, Marilyn Patterson's door on the left. The gold plate bearing the legend of the queen's realm caught and reflected the coach lights through sheer curtains. Kip stood momentarily, running his fingers over the inlaid letters, his mind skipping back in time. Only in recent years, he'd begun entering this office without invitation, and only then to make personal calls if his mother wasn't in attendance. When the queen occupied her office, nothing short of death interrupted her. No wonder Ted refrained from disturbing Bill.

Breaking from his thought, Kip reached down and turned the knob. It caught in his grip—stopped. *Locked?* Doubting, he tried again. *Now, when the hell did this start?* In or out, his mother had never locked this door, had never needed to. No one dared enter without her approval—not her son, not her employees. Probably not even any self-respecting thief, as if anything existed here worth stealing.

On impulse, Kip moved to Bill's mahogany door and tried the knob. Locked.

Now what? Go ask Ted for the key? *Stoned. Grieving. Not incredibly stable.* Asking for a key to his mother's office? 'Sorry, Mr. Patterson, I don't have a key.' Which would be a lie. To hell with a key!

Setting his coffee cup on the stand, Kip checked the hallway toward the parlor more cautiously, then stepped into the secretarial pool. This might be his Home on paper, but he wasn't Marilyn Patterson, and she hadn't passed her staff to him. A wayward Prince, he mused while finding a paper clip in Carolyn's whatnot tray. He brought a credit card from his wallet as he returned to his mother's door. *You always said I was too curious,* he considered while jimmying the paper clip to disengage the lock. *Sorry, Mom.*

Putting his credit card away, Kip stood in the shadows, looking into an eerie bisection of darkness and glowing strips of light within the immense room. Of any room in her palace, this room befitted the queen. Windows opened onto a wraparound porch at two walls, offering a panoramic view of the front lawns and the main entrance, and she'd spent a great deal of time enjoying her view.

Watching him?

Kip remembered her uncanny ability to appear in the kitchen only seconds after he arrived from a sledding adventure or a scouting trip to carry him around the circumference of the Home. She'd never stayed long. Usually breezing into the room while Mrs. Feeney set a bowl of pudding or a cup of cocoa in his hands. Inevitably, Marilyn grabbed a snack and veered close enough to smack the brim of whatever hat he wore over his eyes. 'Hi, there, slugger ... sport ... Injun Joe ... Davy (Crockett) ... Tom (Sawyer) ... Red Baron ... How's your day?'

"Fine," Kip uttered aloud, startling himself in the darkness.

Damnit! Knock it off! You really will end up in a padded room!

Chapter 14

Stepping more fully into the shadows, Kip closed the door behind him. Cold. This room had always carried a chill with winter winds pressed against the windows from either direction. At least one pane of glass needed a strip of caulk. The glass rattled slightly louder than his quickening heartbeat.

Her desk stood against the outside wall, illuminated in the bisecting reflections.

Kip crossed to it, scanning the cleared mahogany surface, his gaze wandering to scan the Victorian chairs and side tables. His mother was here, animated within the rich, polished woods and upholstered chairs. With as much masculine as feminine undertones, her authority and divine rule, her energy and strength abounded. And as he stood, scanning the shadows, Kip knew why the room felt cold to him. This room epitomized the heart and soul of Whistlebrook, and Marilyn Patterson had maintained the pulse.

Whistlebrook's dying.

His fingertips slid across the varnished desktop searching for a pulse. If he'd looked upon the Home in the daylight, would he have seen the gray aura like a storm cloud hovering at its walls? Was that why Marilyn had presented an option? Not just the residents dying. The Home—her home—his home. It was dying with her. No longer would it remain a palace with its motto "A Home for all Seasons." No longer, home-cooked meals, personal care, comfort first. Whistlebrook was dying. Bill Bickerman, Carolyn McAnthony, and whoever else remained would merely pose as guardians of the tomb. The heart and soul had taken their final journey. Is that what she'd intended to show him by trapping him here for three days?

Trapped, damn it. She had trapped him here! She'd known he would leave as quickly as possible. Madison hadn't arrived to tender the Will. '...Personal.' She'd enlisted Madison as a messenger to carry her letter, another symbol of her power and authority, her manipulations. The queen's last act as reigning mistress. Keep the prince here to watch his palace crumble.

Perhaps he no longer hated her ... *but he didn't like her much.*

Even as his thoughts spiraled in anger, Kip heard her written words like a voice in his inner ear: 'Bought you three days ... expected to depart.' John Madison had doubted anything would happen that fast. Marilyn Patterson had believed differently when she wrote that letter. Damn it! Paranoia. *Or was it?*

'Absentia.' Bill used the word, knowing that much about the Will, but unaware of the transition of ownership? Her groomed, second in command, hadn't known the details of the impending sale? Bullshit! Bickerman surely knew the terms, and the bastard had performed one hell of an act for the wayward—*not incredibly stable*—prince.

What the hell was going on here? Why the games? And this felt like a game. Or death. Corporate death. She'd known how her son made his living. Was she attempting a power play from the grave? Or was this truly a game? The game she'd never played with him as a child?

Why now?

'Me, an unwed mother... Ask Mrs. Feeney.'

Unwed mother. She'd waited nearly thirty years to break that news to him, then tossed the announcement in a parting letter like an afterthought? Not even, 'By the way, son, you know Ron E. Patterson? We weren't married. You're a bastard.'

With his thought, Kip sidled around the desk, stooped, and slid the rolling door aside to expose the floor safe. Igniting his lighter, he illuminated the old dial and spun the numbers from memory.

His mother was nothing, if not efficient. The legal folder Bickerman had shown Kip days ago—that very first day—rested against the inner wall of the safe. Bickerman had brought the folder to the suite, saying something about Marilyn's personal papers. 'Thought you'd want to see them.' Birth certificates, hers and his; the death certificate; papers on funeral arrangements: paid cemetery plots; her headstone bought and paid for, ready for delivery; insurance policies that Kip had turned over to John Madison via Bill.

Several of those policies carried his name as the insured. Kip remembered feeling slightly shaken, looking at a life insurance policy with his name on it. Who the hell had she named as the beneficiary? And where the hell was her marriage license that allowed her to be buried alongside Ron E. Patterson with his headstone designating 'Father'—hers 'Mother'? For Chrissake, Ronald E Patterson's birth and death certificates were in the satchel, too.

The flame flickered, burning his knuckle. With a curse, Kip snapped it shut and reached into the safe, lifting the satchel and a handful of other papers that had appeared official in the flickering light. Pushing to his feet, Kip stood for a moment searching the chairs near the windows. Light from the parking lot illuminated a slice of oriental carpet in the center of the room. On route around the desk, Kip lifted the crystal ashtray off his mother's desk, taking it with him to the floor.

Scattering and sorting the documents, he sat cross-legged within the stream of light, scanning one after the other and absorbing the details. The trivial details always told a good story, and in his search for more information, a story unfolded, only beginning with a startling revelation.

Ronald E. Patterson was not his mother's husband. He was her *father*!

"Goddamn it. My grandfather," he uttered aloud. "You didn't even *buy* this damned Home."

She'd inherited the Home from her father, who died the year of Kip's birth. And Bill Bickerman had known that. The evidence rested in the documents Bickerman hadn't carried into the suite, beginning with the original deed along with Ronald E. Patterson's Last Will and Testament. His grandfather acquired the estate in 1897. He'd died in 1957. During the early 1900s, Ronald Patterson had built the mansion's first addition, turning it into a boarding house for the immigrants flooding the valley. In the 30s, it had become a 'poor house' for the penniless throughout the Depression era, and not until the late 40s had his grandfather converted the Home to accommodate the elderly.

Ironic, Kip considered. Some of those immigrants might have spent their first and last days in America within these very walls. Some might have spent most of their lives within the walls. His mother, born in 1922, had grown up in this Home. She'd witnessed all three of its manifestations and transitions.

Dragging from his cigarette, Kip gazed into the graying shadows across the floor, thinking, wondering what his mother must have felt. She'd seen her home filled with immigrants, abounding with hopes and dreams. As a teenager, she'd surely understood the travesties as Whistlebrook became a house of despair with the homeless and starving bodies traipsing through its grand halls. Then later? How she must have ached to see the rooms filled with the dying and deteriorating bodies. Her father had been an octogenarian . And her mother? On the original deeds, the woman's name appeared—Elizabeth L Patterson. But later, as early as 1932, his grandmother's name vanished from the official documents concerning Whistlebrook—known initially as Whittlecreek. His mother would have been ten years old.

Why so much secrecy? Why had she withheld this story from him, not bothering to enlighten him while she could have filled in the gaps? God knows, there were gaps. Like, how did she convince people that her eighty-seven-year-old father fathered *him?* Or did she even try? Did she just become Mrs. by general acceptance? God knows, she was a queen in this house. Everyone loved her and idolized her. Had she feared scorn? The shame of having a bastard? Through her, Kip had become the Prince of Whistlebrook, and Goddamn it, no wonder she'd never tried shielding him from death. She'd survived more than her share, only beginning with her mother at a young age. Why the hell had she withheld this from him? Why hadn't she just talked to him? Confided in him? Had she feared his reaction? Feared his scorn or resentment?

Now what?

Focus clearing, Kip realized the daylight creeping over the drapes, filling the shadows.

Had she intended for him to find these documents? Do something with them? And why the hell had Bill withheld these older documents? Marilyn hadn't asked Bill to withhold these documents, not when she'd written 'unwed' in her letter. She'd known damned full well that her son would search for an explanation. Too many times in his early years, Kip had asked about his father, Ron Patterson, only to watch her bolt as if shot from a cannon. Clearly, she'd known how he would react to that word.

"Goddamn it," he uttered. John Madison knew more than he'd offered. *Twenty-five years, my ass! And Mrs. Feeney?* 'Ask Mrs. Feeney about our first interview.' Damn it! She was playing him like a goddamn fiddle. Toward what end? *What the hell is this? The game you never had time to play with me? And what's the prize?*

Daylight?

"Shit!" In motion, Kip collected the papers scattered about him, replacing them in the order—or disorder—in which he'd found them. As an afterthought, he scoured his personal insurance policy and read the bottom line. No beneficiary? A 100K policy was to be added to his personal assets upon his death. He slipped the policy into the folder. Maybe he should make a bastard, too. A smirk slid into his mustache as he pushed off the floor. *The little fellow would be mean as hell, but financially secure.*

Only one problem, Kip considered while stooping to return the papers to the safe while remembering. Fifteen years ago. Everything seemed to begin and end fifteen years ago. For days, if not weeks, he'd run around with a strangulated hernia. The Prince was going to hell alone. Procreation wasn't likely in the cards.

Snapping the safe shut, Kip heard the rumble of a car engine while too clearly identifying the hazy blue cloud in the room. "Damn it!" Sidestepping from alongside the window, he caught enough of a view to identify Bill's LeMans rolling toward the staff parking lot.

Already in motion, Kip picked the filled ashtray off the desk, swung to the bookshelves, and tugged a tissue from the box on the shelf. Dumping the butts in the tissue, he swiped the ashtray clean and replaced it on the desk. *Details! Details!* He replaced the crystal in its space alongside the phone and strode to the door. With the paperclip, he tripped the door lock in seconds flat.

Pulling the office door shut, Kip started into the secretarial office, swung around, and lifted the plastic cup of stale coffee off the stand, then quickly, but carefully, checked the corridor. At a trot, Kip crossed the opening and ran the length of the hall to his mother's private quarters. As he pushed open the door, he heard an echo of Bill's voice to Jack. Sliding into the room, Kip stood a moment, considering his insanity.

Explain that cloud of smoke in mom's office, Billy boy, and maybe you'll reconsider stability, Kip mused as he moved into the recliner. Considering Bill's first and most logical thought, Kip wondered how long he would need to wait before Bill arrived to check on the wayward Prince of Whistlebrook. Deciding, Kip semi-reclined, canted his hat, and angled his head in a zonked pose. *The Styrofoam cup!* Checking the core for the ring from stagnant coffee, he reached a finger inside and swept away the telltale sign of an upright cup. Finding a natural position for a sleeping hand—a semi-stoned hand—Kip let the cup tilt against the arm of the chair on his thigh with the contents about to spill. Depending on Bill, Kip might need to remove a coffee stain from his jeans, but he'd gladly pay the price.

How long before Bill arrived? A smart man like Bill, he'd notice that cloud, and he might have glimpsed a phantom image at the curtain. *Whose shadow, Bill? Come check. Come find out what the crazy prince is up to.*

Within moments, knuckles tapped the door; Kip relaxed, letting his chest rise and fall with a deep rhythm of sleep. The door opened slowly, quietly. Kip maintained the rhythm, listening and feeling a presence beside him. Several seconds ticked by before the cup lifted from Kip's palm. *No stains today. Thanks, Bill.* Silent and still, Kip listened to the movement in the room. Bill, setting the cup on the coffee table, cloth shifting. Bill returning. A blanket fell over Kip, covering him from his feet to his shoulders. A hand rested briefly on his hat—a heavy hand, seeming awfully large for Bill's hand.

What the hell is this? Damn you, Bill! Touch me—you're a dead man!

Kip heard him moving from the room—

"Is he—"

"Shh, Bill," Mark Frances said in a swift, soft hiss.

In a lowered tone, Bill approached, asking, "He's sleeping?"

Damn you, Dr. Frances!

"Out cold," Frances answered quietly, and the door closed, muffling the voices. "Something wrong, Bill?"

"No, nothing's wrong," Bill stammered quietly. "I just thought I'd check on him. He came in about the time Mr. Calfactor was going out, and I didn't think he'd sleep too well."

"Damn," Mark said softly. "How'd he take it?"

"Who can tell with him? I-I honestly think he was loaded when he came in, doctor, and I don't think he was just drinking, if you know what I mean." Bill paused. "What were you doing in his room anyway?"

"Actually, I was hoping he'd be awake. I wanted to talk to him before I go up to General."

"Anything I can help you with?" Bill asked as they started up the hall.

Mark's voice carried at a more natural pitch. "No—it's not that important. How about leaving him a message to call me when he wakes?"

Fare-thee-well to a great plan, Kip considered while realizing the comfortable warmth under the blanket. The office truly had been chilly. With his thoughts drifting, he was nearly asleep when a sixth sense drew him to a foggy consciousness. Someone was in the room, standing over him, and Kip awoke just enough to catch a whiff of Bill's cheap aftershave. *Shit, should have remembered that detail sooner.* The good Dr. Frances wore a rich musk cologne befitting a high-class lumberjack.

The nightmare was back!

Bolting upright, Kelly heaved breaths; her heart hammered in her chest. The images continued to scroll through her head. A shadowy corridor with single watt balls dangling from wires overhead, swimming and swirling light against the damp stone. Running. Ahead or behind, the slap and slam of running footsteps echoed, and terror raged through her with every clumsy step. Stumbling. Staggering as if through mud, terror flooded her system. Blood and terror. The images faded, ebbing as her mind groped for purchase in the waking world.

The nightmare was back, and its familiar essence was nearly more frightening than the moments inside the darkness. Clumsily, she climbed from the bed. Her flannel gown clung to her sweat-drenched limbs; an instant chill shivered down her spine. Grabbing her heavy robe from the end of the bed, Kelly trembled while thrusting her arms in the sleeves. Pulling the cloth close, hugging herself, she shivered with the force of her heartbeat, sending a quake to her toes. Wide-eyed, still heaving breaths, she scanned her room, identifying her surroundings, her childhood room. The wallpaper, flowered with a touch of pink and soft yellow pastel, had never changed, and for a horrible moment, she felt like a child, one jolted unkindly from sleep in the predawn hours.

Not good, this was not good at all. Internally, Kelly shivered as she focused on the sheer curtains, waking more to the brightening world outside her window. With her room to the rear of the house, she identified the barren spikes of the elm tree from which a tire swing had forever hung in the backyard.

How long had it been? The nightmare. That particular nightmare. Too familiar. She'd awoken screaming in this room, terrified of something chasing her through those shadows. Death, the promise of death, a monster at her heels. How many times in those first days and months inside this room? Too clearly, she remembered waking, sobbing in either her mother's or father's arms. Moving, they were constantly moving, her father's job transferring him. New houses, new friends, new schools, but in this house alone, she'd begun suffering the nightmares. Death, always death, and blood. God, she remembered the blood, blood on her hands, on the walls. Shuddering, she clutched her robe tighter.

Insomnia, she nearly spoke aloud and cursed her latent tremors. Insomnia, personal turmoil, the questions, and conflicts. Rationally, she could justify the nightmares. She hadn't fallen asleep swiftly, nor slept soundly since her arrival three days earlier. Seeing Kip, seeing JD. Too many haunting memories awakened in her subconscious. Why should the onset of nightmares surprise her? Fatigue and mental chaos had combined.

Guilt, too, she admitted silently.

That she'd slept at all should be her only surprise. She'd spent most of the night wondering how to break the news to Richard, thinking about his reaction, his hurt, her hurt. She couldn't marry him, not in good faith or good conscience. Just the memory of her response to Kip Patterson confirmed her thought a thousand times and stirred the turmoil in her mind. If she loved Richard, incontestably, completely, irrevocably, she would never have reacted to Kip, and she couldn't deny her reaction. Without half trying, he'd heated her blood and fired her imagination, and she would have gone to bed with him in a heartbeat.

She loved Richard, too much to lie to him or deceive him. Too much to marry him, knowing she might never be faithful to him. She loved him too much to betray him, and if nothing else, she knew she would.

The mental roller coaster had begun again. The haunting essence of the nightmare ebbed more swiftly, but unfortunately, the alternative offered no relief.

With a glance at the clock on her nightstand, Kelly muttered a curse and turned, stepping into her furry slippers. Rain or shine, day off or duty-bound, she awoke at six a.m. She'd slept in. Nearly seven. But she'd only begun dozing off around four. At 4:12, according to the digital on her nightstand, she'd jolted awake from the brink of a shallow sleep.

Someone—something had moved outside her door. An intruder, a burglar. Then the husky voice muttered a curse, and Kelly remembered where she rested. JD had come home shortly after four.

Annoyed, Kelly suffered the quandary. She'd envied her brother for spending the evening with his old friend, angry that he hadn't invited her, then cursed herself for wanting that damn invitation.

Making her way into the second-floor hall, she considered banging on JD's door just to aggravate the likelihood of a hangover. Forcing herself past his door, if only with a thought of her sleeping parents, she continued through the hall, descending the stairs toward the living room. Apparently, one of her parents was awake. Doubtful her younger brother had awoken this early and made a pot of coffee, but the aroma rather than curiosity lured Kelly to the kitchen.

Nearly as bad as JD, Mike had come home around one o'clock. Shortly after that, their mother had finally stopped wandering around the downstairs and tiptoed through the upstairs hall. Nothing had changed in that respect. Patty still worried when any of her adult-aged children stayed out late. Until Mike found his own apartment to occupy between semesters, he wasn't immune. Patty had probably been awake when JD came home, too, but she'd refrained from waiting downstairs as if he were a child again.

No one occupied the kitchen. Kelly halted in the kitchen entrance, suffering another strangeness. Her attention drawn, she listened. Muffled, the deep voice murmured from a closed door down the hall. Her father in his den? On the phone? At this hour? Her gaze slid to the coffeepot where a single cup waited despite the full pot. Continuing to the counter, she pulled a second cup from the mug tree, then moved to the refrigerator and collected the cream. Her father took cream. She would deliver him a cup and possibly relieve the niggling alarm to find him at his desk so early. Hopefully, nothing had happened at the chemical plant where he headed the engineering department.

With both cups in hand, Kelly passed through the kitchen entrance, almost grateful for whatever distraction her father might offer. As she neared the door and freed a hand, holding both cups by the handles in one hand, her attention froze. This wasn't her father's voice. The pitch was right, the tones wrong. JD?

By natural programming, she lifted her hand to knock, but the voice came clear, elevated slightly.

"Goddamn it, I'm telling you, Patterson's not a player. I don't give a fuck what some asshole said south of the border, I'm telling you what I know... Yeah, so, what did you get on that broad he rolled the other night...? Big surprise, right...? That's bullshit," JD growled. "This bastard has class, Martins, and he probably needed to get laid. What the fuck would you expect him to do? Take a ride down on the strip and pick up a hooker? I spent enough time with him last night to know he wouldn't have to work too hard to get what he wants, and he wouldn't fuck around with some dime-store tramp... We're walking a fine line here, pal, and I don't give a fuck what the State Department thinks it knows. This whole setup stinks"

Kelly had heard enough. *Too much*, by her estimation. As hot coffee slurped over her trembling fingers, she turned from the door and strode a little anxiously to the kitchen. In the stillness, she stood momentarily, drawing soft breaths. Her heart raced for the second time in less than an hour. Only one thought came perfectly clear in her mind. Her brother had not crossed half the states to comfort an old friend, and on the heels of that revelation, she grasped another detail. Her brother wasn't a park ranger.

Who was he? What was he? And what in God's name was Kip Patterson involved in?

Chapter 15

Not fully awake, Kip gathered clean clothes from his larger suitcase and crossed the hall into the bathroom. He hadn't shared a public facility for a shower in ten years. As he stepped from the shower stall, he realized his mistake and halted. A little late to be modest, he stood facing an attractive stranger, and for an instant, he thought of Kelly Mulden, her hair, her posture, her. But this lady was not Kelly. Older. Slightly less attractive. Kelly's dark hair carried that anomaly of a natural brunette sporting just enough deep red highlights to spark fire even in shallow light. Thick, soft waves—he clamped down on the memory, focusing the moment.

She stood between him and the vanity sink where he'd laid his towel and clothes. A faint smile played on her perfectly shaped lips. Her blue eyes trailed down him slowly. No sign of shock or embarrassment appeared as she appraised every inch of his dripping anatomy. Long lashes dipped over stark blue eyes; long, soft brunette curls fell over her shoulders, spilling over a fox fur collar and halfway down the front of her black coat. Diamonds flashed between silky strands of her hair, and more diamonds sparked fire between the open folds of her collar.

Nothing cheap—or shy—about this lady. Genuine amusement rose into Kip's appraising gaze. Of all the insane things to do, to meet a classy lady while spilling a river on the floor? And by her growing amusement, she appreciated either his bewilderment or his vulnerability. "Do you think if I step back into the shower, you could throw me that towel behind you?"

"Don't hide on my account, darling," she said in an oddly familiar voice, still smiling as she half turned, lifted a towel, and handed it to him.

Too late to be modest or embarrassed. He dried his face and swept his dripping curls back before wrapping the towel about himself.

By her posture, her arms resting loosely crossed, leaning against the vanity next to his clothes, she fully intended to watch. Still amused, her eyes trailed over him with an all too apparent appreciation.

"I believe I'm at a serious disadvantage," he decided and glimpsed the wedding band and diamond engagement ring before meeting her gaze. "Possibly, I should take my clothes—"

Lifting the second folded towel, she let it unfold between them, smiling that faint smile as she signaled him to turn around with a manicured finger, a gesture reflective of a swivel stick stirring a martini.

Goddamn, this was odd, but Kip thrived on odd, and he'd forfeited the effort for normalcy long ago. He turned without reservations, watching her over his shoulder, trying desperately to recall if or when he might have met her. The circumstances of this encounter jostled his brain, but little became clear beyond the insanity. Having a married woman—a complete stranger—possibly a daughter or granddaughter of an aging aristocrat touring Whistlebrook ... *drying his back?* Tipping his head to look more fully over his shoulder, he met her brilliant, laughing eyes as the towel continued to slide over him and around him to his chest as he turned.

Maybe this was a dream, an incredibly erotic dream, after which he would need a freezing shower. "Don't suppose you'd mind telling me your name, would you?"

In front of him, now, she handed him both towels, stood on her toes, and brushed a kiss on his cheek. Merely smiling and winking, she commented, "We'll leave that for another time."

He watched her walk out, deciding he was either asleep or hallucinating. Even for him, that experience was a little too weird. Shaking his head, Kip turned to the vanity, finished drying, and began pulling on his clothes. Dressed down to his stocking feet, he collected his dirty clothes and stepped into the hall, unconsciously glancing in either direction for a telltale sign of his visitor. A typewriter pattered. Trays and carts clattered and squealed. No soft, sensuous voice issued from the administration wing secretarial pool. Shrugging, Kip crossed the hall into the private rooms and collected dirty laundry from his disheveled suitcase.

With a bundle of clothes in his arms, he strode through the hall and, if not for Jason following orders, Kip might have run into him a second time. Nodding his appreciation, Kip strode around King, bypassed two other aides who sent him queer glances, and entered the laundry room. Fifteen years and very little had changed. He jammed his shirts and jeans into the drum, added detergent, and started the machine before returning to the kitchen activity.

By the chaos, he'd arrived for the after-lunch rush. Stopping alongside Mrs. Feeney, who stood at the stove, Kip suffered a nostalgic guilt as he watched her flip his eggs in an average-sized skillet. Sausage fried in a second pan. Sliding his hand in front of hers on the spatula handle, he snared her critical gaze, smiling in return; God knows, she worked hard enough without adding further burdens. "I promise not to get burned."

Her attention caught on his cheek, and her eyes twinkled as she lifted her fingers to wipe a smudge. "Now, who've you been tormenting this early?"

Lipstick? Obviously not a hallucination. "An incredibly shameless brunette," he answered with a wink, and flipped the eggs into a proper fold. A married woman who'd probably trotted out, scrambled into a limousine, and raced down the lane. As if that mattered one wit. Scaring off a potential client had been a blast.

His thoughts shifted off the mediocrity, remembering the warehouse of information he'd discovered in his mother's safe. 'Ask Mrs. Feeney.' Dumping his eggs on a waiting plate and flopping the sausage on top, he turned off the burners and moved along the counter to the industrial coffeepot. With his coffee poured, he considered crossing the room to the breakfast nook and decided he'd rather stand for a while. Sleeping on the recliner had given him kinks that neither brunette nor shower had lifted.

Watching the orderly chaos, Kip leaned at the counter, eating his breakfast, appreciating the harmony of the aides. Even Jason had recovered from his clumsiness, hustling dishes from the dishwasher to the cabinet and flopping drying racks of cups and saucers to the counter. The metal food carts were washed, silverware was dispensed to bins, and countertops were cleaned and disinfected. All the while, Edna Feeney stood watch while washing and snapping fresh beans for the start of the dinner fare. Soups, always soups, remained the main staple at Whistlebrook, and no matter how many million bowls of soup Kip had eaten, his mouth still watered at the thought. Nowhere on earth had he eaten as well as in this kitchen.

He'd nearly finished eating when Mrs. Feeney spotted him standing and sent him a scoffing leer with her words. "Now, whoever taught you to eat on your feet?" she asked. "You go on and sit down there and eat proper before you have yourself a case of indigestion."

All three underlings were alerted to her order. They'd spied Kip all along, snatching curious and speculating glances.

Amused, Kip lifted his cup, saluted Edna, and strode around the cute, petite blond. Rather than sit proper, which would likely gain him another mocking scoff, he slid onto the bench, sitting with his back to the wall, his feet crossed at the end of the bench. With a more limited view, he watched Edna Feeney.

'The son she lost when she lost her husband.' Did that mean she'd given birth to a son or merely missed the opportunity to bear a child? 'Her, a widow at 23. Me, an unwed mother at 35.' Something didn't add up. Edna was fifty—fifteen years younger than Marilyn Patterson. She'd lived and worked at Whistlebrook for twenty-six, maybe twenty-seven years.

'Ask ... initial interview.'

As Kip set his plate aside, deciding to ask, another thought occurred. Flashing a glance at his watch, he uttered a curse. 1:05. Father Jordan. Kip barely slid forward when the administration door swung inward, and the priest hesitated in the narrow opening.

"Father," Kip stated, drawing the man's darting gaze and motioning him forward. They could speak here as well as anywhere. Remembering his 'poise,' he continued his slide onto his stocking feet and offered his hand. "Nice of you to come," Kip commented, amused at the reality. Father Jordan had initiated this meeting.

"Looks like I might be interrupting your lunch," Jordan spoke with a comfortable smile, a flashing glance toward the nearly empty plate. The fellow had dressed casual-conservative in the clergy's natural ensemble: black slacks, black shirt, white collar. Rather than shined oxfords, however, he sported a pair of oiled black leather tennis shoes. "If you need a few moments?"

"Coffee? Tea? A soda?" Kip asked while flagging toward the booth.

Edna arrived, wiping her hands on her apron, offering a pleasant greeting, and saying, "Why don't I just make you a plate, Father?"

"Trying to watch my diet, Edna," Jordan laughed while dramatically sucking in his girth and sliding into the booth. "I wouldn't turn down a cup of coffee, though."

Kip barely lifted his plate and cup when Mrs. Feeney slipped both away, telling him, "Sit and relax, dear. More coffee?"

Nodding absently, resigning to the futility of arguing, Kip slid into the booth, resuming his comfortable pose with one heel drawn onto the seat. Catching a light to a cigarette, he met Father Jordan's intent gaze. With his exhale, he asked, "Business or curiosity, Father?"

"Comfort," Father Jordan answered with a natural grin.

"Business, then," Kip commented, indifferently.

"I understand you graduated from St. John's under rather unusual circumstances and special arrangements," Jordan commented.

"Do you like to golf?" Kip asked without wavering.

"Fish, actually. I don't have an eye for golf."

Amused, Kip verified and appreciated his first impression of the priest. Father Jordan's wry grin confirmed his double-entendre. "Trout or Bass?" Kip asked lightly.

"Generally, minnows, but I keep trying," Father Jordan answered easily. "St. John's had an excellent basketball team. Did you play any sports there?"

"Hide-and-seek," Kip answered honestly, indifferently, not betraying his amusement.

"I'd imagine it was difficult attending the academy in your situation."

Mrs. Feeney arrived, sliding cups and saucers before them. Father Jordan was no stranger to this kitchen; his coffee came light. "If you need anything, you just give a holler," Edna offered.

Kip watched her retreat while catching a glimpse of Jason's curious glances. Curiosity. But then, after the round with Bickerman, the kitchen staff might have a good reason for watching him closely. He probably should have exercised control.

"Truthfully, I hadn't meant to bring up the Academy," Father Jordan said lightly, and by the apology in his searching gaze, he meant his words. "I'm more interested in how you're faring."

"Fine," Kip answered absently.

"I spoke to an old friend of yours the other day. Father Richard sends his condolences and prayers. Had I reached him sooner, he would have been here." A soft grin slipped into his lined features. "To hear him tell it, you were quite a character." His eyes darted to the hat that Kip couldn't recall either wearing or removing. The baseball cap rested near his elbow on the table. "I'll have to tell him, you're still a man of many hats." His words trailed, his gaze lingered. "And many burdens, I think," he added lightly.

"Choir ready for Christmas?" Kip asked offhandedly, unwittingly feeling a nostalgic sense of serenity. The Christmas masses at St. John's had remained the highlight of those three years.

"As ready as they'll ever be," Father Jordan mused. "Actually, they're quite good. I'd recommend our midnight service if you'd like to attend."

"Leaving Monday," Kip answered, unconsciously trying to recall the last time he'd heard a church choir or attended a High Mass. He'd heard operas and symphonies in a half dozen countries, but somehow, none had compared to a single choir at those Christmas masses. "I'd never attended a Christmas service," he volunteered lightly, looking to Father Jordan. "I believe I always envied the Catholics their blind faith. I never understood until experiencing a Christmas mass."

"Do you attend mass, Kip?"

"I've caught one or two over the years," he answered and flicked an ash off his cigarette, still looking into the priest's curious gaze. "Programming, I think," he mused. "I met some of your colleagues who could certainly cut to the chase." *And the quick,* he might have added, remembering the welts he'd received after they learned he spent morning mass in the library.

"You were unhappy in St. John's," Father Jordan said knowingly.

"You've been busy," Kip commented. "A reason?"

"Background helps," Father Jordan commented, his gaze intent and faintly amused. "You're a puzzle, Kip. A contradiction, if I may be so bold." His gaze fanned from the booth; a smile haunted his lips. "Not only regarding your faith, if I read the signs accurately." His gaze returned, not quite sober or desperately curious. Reflective. "Your mother spoke about you, and I apologize if I've misled you. I've known for several years that you attended the academy, and you weren't happy with the experience. To the point," he paused, a lingering smile behind his reflection. "When your mother and I met, she was furious. At the time, I believed she was hostile because I'd replaced Father Richards, with whom she had a working rapport. I forced her into a showdown, laying down the facts that I wasn't responsible for Father Richards' transfer. I remember her rage when she called me an old fool and, in no uncertain terms, told me she didn't give a damn which of us righteous fellows came. She went on to tell me of your horrid experiences—none of which she'd known about until after you disappeared."

Jordan's gaze lost the shimmer of both reflection and humor as he continued in a subdued tempo. "You'd turned up by then, but I believe she knew you were lost to her, and I don't think she ever regretted anything more than her decision to send you from here. As much as it hurt her, and you, apparently, I know she made that decision out of love—and perhaps, fear for you. She once admitted to me the terror she felt as she sat with you in the hospital. As I recall, you were in intensive care for several days, and she never left your side. She laughed about it by then, mentioned it was the longest she'd ever spent away from the Home—"

"Excuse me?" Kip asked evenly, his gaze more intent than intended. "The longest she spent away?"

"When she stayed at the hospital with you," Father Jordan answered, studying him. "She slept outside the intensive care ward... And you never knew that before this moment, did you?"

Annoyed and suddenly angry behind his vacant gaze, Kip studied Father Jordan. "My mother never spoke to me, and that episode of my life remains forever awash in a Thorazine—or morphine—fog. No, Father, I didn't know. And at this late date, I fail to see its relevance."

"She loved you very much," Father Jordan said gently. "Though from her and several of your old friends, I gather you don't believe that."

"Comfort is *not* your strong suit," Kip decided calmly, unconsciously lighting another cigarette. He couldn't recall snuffing the first.

Father Jordan smiled faintly. "Then I apologize, son, but I'd rather not let you persecute yourself over your anger at her. I think she understood it and accepted it."

"And that should help?" Kip asked absently, his anger concealed. "I've lived my life not knowing her half as well as you—or a million others—but I should be consoled by knowing she accepted and understood my hostility? Sir, comfort *truly* is not your forte." Had Marilyn ever asked her son to sit with her, he might have forgiven her a thousand injustices. But that wasn't his mother's forte. Sitting, talking to her son was never her strong suit. "If you'll excuse me, now, sir. I have calls to return." Kip started to slide forward.

"Kip," Father Jordan said haltingly, his voice soft, yet commanding. "I didn't come here to upset you, and if those calls aren't pressing, I wonder if I could ask a favor of you?"

Pausing, Kip waited.

"I'm visiting some of the residents upstairs. I'd like you to come with me." Belying his regret, he appeared faintly more troubled.

"A reason?" Kip asked without affect.

"The woman you comforted at the reception, Elsa Taylor, she's been asking to see you. I promised her I'd try to bring you."

Kip considered for a split second, deciding, "Possibly tomorrow." Again, he started out of the booth.

"God forgive me for telling you this, son, on top of everything else, but I don't believe I have a choice. Miss Taylor's filled with cancer, Kip."

Stopped, Kip studied the grim face, understanding the urgency by the priest's tense, sorrowful gaze—he believed the woman was dying. Soon, although her colors contradicted that diagnosis, if Kip recalled those moments in the Oak room.

God may forgive him, but Kip wasn't sure he would.

Silently, he continued his slide from the booth. On impulse, he veered to the laundry room, transferred his clothes to the dryer, and shoved his remaining clothes into a wash cycle. By the time he returned to the kitchen, Mrs. Feeney stood at the booth chatting with Father Jordan. "Wait here," Kip tossed to the priest and continued into the administrative wing.

The last thing he needed was a visit with a terminally ill patient, and another walk down Memory Lane. "Damn it," he uttered while veering into his mother's private suite. Without conscious thought, he pulled on his shoes and exchanged hats.

Rather than collect Father Jordan directly, Kip navigated the loop by-passing the executive offices and stepped into the secretarial pool. Preoccupied, he asked Carolyn, "Any calls?"

She handed him another moderate stack of notes on switchboard stationery and offered him some mediocre comment. "Sleepyhead."

Kip left the office without a return comment and strode into the lobby.

Behind the reception desk, Mrs. Conners—no doubt one of the ambulatory residents if her silver hair and lined face were any indication—sat, smiling and chatting pleasantly with a visitor.

Sidling alongside the desk, Kip sat sidesaddle, ignoring the glances as he turned the 'sign in' ledger toward him. Saturday visitors had begun signing in at 10 o'clock. As many male as female visitors had arrived, not many of either. A couple had arrived and departed early. He checked the names coinciding—either coming or going—with the approximate time of his encounter with the brunette. Two qualified, and of those, Mary Smith, minus a 'reason for your visit,' had entered at 12:10 and departed at 12:20, long enough to dry a stranger's back. Kip considered momentarily, then turned the ledger to Mrs. Conners, who eyed him with a wary smile. "The woman—Mary Smith—do you know her?" he asked lightly.

Her eyes dipped to the ledger, running down the list, stopping as Kip fingered the appropriate name. Her brow crinkled more when she read the absence of either a resident's or a staff member's name on the empty space. Mrs. Conners appeared truly worried, as if she feared her inefficiency could cost her. "I can't imagine how I missed that."

"She was a brunette. Long hair, fur collar, long black coat," Kip supplied. "Possibly she spoke to you, or she's a frequent visitor?"

Her eyes evoked more than Kip needed to know. Mrs. Conners hadn't seen a woman of that description. In fact, she studied the ledger again, still pondering her inadequacy. Her eyes lifted, worried. "I'm sorry, Mr. Patterson. I don't recall seeing her. Is there a problem?"

No, not at all. He was accustomed to wealthy, attractive strangers seducing him in a semi-private john. "Nothing serious. Thank you," he answered and slid off the desk. If he remembered later, he would question Carolyn or Bill. One or the other knew Mary Smith, her given name as well as the proper name of whatever anonymous resident she'd intended to visit. Marilyn truly hadn't forfeited that blasted habit.

Navigating a more direct route alongside the staircase to the kitchen, Kip entered in time to hear Father Jordan chuckling at something Edna, now seated in the booth, told him. "Ready?" Kip interrupted without effect.

Father Jordan wasted no time finishing his coffee and sliding from the booth.

'I'm having second thoughts about getting married!' Kelly had blurted out at the crack of dawn, and resting against her headboard, Kelly considered the insanity. Her insanity. Second thoughts. She hadn't lied. Although when she'd spoken those blasted words, she'd intended subterfuge. With a coffee cup already in hand, she had nowhere to hide when JD walked into the kitchen after nearly catching her eavesdropping. And no other means to explain the tears in her eyes or the blasted tremble in her hands. She wasn't Nancy-freaking-Drew, and she'd never blasted qualify for one of 007's cohorts.

Shaking her head against the headboard, rubbing her temple, Kelly replayed those events in her mind, like an actor reviewing a performance. After that bold outburst, a flood of tears had come naturally, catching her older brother entirely ill-prepared. Who'd become more uncomfortable in those seconds, Kelly couldn't decide even in retrospect, and a wan grin slipped onto her lips. Clumsily, JD had set his coffee on the counter and studied her as if she were a creature beyond his comprehension. And he was too smart to doubt that Kip Patterson played a role in her state of mind, even if she'd refused to consider that detail at the time. In fits and starts, she'd elaborated, dissecting her emotions from the thought of becoming a doctor's wife and never seeing Richard. 'I hardly see him now, and we're only engaged!' What other reservations had poured off her lips in those early morning hours, Kelly couldn't readily recall, now. Somehow, she'd landed in a fold of JD's arms, and for the first time in years, he'd sounded and acted like the brother she'd known. The guy anyone could depend on.

'I can't tell you what to do, Kell, but if you love this guy, maybe you can make it work.'

The tables had turned, then, and Kelly remembered JD admitting, 'I couldn't make it work. I was too screwed up in my head to make anything work, and I'm not much better now. I couldn't give my boys the kind of life our folks gave us. Couldn't give Laura what she needed or wanted.'

The pain in his admission touched her at the deepest level, and Kelly remembered clasping his hand on the table where they'd landed in cater-corner chairs. At that moment, she could have forgiven him almost anything. Sadness haunted his bloodshot eyes; tension gripped his bearded lips. Not the clown, not the prankster or joker any longer. He'd dissected his failure long before reaching that level of remorse.

Did his failure have anything to do with that phone call?

Before the divorce, JD had bounced from one job to another, taking Laura and the boys from one place to another, as if recreating his past, never settling down for long, from security positions in one city to a stint as a dockhand in another. At times, he'd simply gone away for weeks at a time, leaving Laura and the boys to fend for themselves in his absence. In retrospect,

Kelly wondered if his experience in Nam truly belied his irresponsibility. Was he suffering from PTSD? Or was that disorder the excuse he needed to do whatever it was he did?

What was he? Who was he? Who was this older brother to comfort her with such a warm embrace against the quasi-genuine fit in the early hours?

For the first time in years, they'd shared a conversation, and in a way, Kelly knew she'd surprised him as surely as he'd startled her. Not children. Neither of them. At some point, JD had stopped seeing her as a child, started talking to her as a woman who lived alone, choosing a life separate and apart from childhood hearth and home.

'Does Kip Patterson have anything to do with how you're feeling?' he'd asked directly.

Looking into his eyes, Kelly had known the futility of a lie. 'I don't think I'd deny that even if I wanted to, JD, but I don't think in the way you mean. I'm really not a child with a case of puppy love. Once, a long time ago, maybe. But seeing him, talking to him? It started me thinking about the questions I've been trying to push aside.'

'Kell, don't break your engagement or forfeit a chance at happiness over a guy like Kip.'

'The fact that I'd consider doing that—that I'd drop Richard for a man I barely know—tells me more about myself than I wanted to know,' she'd admitted, and in retrospect, she grasped the integrity of those words. 'I'm really not a child, JD. I've been with other guys. I've even gone to bed with a few.' At the shock in his eyes, she'd smiled, 'Honey, men don't corner the market on sex. For nearly every man who's made it, there's a woman who scored.'

Even in reflection, Kelly found those words odd, the conversation unbelievable. She'd spoken to her brother as if he were a friend, an equal, and he'd reciprocated, looking at her in a different light.

A slight reflective grin had lingered on his lips by the time they parted.

'You're a smart girl—woman, Kell,' he'd corrected. 'Just give yourself time to think it through. If this guy's not right for you, someone better will come along, and I'll stand behind you either way.'

The brother Kelly had known, the brother she had idolized, had made his appearance and presence known. If only she hadn't overheard that conversation in the den, if only she could forget the chilling indifference and anger in his tone. 'This bastard has class.' *Bastard. Kip Patterson.* And the words to follow concerning Kip's sex life had sounded like an oratory concerning a stranger. The mention of 'player' and 'the State Department,' and JD's attitude, his deceptively concerned interest in his old friend.

What to do about this knowledge remained the question burning in Kelly's mind. Approaching Kip and warning him that her brother might have an ulterior motive for rekindling an old friendship wasn't an option. Any more than simply confronting JD and demanding answers offered a solution. However, she'd toyed with that idea in a dozen scenarios throughout the morning. Their trust was too new, too tentative, to make demands, and if, as she suspected, JD worked for the government, he wouldn't likely admit the details to her. She'd heard enough, and too much, to accept whatever lies he might be forced to tell.

Uncontrollably, the image of Kip sitting in the recliner filled Kelly's mind. Even in the subdued light, she'd identified the smile in his lips, laughter fleeting through his eyes, and the touch of his lips, his fingertips—

"Damn it," Kelly muttered and pushed off the bed, pacing within the confines of her room where she was supposed to be taking a nap to kick a headache. The headache was real, and the aspirin weren't helping. Tension banged away at her temples. Confronting JD might become the only option, the only sensible conclusion. She might drive herself nuts trying to decide on an appropriate course of action. The only salving factor in that overheard conversation was a subtle indication that JD had attempted to defend Kip, attested to his innocence and suggested a *setup*. Who would be setting Kip up and why? What was he involved in to necessitate the interest of the Federal government? Was JD, as it seemed, attempting to defuse that investigation, or was he simply searching for proof?

'The broad he rolled ... needed to get laid.' He—being Kip Patterson.

Two facts evolved from those lines: JD had apparently known where to find Kip two nights ago, and Kip had obviously found another face.

Which annoyed her more, Kelly remained undecided, but as she muttered another curse, the sound of footsteps outside her door halted her thought. The light tap of knuckles might be her mother, but in a quick assessment, Kelly knew—Richard had arrived.

Chapter 16

Very little of the conversation through the halls qualified for serious thought or consideration, and as Kip stepped from the elevator onto the fourth floor, he'd already begun to doubt his good sense. Had he realized that Elsa Taylor would be found on the fourth floor south, the woman's counterpart to the West Wing where old Irish had lived, he might have declined. 'Spring Chicken,' that was Irish's nickname for the fourth floor. With a faint reflective grin, Kip remembered Irish singling out the South Wing, dubbing it 'Peaches n' Cream.'

'You mark my words, laddy. They're all peaches n' cream 'til you make one a wife.'

Father Jordan barely paused in the doorway to an empty room, then continued forward toward the sound of a shouting match.

Women in wheelchairs rested in doorways, watching the hall—possibly remembering better days when they sat on porch swings, watching old Studebakers passing on tree-lined streets while their children played in nearby trees. So many memories, and how their faces sagged with sad reminiscence. These were the Watchers, Kip remembered as his gaze darted from one to the next, those aged who could physically fend for themselves but mentally resigned to watch, merely awaiting their time as they declined. The Watchers never lasted long on the fourth floor, where the more active aged dwelt; the Watchers slipped away, sinking rapidly to the second floor—'Winter Chicken'—and eventually to the East Wing, where death waited, a living entity between the catheters, oxygen machines, and heart monitors.

If Elsa Taylor lived in the South Wing, things weren't as bad as Fr. Jordan suggested, and Kip needed only recall the pale gray shroud, the mantel of death draped around the old women at the funeral reception. Dying. But not ready to discard her earthly trappings just yet. Others were closer, and as if he needed proof, his attention snagged on the Watcher in the next doorway. His stride faltered. Through the dark gray gauze, he barely identified the gaunt facial features of a once-attractive older woman. As a child, those glimpses and shrouds never disturbed him. Death was natural, and his intimacy with that event was as natural as breathing. When he glimpsed a haze on a crowded street, even now, he barely faltered a stride, willing, able to dismiss the occasional lapses. For a time, that talent had deserted him, and at this moment, he wished it had stayed gone. Returning to Whistlebrook, walking through these halls—?

As if stepping back in time, Kip paused in the doorway to the lounge connecting the four poles of the fourth-floor world. Nearly a dozen men and women sat in wheelchairs or cushioned loungers. A television stood against a far wall with a long window not far away to the left. On that window's circular wide ledge, Kip had rested, sometimes for hours, listening to old Irish's tales. A wing-backed chair stood in front of the window where McGuire's wheelchair had rested, but for a fleeting instant, Kip saw him there, a smile on his gaunt face, a mischievous glint in his brilliant—alive—olive eyes. Irish had become the grandfather of all grandfathers—Kip's friend, his mentor.

Fr. Jordan had continued forward, touching proffered hands, and extending afternoon greetings with quiet God-Bless-You's and the sign of the cross for those who asked. Jordan's interruption barely staggered a heated argument across a checkerboard, barely altered a conversation about the pains of childbearing. The priest had little to no effect on a man shouting at the television or the black woman railing at him.

"Can't hardly hear the set! Ya hush now b'fore I wallop yer tail a good un!"

In a slow scan, Kip recognized the various poles—west and south tower for the most mentally adept; east and north for the physically capable, mentally deficient. By actions alone, Kip knew where each belonged. One old man rested alone in a chair, impulsively swatting the air, batting an imaginary fly, while discussing farm machinery with an old friend who no longer existed;

he cackled a laugh from days gone by. Definitely a North Tower resident, Kip mused, remembering his discomfort when fulfilling his self-appointed obligation to visit north and east wings on all three resident floors. Only that damned East Wing Two had disturbed him more.

Unconsciously, Kip started forward again, following Father Jordan's path, passing the retired farmer who paused to note, "Hired on a new boy. He giving you a fair day, Vern?" In the slight pause, Vern must have answered with an affirmation. Amused, Kip cast the stocky old man a glance as the farmer continued, "Yeah-up, looks like he's got a backbone for it... How's that tiller I sold ya a ways back? Working out for you, then?" He batted a fly on his fleshy forearm. "Bugs been a nuisance this year."

"The Prince," someone hissed in Kip's wake, and by the time he stopped alongside Father Jordan, in front of Elsa Taylor, conversations had faltered.

"Mrs. Taylor," Father Jordan said while holding her tiny hand and opening his other palm toward Kip. "I give you the Prince of Whistlebrook."

Kip flashed the priest a hostile glance before he caught the familiar soft blue, nearly gray eyes. Her awe struck him a momentary blow; his gaze softened on impact. *God, help me, I am insane,* he decided while offering his hand to receive her fluttering fingertips. *Too far gone,* he decided, while he landed on a bended knee in noble fashion. Clasping her fingers gently, he brushed a kiss on the back of her hand. Still on his knee, he lifted his gaze, and a manic amusement danced in his eyes as he spoke in a nobleman's voice. "You honor me with your invitation, Lady Taylor of Richmond. How may I be of service to you?"

No answer. She merely looked at him, blushing and smiling nervously, like a schoolgirl. And what a beautiful little girl she must have been with her petite, delicate features and livid blue eyes. Her white hair would have been auburn and would have fallen in long, silky braids over both of her small shoulders. Pink ribbons in her hair, a giggle in her voice. She tipped her head coyly, eyeing him from beneath sagging lids and graying lashes.

No chemotherapy for this dear woman. An inoperable cancer festered in her frail limbs. The effects of morphine lingered over her faded blue gaze. Damning the sting in his eyes, damning the aura of death he recognized too readily, he dropped his focus, gripping her hand gently, firmly. A month, maybe. Not much more.

"Prince," a husky voice rumbled, and a hand fluttered onto Kip's shoulder. "You'll have to forgive the Lady Taylor."

Forcing his eyes clear, Kip lifted his gaze sideways to Mr. Louten.

Parkinson's disease. Sporadic jitters and twitches in the muscles; the voice vibrated. Only a hint of haze shrouded his salt-and-pepper hair, worn slicked in a greaser style.

"She's a bit under it today," Louten continued. His hand teetered, brushing against Kip's neck and chin as he spoke. "If she could, she'd be telling you how happy she is to have you here. It was a sorry day for the lot of us when your mother passed on. Not a day goes by, we aren't already missing her."

Nodding, Kip caught himself trapped, still on one knee. Mrs. Taylor's hand gripped his palm infirmly; Mr. Louten's hand continued to jitter across Kip's shoulder. Behind him, conversations faltered or lowered, amplifying the labored breaths, rattling coughs ... and his slamming heartbeat.

"Was a long time we been waiting to meet you, boy. Not a one of us didn't know you'd be coming back here someday."

Not back here to stay, Kip thought to shout, trapped between the reality and the fantasy into which he'd readily fallen. Mr. Louten was neither senile nor snowed under a Brompton Cocktail. *Goddamn it*. Regardless of his heritage or that confounding princely moniker, he wasn't taking over this monstrosity. He had his own life. Crazy as that life might be, it had its rewards. No way in hell would he stay here and become reigning lord ... or court jester ... or entertainer! Goddamn it! He'd come too close! Too damned close to losing his sanity in this Home. In less than a month, Kip would be thirty years old, a bewildering *fait accompli* in his opinion. Possibly, he was certifiable, but he wouldn't risk what remained of his sanity by buckling to the whim and whimsy of aged dementia!

Again, brushing a kiss on Elsa Taylor's hand, Kip laid the fluttering limb gently on her flowered skirt. Catching Mr. Louten's spastic hand in a handshake, Kip rose in a balanced turn. "Mr. Louten, truly good to see you again—"

"Oh, Lawrdy!" a resonant voice sent a prickle down Kip's spine. He halted his half turn in time to keep from bumping into a rounded black woman who rock-stopped at his side. A grin slid into his expression as he looked down into her soft chocolate eyes and smooth, rounded face. Gray frost touched the ends of her ebony shoulder-length curls. Her eyes gleamed, sliding upward to meet his gaze. "Lawrd A'mighty!" she huffed, bringing the air and words from a heave at the base of her rounded diaphragm. "Would you lookie here at this white boy!"

An aide, the young aide who'd escorted Mrs. Chelsey in the Oak Room, hurried alongside the black woman, touching her arm. This young woman, Singer, appeared as distressed now as she had on their first encounter—an anxious distress. Her eyes flashed from Kip to the old woman. "Miss Ellie, why don't we go see what's on the TV? I'll quiet down Mr. Mallant for you."

"Just you calm your buns, Missy," Miss Ellie said, and her manic brown eyes danced down Kip again. A smile grew on her mocha face. "A prince I be hearing. Come to rescue the castle. Save all us ole cronies from the state. I be hearing, he's a looker, sure and he is. Got the eyes of a cat. A big cat, I be thinking. Yes-sir-ree, sure as I be standing—"

"Miss Ellie, please," Miss Singer whined while sliding her hand about the wide upper arm. Truly distressed, Singer flashed Kip a furtive glance. A silent warning? *Fear?* "Why don't we go back and see what Mr. Mallant's watching?"

The elder woman's dark eyes blazed, and abruptly, Kip understood. Not a South Tower resident. *No-sir-ree.* Miss Ellie came from the North Pole—or East Pole—despite her comprehensive speech. With his revelation, Kip understood what Miss Singer attempted to prevent. "Miss Ellie," Kip spoke while offering his hand. "It's been a pleasure to make your acquaintance."

Only one hand caught his palm. The lady had a firm grip, a large capable hand. Her free arm circled his waist, wrapped about his back, and grabbed his opposite side. "Why ... I ain't seen man nor beast lookin' so fine," she said while insinuating herself under his arm. "Nosirree, not man nor beast in a lotta years."

"Miss Ellie!" Miss Singer stated as she clasped the woman's broad shoulders.

"Miss Ellie," Fr. Jordan spoke in a calmer, almost amused tone, and he *was* amused, Kip noted in a glance. "This is Mrs. Patterson's son, Kip Patterson."

"Sure, and I know that much, Father Jo'dan," she drawled, dragging Kip's arm over her shoulder before releasing his hand. Even as she looked at the priest, her free hand found purchase on Kip's flannel shirt just above his belt. With a quick firm tug, she yanked his shirttails free, and her hand plunged upward beneath the cloth.

"Miss Ellie—Louise—Baker!" Singer stated.

Oh, yes-sir-ee, one of us belongs on the North Pole, Kip mused as he stood looking down into the blazing eyes while sliding his hand over Ellie's hand beneath his shirt. Was there any point in trying to hold her steady? She plowed an unsolicited path from the center of his waist to his chest and landed over his heart.

"Miss Ellie," Fr. Jordan tried again, possibly not quite as amused, now. "I don't think Mrs. Patterson would be pleased with your behavior."

"Sho are a handsome devil, Prince a men. Sure, and you are," Miss Ellie said up at him. "Sure be nice having a dream-maker about these ole halls. That beau—Billy—he's a mean un. You mark this ol' fool's words, prince-a-men. Seen 'im with muh own eyes how he done 'em up."

"Miss Ellie!" Louten's husky voice vibrated, harmonizing with Singer's.

Despite the opposing sounds, Kip perceived a too similar warning in both voices. Unwavering, he looked into the shining dark eyes, and something—an intensity lingered within the woman's manic shine.

"You mark my words," she said without a trace of madness or southern drawl in her soft words. Her hand stopped and merely pressed against his chest. "There's a devil b'hind that smile a his." As swiftly as her hand had taken root, it slid away, bringing his hand along. She disengaged herself and ambled, batting Miss Singer's hand away and returning to her chair at the TV, shouting at the still rambling old man. "Shut yer trap b'fore I belt ya, ya ole fart!"

Singer cast Kip a swift, alarmed glance, then hurried after Ellie, already calling for Mr. Mallant's attention.

"God forgive her," Fr. Jordan said while turning his concerned attention to Kip with an honest apology. "I should have mentioned Miss Ellie's aggression. She's not generally in this lounge, though. Are you alright, Kip?"

Ellie might be sexually aggressive, but she wasn't senile. Her warning was genuine, then? Real or imagined, the alarm niggled with her implication. About Bill? And why the hell even wonder? On top of all else, did he need another mystery in his life? In the next instant, Kip doubted his sanity even more. Marilyn Patterson endorsed Bill Bickerman as her successor. If a distraught—no doubt, offended—sexually aggressive old woman had a problem with Bill, that was Bill's problem and Miss Ellie's cross to bear. Kip just wished he'd been a fly on the wall when Ellie had tried pulling Bill's shirt open and catching a cheap thrill. Could have been worse, Kip considered while tucking in his shirttails. She might have driven a path in the opposite direction—

A classic, sexually aggressive female would have sent her hand down, not up.

Annoyed with himself, Kip recovered his balance as he accepted another dozen introductions. Formally, Miss Singer introduced herself and apologized for Ellie Baker's behavior. One moment into another, he struggled against the temptation to fall into the fantasies as the elders repeatedly dubbed him, 'Crown Prince of Whistlebrook.' Even those who retained their full mental faculties shared an almost comic pleasure in using his title while asking, "So, Prince, what's your plans for the old place?" Or, "Bet you're considering some changes, eh, Prince?"

Uncomfortable with the niggling at his nape, Kip glimpsed several uncommonly intense gazes and nearly heard them repeating Miss Ellie Baker's warning. 'You mark my words. A devil behind that smile.'

Despite his pressed appearance, from crisp blue jeans and a sweater over his Stanford shirt and Windsor tie, Richard wore a haunted weariness about his eyes and mouth. He hadn't slept. He'd driven five or six hours to be with her, and as Kelly stood looking at him, her heart ached with the news she would impart soon. He smiled, perhaps forcing that curve, and his eyes glinted with a spark of wonder as if he'd found the pot of gold at the end of a rainbow. Kelly felt worse.

Forcing a smile, she accepted his arms about her waist and shoulders, accepted the kiss he pressed urgently on her lips. In his ardor, which might be born of relief to be on solid ground rather than behind the wheel of a car, his lips mashed into her teeth, and in that instant, she knew she was done. This relationship was over. No sparks. No kindling sensations. Almost mechanically, Kelly responded, sliding her lips from under the assault and accepting the insistent need for mouth-to-mouth. At the same time, she remembered how often she'd done precisely this, merely accepted the semantics of a natural relationship, suffering through the clumsy contact of lips and teeth, tongue and hands, bodies pressed with a force to add a new crease in his undershirt. God, she hated this revelation, but it blazed neon. Before Kip's kiss, she'd never known residual sensations should ignite at lip contact. Never experienced the heat at the pit of her stomach; the tingle through her system.

Kissing, until yesterday afternoon, had struck her as a contact sport, a little like football. Slam, bang, winded blows when the contact lasted too long—the initial kickoff before the game launched into play. With Kip ... the first steps to a very long, close dance.

"I missed you," Richard breathed in her ear, sounding as though he'd made the play-offs.

Damn it! Kelly held him just a little tighter, wondering how she could have mistaken this sense of belonging and security for love? And knew abruptly. She'd never kissed a man she truly loved or experienced the sparks ignited through her system. How could she expect to identify what she missed? She knew, now, though. And she'd nearly settled for compatibility and comfort rather than the elusive of all emotions. She was in love with Kip Patterson, probably since first laying eyes on him plastered against their front door. How, or why, she surrendered her heart to him, she couldn't fathom. But the damage was done long before she gathered enough sense to identify the consequences.

The ball was in her court—with Kip—And with Richard, she realized as he eased backward, looking down into her eyes. His eyes dark with fatigue and passion, he studied her. A peculiar, tainted smile eased into his lips, his brow furrowed. He was handsome, more so with his hair slightly mussed, loose dark strands falling rakishly over his brow. Kelly suffered an almost insane impulse to lift her hand and press those strands into the fold over his ear. Not comfortable with his dishevel, he noticed her intrigue, lifted a hand, and brushed his locks into place. Meticulous. A troubled line creased his brow, his worry as apparent as the dark patches beneath his eyes.

"What's wrong, darling?" he asked hesitantly, as if he already knew, merely needed confirmation. A doctor, waiting to confirm a fatal diagnosis.

"You look tired," she said, refusing to oblige. Time—JD's advice. Give herself time. Give Richard time. She couldn't merely hand Richard his ring the instant he arrived.

"I am. You wouldn't believe the roads I've traveled," he said in a huff. Clinically, he studied her, attempting to penetrate whatever barrier had erected. "You don't exactly look well-rested," he said carefully, searching, now, for a new diagnosis. "Your mother mentioned you were lying down with a headache. I didn't mean to wake you, but I—I needed to see you. I am sorry." Already, he backed off and glanced at her bed. "Would you like to lie back down?"

"No, I'm fine, really," she said, suddenly, wanting him out of her room, away from the bed. Too many times, he'd arrived at her apartment after a long shift, besieging her to lie down with him so he could fall asleep, and too tired to do anything else. Too many times, he'd apologized for one thing or another, self-recriminating and needing ... forgiveness? Fleetingly, Kelly recalled him once apologizing for being an intern, a doctor, suggesting he'd change his career choice—if only he could—to please her and spend more time with her. And she'd fallen for it, flattered, before reassuring him, she understood. Of course, she understood. Only a nitwit would expect him to forfeit such a worthy occupation.

Kelly glanced at the door, forcing her mind clear, reining in her start of annoyance. Irish, damn it! She blamed her parents for these quick fits of temper that could ignite instantly. The Irish were never wrong. It was a wonder her parents had survived as long as they had. If not for their love, a tangible thing even when their tempers flared, one of them would have died long ago, slain by the other's waspish temper. Richard was funny, in his own way, sometimes. But he would never veer her from a rage with a quick witticism, any more than he could spark fire from bare rock.

"Why don't we both—"

Before he could voice the suggestion, her mind snapped to attention. "Have you met JD?"

"Uhm, the long-haired gentleman with your hazel eyes who, uhm, called me 'doc?'" His lips twitched, but visible discomfort passed through his eyes.

"What else did he say?" she asked knowingly.

"Nothing really," he said uncomfortably.

"Richard?" she asked, warning him not to lie, sensing he withheld something of importance. If JD had even alluded to the possibility of what she intended to discuss with Richard personally—

"Really, dear, nothing," he said, and Kelly studied him, deciding she would ask JD.

Barely five minutes later, sitting at the kitchen table with her parents, the mystery was solved—both the mystery of Richard's errant strand of hair and his discomfort. Without missing a beat, JD sauntered into the kitchen and scuffed Richard's hair before the poor man could even think to duck. "So, this is your doc, huh, Kell?"

"JD!" she snapped automatically.

"It's all right, Kelly. Really," Richard said condescendingly, as if put upon as he swept his hair into place. "You seem to forget I have two brothers of my own. Older ones are generally the worst."

"Richard, trust me, your brothers—combined—don't compare to the torment of this single one," Kelly warned. "Don't even give him a reason to prove that."

"Is that any way to talk about your big brother, Kell?" JD asked, all innocence as he swiped a coffee cup off the counter. "I haven't so much as tweaked his nose or flipped him over my shoulder and dumped him in a snowdrift yet."

"I'd really rather you didn't, JD," she said honestly.

"I'd have to agree," their father said, but a tiny spark of mischief betrayed his enjoyment. It had been so damned long since any of them had suffered the antics of this wayward son and brother. "There aren't many drifts deep enough to cushion his fall."

Now. Belatedly. Richard seemed to grasp the precarious nature of the Mulden clan as both males chuckled, and Patty slapped her husband's arm. Poor Richard might have fallen victim to older brothers' torment, but his austere, physician-father had never joined in the shenanigans.

Glimpsing the wariness in his blue eyes, Kelly stifled her smile with a serious effort. Richard truly appeared at a loss, and just slightly uncomfortable.

"The way this snow keeps falling, that won't be a problem for too long," JD said with a glance toward the kitchen window, and just for a second, Kelly glimpsed the man to match the voice she'd heard through the den door. More than snow occupied his mind, and these periodic trips to the den or downstairs—where another telephone existed—only confirmed her belief. "You ever play any football, Rich?" JD asked lightly.

From bad to worse. Richard flinched, not hiding how much he detested the short version of his name. His mother, father, sister, and brothers called him Richard. JD should have stuck to 'doc.'

"In high school," Richard answered dryly.

JD looked over, appraising him in a slippery glance. A smile played on his bearded lips. "You'll love playing in the snow. It lends a whole new meaning to the word 'tackle'..."

Chapter 17

Too many stories and fantasies. His senses on overdrive, Kip escaped the lounge and headed for the elevators. Fr. Jordan had abandoned him some time ago, and when checking his watch, Kip halted. For God's sake, no wonder several of the old folks had returned to their rooms. He'd spent most of the afternoon in the lounge. In another half hour, their dinner would arrive, and Mrs. Feeney would prepare his plate a half hour later.

Belatedly remembering the notes Carolyn had given him, Kip slipped them from his back pocket as he stepped into the elevator. Responding mechanically to someone hurrying to catch the elevator behind him, he dropped a hand to stop the closing door, sending it open while reading the top message. Morgan LaMont: Call ASAP. *Shit.* He should have returned her call hours ago. According to the first note, she'd phoned late last evening, early evening California time. Several other vaguely familiar names appeared on the notes, but few numbers accompanied those messages, and most of those callers wore pseudonyms. Amused, he considered the fantasies again. *Too many years in a fairy tale, Kip, my man. Your whole life's one big masquerade.*

"Mr. Patterson?"

Startled, he found Miss Singer's reluctant gaze as the elevator started its descent.

"My uh—" She hesitated, glancing to the elevator buttons as if to verify her limited time or gain confidence. She, in fact, seemed to draw herself up and force the words. "My brother says he went to school with you. He said to tell you 'hi' if I saw you again and he—he hopes there's no hard feelings."

"Your brother's name?"

"Curt. Curt Singer," she said as if she hoped he'd remember.

In a split second, Kip slipped back in time. He stood with his back to a wall of lockers, looking up at six of the most popular faces in Randall High. Curt stood to the left, a sneer creasing his freckled face, but he wasn't smiling or snickering as the seconds grew—

"He sort of asked me to give you his number," Singer said more reluctantly. Glancing at the panel of floor buttons, likely cursing the ancient contraption and praying the door opened soon, she added hurriedly, "I could write it down for you."

"Recite it," Kip said bluntly, looking through her as was his nature. Knowing his effect, he understood her praying for the doors to open while reciting the number, and when the car halted, Kip flagged her out ahead of him. She hesitated in the hall, possibly expecting a conversation. He strode past her and continued down the corridor, veering into the long center hall. Return calls first—*Damn it,* he'd better recheck his messages. Morgan had called twice this morning. Marsh was probably trying to reach him and bugging her. Her last call—at 12:15—had carried a direct quote, which the switchboard operator had cleverly edited. 'If you ever want to see your hibiscus again, you _ _ _. Call me!' In parentheses, the operator had printed, 'Sorry, sir, she insisted I quote her.'

Morgan could be convincing. Two thousand miles would certainly not alter her effect. Kip imagined her anger rolling like steam across every inch of phone cable.

Already smirking with his thought, he strode into the secretarial office. Angie barely paused a tap on her typewriter keys; Carolyn's phone conversation wavered. Her gaze shot in a quick double-take, and she spoke into the phone shortly, "Hold please." Relief swept across her lovely face as she tapped the appropriate button on the phone base.

Settling onto the side of her desk, Kip wondered, "Serious?"

"I was just about to page you. I have an extremely irate young woman on this line. She's called every two minutes for the past twenty minutes, and she refuses to be hung up on."

Kelly? Damn it. "Morgan," he said, and leaned in to accept the receiver.

Carolyn held her finger over the button, a smile quivering on her lips. "Hope you're prepared for an earful."

He nodded absently, amused the instant he heard Morgan shouting, "If you hung up on me, Bitch! I'll fly out there and rip your *hair* out! Do you hear me? You find that crazy bastard and you—Find—Him—Now!"

"Problem?" he asked in the pause, catching Carolyn's laughing eyes.

Morgan's breath caught for an instant. "This *better* be *you*, my darling lover, or he *will* lose his manhood the *instant* I find him!"

"S and M, darlin? Sounds fun," Kip commented. "Vitamins?"

"No! I'm not taking vitamins! I'm taking goddamned phone calls! I feel like that Whistledoodle's switchboard bitch—who by the way, darling, does *not* sound like a sweet little gray-haired old woman—"

"Oh?"

"Don't you even *think* about *Oh-ing* me today!"

"That I know of, I don't."

"Don't *what*?"

"Owe you anything," he said a little vacantly, letting his indifference linger on the line.

Morgan paused her ranting, recoiling silently. Was it possible she knew him and cared enough to want him around a little longer? Doubtful. "Damn it, KJ, I've been going *crazy* here. Marsh called a million times. The poor man's on the verge of a coronary or a nervous breakdown."

"Natural state. Go on."

"You've been getting calls like crazy. I didn't know you *knew* so many people. I was afraid to keep giving them that number, then they scream at me—and, baby? I miss you!"

"Deep six the machine. Take a drive to Tahoe," he mused for Carolyn's benefit.

"You don't want me to take the calls? Or give out the number there?"

"Strawberries," he commented, remembering how she'd worn a strawberry scent the first time they'd met.

"What about strawberries?" she asked lightly.

She'd smelled like ... "Fields and fields of strawberries."

"Strawberry fields? Are you tripping, darling?"

Only a month ago, he'd mentioned that scent after she'd run out of those imported crystals. She hadn't replaced them yet. "Try that shop on Rodeo."

"What shop? Do you want some *acid*?"

"Morgan?"

"What?"

"We tried. We failed. We're finished. Move in with your boxer friend and please...? Water the plants before you leave, will you, luv?"

A long pause came through the line. "I—I think you're serious."

"As a corpse on Christmas, luv."

"Why, damn, you?" she asked on the brink of a shout.

"Use the brain you've chosen to neglect beneath those wonderfully erotic blond curls, and I'm positive you'll understand."

"I can't believe you're doing this!" she stated. "I *will* be here when you get back, you son of a bitch!"

"You shouldn't speak ill of the dead," he commented and leaned, dropping the receiver onto the phone base. Meeting Carolyn's stunned gaze, passing her a faint grin, he asked, "Other messages?"

"Oh, Kip," Carolyn said worriedly. Her gaze shifted from him to the phone and back. Her eyes turned slightly glassy. "Don't you think you were a little hard on her? She sounds like she really cares for you."

"Messages?" he asked evenly.

Carolyn leaned, resting her palm on his arm. "Honey, I know you're hurting, and I don't think you're thinking too clearly. Why don't I get her back on the phone—?" To the sharp ping, her eyes shot downward, and she snapped the receiver to her ear, hissing, "Administration."

Dipping his attention, he spotted the stack of notes and slid them from under the phone as he slipped off the desk.

"Kip, wait," Carolyn stated, covering the receiver with her palm. "This is Morgan. Please, hon. She's crying."

Shifting onto the desk, he lifted the receiver to his ear and heard the snivel. "For Chrissake, Morgan, knock it off. You're annoying me."

"K-Kip, I'm sorry! I—"

"Bad karma," he decided abruptly. "Call you later." He dropped the receiver, continued his turn, and strode from the silent secretarial pool. Before reaching the private room, he turned his attention to other messages. On the first call, he reached an irate Marshal Baxel and suffered the annoyance with Marsh's need for reassurance. Corbin stocks were plummeting. Kefling and Blackwell were showing sure signs of strain. No word, yet, about Elsa Taylor. "Look for a money connection and try other Richmonds. Might not be Virginia." As if it mattered. Undoubtedly, his mother had made provisions for those in Whistlebrook who lingered under alias names. Who was he trying to deceive? He wanted to know Elsa Taylor's history to satisfy his curiosity. At the conclusion of the conversation, Kip commented, "The next time you feel this need for reassurance, Marsh? Call your mother." He depressed the disconnect button, waited through several seconds for a clear line, and released his hold. An odd soft sound slid through the receiver at his ear before he heard a clear dial tone. *A hum and click?*

Glancing at the anonymous name on the notepaper, he decided abruptly and dialed a different number. He waited through several rings, listening and hearing the internal whine. *Paranoia?* Or was someone actually tapping his line? Replaying the conversation with Marsh, he realized, as usual, he'd imparted nothing essential to be understood without prior background knowledge.

"Hello?" a soft voice slipped into his ear.

"Hmm, playing my song again. Hi-Lo."

Hesitation, then, "It does have a nice ring to it."

Just a little on the vampy side, that comment, and Kip found himself smiling. God, this young woman might drive him to drink. Far too swiftly, he recalled the heat of that soft kiss, the taste of her lips, the warmth of her eyes. Not good. He was lucky to remember that Morgan was a blonde. Blue or green eyes? Probably blue, like Carolyn's. "How are you?" he asked listlessly, his rhythm sorely out of kilter with a thought of how much he enjoyed the twinkle in Kelly's green eyes, the feel of her lips. *Damn it!*

"Good, how about you?"

"Couldn't be better," he said smoothly.

"Liar," she said simply.

"Well, I suppose I could be better, but somehow I doubt you'll allow me to prove the sum total of my best. I'll curse myself forever for letting you slip through that door."

"Doubtful, but it's a pleasant thought," she said with a faint smile slipping into his ear, a reserve in her voice. Someone listening? *On her end?* He heard voices in the background.

"I have the distinct impression, you're choosing your words carefully, luv, and as much as I'd love to chat with you, I wonder...? is JD around?"

"Chicken," she laughed.

"Moi? Chicken? For shame, sweetheart, I very nearly needed to enlist the sweeper to clean up the feathers and dust in your wake when you flew. It left me to wonder: Have you ever been kissed before?"

Hesitation. "A time or two."

"Killed them," he mocked dread. "I knew it. You're lethal."

She stifled a laugh, "You seem to have survived."

"Breathing my last," he heaved.

Again, that soft laugh, and he could imagine her eyes crinkling at the corners, her lips quivering on the brink of a smile. "It sounds like it. JD just left, but he should be back soon. Any dinner plans tomorrow?"

"I try not to plan. It's a terrible disappointment when things go awry."

"How about 5 o'clock? Here? My mother's a fantastic cook."

"And I'm to presume, you're not?"

"Never mastered that art. Too busy dancing. My fiancé's coming, too."

"What a thing to mention on the heels of a grand invitation. I'm crushed."

"I thought you should know."

"Practical, I love that in a woman. I'll bring the wine. Tell JD I'll see him tomorrow at five. Tell your fiancé to buy a dueling pistol. See ya."

Hanging up, Kip's hand lingered on the receiver as he uttered a curse. To answer most of the other calls, he'd need another phone, and he might need to meet a switchboard operator.

Lifting the receiver, he called Carolyn's desk. When her 'Administration' came through, he asked, "Still mad at me?"

"You're a brat, but I still love you. What can I do for you?"

"Call Att. Madison. See if he's free for cocktails, his choice of locations, around 8, and find Dr. Mark Frances, have him call me."

"You really are a brat, but I suppose I can handle this."

"Thanks," he said lightly and disconnected.

Three days, Kip considered while his focus slid over the room. Less than two days left to decide if his twilight enlightenment was the extent of the game his mother was playing. A treasure hunt, he considered absently as his focus landed on the framed photo next to the glass dome on the console.

Unconsciously, he stood and strode across the room, lifting the gilt-edged frame. It was the only picture he could recall ever taking with his mother. He stood in a cap and gown, his mother stood, her arm wrapped about his forearm as if he were her escort. Her face tipped toward him, a soft smile touched her lips, her eyes. Behind them, rose vine in livid red bloom, rose up a stone arch shrine. St. John smiled over their shoulders.

In fleeting glimpses, Kip remembered looking down at her, remembered her smile, and she'd said something about pride ... being proud of him. The camera had snapped then, and Dr. Frances laughed as he asked them both to look toward the camera. She'd missed his graduation. She'd entered the basilica shortly after he crossed the stage, and he remembered his anger, his annoyance. He supposed he should have been surprised that she attended at all, after all, he hadn't exactly anticipated her arrival.

Studying the picture, his angled profile hiding the hostility he unleashed in her direction, Kip remembered avoiding that second snap. As a formality, a farewell, he'd leaned and brushed a kiss on her cheek while handing her his cap and tassel, excusing himself to return his gown. 'I'll join you shortly in the reception hall,' he'd lied smoothly.

'Are you angry with me, darling?' Those words echoed over time, and he still recalled her hurt, her concern. Perhaps she's meant to arrive on time.

'Should I be?'

She'd begun to explain, to apologize, but he'd turned and walked away. A scent of roses and lilacs had lingered in the balmy spring air. Scattered in clusters across the lawn, families gathered, laughing, joking, snapping photos. Someone had called to him, a friend, a comrade in arms, but he remembered sending a wave and walking by. No reminders. Kip had wanted no reminders then, wanted none now, but Memory Lane was alive and well in Whistlebrook.

Memory Lane remained the only option for most residents on this final road.

Different roads, those words, too, transcended time, something one of the guest speakers or the valedictorian had said about taking 'different roads.' He'd chosen his own road, called a cab from the lounge in his dorm, and carried his single bag to the curb.

Was this payback time? Had Marilyn waited twelve years to retaliate in a way he couldn't have conspired even in his most creative moods? Dying. Dying without warning or fanfare, leaving him to work through the past, finding the answers to questions he'd believed long ago forgotten. She'd known how he would react to those words, damn her. And a certain irony, or justice, existed in this lousy game. Three days, three days of hell—one for each year she may have wondered if he were alive or dead. How she must have hated him throughout those three years. No phone calls, no postcards, not a hint of communication, and later, he'd never admitted where he'd spent those three years. She'd asked. He'd never answered.

Different roads. Those words echoed in Kip's mind even now. He couldn't recall what the dean, valedictorian, or any other speakers said at his commencement. Someone had said 'different roads'—that was all he heard while searching every row for a face he might recognize. He remembered fearing he might not recognize her in the crowd, but he'd spotted Mark Frances, the lumberjack, the 'good doctor' when he ushered Marilyn into the Basilica about thirty seconds before the bagpipes started playing the march. On top of everything else, her late arrival should never have bothered him, but it had.

He remembered that feeling even now, as if something violent had curled up inside of him. The shy, quiet little kid raised in Whistlebrook had died right there on that stage—

The buzzer jolted Kip from his reverie. He set the picture down clumsily; it clattered, skidded, and lay down alongside the Wallendorf's tomb. In two strides, he collected the receiver on the second ring. "Yes?"

"Kip, Att. Madison offered to pick you up at 7:30. I left a message with Dr. Frances's answering service for him to call you. Is there anything else I can do for you before I take off?"

"Where's Bill been hiding?"

"He, uh—he had business outside the Home today."

In a split second, Kip remembered Calfactor. "At Stone's"

Dread poured through the pause. "Uh, yes."

"Thanks," Kip said lightly and hung up, glancing at his watch. Almost 5:30. No blue jeans and tennis shoes tonight.

Even in retrospect, Kelly couldn't decide why she'd done it, why she'd invited Kip to dinner. Lingering in the kitchen, she tried to make sense of her intentions. Taunting, teasing a man like Kip Patterson could be the equivalent of lighting dynamite, and as much as that event might thrill her at a primal level, she couldn't help realizing how many others could be hurt in the blast. Richard, her intended, would be slammed the hardest, and for a moment, she listened to his reserved laugh from the living room, feeling miserable. He never laughed often, usually in reserve. He wasn't a man to tease or taunt, but not for the same reason as Kip. If she ever called Richard 'chicken,' with the implication applied to that single word, Richard would have been wounded, if not offended; then he would have apologized and attempted to make amends by proving his manhood with gusto. He never would have gotten it, never would have laughed, or tossed the ball back into her court. She'd never heard Richard really laugh—

Blast! This wasn't fair. In Richard's career, he found very little to laugh about. But how many times had she relied on that excuse? Richard's career, his exhaustion after so many long hours at the hospital, his fortitude to juggle a personal life with a demanding professional life. Richard never joked, and she'd read his wariness, his discomfort in the kitchen when her brother and father had tormented him.

Kip Patterson had just lost his mother, and the man tossed out enough zingers to make her laugh, even managed a genuine smile when they'd talked the day before. Death was never far from his thoughts. She'd heard it a dozen times already. His references to death slipped into the conversation in a way that sounded amusing rather than morbid or depressing. Belying those jibes, his depression lingered, but on the surface, nothing remained visible. He would probably laugh a great deal under better circumstances.

"Who was that, hon?" Patty asked as Kelly meandered, distracted, into the living room.

Richard had chosen a corner of the couch, his face more haunted than Kip's at his worst.

Barely glimpsing Richard, Kelly settled onto the couch in the space alongside him, wondering how this had happened. How had she fallen so hopelessly in love with another man that the mere thought of playing out the next hours or days with Richard seemed like a curse, or penance? "Kip," Kelly answered, looking at her mother. "I hope you don't mind, I invited him to dinner tomorrow night. He said he'd come, but I don't know if he will."

Patty's reaction spoke volumes. The subtle glance toward Richard and the soft crease in her brow as she offered, "Of course, I don't mind."

Kelly had seen that expression often enough to know exactly where her mother's thoughts had gone and recognized the worry. For a moment, Kelly considered discussing her plans, weighed the odds of seeking advice from her mother, and knew exactly what her mother would say.

Follow your heart—

"Kip," Richard said thoughtfully. "That's rather an odd name. English, isn't it?"

"English or Scottish," Jarred agreed.

Noting Richard's apparent intention to find common ground with a stranger, Kelly asked herself again, *why*? Why had she invited Kip here? What fit of madness or inspiration had sent those words off her lips before she considered the consequences? Distracted, her focus drifted over the living room, scanning the family photographs hung in neat clusters on the walls. Insanity. Inviting Kip to dinner, not knowing exactly when or how she might break off her engagement ... and suddenly, her focus cleared on the pictures on these walls.

The faces of children and grandchildren, a tribute to the Mulden family history, family and extended family members, a chronicle of their lives from sports poses to portraits. Kip had no family, and despite the catty rhythm of his voice, he'd sounded depressed, distracted. Just thinking of him within that small, windowless apartment alone had triggered her banter. If she could have held him on the line longer, she would have, and to hell with the consequences. Inviting him might have been a spontaneous decision, one with a couple of tricky catches, but she knew it was right. He needed a friend, and damn JD. Just *damn him* for whatever ulterior motive had brought him here.

Chapter 18

"Hot date?"

Genuinely startled and instantly amused, Kip read young Jason's regret. The boy nearly lost his grip on a canister of spoons, fumbling to land it in the holder as he fought to recoup his sanity. "Confidence is a virtue, Mr. King," Kip said as he plucked a fork from the canister and caught the boy's semi-amused, less anxious glance.

"Gets me in trouble sometimes," Jason commented by way of apology.

"Girlfriend?"

"None steady," he answered, shrugging indifference.

"Bachelorhood's an art form," Kip smirked and carried his plate to the booth. Eating was such an awful waste of time, or was it something else suddenly affecting his appetite? God knows, the bowl of soup smelled good and tasted all right, and if the baked chicken breast was half as good as it looked, it would satisfy the Pope. His stomach gripped after the first swallow of soup, and before he swallowed the first piece of chicken, he knew the futility. The reason came to him as he considered King's comment. Hot date. He wore one of his black suits, the only one he hadn't worn during those two dismal days. Sliding from the booth, Kip moved to the trash bin, scraped the plate clean, emptied his soup bowl, and carried them to Connie to add to the last dishwasher load.

As he turned, he ran into Edna's intent gaze and sent her a silent shrug. *I probably still cry on Christmas, too*, he admitted silently as he scanned the kitchen. Nearly spotless. By 6:30, the floors would be scrubbed, and Edna would douse the lights. Not like the old days. Edna no longer needed to spend every waking moment in the kitchen. She relied more on aides and her assistant, Maggie something-or-other, who'd nearly run the kitchen solo if he remembered anything of those first foggy days of his arrival.

Mrs. Feeney could take a break. Kip strode around the worktable, cater-corner to where she stood, folding dish towels. In an easy slide, Kip landed on the corner of the table, watching her dark brown eyes glint and curiosity mount.

"When a boy sits like that, he has business in mind," she played.

Absently, he lifted one of the rumpled towels and whipped it into a fold, slapping it onto the rising stack. "Predictable," he commented and lifted another towel.

"You were once," she said lightly, eyeing his fold for perfection. Apparently, he passed. "You're far from predictable, now, sweetie."

"I need a story, Mrs. Feeney," he said lightly, deliberately enlisting the old address. "Over coffee?"

She studied him momentarily, then scanned her workforce. Fighting against tears, her voice quivered, "Those words surely bring back some memories, sweetie. Why don't we go to my parlor?"

An unexpected suggestion, but a pleasant thought. Sliding off the table, Kip returned to the booth for his coffee cup and his hat. By the time he joined her, she'd issued instructions and collected her cup.

As he followed Edna through the back hall, the first flutters of déjà vu slid through his mind, pulsing with long forgotten memories. Like his home within the Home, Edna's private suite comprised a single large room. At least two decades ago, Marilyn renovated the rooms to accommodate a bedroom and a sitting room, which Edna referred to as her parlor. A single window offered a view of the rear lawns, footbridge, and creek, and stepping into her parlor, Kip sensed the warmth, remembering how often he'd peered through those windows. Long-forgotten feelings of comfort swelled through him. Once upon a time, he'd spent hours inside this room, curled up on her lap in the rocking chair by the window. She loved to read, and oh, the adventures contained on the built-in shelves from floor to ceiling on the inside wall.

'I need a story, Mrs. Feeney,' he would say.

'Find us a good one, sweetie,' she would answer while pulling her footstool to the shelves.

"You always wanted one from the top shelf," Edna said, apparently following his reflections.

His gaze focused on the top shelf. A lighthearted grin quivered on his lips as he found her watching him. "Tis the best yee find at the top, sure an' it tis."

She touched his arm, motioning him to one of her comfortable chairs. "It was a sorry day for me when you learned to read," she said lightly. "I missed those early days." She settled into her rocker, setting her cup on a delicate stand beside her. Her eyes misted as she looked toward the window, through the glass. "We'd sit here, you cuddled in my arms, those big gray eyes looking up at me." Tipping her head, she spied him, trying to draw from her reflection, smiling sadly. "A lot goes on behind those eyes of yours, and you've always had that way of looking through people. Think that look—it scares some people."

"People with things to hide, possibly," he commented absently, half wondering if that 'look' as Edna called it, might have scared Marilyn. God knows, she never stuck around long enough for more than a quick glance. "A story, Mrs. Feeney?"

She smiled more, relaxing in her chair. "Which story, sweetie?"

"You and my mother were close. How did you meet?" Kip asked directly, and her eyes misted with sadness and reflection.

Her focus slid to the window, her thoughts drifting as a faint grin touched her lovely face, as open and honest as a child, and yet, somehow weighted with wisdom, haunted? Born of despair? Or grief. "Your mother," she began softly, reflectively. "A stronger woman I'll never meet. Strong in a way I could never be. I came here in late fall with the world on my shoulders. Your mother ... I think she took one look at me and decided I belonged here. The good Lord knows, I felt old—old as the hills at twenty-three. Barely a sole left on my shoes; a dress I'd mended so often it was more thread than cloth.

"I was a carpetbagger back then. Of course, I suspect I'd been considered more of a flower child. Had a cloth satchel carrying the only other dress I owned and a handful of photos," she paused, remembering. "I was looking for a couple days' work. Some folks in town sent me out this way . A pawnshop owner as I recall. I believe I went into that old store intending to pawn my old bag and buy a hot meal. That old bag wasn't worth a thing. I don't recall what all that old man said, but he must have mentioned a hot meal.

"So, I walked out this way, thinking that if that doggone driveway got much longer, they'd be picking up my bones out there on the lane. I got about as far as the front steps, having a load of second thoughts. Stood out there a good long time, just looking at those double doors... The glass doors came later. When I came, those original frosted glass oaks filled the front entry. About the time I started looking over the windows, I spotted a woman looking out at me. A finer looking woman, I hadn't seen since leaving Norfolk."

Edna looked at him, smiling faintly. "Your mother, she was something to see, sweetie. Her with that long dark hair and a body to make any sensible man pay attention ... and a look of sophistication to intimidate any woman. One look at her, and I decided I'd go on back to town and take my chances. This Nursing Home was too rich for my blood, and that lady looking down at me was more than I needed to see to know it."

Her focus drifted again, flowing through the window, her smile shadowed. "Well, I got turned around, and I started back down the walk, and don't you know, your mother got one of those windows open and she called out to me. Maybe she called a few times before I turned around, and there she was, hanging out that window asking me if I was looking for someone. Don't suppose I was very good at lying. I think I called back that I was looking for work and had been sent out by that pawnshop owner in town. Here she is, this beautiful, high-class woman, leaning on her forearms on a windowsill, asking, 'What can you do?'"

Kip's focus drifted, following Edna's gaze through the window, seeing an elegant young woman leaning on a windowsill, her blue eyes shining. *Was it*? "Sunny?" he asked absently.

"Believe it was," Edna answered. "I was sweating something awful from the walk, but the air was cool that late in autumn. Most of the oaks were a fire red."

More! Tell me more! At the echo of his child's voice, Kip withdrew from the edge of nostalgia and smiled. "What did you say to her?"

"The only two things I knew, I called back, 'I can cook and clean.' She rested there for a moment, then called, 'There's a door around the back. I'll meet you there.' So, she went back inside and shut the window, and I walked around to the back entrance for the first time. Here comes this pretty lady, and she's holding about the handsomest little tyke I'd seen in a long time.

"We came into the kitchen there, and I can tell you, sweetie, the smells in there had my head reeling. There was an old woman—Briggs, her name was—remember I took to calling her Bags... Your mother put you down then, and I couldn't take my eyes off you. You were scooting about under tables, took up a spoon off the floor, and started banging on pans. And all the while your mother's asking me questions. Bags was yelling at you, and a young helper—don't think she could decide which of you was the most trouble. Couldn't take my eyes off you."

She paused, letting the memories flow through her mind, the weight of nostalgia wearing on her faint grin. "I wasn't much on talking about myself, and your mother never let on that she was interviewing me. She wasn't all that confident back then. The whole time we were talking, I was thinking she was the lady of the house, and I wasn't looking forward to meeting her man...

"Was old Bags that cracked the whole ball of wax with a little help from that little terror running around the kitchen. It was that old metal cabinet we used to have for the dishes. I saw you reaching up there, trying your darndest to get that door open. Hit me funny—you hadn't said a word, and nobody seemed to notice you, not until you got that handle and tugged. That whole cabinet started coming down on top of you. I don't know to this day how I got there in time to catch that cabinet. The next thing I know, maybe a dozen dishes had fallen out, and there's Bags, grabbing you up, laying you over her arm, and you..." She paused with her memory. "You started kicking and screaming, but Bags managed to tug your britches down and took up a spoon.

"Wasn't that long since I lost my own little boy." Shadows ran into her profile; her smile twisted unnaturally as she continued softly, "Timothy John Feeney. Named after his daddy. Buried them both. And here was this old hag putting welts on this beautiful little dickens. No vengeance on earth like the vengeance of a mother who's lost a child," she said solemnly. "Your mother, she was standing there looking as helpless as I'd ever seen a woman, not knowing whether to stop Bags or cry over the dishes.

"Needless to say, sweetie," Edna looked to him directly, a chilly glint in her eyes. "I went to your rescue. Grabbed you off old Bags and hugged those tears away while giving that ole bag a royal chewing out. Me and that Bags, we exchanged a whole lot of words before your mother stepped in and ordered her to clean up the dishes. Me and your mother finished that interview with you hanging onto me for dear life. By the time you drifted off to sleep, your mother knew my life story and hired me as kitchen help and ... and your nanny, I think now. I spent an awful lot of those early years chasing after you and doing a great deal of healing."

His mother had been right, Kip realized in the pause. He'd enjoyed the story, though, honestly, he couldn't recall a metal cabinet, not its existence or that accident. He remembered old Mrs. Briggs, though—her and her long wooden spoon. "She was always after me with that damn spoon," he commented absently.

"She was a hateful old woman, the way a lot of folks get mean when they get up in years," Edna said quietly, her gaze shadowed. "I sure tried to keep you safe from that type, but Lord knows, you took some walloping you never deserved."

Kip met her gaze. "Briggs knew, didn't she?"

"Knew what, sweetie?"

"That I was a bastard. That Ron Patterson was my grandfather, not my father?"

Edna studied him for several seconds; no surprise appeared in her expression. Only an odd intensity lingered behind her gentle eyes. "I'd imagine so, sweetie. She was here a long time, and I remember some talk about her and your grandfather."

Her casual tone implied the reality. Edna had believed that he'd known his history long before now. "Did my mother ever mention him? My real father?"

"Your mother was never one to talk about herself much," Edna said with a dismissive, decisive tone. "I know she was a dancer, and she left the Home for a lot of years. I think she left when she was still a little girl. I know she lost her mother when she was young." Pausing, she considered his question as well as her answer. "I remember her telling me once, you have your father's eyes, and I think she must have loved him very much. I remember how distant she'd seemed, and there was no mistaking her smile."

"She never mentioned his name?"

"Not to me, sweetie," she answered rhythmically, studying him carefully. "You're going to search for him, aren't you?"

"Actually, no," Kip answered honestly. Thirty years too late for that. "I'd just like to know his name." And to know why his mother hadn't taken this secret to her grave. God knows, Kip could have lived without this enlightenment.

With his thought, he dismissed the comfortable aura of Edna's story. Nothing in her dialogue added insight to his quest. Whatever the hell quest he'd begun. Three days of bought time. To discover he was the only idiot to believe she was a Missus rather than a Miss? Was that supposed to explain something?

"What's bothering you, sweetie?"

Kip met Edna's concentrated gaze, thinking, wondering, "You assumed she was a Mrs. When did you find out differently?"

She considered for several moments before answering, "Not too long after I came." Looking at him, her worn smile returned. "See, sweetie, your mom and me, we hit it off that first day, and I think, from then on, we became like sisters. This old place," her eyes misted, trailing fondly over her comfortable room. "I couldn't imagine a life anywhere else. There's always been a lot of suffering here. Your mother... Not too long ago, she and I were sitting about like you and me, now. She'd come over here quite a bit the past while back, and I think she said it best. Whistlebrook's always been a place for the castoffs and forgotten. They come here in the twilight of their life—"

His gaze shifted, hearing his mother's voice, her words rather than Edna's, remembering the loss, feeling the pain.

"—They come here to die, but they find peace. There's peace on this old hill." Again, Edna paused, drifting her gaze through the glass. "Your mom and me, we both had a lot of heartache. I think that's what drew us together. That, and you, sweetie." Her attention returned with a fond smile, meandering scrutiny. "You brought us together and held us together. In a lot of ways, I became your mother. Your mom became your father. And I think between the two of us, we did okay." An old smile tipped her plump lips, her gaze listed over his face before landing on his eyes. "Yes, I think between us, we did just fine. Looking at you, a grown man—a fine man you've become. What a joy it is to look at you, Kip."

Somehow her words sent an uncomfortable wave through him—a wave of remorse that only she could create. Doubtful, he'd become a man that every mother could love. He thoroughly enjoyed devastation and destruction, and Edna, his mother's closest friend, knew at least that much about him. *Damn it! The story. Ask Edna.* Kip cleared his focus, dismissing his guilt as he snared

Edna Feeney's fond gaze. "My mother wrote me a letter. Did she talk to you about me—about Whistlebrook—in the event of her demise?"

Her eyes betrayed her in her pause. Sadness, more sadness slipped across her drawn features as she lifted her lukewarm coffee. She sipped her coffee, holding the cup before her as if it were fine china rather than glazed, heavy pottery. When her gaze returned, she was a mother—his mother—torn between her desire and his. "Your mother did speak to me, sweetie. For all the world, she wanted you to take over Whistlebrook, but she said she made too many mistakes. Too much came between you and the man—Kippen James Patterson—had a life of his own.

"I know you have options to free yourself from this old place. I promised your mother I wouldn't interfere." Her eyes welled with tears. Taking a swallow, she cast her shiny gaze through her window.

"Will you remain here after the title transfers?"

Blinking, she lifted a hand to clear her vision, an apology in her sad smile. "Some months ago," she said while studying her cup, then looking again to him. "Your mother had several properties besides the Home. One she particularly liked. She offered me a fair price, and I bought it from her. I won't be staying on long here, and I'm not a woman without means, sweetie. I've been putting away a nest egg for a long while. I'll just be retiring early."

Not happily, Kip understood from her expression.

"Don't you worry about me, sweetie," she said kindly. "I've had a lot of good years here. Happy years, for the most part. I'm going to miss this old place, but life thrives on change."

With crystal clarity, Kip remembered the clause concerning Edna Feeney in the Will and transfer papers. He understood it better, now. His mother's dearest friend would decide for herself when to depart Whistlebrook. Under the provisions, the new administration would continue her salary indefinitely, but Edna would need only submit a ten-day notice before leaving.

"Kip, your mother wanted you happy," Edna said quietly.

"How many others know about my option, Mrs. Feeney?" he asked, meeting her gaze.

She considered for a moment before answering. "That I know of, me and Attn. John Madison. Frank Culver might know. I think your mother offered him one of her properties."

"Bill Bickerman?"

Edna smiled, an odd smile for her gentle face, one that conveyed as much dread as anger. "He might know, Kip, but truthfully, I doubt it. When your mother spoke to me, she asked me not to repeat what she was telling me. I know there's a lot of speculation about what's going to happen between you and Bill, and I know you don't trust him. You are your mother's son," she mused. "Bill's a good administrator when it comes to taking control and getting things done, but I don't think your mother ever quite confided in him. She kept him at arm's length if you know what I mean."

"That seems a little odd."

"Not for your mother, sweetie. There's only one person I know who's more private than she was." She hesitated, with the implication in her gaze and grin. "And I think I'm looking at him."

Mrs. Feeney wasn't guessing. She'd become his mother and his mother's confidant. Doubtful, she knew the extent of his activities, but she knew as much as Marilyn Patterson. She probably expected this conversation. Not much had changed. *Ask Edna.* Had Marilyn offered that suggestion for him to confirm Edna's trust? To make her his confidant? *Damn it.* Why did he *need* a confidant?

"You have that look again, sweetie. What's bothering you?"

At her interruption, he glanced at his watch, amazed at how much time had passed. John Madison would arrive soon, if not already. "I'd better get moving," he decided aloud and set his cup aside as he pushed from his chair. With a natural ease, he strode to her, leaned and brushed a kiss on her cheek, looking into her troubled gaze as he straightened. "Thank you for the story, Mum."

"Kippen," she stopped him, sliding her hand into his and smiling fondly. "No matter what becomes of Whistlebrook, my door's always open to you."

He squeezed her hand lightly. That much he'd known. Leaning, he brushed another kiss on her cheek, and as he lifted, a glimpse of odd color swam through his vision. As confusing as it was unsettling, the color yellow flashed within swirls of red and purple, a conflict of lies and anger, deceit? But this was Edna Feeney. She knew him, likely reacting to his conflicts. Was she angry? At him? Or disappointed? Only time would prove her fears unjustified. Recovering in an instant, he managed to wink and smile as he slid his hand free of her grip. "Thanks, Mum. Maybe we could chat again before I leave."

"I'd like that, sweetie," she said serenely, leaving no doubt of her thoughts drifting toward the past.

Winking, he turned and strode to the door, collecting old Irish's brimmed hat from the chair before stepping into the hall, pulling the door closed in his wake. His 'funeral' hat, Kip mused as he pulled the brim low, gangster style, and started down the quiet corridor.

Despite himself, he paused, momentarily enthralled by the truly deceptive quality of this rarely traveled section of Whistlebrook. Preserved, a thin carpet extended the length of the narrow hallway. Wide mahogany baseboards stretched between the floor and faded, flowered wallpaper: several doors indented either wall. His attention lingered briefly on a door clearly labeled, 'Basement.' Unconsciously, he recoiled, faintly aware of his muscles cramping against an internal alarm. In a 1920s style, glass domes covered the single bulbs, dangling every fifteen feet from the tin-type ceiling. Shadows and soft light spilled along the walls. How easily he could imagine the immigrants striding through this hallway and the poor... How the poor must have marveled at the opulence as they wandered, uncertain of their future and the strife cast upon them.

Tense for no apparent reason, Kip continued his stride, entering the kitchen at a slightly harried pace. The floor had dried. The smell of disinfectants wafted within the subtle glow of a small fluorescent lamp above the industrial sinks.

What had he accomplished by speaking to Edna? Insight into his mother as a person? As a young woman with the burdens of a child and a business? Insight into why an old woman had terrorized him as a child? How he had feared and hated that old woman with her ever-ready spoon. Was it any wonder he'd never run inside this kitchen? Even now, he avoided the kitchen within the hour of hiatus when the residents dined. Edna and his mother had always dined within that comfortable lull between delivering the meals and recovering the trays. Alone, Kip had blended into the chaos of the cleanup and wolfed his meals while old Briggs was busy snapping orders at her underlings. In the shuffle, she was mean—alone in that quiet break, she'd been vicious.

Again, Kip halted, seeing himself huddled in the corner between the refrigerator and the wall. If he could have crawled through a crack, he surely would have. He couldn't remember what he'd done. He remembered staring up at that old woman's gnarled face, feeling her contempt in her glowering eyes, and knowing that spoon—tapping idly on her palm—would find its way to his backside.

'Mourning child,' she called him. 'You're a no-good mourning child.'

Not 'mourning'—he realized for the first time in his life. Morning!

'Your momma never thought about you 'til morning.' Cackling laughter echoed, bouncing off the wall, chilling Kip's spine before his backside heated under her spoon.

"Bitch," he uttered aloud and strode across the kitchen. Was it any wonder he believed himself certifiable? For Chrissake, he'd grown up believing his mother only thought about him at funerals, and God knows, there was plenty of mourning.

Bitch. Bitch. Bitch, Kip chanted while collecting his coat from the PRIVATE suite and *thanks a whole helluva lot, Mother! I'm truly enjoying this three-day blitz.* If he retained any common sense, he'd fly to New Jersey, take a walk on the Boardwalk, find a brunette and a slot machine, and fly back Monday afternoon. With his luck, the brunette would be married, and he'd hit a bundle on the machines. Inevitably, he'd offer his accountants something else to worry about—

Whatever happened to Briggs, he wondered absently. And for one fleeting second, he saw a twisted, tangled image of spindly legs and cotton material that reminded him of old mattress ticking. Blood—the basement—crumpled at the base of the rickety stairs.

He shoved the image away, drew breath, and headed for the lobby to find Madison.

Chapter 19

As quietly as she could, Kelly slipped off the bed where Richard had finally fallen asleep. He looked like a child sprawled under the cartoon character quilt, and in an odd moment, Kelly realized her resentment. Without a doubt, he was exhausted, and she found no fault, would never forbid him to sleep or resent him for his need. He, nearly begging her to join him as if he feared falling asleep in a strange room alone, annoyed her beyond measure. What did he do in the hospital lounge? How did he manage that feat? Or did he ask a nurse to lie down with him? Not fair! Not fair at all, but suddenly, Kelly analyzed this relationship more critically and realized what her subconscious might have known all along. He was needy, and demanding, and sometimes she felt more like his nanny than his fiancée.

Watching him dozing off on the couch in the middle of a conversation with her father, she'd been irritated. Then, inevitably, he jolted awake as if stuck with a hot poker before donning a sheepish expression of apology. Still irritated, she spied his sleeping form. At nearly thirty years old, he shouldn't need to be ordered to go to bed, any more than he should have worn a pout while whispering—about as inconspicuously as a rockstar in a confessional—for her to join him. Unlike her parents, who suspected an ulterior motive for his request and suffered to appear oblivious, Kelly had known Richard wasn't offering a lewd invitation in her ear. Necking remained the furthest thing from his mind and ranked right up there alongside cuddling or sharing a serious conversation. He needed his hand held when falling asleep—as he'd needed his hand held a hundred other times when arriving unexpectedly on her doorstep. In the morning, he'd apologize profusely for his negligence and make her feel like a heel for entertaining the notion of a carnal moment. As if she were the only girl on the planet who might like to share an intimate experience with her boyfriend rather than watch him sleep.

Annoyed, Kelly moved through the shadowy room, stepping into the hall and closing the door as gently as she could. At the motion in the corner of her eye, she nearly jumped free of her flesh before recognizing her mother. God. She'd done this so often in her own quiet apartment that for a moment, she'd forgotten where she was. Aside from all else, Richard was a light sleeper, jolting awake at the turn of a key, needing the telephone unplugged and the television turned off, provided he wasn't dozing in front of it. Growing up in South Carolina, he explained, his parents' plantation house stood far enough from the highway that he'd never heard the constant hum of city life.

Focusing, Kelly noted the worry in her mother's eyes, across her brow, and decided, "Think we could talk a moment?"

"I was hoping we could," Patty said with soft relief, and glanced down the hall to the stairway where the television remained at a normal decibel. "My room?" she offered.

"Great," Kelly said and followed her mother down the hall. The house wasn't that large, the walls not too thick. Thinking about the words she'd accidentally overheard in the early morning hours, Kelly vowed to keep her voice low.

Like old times, Kelly flopped across the end of her mother's king-sized bed as her mother propped the mound of pillows and settled against the headboard. They'd been friends, as well as confidants in recent years, but not always. Throughout her teenage years, Kelly struggled to find her identity amid dance lessons, schoolwork, boys, and sports. Looking at her mother, now, Kelly regretted those battles and thanked God for the woman who'd stuck by her regardless of her tantrums. "Guess you know, I have a problem," Kelly began simply.

Patty's lips twitched with a slight smile. "I wondered," she said, tongue-in-cheek.

"Remember when I told you I was engaged, and you said something like, 'As long as he's right for you?'"

Patty nodded, her pensive gaze and faintly troubled smile undiminished. "Are you sure he's not?" she asked quietly, summing up the total of Kelly's emotions.

"I didn't realize it until—" God, this was more difficult than she'd expected, but her mother knew. The soft shine of understanding, as well as concern, urged Kelly onward. "Until I saw Kip Patterson," she admitted. "I honestly didn't come here for this, Mom. I believed fully that I was over that silly crush years ago, but ... but I think I knew the instant I saw him, I was in big trouble."

"He was a handsome boy. He's a more handsome man," Patty conceded. "But then, Richard's certainly no slouch, dear, and I do think he's in love with you."

"I'm sure he is, Mom," Kelly said, and her focus drifted. Just like old times, her fingers played with a piece of fuzz on the flowered quilt in front of her. "I'm sure I love him, too, but not the way I should. Not enough."

"It's natural to have second thoughts. But I think you need to consider why you agreed to marry him in the first place, hon. Did you have any doubts then?"

"More than I cared to consider," she admitted. "I've been thinking about this for months. About being a doctor's wife, making concessions for his profession, about the long hours, and the long nights I spend alone already. I tell myself, when he finishes his internship, things will be better; we'll spend more time together. But you saw him this evening. Falling asleep on the couch? That's our general routine."

"Kelly, don't take this wrong, dear, but I wonder how much of what you're feeling, thinking, truly has to do with Kip?"

"A whole lot," she said smoothly, honestly, catching her mother's critical gaze across the span of quilt. In the lamplight, Patty appeared older. Shadows collected in the soft lines to trouble her brow. Honesty. "When I realized it wouldn't take much for me to be attracted to Kip—that I am attracted to him—I started really looking at what kind of relationship Richard and I have. I started thinking about all the things that I've been trying not to think about, and I realized one basic truth—I don't love him enough. Not when a perfect stranger can step out of the past and I'd race a three hundred miles to be there for him. Not when I know, given a certain set of circumstances, I'd betray Richard's trust in a heartbeat."

"Knowing you, honey, I don't think you would, no matter what you're feeling."

"Not physically, no," Kelly said and sat up, unable to remain relaxed any longer. Her gaze drifting, she sought the words, wondering if she wanted her mother's advice or simply her approval. Not sure of anything at this moment, Kelly commented, "Mentally, I've already betrayed him."

"I don't think that counts, hon," Patty said with a slight smile.

"Let me ask you, Mom, all kidding aside. If some guy stepped out of your past, somebody you believed you loved, would you drop dad for him?"

Patty considered the words, her gaze adrift and pensive, lips quirked. A spark of mischief in her hazel eyes, she commented, "I'd probably have to think twice if Paul Newman came to our door."

"Mmmom."

Patty stifled a laugh and sobered. "No, honey. When I met your father, I knew he was the one. He makes me mad enough to spit, but there's no one I'd rather be with. And I know how rare that is. I watch other people in relationships. I wonder how some couples can simply walk away from five, ten, or twenty years of marriage. Sometimes I wonder if we're just too stubborn to give up or too comfortable with each other, and then I realize that's part of what we have, what we share. I wouldn't give it up, even for Newman."

"There's my dilemma, Mom," Kelly said quietly, feeling the ache. "I like Richard—when he's awake—but I'm not sure I love him. I uh … I went to see Kip yesterday," she admitted and noted her mother's lack of surprise. "We just talked for a few minutes, but—but this is nuts. I hardly know him, but that's not how it felt. I kept telling myself, 'He's a stranger.' But that didn't help a damn bit. He's … a major flirt," she said with a slight smile. "And that doesn't help either, because I caught myself thinking, I'd fall for his line anytime.

"What's that say about me, about my relationship with Richard? It's like I'm caught in the middle of this mess of my own design, and I have some Almighty Power giving me a choice—a doctor's wife for the rest of my life or a wild one-night stand. One or the other—not both. I can't have both, and I know it, and the problem is … I'd take that one-night stand any time because maybe that's all I'm supposed to have. Maybe I've been kidding myself that I could settle down with one man and build the kind of life you and Dad have. I think about having children, me raising them, taking time out while I'm fat, then going back to my studio. And I think about Richard popping in on occasion. Then I think, what if a guy like Kip comes calling when Richard's too busy to be a father and husband, and if present circumstances are any indication, Mom, I'll be a lousy wife."

Patty's eyes crinkled; a smile quivered on her lips. "I don't think you're giving yourself enough credit, honey."

"I feel like I'm trying to justify a decision I've already made," she said and leaned back, hooking her elbows on the footboard, looking at her mother with open frustration. "And I don't like this feeling. The bottom line is, I've never felt with Richard how I felt with Kip in those couple minutes. He uh ... he was teasing, but he landed a kiss that knocked my socks off, and that's never happened. I've never felt that kind of attraction with any man, and I feel like crap because I wouldn't mind exploring that feeling a little more. So, what do I do? One or the other—not both. I can't have an affair while I'm wearing Richard's ring. About that, you're right, but if I don't find out what this is between me and Kip—if it's anything—I'll wonder what I might have missed for the rest of my life. How do I handle this?"

"Tell me something, hon," Patty said thoughtfully. "Have you already made up your mind to break your engagement?"

"Yes," Kelly said before she could even think twice. If nothing else, she knew she wouldn't spend the rest of her life with Richard.

"Even if you don't see Kip again?" Patty asked quietly.

"I'm going to see Kip again," she said with equal resolution.

"Then it sounds as if you've already made your decision."

"The wrong one, huh?"

"Does it feel wrong?" Patty asked carefully.

"That part doesn't," Kelly considered. "I'm just not sure how to tell Richard or what to tell him. I feel like I'm shafting him for another man, and in a sense, that's exactly what I'm doing. In the same respect, I've been having doubts and making excuses for a long time, telling myself I could make this work, that marriage won't be so bad, it'll get better once Richard finishes his internship."

"You're not excited at the prospect of marriage?" Patty asked with a peculiar gaze.

"It sort of feels like I'm looking at life to begin about two or three years from now," Kelly admitted miserably. "After his internship, after he opens his own practice, after we have the two children and a dog, he's mentioned on occasion. No, I don't think excitement comes into play. My saving grace is my studio. I'll still have that to keep me busy, and even that pisses me off," she said irritably. "Richard claims to support me, but he comes off so damned condescending, as if he's humoring me—letting me keep my identity out of the goodness of his heart."

"This has been bothering you for a long time, hasn't it, honey?" Patty said quietly.

"It's been building," Kelly admitted.

"Kelly, I can't tell you what's right or wrong," her mother said gently. "But I can tell you, it doesn't sound like you're ready to make a commitment to Richard, and it sort of leads me to wonder why you agreed to marry him."

"I'm twenty-seven," she said absently. "It seemed like I was running out of time."

Patty tried, but she couldn't stifle the soft laugh or quench the twinkling in her crinkled eyes. "Honey, you're not over the hill," she said with a quiver in her voice.

"Kip's only staying until Monday or Tuesday," Kelly said quietly, and her mother's laughter ebbed. "And now I really feel like a heel. I'd like to walk in, put this ring on my nightstand, and then go find him. And I can't do that either."

"Kelly, one little word of advice," Patty said quietly. "Don't rush into a situation where you could end up hurt. You really don't know Kip, and from what JD said, I don't think Kip's the kind of man who'd consider a serious relationship."

"Was dad?"

Patty stopped, and didn't need to answer. Her eyes transformed from pensive to a soft shine of amusement. Kelly had heard the tales often enough. Jarred Mulden had been the ultimate lady's man, wild and unruly, smart and witty, and considered a rogue in the decent little town where they'd both grown up, right up until one saucy little Irish girl turned his head and stole his heart. "Don't leave Richard hanging too long, dear, but do be gentle. He seems like such a sensitive young man."

"Do you think I'm a bad person, Mom?" Kelly asked quietly.

"I think you're an intelligent young woman who knows what she wants, and I think I feel a little sorry for Kip. That poor boy has no idea who he's dealing with."

At the sigh in her mother's voice, the mischief in her hazel eyes, Kelly stifled a laugh, but they were too much alike. Neither one could keep a straight face, and it seemed like an eternity since Kelly had truly felt like laughing. In fleeting seconds, they were both laughing, and it occurred to Kelly. That's what was missing the most in her relationship with Richard. Laughter. He never made her laugh.

Another snowfall had begun, but John Madison seemed not to notice the backwash of splatters between his flopping wipers. In fact, he appeared oblivious to holding the wheel of his Eldorado as he adopted his counselor's nuances to persuade Kip against stopping at Edgar B. Stone's Funeral Home. 'You didn't know the man personally, did you? Did Bill give you any indication that your presence was required?' When both his cross-examination and rebuttal had failed, Madison had simply relied on the most basic of excuses. 'We have reservations. We shouldn't be late. Saturdays are generally hectic even without Christmas so near.'

With the Eldorado stopped at the curb, Kip commented, "I won't be long."

"Be careful on that walk. It looks slippery," Madison commented, gracefully accepting defeat.

The roads were more dangerous than the sidewalk, Kip considered mentioning while stepping from the car. The walk was wet, not slippery. Rock salt crunched underfoot as he crossed the pavement to the grass-rug-covered steps. Pulling his coat closed against the winter chill, Kip ascended the steps beneath the burgundy canopy. Stone's wasn't as elegant as Fitzpatrick's parlor, but the aura of sophistication lingered—excluding the snap-in bulletin designating Victor E. Calfactor on display. Viewing: Saturday, Sunday 2-4, 7-9. Service: Monday 10 a.m. Kip slid his hat off as he opened the aluminum storm door. Judging by the empty spaces at the curb, the silence inside the receiving hall was no surprise.

Edgar B Stone, lean and sturdy in his black suit, stepped from his office doorway on the left, no doubt intending to hold the door. His solemn grin, a mourning grin, wavered with a glint of honest surprise. "Mr...."

Kip glanced at the two archways—one directly ahead, one to his right, parallel to Edgar. Accenting the burgundy colors, the walls were a pale pink with a paisley pattern. Another black, snap-in bulletin seemed to jump off the far wall, and again Victor E. Calfactor remained temporarily famous. Glancing off Edgar's gaze, Kip nodded acknowledgment and strode forward.

Within an undertow of subdued voices, Bickerman's low, reverent voice echoed, only slightly off-key from those days at Fitzpatrick's. A half-dozen visitors loitered in the parlor, suggesting that Mr. Calfactor hadn't been entirely forgotten. Several flower arrangements stood at either side of his casket. Beloved Husband. Brother. Grandfather. The accolades shined crimson from the arrangements on the gold silk lining of the open-lidded casket.

Too readily, Kip remembered the long fan of red carnations spread across the white satin-glossed lid. Beloved Mother. Her face—always faces—a strong, faintly lined face with only a hint of her actual age. He could imagine how she would look beneath that lid, but in his memory, she remained alive and well, awash in the glow of ambient lighting in the airport restaurant. He'd never seen her in repose. Would she have looked like Victor? As if she would awaken at any moment? Vaguely, he recalled wanting to yank open the lid. He'd started to turn, but Edna and Robert Fitzpatrick had stopped him. He'd meant to grab the emerald lid, reach inside, and shake her—maybe yank her out.

All right, Mother, the joke's over. You blew me away. Now, get up. Get out of there. Surely there's a meeting you're missing. Someplace to go. Something you must do. Wake. Up. God. Damn. You!

Jolting from the memory, Kip found Bill's startled expression. His lips parted beneath his thin mustache, apparently forgetting whatever he meant to impart to the old woman seated near the coffin. A wife? A sister? Kip cursed himself for not reading Calfactor's records. Instantly, he countered his thought. This was a courtesy call—a whim—and so what if he had no idea who survived the old man? The survivors had never mattered to him.

Bill shook from his surprise, striding forward with one of his most queer grins to date. Meeting halfway, Bill thrust out his hand, speaking in a discreet, anxious whisper. "Shit, buddy, you didn't have to come here. After this week, you don't need something like this."

"His wife?" Kip asked, glancing off Bill's intent gaze to the old woman.

"His sister, Ellen Braden," Bill said offhandedly, her name incidental. "Really, Kip. Why don't we step out? This can't be good for you—"

"Excuse me," Kip said and sidestepped, continuing his stride to the coffin. Victor Calfactor's color had improved to a waxy white. Edgar Stone hadn't altered the tranquility on his face. With no trace of amusement in his natural grin, Kip moved to the wet-eyed woman who sat gripping the hand of another younger woman—a daughter, perhaps—who appeared bored. She'd probably prefer to be home watching television or washing dishes. The older woman lifted her face with a broad, weird smile, the kind reserved for a ladies' social hosted in her honor. Odd—odd—odd—how differently human natures reacted to death. Only her dull blue color indicated her current state of distress. "Mrs. Braden?" Kip spoke while offering his hand. "Kip Patterson. You have my sympathies."

A startled expression swept across the round face. The daughter no longer appeared bored. "Th-thank you, Mr. Patterson," Ellen said in a fluster. "You know my daughter. Elaine Billings."

Why she believed he should know her daughter, a middle-aged woman of considerable size, Kip had no idea. Still, he remembered abruptly—the peculiar nuances of grieving loved ones. Extending his hand, he offered, "Mrs. Billings."

"It's Miss. I'm divorced," the daughter said dryly and grasped his hand firmly, her gaze intent. "I was sorry to hear about your mother. You have my sympathies. I know how difficult it must be for you to be here."

This niece of Victor Calfactor was more in tune than her mother; his initial impressions had deceived him. This woman had cared for her uncle; her misty eyes were anything but bored. "My mother would have wanted to be here," Kip said absently, honestly, and looked again to Mrs. Braden. "Again, my condolences." Excusing himself, he turned, nearly running into Bill, who started to touch his arm but retracted sharply.

"Could I speak to you a moment, Kip?"

"Tomorrow, Bill," he answered and strode across the thick burgundy carpet. Edgar stood in the entrance, his solemn grin intact, his aging face stressed. He extended his palm, clasping Kip's hand, then oddly, covering his second hand over Kip's. Something in his dark eyes conveyed approval; his voice carried a practiced soft sorrow. "Will you be here for the service on Monday?"

Not if I can help it, Kip nearly spoke aloud, but this aging mortician expected an affirmation. "I can't say for sure."

Edgar patted his hand, nodding and releasing his hold. "I'll see you then, Mr. Patterson."

Then? As in—*Monday*? Or *then* as in—*sometime*? Undecided, Kip strode to the arched entrance and stepped into the cold night air. Snow blew beneath the awning in thick flakes; a pickup truck passed the Eldorado, moving at a pace slower than an otherwise empty street should dictate. As Kip started down the steps, thinking he should postpone the meeting with Madison and be driven to the Home, his gaze caught on the blinking lights across the street.

Colored lights and the sudden revelation nearly halted him. Christmas. In four days, it would be Christmas.

Six days ago, Kip had planned to spend Christmas in a beach house with Morgan and her brother's family visiting from Washington state, not the district. Life certainly had taken a violent twist. No Morgan. No Mother to be annoyed with. No beach house plans. No dancers to buy, despite the one wrapped and nestled in his suitcase. He couldn't even remember why he brought the glass-blown ballerina with him. Another flea market find—

"Are you alright?" John Madison asked, breaking the silence within the car.

"Fine," Kip answered, doubting it. When the hell had he climbed into the car or lit a cigarette? Already, the Eldorado moved steadily against the splattering snow. In a swift, limited scan of passing houses, he recalled the trip to Stone's and his second thoughts on the front steps. "How far are we from the restaurant?"

"Not too."

"Lousy weather. I still have some scotch at the Home."

"Weather doesn't bother me if it doesn't bother you," Madison commented.

"The man doesn't like my scotch," Kip mused.

"The way you mix them, I'd pass out after two," Madison answered. "I prefer to battle the elements rather than a hangover. Besides, I have yet to be stranded in this car."

"The world was built on firsts," Kip answered while watching the windshield wipers. How did one manage to see beyond the splatters, wipers, and hypnotic glimpses of heavy flakes within the headlight beams? And concentrate on the highway? More than once, Kip caught himself more intent on the flakes than the road, only to snap to attention as Madison braked for a stoplight or a slower car in their path. Muttering a curse, Kip turned his focus through the side window. Madison's confidence offered no relief, but who was Kip to argue? God knows, he'd probably destroyed the rental's front end on his single jaunt, and at least another three inches of snow had fallen.

By the time the Eldorado stopped at the valet curb, Kip was grateful to climb from the velour seat. Without a doubt, Madison was no stranger to Le Chateau; both the valet attendant and the maître d' addressed him by name, and neither wasted time. Following Madison, Kip appreciated the quiet atmosphere. Despite the weather, many of the booths and tables were filled as Madison had anticipated. Conversations remained subdued between high-backed booths and candlelight, all set against a backdrop of soft, inoffensive music. Christmas music. Before they were fully settled in a private, corner booth, an attractive waitress arrived to take their drink orders and deliver the wine list and leather-bound menus. Candles burned in red tumblers on the table, and soft amber shaded fixtures hung over the center, offering just enough illumination to read the gold print.

On the doorstep of Whistlebrook, John had begun, 'I don't imagine this is a social visit.' And Kip had interrupted him then, asking if he'd mind detouring by way of Stone's. John hadn't spoken again, but in the brief silence after the waitress departed, Madison's curiosity returned in force. As Kip glanced over the wine list, he sensed John's scrutiny before the attorney spoke.

"I doubt you invited me for cocktails because you needed a drinking partner," Madison commented. "You have questions regarding your options?" he asked directly.

Shaking out a cigarette, Kip snagged a filter between his lips, still scanning the wine list. "Decent selection," he commented and held a flame to the butt.

Madison leaned back in the comfortable leather and lifted the dinner menu. "If you're hungry, the lobster's excellent here."

"Love lobster. It's the fresh scent of death that destroys my appetite," Kip answered and glimpsed Madison's startled eyes. "I'm not hungry," he added with a faint grin.

"After that comment, neither am I," Madison decided and folded the menu. "Somehow I don't believe you were merely referring to lobster."

"Suppose not," Kip commented while flipping the wine list shut, and glancing in time to see their drinks arrive. With slightly more interest, he noted the woman's smile, her straight short hair, and plain build. Lovely eyes, he decided, and turned his attention to his Manhattan. Not bad—not the drink or the brunette sliding into a chair two tables away. What *was* this new attraction to brunettes? A latent mother fetish? An after-effect of the stranger? *Kelly Mulden?*

"How are things going at the Home?" Madison asked lightly.

Turning an abstract focus to the attorney, Kip commented, "I'd prefer to discuss client-lawyer relationships, Att. Madison. More to the point, your loyalty to Marilyn Patterson versus your honesty with her heir."

For a moment, Madison held his glass, undecided whether to lift it or leave it rest. His gaze held steady, bathed in flickering firelight. "That I'm aware of, I've breached neither."

"Ronald E. Patterson. Tell me a story."

Madison's reaction was subtle, a mere shift of his focus, an indifferent waver in his cultured features. "I'm afraid that's not a long story. He was your grandfather. Marilyn's father."

"You're an attorney. You condone falsifying official documents?"

"Before my time, Kip. I only learned of your mother's deceit when we began the title search on Whistlebrook." He turned his glass, looking into it a moment, then lifting his gaze across the table. "As I understand it, you weren't aware of the deception, and although I wrestled with my moral and legal conscience, I saw no reason to publicize the facts. For your mother's sake, as well as yours, I've kept my knowledge to myself. If I've offended you and lost your trust at the same time, I apologize."

The words and expression dripped with sincerity.

"Tell me what the hell's going on here, John," Kip said evenly, dropping all pretense and theatrics. "Tell me why my mother chose to keep her right-hand man in the dark about the arrangements. Tell me why she went to the trouble she's gone to."

"Your mother was a private woman," Madison said, over-simplifying an answer. "She insisted we play this close to the cuff. And don't ask for an explanation, I don't have one. What I know is that the negotiations were sent through my office. The papers I brought to Whistlebrook were a fraction of the compiled data, and frankly, we'll need several hours on Monday before the public reading. I'd like you to see the financial reports and records before you finalize your decision."

"You've scheduled the event."

"Monday afternoon at 4 o'clock," he verified.

"Any plans for tomorrow afternoon? Say, one?"

"I imagine I'll be free. My office?"

Kip nodded, considering, "What do you know personally about Bill Bickerman?"

"He holds several degrees, and he had a background in hospital administration before Whistlebrook."

"Were my mother and he romantically involved?"

Madison hesitated, undoubtedly annoyed. *Jealous?* "I'm sure they were for a time; however, I made it a point never to ask."

"Strong vibes," Kip said absently, thinking about Ellie Baker without fully rationalizing his thought.

"I'd like to reverse the tables for a moment," Madison said lightly, his gaze intent. "Why do you play the fool with him? Why not allow him to realize you're potentially of sound mind?"

Faintly amused at the 'potentially,' Kip asked, "Don't you find it odd? My mother's second in command—and lover—believes her son's a moron?"

"Odd," Madison agreed, and wore an annoyed expression. "Extremely odd, considering the fact that she warned me never to underestimate you." An amused glint ran into his gaze. "Frankly, her words—He may look like a beach bum, but his top floor's loaded.'"

His mother thought he looked like a beach bum? "Apparently, she noticed my tan," he commented without affect.

"She didn't miss much, Kip," Madison said lightly and lifted his drink in salute before downing a swallow.

What else hadn't she missed, Kip wondered absently as he tipped his glass in response. *To you, Mother. May all your old lovers forgive you.*

With the decision made, Kelly relaxed long enough to join her family, which had multiplied by the time she and her mother emerged from the bedroom. Unfortunately, as she listened and engaged in more mundane battles with

Mike and his college roommate, a spicy little fellow with a crew cut and quick laugh, her thoughts inevitably turned to JD and Kip, the trouble that might ensue from that damned overheard conversation. JD hadn't returned from his alleged run to the mall hours earlier—a lot like her trip to the mall yesterday, no doubt. Whether he was meeting a stranger, or worse, spying on Kip from some dark corner of the Home, the thought annoyed her, distracting her enough to miss the youngster avidly—carefully—flirting with her between rows. Only later, after Tim departed, Mike cornered her in the kitchen and chided her good-naturedly.

"You do realize, you just broke my buddy's heart, right?"

"I'm turning that into an art form," she said without thinking. Her attention snagged on the heavy white flakes beyond the window. Catching up to her words, she found Mike's blue eyes sparking with a peculiar intensity. "But I'm not sure I'm following you. How did I manage that?"

"For starters," Mike said with a wry smile. "You didn't race upstairs and throw that ring in your fiancé's face the instant you met Tim. He's had it bad for you ever since I showed him that picture of you on Broadway." Smiling more, he commented, "You're the only famous person he's ever met, and I guess, in the looks department, you're no schlep."

"Ohhh, thank you. I don't think I could have lived without that compliment."

With the bravado and nonchalance of his twenty-two years, his face a close reflection of their father without the maturity, he shrugged, "Don't mention it. What are brothers for?"

She reached over, smacking him in the head, watching him duck and laugh, breaking his macho attitude.

"Seriously, Kell," he said, and she knew to expect the opposite. "You ever decide to drop your doc, Tim would marry you in a second."

"Now, you've really made my day," she said, enjoying his smile and mischief.

"Always willing to help," he said and sauntered from the kitchen.

Had her mood become so obvious that even Mike—who generally sailed in and out of the house like a tornado, pausing only long enough to wolf a meal—had noticed? In JD's absence, she and Mike had become close, close enough for him to read the signs without spoken words. Unless she confronted Richard soon, one or another of her brothers would apprise him of the situation, and God help him if any of them believed him responsible for her disposition. Defusing the Mulden boys could be pure hell, and that wasn't even counting her father.

In retrospect, Kelly considered the speculation in her father's eyes more than once during the afternoon, and Richard had won no points when asking her to tuck him into bed. Catholic. Good Catholic girls, raised in a family of good Irish Catholic parents, do not snub their faith under their father's roof. Ironically, she hadn't even considered how it might appear to them. Not once had she suffered an ounce of reluctance, knowing damn full well that she and Richard wouldn't do a damn thing in her room. She couldn't have been safer if she'd trucked up those steps with the parish priest.

Living alone, responsible for her own decisions, following her own set of principles ... never was she more grateful for her mother's ability to influence her father. Neither of her parents was naive to the ways of the world, but neither condoned the morals promoted by the sixties. It was one thing to know their daughter wasn't living the chaste life of a nun, another to have that detail crammed down their throats.

"What's the trouble, Kelly-girl?"

Startled, Kelly focused as her father continued into the kitchen. "Funny, I was just thinking about you," she said as he leaned at the counter.

"That explains the ears," he said as he crossed his arms, canting his head in a comic rendition of a man who might be 'all ears.' His near-sober expression foretold what Kelly expected. He hadn't failed to notice her mood any more than his sons. "Things all right between you and your beau?"

Sometimes the closeness of their large family could be too much to bear, and by no surprise, her father relied on a colorful word or phrase to break her mood. She smiled faintly. "Wouldn't surprise you one bit if I said, no, would it?"

"Don't suppose it's any of my business, me being an old man and all, honey, but I'll tell you true, I've seen more sparks fly between your Aunt Thelma and Uncle George than between the two of you."

Now she did smile, thinking of her dogmatic aunt and uncle who generally sat at opposite ends of any room they entered together. "That's not very nice."

"You're not happy with him, are you, hon?" he asked in a rare, entirely sober tone, his gaze searching and studying.

"I thought I was," she said carefully.

"You know, I was thinking, watching you two today," he said and turned, reaching for a mug, sidestepping to collect the coffeepot. His gaze darted over, bemused. "When I met your mother, hell, I couldn't see straight. I'd be sitting around with the guys, having a few beers, next thing I knew, I'd be on the phone or hot-rodding it into her driveway. If I got within fifty feet of her, I had to be touching her. Couldn't sleep some nights, thinking about her. It was pure hell."

Kelly smiled, thinking of her father getting tortured, and not finding it hard to imagine. For all her father's rugged charm and devilish nature, she'd grown up secure in the knowledge that a connection, untouchable, unbreakable, existed between her parents. When they looked at each other, even now, a certain secret seemed to exist between them, a shared knowledge, a spark.

"The point is, honey, I'm not feeling those vibes between you and Richard. He seems like a nice enough guy, a little on the stuffy side—and there's no denying, he looked tired when he came in," her father leveled his gaze, his voice hesitant. "But I'll tell you, honey, if I'd have driven five hours to be with the woman I loved, I damn sure wouldn't have spent that time falling asleep."

"He's been on a long shift, Dad," she said, cursing herself for defending him.

"Sweetheart, you've been here for three days," he hesitated again, seeming to weigh his words before resigning, continuing. "You've spent more time on the phone with Kip than with Romeo upstairs—"

"Dad—"

Her father donned a cocky smile and shrugged. "I have excellent hearing, Kelly-girl. Besides which, you're too much like your mother for me to miss the signals, and I'll tell you, I might not know Kip well, but I think you'd better watch your foot tomorrow, honey. I don't think he's nearly as shy as he was fifteen years ago, and he strikes me as a man who might be accustomed to getting what he wants."

Was her father warning her? Or encouraging her? That Kip had said nearly those exact words three nights earlier occurred to her. "I think you're right."

"Honey, if we have a brawl in the living room tomorrow, I'm holding you responsible," her father said with a kink in his lips. "Just bear that in mind."

"Richard's not a fighter," she tossed back offhandedly.

Her father's brow lifted; his eyes twinkled. "It's the quiet ones you have to watch out for, honey."

Kip. "You're probably right about that, too."

"Children," Jarred huffed and shook his head, taking his cup as he turned. "They do make life interesting on occasion." He stopped and looked back at her, a glint in his eyes. "Just don't sit Richard anywhere near the Christmas tree if you can help it. We have some family heirlooms we'd have a helluva time replacing."

"Dad!" she huffed.

He completed his turn, chuckling, "Don't say I didn't warn you, honey."

Part Three

Closure

Chapter 20

Behind the wheel of the Regal, Kip rested momentarily, considering the details contained within the files he'd spent the afternoon reading. That he found the Mulden residence remained secondary to the activity scrolling through his mind. Too well, he knew the hours upon hours of negotiating, researching, and planning that had compiled into the proposals John Madison had placed before him. Damn it! That sort of market analysis and planning only verified the reality. Marilyn had known she wouldn't walk the earth for an extended length of time, and with that revelation, as much anger as critical thought spiraled in his busy mind.

Automated, Kip stepped from the rental, bringing the wine bottle with him as he scanned the Early American-style home and accumulated vehicles in the driveway. For a moment, lost in thought, he stood, feeling the snow and the cold, wrapped within an abstract chill. A Datsun with Maryland plates, a Blazer … Jarred Mulden's Blazer. A late-model wagon, another rental, a white New Yorker with Maryland plates, and a black, sporty-looking Chevy.

Only as Kip passed the Chevy did he consider its resemblance to a car of yesteryear. Wrong year, but someone in the Mulden family shared JD's fascination for fast cars—a Camaro, Z-28.

By the time Kip reached the door and pressed the lighted doorbell, his thoughts had shifted, returning to the data. Preoccupied, he entered the house, extended greetings, and accepted introductions to Bryce Mulden and his wife, Arlene, as well as their children. In a formal cordial greeting, Kip logged Richard Whitman's name while accepting the offer of a cup of coffee.

Autopilot.

An atmospheric chill brought Kip closer to his reality. Across a comfortably large room, Kelly Mulden—magnificent in another fashionable skirt and blouse ensemble—rested alongside her lean, collegiate-dressed fiancé. Whitman wore a tie, expertly tucked down the point of a V-neck sweater, and that was some crease above his boat-style leather loafers. Amused, Kip realized he'd stepped out of his shoes at the door despite wearing a three-piece silk suit and tie. JD had made some comment about his suit—something about dinner being informal. Was it his clothes or preoccupation that faltered the conversations?

Undecided, Kip dragged a flame into a cigarette and found JD studying him from a cater-corner chair. In a split second, Kip remembered their last parting moments between the gates of Whistlebrook, and he understood the scrutiny, as well as the uncomfortable, forced conversations, trying to bear fruit. *Not mourning*, Kip could have explained, *information overload, JD*

Unfortunately, or fortunately, as the case might be, the instant Kip stifled his mental commiserating, his attention fell on the couple on the couch. Far more interested than he cared to analyze, he studied Whitman behind an abstracted gaze. What had Kelly found attractive about this starched shirt? She could do better. Much better. Nearly a full three inches separated her hip from his, and there was something in her tense posture to suggest his proximity disturbed her—and not in a good way.

"Did you get around to calling Darcy yet?" JD asked, attempting to sound offhanded.

"There's a Camaro in the driveway," Kip commented.

"Mike's following in my footsteps," JD mused with a glance at his younger brother seated across the room.

Kip glanced toward Mike, scanning the room and becoming more aware of his immediate surroundings, picking up subtle vibrations. Jarred and Bryce Mulden were seated close to each other, neither speaking. Bryce's oldest daughter, mid-teens, rested on the floor, staring at him rather than at the checkerboard between her and her brother. Richard should be playing the game—he leaned on his forearms, studying the moves. Momentarily, Kip focused on the board, sizing up the game, watching Whitman silently signal the boy, Bryan, on his next move. Bryan took the move Whitman suggested. Kelly seemed to be watching the game as well, but Kip wondered at the pensive expression on her lovely face. Not the same young woman who'd visited him two afternoons ago. In his living room, she'd been playful, smiling. Electric. Damn it, the last thing he needed was an infatuation. But to his sudden revelation, he knew he had never suffered infatuation. Romantic endeavors were convenient. He'd sworn off serious interest years ago. But if ever a young woman could turn a head. *And this asshole was playing checkers with teenagers?* A doctor. Dr. Richard Whitman, someone had said, and the fellow had strained, all blushing and modest, admitting, "Intern."

Dueling pistols, Kip recalled, and flashed another glance to the checkerboard as the teenager contemplated her next move.

On impulse, Kip pushed off his chair and stepped closer. Stooping opposite Whitman, noting Kelly's swift tension, nearly feeling it, Kip looked into Abby's startled, swooning gaze. "Believe it's your move. Mind if I assist?"

"Uh, nn-no," she stammered, looking down, trying to focus, and blushing. Her soft blue eyes lifted, pleading in a naive attempt to appear coy. "What do you think?"

Kip touched a finger into a checker and slid it into position before tipping his head to spy Whitman's condescending gaze. Doctors. What was it about doctors that created instant alarm? "Your move, doctor."

No blushing or modesty, now. The fellow accepted his apparent due and accepted the challenge. With a touch of arrogance, Whitman coached Bryan to jump the bait.

Knowing what to sacrifice and when was the key to victory. The game was technically finished by a single move; however, Kip dragged it out, coaching Abby in two more moves to remove five pieces and lock another four into jeopardy. Kip rose smoothly and started to turn.

"Wait," Abbey said anxiously. "We're not finished."

"You won, luv. Clean house," he answered, winked at her, and completed his turn, aware of Kelly watching him, more aware of his concentrated effort not to look into her magnificent eyes.

"Bet you're hell on a chessboard," Bryce mused.

"Shit," Richard said absently, only now realizing he'd lost the game.

Kip flashed an honest doubt over his shoulder, shrugged to Bryce, and returned to his chair in time to notice JD's amused glint.

"You really are a smartass," JD commented, casting his glance toward his sister, returning, more amused. "So, did you call Darcy or not?"

"Haven't had the time," he answered honestly, recovering his smoldering cigarette from the ashtray.

"You're leaving tomorrow," JD anticipated.

Hard to say. Informational overload. All circuits humming. Between the hospital files that Kip had read throughout the night—beginning with one puzzling, sexually-aggressive Ellie Baker, ending with Victor E. Calfactor—and the four and a half hours of reading in Madison's office, Kip suffered only bad vibrations. Something felt wrong—terribly wrong.

"You really ought to consider laying over for a couple days," JD said lightly. "You could always invite Morgan to fly in."

Vaguely, Kip recalled mentioning Morgan sometime after leaving Darcy and Rachel at the Ironside. "Morgan's no longer an issue," he commented idly.

JD studied him. "You broke up?"

"Obsolete," Kip considered, thinking about the old slang term, 'broke up.'

"What's that supposed to mean?"

"Why does a man choose Colorado to be a Ranger?" Kip asked and held JD's gaze, seeing thoughts spinning behind the hazel eyes. *Paranoia?* Something wrong.

"I like the mountains," he answered absently.

"Barring blizzards and possible frigid winds," Kip commented, remembering JD telling him to get in the Blazer, out of the cold air. Something ... what was it? Something out of sync. Out of tune. Without fully identifying the sensation, Kip noted Kelly's eyes fleeting, worry flashing. Informational overload. *Paranoia?* JD appeared nervous, seemed tense. Older.

"Take the good with the bad, I guess," JD said lightly. "What happened with you and Morgan?"

"You've always had an incredibly one-tracked mind," Kip said with a faint grin. "One of us put far too much emphasis on Morgan's existence in my life, and I doubt, I'd have made that mistake."

"You did happen to say you lived together," JD said with a fair amount of annoyance.

"Have I mentioned my terrarium?"

"Another subject change, or should I look forward to a lesson in Botany?"

"Metaphors, my old friend. I live with a variety of plants. I have different favorites about every two months." And hopefully, Kelly heard the message, loud and clear.

Mulden hesitated, understanding thoroughly, still annoyed. "If we hadn't gone out the other night, I'd probably doubt that."

"Hell of an attitude, Kip," Bryce mused. "Bet it gets you—"

"A male chauvinist attitude," the lyrical soft voice interrupted, drawing Kip's attention. By the lovely lady's steady gaze, his words had struck a nerve. Maintaining indifference, he enjoyed the hot glow of her eyes as she continued in a dry tone, "Do you consider all women shrubbery? Or possibly 'fish' would be a better metaphor? Reel them in on a good line, play them until you're bored, and throw them back."

"Certainly depends on the fish, I'd imagine," he said without offense, his gaze dueling hers. "Docile—*contented*—fish don't generally hit on any line." And she'd visited him at the Home.

"Is that right?" she asked dryly.

"Actually, no," he answered, truly enjoying her brilliant, angry eyes. "Most fish are governed by their stomachs. They bite on any edible bait; however, like all practiced fishermen, I live by certain rules of the sport. I'd certainly never reel in a Great White Whale. They mate for life."

"Like to fish, do you?" Jarred Mulden asked with subtle amusement.

"Certainly a satisfying sport," Kip answered easily.

"Sounds dangerous," Richard Whitman commented in a deeper tone, not blind or nearly as foolish as he appeared.

"Did you drive from Baltimore in that Datsun?" Kip asked.

"Yes," Whitman stated.

"Value your life, do you?" Kip commented and held the man's tense gaze.

"Kip," Kelly said bluntly and drew his gaze.

The word games, the sport of antagonizing a man he'd only just met, the nonsensical conversation... One look into her incredibly soft eyes and his indifference shattered. She was the same young woman who'd brazenly strode into his realm, throwing caution to the wind and pushing a few weird buttons. Had he attempted to fill his head with facts and figures only to combat this moment? Odd, very odd. She managed to distract him just long enough to realize what he was about to do, where this game had headed. Engaged. She was engaged. This pompous, lofty fellow with slicked black hair and a college education was her intended.

"Poor form," Kip commented with a slow donning smile as he continued to look at her. "Pistols would have been so much more fun," he said, and read her attempt to cover her smile. Relief and a spark of laughter ignited in her eyes.

Sighing, Kip looked at Whitman, who appeared lost. "Do forgive me, old chap. Kelly and I have been at odds since she sicced the family dog on me years ago. Afraid you've caught the fallout of that long-ago mishap."

"I didn't sic the dog on you," she protested with a bemused smile.

God, she was lovely when she smiled, and he'd apparently chosen the proper course of action despite the gut-wrenching anger behind his smile. "Did to," he said smugly. "I saw you. You took one look at me and sent that monster flying."

"I vaguely recall apologizing," she said.

"Ahh, yes, fifteen years later. And far too late. The damage was done. I'm stuck talking to plants and carting them around in my car for company." As several chuckles erupted, Kip turned his gaze, not missing the teenager eyeing him with open adoration. His attention landed on JD, who remained unusually quiet. "And on that note, JD... *Changes.*" The word dropped out of his subconscious like a rock.

"Excuse me?"

"Life thrives on change," Kip said as he heard Edna's voice. His thoughts shifted, suddenly, as if changing tracks. Several realities spilled from his subconscious as if scrolling onto a computer screen. In five years, Whistlebrook would have bankrupted itself and Marilyn Patterson. The Home had steadily lost money for the past several years, declining despite his mother's inflationary tactics. The death ratio ... *coincidence, damn it!*

Unconsciously, Kip stood up. Financial reports. The resident files. His mother's clientele hadn't changed over the past dozen years. The residents were still screened for solvency, a policy obviously initiated by his grandfather in the wake of the Depression. "Life thrives on change," he uttered as he strode to the door, leaning against the wall to pull on his shoes. His mother hadn't changed. She was not a creature of change—not in thirty years.

"Where the hell are you going?"

"Raincheck on dinner," he said absently. Sunday evening. The offices were closed. He needed to get into his mother's and Bill's office. The current resident files weren't the ones he needed to see. His focus found the closet. He reached for the sliding door. JD touched his arm.

"Hold on, Kip. Dinner's almost finished, and I promise, I won't pry into your love life."

Kip focused on JD. "Who told you—or implied—I wouldn't remain at Whistlebrook?"

JD considered a moment. "Aside from you, I overheard a couple conversations at the reception," he answered, suddenly intent. "Dr. Frances and uh...? Carolyn, I think. That Bickerman character alluded to the fact."

"You sat with Edna. Did she comment?"

Again, JD considered before answering. "I don't think she said one way or another. And you're not asking this out of general curiosity. What's bugging you?"

"The winds of change, possibly," he answered and slid open the closet, lifting out his long cashmere. As he slipped into it, he met JD's curious gaze, realizing abruptly, "I probably won't collect on the raincheck, JD, and I probably won't see you again." Holding out his hand, he read Mulden's sudden confusion as profound, now, as fifteen years ago when Kip had spoken nearly those exact words.

"Bullshit!" JD echoed the word from the past; his grip firmed. "Aspen and L.A. aren't that far apart. Why don't you give me an address—

"Like my favorite plants, JD, that changes rapidly."

"Then I'll give you my address," JD stated, his eyes changing, becoming annoyed.

"I'd only disappoint you," Kip answered and scanned the curious, confused faces. His gaze snagged on the magnificent green eyes across the room. "Broadway," he stated and winked at Kelly before landing on Jarred Mulden, who pushed from his early American rocker. In the same instant, Patty Mulden came into the doorway across the room. Kip glanced at her, then back to Jarred. "Thank you for the invitation. It's been a pleasure seeing you both again," he said as he shook the proffered hand.

"You're leaving?" Patty Mulden asked as she started forward, her curiosity rising. "We're just about to sit down."

"Accept my apology, Ma'am," he said. Glancing at JD's angry gaze with a faint pang of remorse, Kip clasped the door and started out. Behind him, JD grabbed a jacket and followed onto the porch. Halting, Kip caught the angry gaze, offering his hand. "Thank you for being here, my friend. Despite what you believe at this moment, your friendship has meant a great deal to me—"

"Bullshit," JD stated in a low, angry tone. "Friends don't burn new bridges. The last time, you didn't have a choice. You do this time, and I probably should have remembered the past. You didn't want friendship then, and you want it even less now. It still scares the hell out of you, doesn't it? It's still safer not to get too close."

"I wondered then, how long it would take before those words came back to haunt," Kip commented reflectively, studying JD's angry gaze. The past was gone, and he wasn't the same child who'd stood out of sorts in JD's company long ago. "Frankly, JD, I should have added several more words to those. I had no idea how to be a friend. To me, the words evoked thoughts of funerals. 'Undertaker' was a fitting nickname. I buried 232 friends before you and I met. Nearly attended my own funeral before we parted company." Looking into JD's hot gaze, Kip spoke simply, "Forgive me, my old friend, but I've come to prefer live departures. It leaves far more to the imagination and leaves less of a burden on the spirit. Now, if you'll excuse me? I have a prior engagement I'm obligated to attend."

"You know, I buried a lot of friends, too," JD said without a trace of emotion in his eyes. "I watched seventeen of them being picked up and put into body bags. There's not one of them I would have avoided knowing for a while."

"If you thought it would have kept them alive, would your opinion have changed?" Kip asked, watching Mulden's wheels turning. No more needed said.

Before he climbed into the Regal, Kip's thoughts had shifted into subconscious overdrive. No games tonight, no picking the lock to his mother's office and reading under limited light. No hiding under her desk in case Jack Gardner decided to open the door rather than jiggle the locked knob every half hour. A brief stop at the Presbyterian Church hall—he would make his appearance at the luncheon as promised—after which, he would find out where his mother had gone wrong.

Chapter 21

"Well, that was rather rude," Richard said quietly, interrupting the odd silence.

Not sure whether to be disappointed with Kip's departure or annoyed with Richard's comment, Kelly glanced at him.

Before she could raise a defense, her father commented, "Didn't think he'd stick around too long. Think it's probably starting to hit home."

"Think Uncle Justin will convince him to stay?" Abby asked while pushing off the floor, oddly glancing at Kelly for an answer.

"Doubtful, hon," Kelly said automatically and likewise pushed off the couch, deciding she better assist in the kitchen before she said something she might regret. She was halfway across the room when JD stepped into the house, and for a split second, she saw her brother's eyes, the eyes of a stranger. What was he really doing here? Why had he come? A setup?

Preoccupied, she joined her mother in the kitchen, catching a flashing glance of Patty's likewise distracted gaze. At least the Christmas tree was still standing.

From the living room, Jarred's voice carried, "I wouldn't be too hard on him, JD. Doubt he's thinking too clearly at the moment."

"Probably right," JD said and continued into the kitchen, striding to the coffeepot, and forcing a smile in Kelly's direction. "Pistols?" he asked discreetly. "As in dueling pistols?"

"Probably something like that," she said and smiled faintly.

JD shook his head, glancing toward the living room soberly. "Don't let it get that far, Kell," he said lightly and picked up his cup.

The warning again. What exactly did her brother know—or suspect—about Kip to worry him this badly?

Coming into the kitchen, Richard sidled behind her, clasping her hips and leaning over her shoulder as she emptied steaming corn into a larger bowl. "Can I help with anything, darling?"

"You could call everyone else in. It's time to eat," Kelly said distractedly, all too aware of the absence of sparks. Truly, there were no sparks. And Kip was leaving tomorrow.

Damn it, she had it bad. Just watching Kip enter the house had elevated her blood pressure. Between that cocky smile and his lyrical deep voice ... damn it. She needed only to think about the distance in his eyes. He'd seemed far away when he entered, as if on autopilot. Briefly, though, he'd loosened up to stomp Richard at checkers. At least that was better than dueling pistols.

She should have stayed in Philadelphia!

She should have spoken to Richard earlier, she countered silently. Whatever she thought they shared before today, it was gone, if it had ever existed.

With Sunday's extended visiting hours, Angie manned the reception desk, currently chatting with a lanky man wearing the familiar beige and brown security uniform. Preoccupied, Kip strode through the glass doors, barely glancing at her and Ted Dorsen, one of Frank Culver's underlings. The Oak Room doors stood open, and if the soft chatter echoing into the lobby was any indication, a half-dozen fourth-floor residents had come downstairs for an evening visit with friends and family. As Kip strode through the administration entrance, continuing into the secretarial wing, he halfheartedly wondered if he would soon hear the echo of the Baby Grand. How he'd loved to listen to that old piano and the rusty voices lifted in song. Shaking away the start of nostalgia, he switched on the overhead lights and continued to Carolyn's desk. Flipping through the address roll near the phone, he found Mark Frances's home number, memorized the number on impact, and lifted the receiver. A half dozen rings later, Mark's hearty 'hello' transcended the line, and Kip asked, "How soon can you arrive?"

"Kip?"

"Court jester," he answered. "How soon?"

"Twenty minutes. Is something—"

Kip dropped the receiver into its cradle and strode to the doorway, flipping off the light switch in his wake. In his room, he discarded his suit, changed into jeans and a flannel shirt, and remembered to put on his shoes. Someone was still in the kitchen. The familiar rattle of an industrial mop roller echoed into the corridor. With a glance and nod, Kip acknowledged Jason King while striding around the center island, taking the dry floor route to the refrigerator. Edna had taken the day off. No aluminum-foil-covered plate awaited him on the nearest shelf. A bowl of fresh fruit, several pans of various vegetables prepared for soups, cooked bouillon for a quick start on tomorrow's lunch menu, all on neat display and clearly labeled. On the bottom shelf, Kip found a container of cold chicken breasts.

Where did the leftovers go these days? Remembering, he rose with a piece of chicken in hand and snatched a couple of carrot sticks. Fifteen years ago, several of Randall's less fortunate residents had come to the kitchen door. His mother had never tolerated beggars, but a mother with mouths to feed or a father who'd lost his job...

Turning with his collection in hand, he nearly halted. Jason leaned on his mop handle, watching, wearing another curious grin. Shrugging, Kip moved to the silverware bin and snagged a fork before sliding into his private booth.

"Want a cup of coffee?" Jason asked.

Kip glanced at the industrial pot.

"I can get you a cup from the lobby," Jason anticipated.

Nodding absently, Kip turned his attention to the cold chicken, his thoughts turning inward to his revelations. When the cup arrived, he acknowledged Jason with a nod, still preoccupied.

"Is everything okay?" Jason asked.

Looking at the faintly worried youth, Kip understood. King attributed the abstract focus to mourning. Or drugs, considering some of the conversations the boy had overheard. "Thanks for the coffee."

"You're welcome, sir," he said politely, not reverently.

Strange kid, confident one moment, reluctant the next, but then, at seventeen or eighteen, that was fairly normal. Jason started to turn; an uncomfortable half grin lingered in his lean young face.

"You've heard a lot of rumors, haven't you?"

King halted, shrugging slightly. His expression conveyed a paradox of amusement and intimidation. "Probably a few."

"What do you find amusing?" Kip asked.

"It's uh—it's not really funny," Jason said lightly, leaning against the metal storage cabinet, apparently attempting a casual pose. His brown eyes betrayed his denial. He was still amused. His attention darted a moment before he decided, "It's sort of cool. They call you the Prince of Whistlebrook."

Concealing his momentary surprise, Kip commented, "An old title." He would have thought Jason reflecting on Bill sprawled on the kitchen floor. "What else have you heard?"

"A lot of people saying different things," Jason said while looking across the room, visibly uncomfortable. "I better get back to—"

"Elaborate. You won't offend me or risk your position here."

Hesitating, Jason weighed his options and the consequences. No doubt, now, he was thinking of Bill's demise. Decidedly, he met Kip's gaze. "A whole lot of bullshit. Some people think you're taking over here. Some people think you're a little ... crazy, meaning no disrespect. I think you're pretty cool. Other people," he shrugged. "They say you're gonna leave and not come back. I've even heard shit like you work for the government—some kind of secret agent." He appeared to regret those last words and hurried on. "The old folks, they idolize you. Like you're their savior. They uh—they say how things will change now. Some shit about the queen. Well, you know how they talk. I mean your mom—Mrs. Patterson—they really loved her."

"Something about the queen?" Kip urged.

More uncomfortable, Jason continued, "Just some shit. Like she promised them." He stopped abruptly and glanced about the room far too critically for his young face. His gaze returned, alarmed, concentrated. "One old guy...? He uh ... shit. This is probably nuts, but he pulled me aside. He asked me if I knew the Prince. Asked me if I'd deliver a message. I didn't think too much about it. Told him I didn't know you personally."

"The message?" Kip wondered absently.

"Maybe just forget it, ya know?" King said with a peculiar embarrassment flushing his face. "He was probably just pulling my chain because I'm new. The nurses upstairs… They warned me about taking anybody too serious up there."

"The message, Jason," Kip asked again, unwavering.

Shifting uncomfortably on his feet, he started off the cabinet, then settled back with a nervous grin. "Okay. But don't take it serious, okay? I mean, I wouldn't have given it much thought or uh … or gone out of my way to tell you this. Anyway, he said, 'The Prince is in danger. Someone's trying to destroy his castle.' Quote, unquote, if ya know what I mean." Jason appeared more apologetic, still nervous, possibly considering it a coded message. *Secret agent*? "Told you it was nuts."

"Did the message come from a man with Parkinson's disease?"

"He shakes a lot," Jason said with a shrug, his gaze more intent than he wanted to convey.

Louten wasn't senile. Vaguely, Kip recalled the rainbow colors of his aura, the predominant yellow in the halo. "When did he speak to you?" Kip asked lightly.

"Last night. About snack time. You uh … you don't think he was serious. I mean, there's—"

"Paranoia manifests early in stages of senility," Kip commented with an air of dismissal, his faint grin emerging. Glancing at his watch, he slid from the booth, handing his dish to Jason. "Put that in the sink, will you?" With an amused wink, he turned and strode through the administration door.

Just what he needed. An old man sending him a cryptic message via a kitchen aide as if his paranoia needed any fuel. Wire taps? Security guards casing the office? Official documents withheld and others fraudulent? And an uncanny feeling that something truly wasn't right in the kingdom. His mother had turned a profit in this Home for years. Maybe not a financial wizard, but she'd never lost a dime. God knows, she'd taken in residents whose bills had survived them, but she'd always balanced the scales in her favor. Ninety-four paying residents,. Add government grants and sizable donations of civic groups and private benefactors in need of tax write-offs. Whistlebrook should be solvent.

Kip strode around the corner in time to hear Angie giggle at something Ted said. At the sight of him, both sobered. Angie sat forward at her desk, almost comically trying to appear occupied; Ted started toward the coffeepot.

"Ted, hold up a moment," Kip commented. "I need assistance."

"Sure, Mr. Patterson. What can I do for you?" he asked, halted in a half turn, his face grim. His dark eyes darted, piercing the sudden haze of bright orange—further indicating his tension as he glanced at Angie, possibly to reassure her, and for just a moment, he looked as though he might reach for a weapon.

Ignoring the signs, concealing his annoyance at the cost of his little showdown with Bill, Kip commented, "Find the keys for the executive office, will you?"

"Sorry, sir, can't help you with that one," he said as if he'd rehearsed that line.

"I'd imagine Mr. Bickerman left orders to refuse my request," Kip said and watched closely, recognizing the lie in Ted's eyes. "May I remind you that I own this facility and I'm a vindictive son of a bitch when I don't get what I want."

"Sir, I'd really like to help," he started.

"The key, Ted, or I'll phone for a locksmith, and I can guarantee you won't have the certification to guard a rat's ass in the morning."

In a paradox of anger and intimidation, Ted decided, "I uh...let me see if I can find one."

"And Ted?" Kip waited for the dark eyes to focus, momentarily ignoring Angie's intimidation. "If you feel a need to call someone for advice, I suggest you speak to Frank Culver."

"I'll find a key," he said tensely and completed his turn.

As Ted strode across the lobby, Kip turned his attention to Angie, who dropped her gaze to an open ledger. A visible cringe stiffened her thin shoulders behind an aura of fear; her dark bangs failed to shade her tense brow. "Has Dr. Frances arrived?"

"N-no, sir," she answered with a sharp upward glance.

"When he arrives, send him to my mother's office," Kip commented before spotting the immense figure outside the glass doors. "Never mind," he tossed to her and strode past her desk, noting her shy sideways. He would love to know what rumor had spurred these young women to cringe from the sight of him. As far as he knew, he'd never so much as lifted a hammer, much less an axe, to be considered a murderer. Shaking his head absently, Kip continued to the courtesy table in the far corner. As he filled two Styrofoam cups, he listened to the voices echoing from the Oak Room. No piano sounds. In a vacant glance, he noticed the two elder women paused in the doorway, chattering softly.

"Prince of Whistlebrook," the words echoed softly, clearly.

Annoyed, angry, Kip retorted silently, *I'm no Goddamned Prince, ladies, I smash small companies for the hell of it, and my mother was probably afraid I'd tear down Whistlebrook before the ink dried on her death certificate. And I'm still not sure that I won't do exactly that.*

Dr. Frances stalked forward, his expression anxious and curiosity apparent under his arched brow. His bearded lips parted—

"Cream or sugar?" Kip interrupted idly.

"I thought, by God, this was an emergency!" Mark stated. "Cream!"

Ted emerged from the arch alongside the staircase, not happy, but holding the skeleton key in hand. He'd spoken to Culver. "I found it."

Kip held out his hand, his grin not friendly, his dry tone less friendly. "I had faith in you." With the key in hand, Kip lifted both coffees, handing one to Mark and motioning him to follow. "Glad you could make it," he said as they started into the administration wing. Without pause, Kip flipped light switches en route to his mother's door. No one had removed her nameplate, but that would undoubtedly be Bill's first official act tomorrow after the public reading of the Will.

"I hope you don't intend to keep me in suspense," Mark stated. "Not when I just spent an hour cooking and left my steak sitting on the table."

"Steak sounds good. Should have brought it along," Kip commented as he pushed open his mother's door and ignited the wall switch. "I attended two dinners this eve and just dined on cold chicken and celery sticks." No heavy lighting in this room. Standing lamps ignited, one behind the desk and the other by the front window alongside a comfortable upholstered armchair. Motioning Mark inside, Kip nudged the door closed as his focus wandered.

For two nights, he'd entered this room in the dark. In the soft light, a comfortable strength emanated, stirring thoughts of quiet evenings of reflection and intense conversations. His mother was here. Her aura remained as powerful in death as in life. In this room, within its conflicting masculine-feminine tones, she'd charmed or coerced at will. Dominated—

Yanking himself from his reflection, he caught Mark watching him and motioned the 'good' doctor to a chair near the desk. Sipping his coffee, Kip moved to the bank of the filing cabinets. He'd devoted the early morning hours to the latest files. The living residents. Setting his coffee atop the earliest dated cabinet, Kip stooped, scanning the designated dates in the small windows on each of the five drawers. Denominations of five years, he noted, and found the appropriate drawer at the bottom of the second cabinet. 1975-1980.

Pulling the drawer open, he scanned the cramped space within, impulsively pulling open the bottom drawer of the first cabinet. Not nearly the files in that drawer. Tipping his head, he read the date: 1960-1965. Not as many residents, more paperwork, All sorts of explanations could exist for the thin files. Pulling out each drawer of the first and second cabinets, Kip judged each one by its depth. Standing again, he looked into 1970-1975. Those five years hadn't shown any significant change. Only the 1975-1980 drawer maintained a cramped appearance. The turnover accountable to what? Social? Economic conditions? Paperwork? Impulsively, he pulled a random file from the pre-75 drawer and fanned through the forms. Replacing it, he stooped and pulled a file from 1975 at random. In a rapid fan, he verified—no added paperwork.

Focusing his attention, he fanned the 1975 file a second time. Slightly more slowly, he recorded dates, financial figures, billing schedules, added expenses, and the names of surviving relatives of Mrs. Rita Hamilton. Turning to the financial report, he read her assets. Loaded. Three houses, several cars, savings accounts, bonds, and insurance contributed to her wealth, and she represented Marilyn Patterson's typical resident. Smiling faintly, Kip stooped to replace the folder. Abruptly, he opened it again and flipped through the pages. He found the final billing statement and stopped. Unpaid? This typical wealthy woman had departed the world owing Whistlebrook twenty-nine thousand dollars?

Looking down at the cramped drawer, Kip frowned. Nothing's ever easy. Lifting out a handful of files, he settled onto the floor.

"Are you looking for anything in particular?" Mark asked.

With a mild start, Kip flipped open the first file while asking, "Did you and my mother have a falling out?" After several stopped seconds, he glanced over to read Mark's curious gaze—no alarm there.

"No," Mark answered. "What makes you think so?"

"You don't like Bill Bickerman," Kip commented, watching Frances attempt to disguise his disgust and dislike. A futile attempt with his colors shifting in the lamplight, becoming more curiously dark to signify his contempt.

"I respect him as an administrator," Mark answered, his entire relaxed pose becoming a practiced deception, as if trying to convince a family that cancer isn't an end-all.

"Your eyes betray you. Stop lying. You're lousy at it."

"All right," Mark commented with a faint grin. "The man's an ass. Better?"

"On principle? Or do you have a specific reason for your opinion?"

"He smiles too often."

Kip smirked a grin. "Certainly, concrete evidence to support your claim."

"I don't trust him, Kip. And I don't think you do either."

"You wanted to speak to me yesterday. About what?" Kip asked, remembering the message he had never received.

"I honestly didn't think he'd tell you I was here."

"A reason?"

"Because he probably assumes correctly that I'd try to convince you to stick around here, and I doubt he wants that to happen."

"Why would you?"

Mark shifted his gaze for the first time, his gaze distant with abstract thoughts. When his attention returned, his concentration returned, penetrating the gloomy light. "It's your home and I believe you need it as badly as it needs you."

Sincerity reigned in Mark Frances's gaze; Kip bayed his annoyance at the implications, remembering the absence of Mark's name on his mother's Will. "You and my mother were close."

"Extremely," he said lightly and tried to cover the well of sadness in his gaze.

"Romantically and professionally involved," Kip commented and watched the verification in Mark's disheartened gaze.

"Both for a time," Mark answered quietly.

Anger spiraled down Kip's spine, barely contained as he asked, "When did you meet her?"

"Twenty-one years ago," the doctor answered without pause. His gaze drifted, betraying his attempt to appear unaffected. He'd spent a lot of time thinking about Marilyn Patterson. Sipping his coffee unconsciously, his focus trailed to her empty chair.

Twenty-one years was about right, Kip realized, calling on his memories of the *good doctor* Frances. An older doctor ... Cullugan. Dr. Cullugan. The image materialize. A thin, angry face, dark eyes, a gray swatch of hair above either of his prominent ears. Papers fluttered in Kip's hands; an abstract chill yanked him to the present. "You—you replaced Dr. Cullugan," he said absently.

Mark's gaze returned, glancing off Kip's hands to his eyes. "I'd love to know what that man did to you," he said evenly.

Nothing in particular came to mind, but the chill lingered at his nape as he held Mark's focus. "What are your plans, now, doctor? Are you staying on as a resident physician?"

Losing all traces of either reflection or curiosity, Mark's voice became as concentrated as his gaze. "That'll depend on you, Kip."

"Excuse me?"

"I know that you have options," he said directly. "Your mother and I discussed those options, and frankly, son, this isn't something I'll discuss with you in this office."

"Excuse me?" Kip asked with only slightly more affect.

"Your mother and I took our conversations elsewhere at her request," he said soberly. "If you'd care to take a walk in the snow, we could continue."

A walk in the snow? Conversations elsewhere?

'Everything went through my office,' Attn. Madison had said. And Edna Feeney: 'She came here often the past while back.' "What the hell's going on here, Mark?"

"I wish the blazes I knew, son," he stated honestly, his eyes angry, too angry before he tore his gaze away and studied the window beyond the desk. "Damn it," he stated and pivoted his livid blue eyes. "Whatever the hell it is, I think it had a helluva lot to do with your mother's failing health, and I probably shouldn't be telling you this. The fact remains, your mother had a heart condition for years. I tried convincing her to retire as much as five years ago. We compromised. She slowed down a little, and we had her condition under control until about a year ago. I noticed a problem developing and tried my darndest to slow her down. I thought about contacting you," he paused, only anger lingered in his eyes. "She threatened suit under doctor-patient confidentiality, which—despite her sincerity—was *not* the reason I didn't speak to you. Specifically, I forfeited the argument when it nearly sent her into cardiac arrest.

"Something is going on here, Kip," Frances said gravely. "She was under too much stress, and she refused to speak to me about it. Always some off-the-wall explanation—oh, the usual, Bills need paid or one of the resident's failing health—or she was just feeling her age. And that was hogwash. She was back to smoking three packs and drinking four pots of coffee. And she resigned to dying."

"Did she happen to say why she didn't want me contacted?" Kip asked in a dead tone; anger and a strange boiling pain flowed beneath his surface calm.

"She said the words that convinced me about a serious problem. She said she didn't want you involved or hurt. After which, she tried convincing me that you hated Whistlebrook and you were hurt too badly as a child."

"That seemed odd to you, considering the fact that I nearly died that fall?" Kip realized.

"That you were hurt here, I have no doubts. That you were angry? Irrefutable. But you were also one of the most—if not the most—astute young men I've ever had the pleasure to know. You loved this Home. You loved the people here, Kip. Death, I believe, came secondary to that love.

"To answer you. Yes. I considered her reason odd," Frances admitted. "You're not an introverted adolescent suffering the pains of puberty. You haven't been a child since the day of your graduation and exodus.

"Besides which, until a year ago, your mother and I spoke a great deal about her plans to talk to you. A grand affair," his gaze shifted into abstracts. He played with his coffee cup, swirling the contents, watching the motion. Sighing heavily, a weariness haunted his bearded face, betraying his forty-nine years. "She was planning to invite you here for her sixty-fifth birthday. Thirty, she said. Old enough to have sewn plenty of wild oats." Mark's attention drifted with his thought, a soulful smile touched his lips before his gaze returned directly. "She knew you hadn't forgiven her for sending you away, but she also knew you'd forgive her when she invited you home to take the reins. That was her plan, Kip. Until a year ago," he finished heavily.

"Why are you telling me all of this?" *What's your game, damn you?*

"Because you're not an irresponsible, strung-out teenager," Mark said bluntly. "And I wish, by God, you'd have clipped that imbecile when you held him down."

"Good news travels."

"Edna worries," he said, his grin shadowed. "She wasn't quite sure if you were faking despondency or genuinely devastated, and though she enjoyed your performance, she didn't think it would be kosher if you landed in jail for assault."

"Do you think he'd have filed charges?"

"I don't have to think, Kip," Dr. Mark Frances said simply. "I paid the little weasel five thousand dollars in damages for throwing him a measly ten feet four years ago."

Abruptly, Kip's memory surfaced. His mother had spent ten minutes of an hour-long dinner telling him what an overgrown child the good Dr. Frances had become. 'With all his brilliance, you'd think he'd have more sense. Can you imagine? A *doctor!* Throwing an administrator! Thirty feet down a hospital corridor! Only at Whistlebrook—' "Why?" Kip asked.

"He smiles too much," Mark answered with a faint amusement and a shrug. "Aside from that, the ass threatened to sue me for lowering an anti-psychotic." Again, he shrugged, enjoying his memory. "Suppose I should have belted him."

"I'd imagine it would have cost you more than five thousand," Kip commented indifferently. "How many patients do you have here, now?"

"An even dozen," he answered, faintly amused again. "I have a decent private practice. Truth be known, I keep a dozen to annoy Bill. Your mother and I haven't negotiated a written agreement since the day she threatened to sue me for malpractice over you."

"You called her a bitch."

Amused, Mark nodded absently. "Doubted you'd forget that; however, she was behaving accordingly as I recall." His focus misted into abstract thought, trailing toward the window.

Kip remembered, too, through a fog. Lying on an examination table, floating on valium. Dr. Frances had wanted to ship him to Richland Hospital; Marilyn had refused and called the good doctor a quack. The memory stuck as one of the few times Kip had ever witnessed anyone other than Edna Feeney stand up to his mother. "She threatened your license," Kip remembered.

"She did," Mark confirmed, suffering a smile with his reflection. "And I believe that was the day I realized how incredibly bright you were. You knew you were—"

"Bill believes I'm a moron. My mother's doing?"

"I'd imagine so, but don't ask me for an explanation. I don't have one," Mark said honestly, shrugging as he collected his thoughts to the present reality. "Perhaps, she simply didn't like to share you with strangers. She had a habit of keeping her greatest loves private."

Private. But she certainly spread it around. Damn it!

Should her discretion console him? Her privacy? Her secrets? For Chrissake, what was it? Some warped obsession with love? The great Queen of Whistlebrook couldn't be caught loving someone? Not even her own son? Or was that another quirk? Possibly the explanation? What had Mark just said? Not what he said, Kip realized, the way he'd said it. Mark knew her past? Her mistake? With greater intent, Kip studied Dr. Frances' misty gaze, which was once again focused aimlessly on her empty chair. *Damn it. Quite a harem you had, mother. And they all still love you.*

Shaking his head, Kip dropped his attention to the folder on his lap. Without a doubt, she'd never wanted him to return, and that detail made perfectly good sense. She knew he'd uncover all her goddamned secrets. What was this? Her ultimate idea of justice? Her ultimate hit and run? From the grave? All this Prince of Whistlebrook shit. A Goddamn Fairy Tale! Maybe *she* had believed him a *moron!*

Abruptly, Kip stared down at watery print, unable to decipher a single word. *Bankruptcy. Damn it, concentrate. Find the cause—*

"Why?" he uttered aloud.

"Kip?"

Impulsively, Kip slapped the folder shut and slid the stack to the floor, pushing to his feet. He needed some time to think, to be alone with this new wave of—of *annoyance.* "Why don't you get us another cup of coffee?" he spoke as he strode to the door, not looking back. "I'll be back in a moment."

Without awaiting a reply, he sped from the room and passed through the adjoining rooms. Too much. Too many walks down Memory Lane. He should have gotten the hell out of here two days ago. Secrets and lies. His entire life had evolved around secrets and lies. Fairy tales! Inside the private suite, Kip leaned, his back to the door, staring vacantly at the floor as the anger spiraled through his taut lean frame. Secrets and lies! Deceptions! Was it any wonder he thrived on conspiracy and deceit? Was it any wonder he thrilled to watch buildings destroyed, never waiting around to watch the reconstruction. Buy cheap. Blast the fuck out of things. Sell high. *I'm no moron, Mother, but I do love destruction. And that much you knew.* She'd probably known he kept watch over this white elephant. Like the specter of death, keeping silent vigil, becoming the gray cloud to hang over the roofs and eaves. An Undertaker.

He could have buried her! He could have buried her and this whole fucking Home; the same way he buried her goddamned prehistoric dance studio!

Rage swept through him, a need more potent than ever before, and with a subtle shift, his coal-gray eyes fell on the dancer, standing so arrogantly within her glass crypt. Destruction! He *needed* to destroy something, and how much that pert-faced statue reminded him of Marilyn Patterson. The coquettish tip of her head, aloof and scoffing!

"Bitch!" he snapped and pushed off the door, striding to the console. Like a Queen in an ivory tower. But this was glass ... and glass breaks! He lifted the dome, his hands trembling with fierce restraint. With a controlled, careful hand, Kip set the dome aside and reached, tentatively touching an index finger to the cold porcelain. Oh, this one's dead—no doubt about it—and the queen had loved this one. In a firm, angry grip, he held the Wallendorf in one palm, feeling the curves of the scantily dressed frame against his sweated palm.

Poise! His mother screamed inside his reeling mind. No tantrums. Never allowed to throw tantrums. *Quiet, Kippen!*

"Fuck you!" he demanded and lifted the statue, his gaze falling unwittingly to the photograph of him and his mother, his graduation. Another joke! A seminary prep school! He hadn't even been baptized a Catholic until *after* his enrollment! "Damn you! Just *damn* you for creating me!"

He barely started to slam the statue down, his action halted, frozen against the tremble racing through his heated muscles. A greater rage swept through him as he realized his inability to smash the figurine—his mother's favorite—as if he'd smash Marilyn Patterson through the statue! In a violent paradox, he gripped the chilled china in his left hand as his right swept down, grabbing the wooden base instead. Pivoting, Kip propelled the ornate disk across the room, watching, not thoroughly satisfied, when it shattered against the shiny oak door. The statue would have created a louder blast. The wood emitted a mere thud and thump-thump as it landed on the carpet. Minor chunks of carved cherry wood rained down on the soft brown carpet. Not nearly as satisfying as a thousand shards of glazed pottery exploding. With his mind fine-tuned to notice discrepancies, he barely shifted his focus to the statue when his attention pivoted to the scattered base. The base had been almost featherweight in his hand, not weighted as it should have been to offer the delicate figurine a safe pedestal, and what was that thick white corner jutting from beneath the chipped disk?

Chapter 22

My Darling,

I pray you have found this, and my words are not falling on the wrong ears. If it is you, Darling, then I assume you have received my letter from John. There are so many things I wanted to say in that first letter, but I dare not write too much. I feared that letter might see other hands by no fault of John's.

If you've found this while packing to leave, then goodbye, Darling, and have no regrets. In my absence and yours, whatever's going on here will cease under the new policy.

If you found this note in a deliberate search for answers, then you are considering taking control of Whistlebrook. As much as that pleases me, it also worries me tremendously.

Something's happening in our home, Darling. As much as two years ago, I noticed my books not balancing as they should. An indicator, not a serious problem. An increase in debt and inflation, an increase in services and staff to accommodate the cancer and physical therapy areas. I expected that. And truthfully, the decrease in profits wasn't a serious concern. We Pattersons have never remained destitute for long. Your grandfather used to say we had the Midas Touch.

The problem then wasn't a loss in profits, though, should it continue, I don't imagine I'd have kept the Home too long. I let it ride and watched the books more carefully over the course of several months. Check the d. resident files, Kippen. You've always had an eye for detail. You'll see what I saw.

I should have gone to the police. Considered it, truthfully, but I don't know to what lengths these people will go. If you've been here any length of time, Darling, you might have noticed the atmosphere. Our residents are scared. They're old. They're not ready to die. Those who will talk will not talk to the police. They may speak to you as they have me.

A ring of thieves exists in our home, Kip. They're stealing our residents blind. I've tried finding out who's involved, only to question my own paranoia. I'm an old woman. Perhaps I am paranoid. Perhaps, there's nothing at all going on, and it's my age showing. God knows, the cases are sporadic. It's the pattern that disturbs me. Two or three a year, always in declining states, not many surviving relatives.

Paranoia again, perhaps, but I feel as if I'm being watched—monitored. I don't want you hurt, Darling. I've kept you in the dark, hoping to protect you through ignorance. I truly don't know if you want Whistlebrook. If you do, then be careful. Trust only the names I give you now—Edna Feeney, Mark Frances, John Madison, and Frank Culver. No others until you find proof of their innocence. God knows, I'd like to add Bill's name, but he's an odd man. I've tried determining his innocence. Evidence points to him, then away from him. I just don't know, but don't judge him on appearances. He could end up a sheep in a wolf's cloak.

Again, my Darling, if you have opted not to accept Whistlebrook, have no regrets. In our absence, Whistlebrook will change. There will be no opening for thieves.

If you have decided to take up the staff. Welcome home, Prince of Whistlebrook.

All My Love, Mother

"Damn it," Kip muttered absently. "You, too." *Prince of Whistlebrook.*

Letting his hand drop with the letter, he rested on his knees, momentarily gazing at the fallen—damaged—base. Ellie Baker's warning—Mr. Louten's warning via Jason King, a new employee. The names his mother designated, three of whom he'd already spoken to, deciding for himself, their innocence and their loyalty. She hadn't entrusted them with her problem, but each had stood beside her. *Protection.* For their protection, she hadn't confided in them. Keeping them in the dark for their safety. *Paranoia.*

Dr. Frances knew more. 'A walk in the snow.'

Folding the two pages, Kip tucked them into his back pocket, pushed into a stoop, and collected the pieces of the base. His anger had disintegrated; he picked the Wallendorf from the carpet, more carefully lifting her as he pushed to his feet. Automated, he returned to the console, fitting the base together, replacing the statue and glass dome.

As Kip strode up the hall, he heard Angie offer a departing visitor a pleasant "good night" and "Merry Christmas."

After a talk with Mark, he'd go through the files, the d. resident files and current employee records. Less than twenty-four hours. Preoccupied, he strode into his mother's office expecting to see Mark Frances. Less than twenty-four hours to find enough evidence to call the police and clean house. Which is what his mother should have done.

She might still be ali—

No. He pushed that thought aside, concentrating and realizing Mark's absence. Still out for coffee? No. Both cups had been refilled. One rested on the desk, one on the floor near the folders. Keeping his coat over his arm, Kip strode out, closing the door behind him and striding through the secretarial pool.

A mid-aged couple stood signing out at the reception desk. Angie extended another "Merry Christmas" along with a cheerful, "See you next Sunday." Apparently, she often covered the Sunday visitor hours. The elder man tossed his words lightly, "Have a good Christmas, Ange."

Only as she spotted Kip, her friendly smile wavered into a wary grin. No others occupied the lobby, and by her desperate glance at the departing couple passing through the glass doors, Angie harbored a serious fear of the Prince of Whistlebrook.

"Did Dr. Frances leave?"

"Oh—" she appeared almost relieved. "No uh. I mean, he's still here. He got beeped."

Beeped? As in paged?

"I mean, his answering service called. He used this phone. Turns out it was for here. Dr. Nagel phoned. Anyway, he went up to check on one of his patients," she huffed the words, her voice racing. "He said he probably wouldn't be long." Her glance darted past Kip toward the entrance; her attention divided with a flash of appreciation, then too abruptly—alarm?

By her focus lancing him, Kip suffered a chill before turning to see JD Mulden striding toward him. In Mulden's wake, the glass door snapped shut and halted the cold blast of winter air as effectively as an air conditioner vent closing. Mulden's smile wavered, an expression of apology combined with his 'So, I shouldn't have come. Never stopped me before.'

"You were wrong. Can we talk somewhere?" JD said as he stopped three steps away.

Knowing Mulden even slightly, a simple 'no' would be futile. Faintly annoyed, Kip glanced toward the complimentary coffee table. "Coffee?"

Mulden glanced at the coat in Kip's hand, "Going out or coming in?"

"In," he answered absently, ignoring Angie's curiosity. "Get a cup. We'll talk in the office." Turning his focus to Angie, he commented, "Send Dr. Frances in when he comes down."

"I will, sir."

Sir. Sir Patterson, Prince of Whistlebrook. *Bullllshit!* Masking his annoyance, he stood momentarily gazing into abstracts toward the front door. When JD came beside him with a cup in hand, Kip turned, motioning him to follow.

Holding the office door for JD to pass, Kip stepped inside behind him, hooking his coat on the brass stand before striding to the file cabinets. Stooping, Kip collected the folders and his coffee from the floor, then meandered to his mother's desk. For a long moment, he stood, not entirely sure why he paused. Her chair. Never once had he sat in her comfortable leather chair. Even when he used her office on his brief stops, he generally sat on the desk while placing his calls. The high back chair was her throne—

"Your mom's office," JD intruded deliberately, his gaze darting, admiring. "I came in here once. It's still as grand as I remember."

Appreciating the interruption, Kip shot Mulden a glance, then, a little awkwardly, delivered the folders to the felt mat and sat sidesaddle on the desk while lifting a cigarette pack from his shirt pocket. Mulden loosened his leather jacket, settled into one of the receiving chairs, and set his coffee near Mark's cup.

As their gazes met, Mulden's sobriety intensified. "I was going to say okay and let you walk away again, then it hit me. You had the last word again, and you were always a little left of center."

Indeed, not a compliment. "Insane?" Kip wondered.

"Off center," Mulden repeated. "Not insane, at least not completely. In any event, I have no intention of dying young, which means we have a helluva long time to enjoy a lasting friendship. It's not as if I'd make any heavy demands on you. Christ knows, I'd never hold my breath for a letter from you, and you apparently haven't changed your opinion about returning calls."

"I return calls," he said in his defense, annoyed at reacting.

"Right," Mulden mused. "You probably still let them pile up on your desk. Until you arrived tonight, I wasn't sure you even got the directions I left for you."

Directions? Messages? *Damn it*. Probably on Carolyn's desk. Impulsively, Kip pushed off the desk and strode through the offices to Carolyn's desk. His messages rested in a neat pile under the corner of her telephone base. Dr. Frances had returned his call three times. Once last evening, twice today. JD had called twice; the second time, he'd left directions to his house. Morgan had called once today and left the number to reach her at the Cabana. Marsh had called twice, leaving no number or message. Several other familiar and unfamiliar names scrolled in Carolyn's neat script—she should have been an artist. As Kip turned to return to the office, he spotted Dr. Frances coming through the doorway.

A heaviness appeared in the good doctor's eyes. Something wrong. With an internal alarm, Kip halted, his attention riveted on Mark's grim attempt at a smile through the dull rainbow colors. "A problem?"

"Unfortunately, yes," Mark answered. "Bill's on his way over." He stopped; his gaze evaded Kip's momentarily, glancing at the notes, then toward the office doorway. "Why don't we continue our discussion in your rooms? I'm sure we'd both be more comfortable."

Comfort was the least of Mark's concerns. Bill coming? Unfortunately? "Someone passed away," Kip commented absently and read Mark's disheartened verification.

"Unfortunately, yes," Mark repeated quietly. "A woman I didn't expect to last as long as she has."

"The holidays are a bad time to die," Kip commented offhandedly, watching Mark's dread. *Mrs. Taylor?* "Her name?"

"Why don't we let Bill handle this, Kip?" Mark suggested in a more assured tone, his gaze steadied by force. "Really, son, I don't think you need anything else on your mind at the moment."

"Her name," Kip repeated.

Dread rolled across Mark's dark blue eyes as he realized the futility of evasion. "Elsa Taylor," he said heavily. "Kip, she's been terminal—critical—for months. There wasn't anything we could do except make her as comfortable as possible."

A flash of the lovely little woman's face swept through Kip's mind as he nodded, completed his turn, and strode to the office. Father Jordan had anticipated Mrs. Taylor's end, and even without his talent to see the gray shroud around her silver cap, Kip had recognized the signs. Her little-girl eyes glazed on morphine, struggling with pain and reality, able only to grasp his hand in a meager touch. But her shadow, the cloak, wasn't dark, not as dark as others. He'd seen her. He'd sensed her impending death, but not ... *damn it*. He would not, could not allow himself to think about his blasted talent. She was dead. Her time had come.

Automated, Kip moved to his mother's desk, lifted the stack of folders, and returned them to the appropriate drawers. He barely started toward the desk but halted. Impulsively, he turned, strode to the current resident cabinet, and waded through the second drawer, finding Elsa Taylor's file. With it in hand, he moved to his mother's desk, not fully considering his actions as he turned the chair to receive him. Unconsciously, he lit a cigarette, crossed an ankle over his knee, and opened the folder on his lap.

"Kip," Mark spoke quietly. "If that's Mrs. Taylor's file? Why don't we let Bill take care of this?"

Mrs. Taylor's paperwork remained in order; her bills paid by a surviving son who held power of attorney. Doubtful this was the son's real name. As Kip had verified only the night before, this file was a dupe to cover the old woman's true heritage. Marsh had probably collected the facts by now. Lifting her alleged personal history from the folder, Kip slipped the pages to the felt mat beside him. Still in automation, he rolled the chair backwards a step, opened a drawer, and fanned over folders before finding 'Death Certificates.' He lifted one and sent it sliding across the mat toward Dr. Frances. Ignoring both gazes, again looking at Taylor's file, he commented, "I'd imagine you need to fill that out."

Glancing over the pages in Taylor's file, Kip removed another sheet, then closed the file and rested, reading over the death arrangements. Mrs. Taylor, of the Richmond Taylors, would be laid out at Fitzpatrick's and buried in the Catholic mausoleum in Mt. Oliver Memorial Park. Kip's gaze trailed off the page, through the side window into darkness. How would Marilyn Patterson manage this event? What did she say to a husband, son, or daughter, a grandchild, when this moment came? What did she say to Fitzpatrick or Stone?

"Kip," Mark said quietly. "Bill should be here at any moment."

Kip glanced at Mark, understanding his genuine concern. The death certificate was filled out. "Let me see that, will you?"

Hesitantly, Mark leaned forward, handing the certificate across the desk.

Mulden sat uncomfortably, unusually silent, glancing between Mark and Kip, sipping his coffee.

Cause of death ... ultimately, cancer. Lifting his attention to Mark, he asked, "What took her? Kidneys, lungs, heart?"

"Cardiac arrest," Mark answered quietly.

Nodding, his focus trailed over the desk. Less than a week ago, the woman had grasped enough reality to make a connection between his name, his unfamiliar face, and a collection of old stories. Only yesterday, she hadn't retained even the ability to speak her name. Again, focusing on Mark, Kip asked, "Did she take a sharp turn for the worse this week, doctor?"

"Kip, she's been steadily declining," Mark said quietly. "There wasn't a thing we could do for her."

Nodding again, he laid the certificate on the folder and started to lift both to the desk as the telephone buzzed an inoffensive note. He hesitated before lifting the receiver and pushing the lighted in-house button. "Yes?"

"Mr. Bickerman?" a hesitant voice asked.

"No, but you've reached the executive office. Do you have a problem?" As if he needed to ask. Anyone calling this number at this hour on a Sunday evening would have a problem.

"This is Dr. Nagel, intern in residence. Could I speak to Mr. Bickerman or er ... Mr. Patterson?"

"You're speaking to the latter of the two. Problem?"

"I'm in North Tower Three, Mr. Patterson. I've sent for Dr. Sheffield. Mr. Seratti just passed away."

A cold knot gripped the pit of Kip's stomach as if he'd just swallowed—or been struck—by one helluva snowball. Another one. Two in one evening? "How long ago and what cause?" he asked in calm control that he no longer felt.

"Ten minutes, sir. Cardiac arrest. And, sir?" Nagel paused. "Mrs. Lonnigan on E-Two is going into renal failure. I doubt she's going to survive the night. If she has family, they should be notified."

God Almighty! Three? "Anything else?" Kip asked in a deadened tone, his stomach wrenching, twisting into a tighter icy ball.

"I'm going back down to E-Two. I've had Mr. Seratti sent downstairs."

"Thank you," Kip said absently and lowered the receiver. Seratti. Lonnigan.

"Kip?" Dr. Frances asked lightly. "Is everything all right?"

No. Everything is not all right, he might have answered. Instead, he pushed from his mother's chair and strode silently to the current cabinet—emptying rather quickly, it seemed, as he located both names and removed the files. Returning to the desk, he set Seratti's file aside and opened Lonnigan's file. As he sorted through the admissions records, he prayed that no one needed to be contacted. Oh, but of course someone required notification. The woman had a husband. *Good God, she was only sixty-two!* Young compared to the median age of Whistlebrook's residents. Survived by a husband and four children. The eldest son's name appeared first on the emergency contact list.

Without thinking, Kip lifted the receiver, connected an outside line, and dialed the son's number. Christmas raced into Kip's mind as he waited through four rings. At the child's 'hello,' Kip asked, "Could I speak to Paul Lonnigan?"

A screamed "PAAAUL" pierced his ear. Seconds passed before another young voice asked, "Yeah? Mat?"

Wrong Paul Lonnigan. "Is there an elder Paul Lonnigan I could speak to?" he asked before a second scream assaulted his ear. "DAAAD! It's for you!"

More seconds passed before a husky voice drawled, "Y-ello"

God. "Mr. Lonnigan? This is Kip Patterson from Whistlebrook Nursing Home. I've just been informed that your mother's condition is declining rapidly. I'm sorry, sir, but she's not expected to survive the night."

"Oh, Jesus," the son hissed softly, his cheer abandoned, crushed. "Uhhh … I have to call … have to go pick up my dad. We'll be there in a half hour."

At the clatter and silence, Kip replaced the receiver, glancing down the admissions sheet. Again. Cancer. Shaking his head, he closed the folder and slid Seratti's file in front of him. *Shit—shit—Shit!* Mr. Seratti was only sixty-five. His wife, fifty-eight. Survived by a mother, four sons, and two daughters. Again, the oldest son was listed to be notified.

He hadn't called Elsa Taylor's son.

Automated, Kip lifted the receiver and dialed. A man answered. "Emmett Taylor?" "Yes?" the surly voice asked. "Kip Patterson from Whistlebrook Nursing Home. I'm calling about your mother, Elsa Taylor."

"Yes. She passed away?"

Indifferent? "I regret to inform you, yes, sir."

"She still there at Whistlebrook? Or at Fitzpatrick's?"

"You're the first to be notified, sir. I'll be speaking to Mr. Fitzpatrick in a moment."

"Well, then, tell him I'll call him in the morning," the man said heavily and hung up.

"Bastard," Kip commented and dialed the number from Seratti's sheet. Again, a child answered, and Kip listened through an echo of shouting and laughter before a friendly voice stated, "Eh, Pisano. Merry Christmas."

Damn. "Vincent Seratti?"

"Yes?" the voice sobered abruptly, alarmed.

"Kip Patterson from Whistlebrook Nursing Home. I regret to inform you, sir, your father, Vincenzo Seratti, passed away a few moments ago."

"He...? Goddamn it! No!" the man demanded. "If this is a fucking joke—" The man had reverted to Italian; his voice stopped, the silence deafening through the receiver. Even the background din had silenced.

Speaking in Italian, Kip stated, "My apologies, sir. Truly. This is no prank, I assure you."

"H-how, for Chrissake, I just saw him a couple hours ago! He—he was fine!"

If Vincenzo Seratti was 'fine' at sixty-five, he would be home with his wife, not in Whistlebrook. With his thought, Kip answered, "Regrettably, sir. It happens that way sometimes."

"Who...? Who did you say you are?" the strained deep voice asked.

"Kip Patterson, acting administrator." *Acting* was right, *Goddamn it*! He should have left this to Bickerman!

"You ... shit. Yeah. Did you...? My mother wasn't called, was she?"

"Not yet, sir. Would you like me to place the call?"

"Uh ... no. I better—better go see her in person. They had the arrangements made, though, right?"

Kip flipped the folder open, reading swiftly, "Yes, sir, they do. I'll contact Cellini's." *Right after Fitzpatrick's.* As Kip completed the call with Mr. Seratti, he flipped open Mrs. Lonnigan's file. Edgar B. Stone. Replacing the receiver, he leaned back, barely glancing at the flame as he lit a cigarette. His stomach hadn't lost its fitful knot, but for the moment, he could refrain from vomiting.

"Are you all right, Kip?" Mulden asked carefully.

Nodding to JD, Kip found Mark's studied, worried gaze and grim smile. "There's a Mrs. Lonnigan in E-Two. I'm ringing the station, and I'm authorizing you to review her chart. If there's anything you can do for her, do it. The woman's only sixty-two."

Mark stood up from his chair. "What's her condition?"

"Renal failure," Kip answered as he lifted the receiver, punching the code for the second-floor nurse's station. "Kip Patterson," he stated. "Your name?"

"Allison Hawkins."

"Allison, Dr. Frances is on his way. Have Mrs. Lonnigan's chart ready for him. He's accepted the position of Chief Physician of Record. Supply whatever he needs."

"Ye-es sir, Mr. Patterson."

At the door, Mark Frances halted shortly, wearing one of his more cautious expressions. "When, exactly, did I accept that position?" he asked.

"When you stood up," Kip answered and held his gaze. "After you've seen Mrs. Lonnigan, contact me here, doctor."

Frances hesitated, then spoke as he turned, "Will do, Mr. Patterson."

Not Kip. Not son. Not Kipper. Kip uttered a curse after him, then looked down at the files. First Fitzpatrick's, then Cellini's. Automated, he placed both calls, not exactly sure of what he'd said but reasonably certain that he'd related the respective information to both morticians. Sitting back, he found Mulden watching him with a faint grin. "We're certainly having fun now, aren't we?" Kip asked, his gray eyes dark and heated, a wave of sarcasm rising.

"Guess I never thought too much about this end of Whistlebrook, but you have, huh? And it's one of the reasons you don't plan on taking over here."

"Seems odd to you?"

"Not odd. I think it's real normal," Mulden commented. "But if it's any consolation, the way you're managing it is mighty impressive."

"I don't need a fucking pep talk, JD," Kip stated while considering the odds of losing three residents in the course of a single evening. Five, counting Calfactor and Marilyn Patterson, in the space of a week. Swaying with the thought, bits and pieces of warnings, along with his mother's paranoia, took shape in his mind. "I need some air," he decided abruptly and pushed off his chair. Motioning Mulden to follow, Kip strode around the desk, snatching his coat from the ornate wooden coat tree at the door.

Barely pausing at the reception desk, he told Angie to page him over the external p.a. then strode to the front door. Against the instant chill, Kip pulled his coat together as he stepped onto the porch and spotted Bill ascending the steps at a trot.

"Kip, what's—"

"Mrs. Taylor passed away. Mr. Seratti joined her. A Mrs. Lonnigan's attempting to buy a seat on the same train. Their files are on my mother's desk. I notified the families and respective morticians. I'm taking a walk," Kip barely paused then added, "Oh, and I've hired Dr. Mark Frances as Chief of Staff. He's with Mrs. Lonnigan—"

"You can't do—" Bill halted.

Kip hesitated, his tone low and as cold as the chilled wind. "You will assist him and see that he has the cooperation of the staff, won't you, Bill?"

"As acting administrator in your mother's absence, I must advise you, Kip, that could be a mistake. Dr. Sheffield has been our—"

"Don't fuck with me, Bill," Kip stated, his gaze level on Bill's shining glow. "Three in one night is a bit much." With his words, he motioned to JD and continued across the porch, striding down the steps.

With no direction in mind, Kip veered toward the entrance lane, striding on the cleared sidewalk across the front of the Home. Uncontrollably, his thoughts spun over the details compiling in his mind. First, his mother's paranoia, then warnings. Now, death?

"You know, I meant what I said inside," JD interrupted. "You handled that well."

"You're a ranger. Police training?" Kip asked absently, catching Mulden in a side glance.

"Among other training, yes," he answered.

Two—possibly three in one evening? *Damn it! In the space of an hour?* Kip continued walking, his focus drifting over glowing white lawns, his mind in an uncomfortable gridlock of déjà vu and his present reality. His mother's second letter—*the wrong hands.* Dr. Frances—*a walk in the snow.* Bill Bickerman—*a sheep in a wolf's cloak?* Three deaths in one evening? Five in a week? Fifteen years swept away...

Five in one week. One after the other. People were dying one after the other, and Kip had never seen it coming. No warning. He'd known about death, lived with it, and saw it in the auras. Forever, he knew when his friends were slipping away. Whatever the strangeness in his vision, he'd always known when to sit with a resident a little longer, when to offer quiet words and hold hands. God, he hated watching them go, but he'd learned to accept it, learned to be glad for whatever warning signal allowed him to recognize the gray mist darkening around their shoulders. He'd learned to read those signs even before he could walk. But now, like then, it was all wrong. In those three weeks, he hadn't seen the cloak thickening or darkening. Too many of them, too close together, and no one to talk to about the strangeness—

Mrs. Ramsey. The name erupted within his mind, as clear as the image of her face the day she'd handed him the checkered quilt, a quilt painstakingly knitted by her arthritic hands for weeks, if not months. Black and white, like a checkerboard, almost like the checkerboard that he and Irish had hovered over for hours, and Mrs. Ramsey had told him she was knitting it as a gift for someone special. For weeks, she'd led him to believe the quilt was for her grandson as Kip had sat next to her, letting her use his hands to roll the endless balls of white and black yarn. 'I did tell you it was for someone special.'

"God, I loved that quilt," he said absently, belatedly aware of his breath condensing and smoking in front of his eyes, aware of the cold sending his fisted hands deeper into his pockets. The last image, though, the last time he'd seen her with the pale gray cloud swirling. He'd known, even before Mark Frances, that Mrs. Ramsey's condition had become terminal. Kip had known before she ever transferred to the East Wing, and he hated to visit that ward...

She was so swollen. Her rheumy eyes glazed with pain and fright as she struggled to cling to the side of the bed, and he'd lost so damned much weight by then. When she came into his arms, her strength expired, his knees buckled, his system wrenched with a blinding pain as he carried her weight to the floor.

Stopping, Kip gazed into the past, an overlay of the dark, snowy lawn filled his mind's eye.

Five in one week, and Mrs. Ramsey was the first. His fault. Somehow, that had been his fault. He'd been accused. The rumors had run wild through the staff ranks thanks to Janet Cross, one of the attending nurses at the time.

Cross had risen to head nurse status later, long after he'd gone. And she remained employed even now, although he'd made a point of avoiding her on his brief excursions through the hallowed halls.

Chapter 23

"**W**hy'd you ask me about my training?"

Yanked from the past to the present, Kip fumbled his cigarettes from his coat pocket. With the lingering effect of nostalgia, he cupped a flame against the wind, absently watching the main entrance ahead. Three cars, headlights blinking between barren branches and trunks of trees, passed slowly along the slope of the highway. Beyond the cars, across the highway, residential houses tucked within more trees and shrubs. Christmas lights twinkled in shapes of porch roofs, windows, and doors. Sounds had carried across the slopes. Children laughing, dogs barking. He could almost hear them even now, tiny snow-bundled figures trundling sleds or erecting snowmen on their long front yards. Almost too readily, he imagined a young Edna Feeney, lean and trim, tattered, toting her battered carpetbag as she trudged the last steps of her journey beneath blazing colorful bows of autumn oaks.

Hearses came, though. So many hearses.

Had three ever arrived in a single evening?

Not fully recovered from his lingering nostalgia, Kip watched two more cars ascending the hill coming from town. A third trailed behind, breaking almost lazily from thick woods beyond the gully. The first two passed the pillars; the third slowed. Mrs. Lonnigan's family? They'd arrive soon, if not now, pulling between the pillars. Paul Lonnigan, a faceless man of indeterminate age, would lose his mother tonight, if not already.

"Kip, are you alright?"

No, he wasn't all right. As if he were thirteen again, he feared to enter those glass doors, terrified by the prospect of facing another death, donning his black suit, riding in another hearse, carrying another coffin. Five deaths in less than two weeks. Six, he corrected silently. Mr. Hammond had become the sixth in less than a month, and mourning had become—

"Damn it. Even for Whistlebrook—" *Five in two weeks…? Three in a single evening?*

'Elsa, it's the Prince,' Mrs. Chelsey had said less than a week ago. Yesterday, Elsa Taylor had looked into him, tried holding his hand, her fingers infirm, fragile, under heavy sedation. The *Prince*.

'The atmosphere … our residents are frightened … the police … what lengths these people will go … They're old. They're not ready to die.'

Was it a coincidence that Mrs. Taylor—terminal for months—chose tonight for her final journey? Taylor, the first resident with whom the Prince had publicly interacted? A coincidence? Elsa Taylor, of the Richmond Tailors.

Headlights blinded him momentarily. Blinking spots as the car swept past him, Kip turned, unconsciously, watching the sedan stop at the main entrance. Only vaguely aware of his chilled fingers, smoke, and condensed breaths mingling and sweeping away from his cold lips, Kip watched a lean man step from the driver's door and hurry around the front end. The fellow arrived at the passenger door in time to assist an elderly man. Another woman climbed clumsily from the rear door. The trio hurried up the front steps in a cluster. Husband, mother, father. Lonnigan was only 62.

Was Mrs. Lonnigan, another terminal patient, merely a random choice from the countless possibilities within the castle walls?

Even in the hollows of his own mind, he knew what that question implied. *Murder.*

But why? And why, now, goddamn it! Why? To tilt the balance of a wayward prince? To send him fleeing? To convince him that his Home hadn't changed? That death is Whistlebrook's prime investment? To send the prince packing and prohibit him from meddling in…*in his mother's office?*

His thought halted abruptly. Only an hour ago, Kip had asked Ted for the key to Marilyn's office. Less than an hour ago, Mark Frances had stated, 'I'm not going to discuss this with you in this office.' But they'd begun speaking, and the call for Elsa Taylor had come during Kip's absence. Elsa resided on the fourth floor; Mr. Seratti on the second floor. Mrs. Lonnigan lay dying, even now, on the third floor. And Mr. Calfactor lying in state at Edgar B. Stone's?

"Kip, damn it," JD stated while touching his arm. "Snap out of it."

Jolting slightly, Kip pivoted his gaze, remembering a day—that day so long ago when he and JD had walked these grounds. Mourning. In mourning, Kip had fallen into mindless dazes. Until that day with JD, he'd always mourned alone. Until those five weeks before he departed from Whistlebrook, others had seen him in mourning, but none had ever gotten as close to the Prince of Whistlebrook as JD Mulden in those brief five weeks. But they're friendship had been too new, too tentative, to share his fears.

"I know this kind of shit blew you away, way back when, and I know you're already hurting over losing your mom, but you'll get through it, Kip," Mulden said carefully, his face flushed from the cold. Under the fluorescent glow from the parking lot, genuine concern animated his disheartened smile. "I know it's not easy—"

"Have you decided how long you'll be staying?" Kip interrupted.

"At least through Christmas," JD answered hesitantly.

Remembering why he'd asked JD about his training, Kip asked, "Would you mind moonlighting through your vacation?" He might just as easily have admitted he needed an ally or *police protection.*

"Moonlighting?"

"Temporary Assistant Chief of Security, beginning now, if you're interested," Kip answered, watching JD's curiosity and slight surprise. "The position may only last for a day; however, it will pay well if you accept."

"Something's wrong with this picture," Mulden said carefully.

"Do you accept the position?"

"A day," JD considered. "Yeah, I'll accept the position."

Unconsciously, Kip started moving toward the main entrance. "As your first order of business, I'd like you to find the taping device and phone tap in my mother's office."

"Want to run that by me again?"

"What didn't you understand?" Kip asked absently, glancing sideways to spy Mulden's critical gaze.

"The office is wired?" Mulden asked. "You're sure of that?"

Ignorance? To protect the innocent? To adhere to his mother's privacy policy? With a mental shake, Kip commented, "I don't stutter." Maintaining only indifference, he continued, "My mother had several quirks, one of which obviously included recording her conversations for later reference. Find it. Dismantle it. Within your area of expertise?"

"No problem," JD said with an echo of youth in his voice.

"How long will it take you?" Kip asked as they strode up the steps.

"Depends. As Assist. Chief, do I have access to your security records? There's probably a schematic—"

"Won't help," Kip interrupted. Stopping them under the porch roof, he studied JD's intent gaze. "The system was installed by an outside contractor. I don't have the time or desire to disrupt their Sunday evening. Besides, I'm placing you in my trust, and frankly, I don't want anyone to know what you're doing. You report to me, exclusively."

"Now I know there's something wrong with this picture," Mulden stated carefully. "You want to tell me what's going on?"

"That I know of, nothing," Kip lied without wavering. "I'd merely like more privacy. Is it within your expertise to assist?"

Hesitating, JD decided before nodding. "No problem, but it might take a little while unless you know where the base system's located."

"I don't, but I doubt you'll find the recorder in the office," he admitted. "As I recall, she mentioned remote devices."

JD hesitated, his hazel eyes intent. He wasn't stupid or slow by any means. "This sounds a little screwy, Kip. Taping devices is one thing. But bugging her own office?"

"Hereditary insanity," he commented indifferently, shrugging as he scanned the parking lot. An abundance of cars occupied the lot, likely in proportion to the number of visitors. Despite the busy day, it was still only early evening. "And different strokes, obviously," Kip continued as he leveled his gaze on Mulden. "I don't like recording devices, not even answering machines. God knows, I'm considered certifiable. I'd rather not have evidence on hand."

Conceding, JD commented, "All right." His attention shifted absently toward the lot, returning directly. "But for the record, Kip. I don't buy that story. Something's been bothering you for days. Now you're asking me to find wiretaps? I *have* had police training, and this rings a bell."

"Are you on my payroll?" Kip asked simply, studying Mulden's tension.

"By temporary arrangement, yes," Mulden answered carefully.

"Then find the taping devices and page me when you're finished," Kip said lightly and moved toward the door.

For now, Mulden would keep his confidence, but in his words and tone, he implied that his position could change. If whatever was happening here skirted the law, JD would act in an official capacity. Their 'temporary arrangement' would be terminated. As it should be, Kip decided as they strode into the parlor-lobby.

Two more visitors stood at the reception desk, signing out. Kip barely glanced toward them as he started Mulden toward the administrative area.

"Mr. Patterson?"

Effectively halted in a half turn, Kip spotted the two older women, neither of whom was far from the median resident age. The slightly less gray-haired woman started toward him, scanning him from head to toe as she donned a grim smile. By her expression alone, Kip understood the nature of her interruption.

"I'd just like to extend my sympathies," she said with an uncomfortable voice, offering her plump hand. "I didn't know your mother well—"

That makes two of us.

"—but as long as my sister's been here, your mother was always dear to her. She's going to be missed."

"Thank you," he said vacantly, wondering what else needed said.

The woman squeezed his hand, her smile twisted into a grimace. "Sir, if you don't mind me asking? Will you be taking over, now?"

How many times had someone asked that question? Absently, Kip recited his natural response. "Mr. Bickerman will be stepping into the executive administrative position, ma'am. If you have any questions, I'm sure he'd be happy to speak to you if you phone him during business hours."

"My sister's concerned," she persisted, still clasping his hand. "You understand, sir. At her age—"

"Just tell him, Cora," her elder companion interrupted as she joined them. With a brassiness inherent to advanced age, she stated, "Lena's afraid the Home's going to shut down and she'll be out on her ear. Is there any truth to that?"

The last thing he needed was to be cornered and accused of something or other by two elderly women who retained their full faculties. "I'm sure there are several rumors abounding," Kip spoke with a thin rein on his patience, glancing between them and focusing on Cora, the sister. "Assure your sister, the Home will perpetuate in my mother's absence. She has nothing to fear. Whistlebrook will continue to accommodate her."

"But are you—"

"If you'll excuse me," he slid his hand free with a faintly apologetic grin. "Again, thank you for your condolences, and please, do assure your sister of her well-being." Hopefully, he wasn't lying. Turning, he found JD watching, waiting just inside the hallway and holding the administration door open.

Mulden's curiosity lingered silently until they strode into the secretarial pool. "Is Whistlebrook really going to perpetuate, Kip?"

"Without a doubt," he answered without inflection. Whether the Home would perpetuate in its present capacity remained the only question. Privately owned and operated, catering to the elite, or a state-operated facility, open to whoever qualified, physically or financially. *Winds of change. Life thrives on change.*

The office door remained unlocked, but Bill wasn't inside. Pausing, Kip found the light switch while looking to JD as the lamps ignited. "Do your thing. You'll find an intercom button on the phone to page me. If Bill returns before me, have him ring me and I'll confirm your position and clearance."

"Will do."

Kip pulled the door shut between them and strode through the offices. In the junction between the offices and parlor entrance, he paused, considering another unnecessary interception. At the sound of Ted's voice, he veered toward the parlor. Undoubtedly, he would need another set of keys.

Angie started, "I thought *last* Sunday was bad—" She halted her words at the sight of Kip. Her relaxed smile stiffened.

Ted had been about to sit on the desk, thought better of it, and straightened as if he might salute at any moment.

"Do you have the keys to the switchboard room?" Kip asked.

"Uh? Yes, sir," Ted said as he reached for the set of keys attached to his belt, unsnapping the entire wad. "Do you want me to open it?"

Turning his focus to Angie, Kip asked, "Any word from Dr. Frances?"

"None, sir."

Kip nodded as he looked at Ted. "Is Mr. Culver on the premises?"

"I think he's at his house," Ted answered and handed Kip the key. A subtle beep drew his attention to the security monitor over Angie's desk. By apparent habit, the security guard lifted a walkie-talkie from his belt. "Station two, a wagon's pulling in now. Better get to the dock."

Kip spied the monitor, recognizing the glimpse of emerald as the hearse rolled through the front gates. Fitzpatrick's. Toward Ted, Kip asked, "Has anyone picked up—or delivered—Mrs. Taylor's paperwork?"

"I think Mr. Bickerman took it," Angie offered before she appeared to regret drawing Kip's attention. In a fleeting glance, she sought Ted for assurance.

He should have enlisted an aide to collect the proper forms and death certificate, and should have alerted the security station to expect the hearses.

Damn it! So, what? This is not my line of work!

With his thought, Kip turned from the desk and crossed the parlor, passed the elevators, and entered the brief alcove beneath the staircase. Fitting the skeleton key into the old door, Kip unlocked another blast of nostalgia.

The room, six by three feet, hadn't changed. One wall contained a slotted corkboard, resembling a pegboard, which originally accommodated the obsolete system. His mother had periodically updated the system, eliminating the old terminal board and the need for two operators. At least twenty years ago. she'd semiautomated the switchboard, and the updated system had fascinated a little boy with an insatiable curiosity. Semiautomated, the new system required only one operator for the designated business hours.

Hiding. Kip remembered sitting in the single swivel chair. He'd been hiding in here when the flashing lights had snagged his undivided attention. More than twenty years ago, he corrected silently. He could have been no more than seven or eight when he jammed the new system, and telephones erupted on two floors, ringing for over an hour. *Goddamn, was she ever pissed.* When the aides had found no other means to offer the residents peace, they'd ripped over two dozen phone lines from wall sockets. For weeks, residents had complained about hearing phones ringing in their nightmares. But nobody had suffered more than one Kip Patterson. Not only had his mother personally attended to his backside, but once news traveled, very few residents let him forget his mischief.

One though—one resident had snatched Kip off his feet—

'Heathen!' The words quaked, transcending time and space. Wheezing breaths swam against him as blisters electrified, his muscles quaking beneath another strike. 'Little Heathen! Creating all that racket! No father! You'll get up to no good! You come here!' Hammond, Bill Hammond. Shame and humiliation coursed through Kip's mind as he remembered ambling through the crowded recreation room, answering that summons. In one wrenching tug, the old man had dragged him over his sturdy legs, whacking him as a dozen spectators—

'Bill! Goddamn, you! Put the laddy down!' Irish stormed, wheeling his chair in an angry advance. 'That youngster didn't do you no harm!'

Through a haze, Kip remembered the old man landing a dozen swift swats before ole Irish belted Hammond in the mouth. For an old man, Irish's arms were strong, his temper fierce only until tugging Kip off Hammond and landing him on his stump thighs, holding him—

"God," Kip uttered. "How I loved you, old man."

At the sound of his voice echoing in the compact silence, Kip jolted from his reflection, cursing his momentary lapse. Clearing his focus, he scanned the modern switchboard. Was it any wonder he hesitated before sitting in the operator's chair? Old haunts.

Semiautomated still applied. Calls transferred via automation from 5 p.m. to 8 a.m. At 8, the operator began answering and transferring calls through the main board to every section of the Home. A lonely occupation, Kip considered unconsciously spotting a notepad, noting the doodles across the letterhead. On a corkboard on the inside wall, school photographs of the operator's children and dozens of children's drawings hung in no particular order, along with numerous family photos. One little boy, around six or seven years old, smiled despite his empty incisor sockets.

Obviously, the operator was married, had three kids, and a schnauzer. *Thanks, Morgan, but no thanks.*

With his memory still lingering, Kip hesitated before flipping switches and lifting the headset. A dozen buttons glowed on the board. On impulse, he pushed one randomly, hearing a pause in the conversation, then an old voice squawked, "You still there, Harry?"

A return voice growled, "Sure am. Sounds like the phone's on the fritz."

Apparently, the operator wasn't responsible for the glitch on Marilyn's private line, as at least one elderly gentleman had identified the interruption.

Deciding, Kip connected an outside line, then dialed a number from recent memory.

"Fitzpatrick's Funeral Home," a husky familiar voice answered.

The elder Fitzpatrick, Kip recognized, "Mr. Fitzpatrick, Kip Patterson here."

The voice paused then. "Yes, sir, what can I do for you? My man should be out there by now."

"He's here, Mr. Fitzpatrick; however, there is something I'd like you to do for me."

"Name it and it's done."

An odd comment. Hesitating, Kip decided, "I need your assistance in a highly sensitive and confidential matter, Mr. Fitzpatrick. Understand, there's some risk involved. If you decline, it won't reflect on future association."

"Son, the Fitzpatricks and Pattersons been doing business for close to a half century. If you need something, you say whatever it is, and it'll be between us."

Fifty years. Fitzpatrick had probably known his grandfather, Ronald E. Patterson, along with Marilyn's unwed status despite the Mrs. address. "Mr. Fitzpatrick, I'd like you to run blood tests on Mrs. Taylor. I need to know the chemical content and level of morphine in her system if that's possible."

Fitzpatrick held silent for several seconds before he spoke quietly, "You wouldn't be asking this without a damn good reason."

"Undoubtedly, sir. And bearing that in mind, I'd appreciate your confidence regardless of the results."

"You're thinking this woman might have been overdosed."

"I can assure you, sir, if that's the case, I will see that the responsible party is held accountable. So saying, take whatever necessary precautions to document your procedure."

"If you suspect malpractice, we should call the proper authorities and ask for an autopsy, son. That's proper procedure."

"I would like nothing better; however, I don't believe that would be in anyone's best interest at this moment. If the evidence verifies my suspicion, I assure you, Mr. Fitzpatrick, I will notify the proper authorities."

Fitzpatrick hesitated, his voice conceding, "I knew your mother for a lot of years, but things haven't been just right out there for a while. I'll get these tests run and contact you with the results. It'll take some time, though. Could be morning before I have anything to tell you."

"Contact me, regardless of the hour, and thank you, sir."

Disconnecting the call, Kip heard the page echoing outside the door, not sure how many times it might have been spoken. "Mr. Patterson, please contact the executive office."

Returning the switchboard to automated capacity, Kip tried to decide which male voice initiated the page—Mark or JD? Stepping into the alcove, he locked the door, realizing as the page echoed a second—or tenth time—that was Bill's voice paging him.

Angie sat alone at her desk, looking more worried than she had ten minutes earlier. She shied visibly as Kip approached, trying hard to concentrate on something in front of her.

"Phone Mr. Culver, will you?" Kip asked in passing. "Have him come over immediately and send him into the executive office."

"Yes, sir!" she snapped and reached for her phone.

His request hadn't demanded panic; he hadn't even raised his voice. Kip cast her a more peculiar glance as her dark eyes darted away from him. Apparently, naturally excitable, or she suffered a nervous disorder. As he strode into the administrative area, he heard the voices echoing. The sounds cleared as he passed Carolyn's desk.

"—Your friend may *own* this facility, young man, but I am acting administrator. I could very easily have you both removed—"

"I hope you have a good attorney if you intend to carry out that threat," JD returned in a calm, dark tone.

"You'll need the attorney when I have you arrested for trespassing!" Bill seethed.

Stopping in the doorway, Kip leaned against the doorframe, lifting his lighter to a cigarette. His back to the door, Bill stood facing JD, who rested comfortably in one of the receiving chairs in front of the desk. Only his ankle-crossed jeans remained visible between Bickerman and Ted, who stood, unwisely positioned as if he would physically accost Mulden on Bill's command.

"As it stands, I'm reasonably sure that your friend's suffering the equivalent of a nervous breakdown, which is the only reason I don't have the police on their way already. If you have any decency, you'll refrain from humoring him and assist me in convincing him to speak to our staff psychologist."

"Seems to me, if he needed a shrink, he'd make the appointment himself," JD said with a hint of amusement. "And if I were you, mister, I wouldn't suggest that to him again, unless you'd like another great view of the ceiling."

"Dorsen, radio your associates. I want Mr. Patterson found and brought to this office—"

Kip flicked his lighter, catching a flame to his cigarette while watching Bill and Ted pivot, parting a clear view of Mulden. Amusement washed over JD's bearded face. Ted appeared stricken, possibly terrified despite his solid stance. *A karate stance?*

Bill halted with a strained, bitter smile, but heaved a sigh, nearly managing an expression of relief before remembering his anger. "Maybe you'd like to explain to me what the blazes is going on here, Kip? I came in here and found your alleged friend snooping around your mother's desk. He suggested I speak to you—"

"Bill," Kip spoke with a smoky exhale, his gaze steady. "As of an hour ago, you are no longer acting executive administrator of Whistlebrook. As my mother's favorite son and single heir, I am within my legal bounds to take the reins until such time as my mother's Will is executed.

"You have two options," Kip continued as he eased off the doorframe.

Bill stepped back despite the considerable distance between them and bumped the desk at his hip. "Kip."

"It's in your best interest to be quiet," Kip said simply, continued past Bill, and rounded the broad shiny desk. All too naturally, he slid into Marilyn's chair, leaned back, and lifted his feet, crossing his tennis shoes on the corner of the desk. Noting Bill's outrage and shock, Kip smirked, "You can humor me for the next dozen or so hours, after which time you will, in all probability, resume control .

"Your second option is more complicated," Kip continued simply. "You can attempt to have me incarcerated or removed from these premises. At which time, you will find yourself in need of bail. Simply, old man, I'll have you arrested. Trespassing, I believe you called it. Private property and all that nonsense.

"You see, Bill, this is private property. *My* private property. But I'm generally not that difficult to get along with. You do your job, and I'll do whatever the hell I feel like doing for the next several hours, which includes hiring Dr. Frances as Chief of Staff, and hiring JD, a licensed law enforcement officer, as Assistant Chief of Security.

"Do you understand me?"

Bill chomped on his tongue, restraining his outrage as his pudgy cheeks flamed blood-pressure red. Seconds passed before he forced a thin smile. "Kip, I know you're under a great deal of stress, but throwing the Home into chaos won't relieve your pain."

"Indulge me, Bill, or I'll have you removed, and God only knows how much chaos I could create in a day without your expertise." In slow deliberation, Kip drifted his focus over the office. "This room's always needed greenery. Actually, several rooms could use a change, and plants certainly need sunlight, don't you agree, Bill?"

"Kip—"

"What we need on the premises is a greenhouse or a terrarium," he considered as he swiveled his chair enough to scan a windowed wall. "A terrarium. My mother should have thought about it. That wall looks about right. Of course, we'd have to move out all this shit, and we'll need plastic." His gaze lifted to Bill, who studied him critically. "Surely, you know a good contractor who wouldn't mind picking up a little pocket change this close to Christmas? No, I don't suppose you do, but I'd imagine I could find one in the Yellow Pages—"

"Kip," Bill interrupted carefully, his voice wavering between fear and doubt. "Why—why don't we discuss what your friend was doing in this office. If there's something—"

"A mouse," Kip said vacantly. Clearing his focus sharply, Kip pivoted his gaze to JD. "You did find the little bastard, didn't you?"

"Not yet," JD mused. "I thought I saw it run behind the desk. God knows where it—"

In one swift motion, Kip scrambled, bringing his feet onto the chair, rising and stepping onto the desk. "For Chrissake, JD!" he demanded while bouncing manic glances between the back of the desk and Mulden's suddenly startled gaze. "You let me *walk* back there? Knowing that hairy little beast could be *lurking* beneath me! For Chrissake! I thought I could *trust* you! After everything else tonight, I don't need a fucking *coronary!* Goddamn it, maybe you shouldn't be a security guard if you can't even protect me from a fucking rodent!"

Bill and Ted both darted glances about the floor and up to Kip.

Straining against amusement, Mulden commented lightly, "Calm down, Kip, I promise, I'll get the little varmint—"

"An exterminator!" Kip stated, leveling his gaze at Bill. "Tomorrow, Bill! You'll call an exterminator! I want the entire Home exterminated! Top to bottom! One end to the other! We'll call all the families! Have them take their loved ones home for the holidays! Make arrangements! I won't have *rats* in my Home! We'll have the terminally ill transferred to other facilities. You can arrange—"

"Kip!" Bill stated sharply. "Calm down, buddy!"

"Calm down?" he asked in a faltering, shocked voice. "Rodents, Bill! We—can—not—have—rodents!"

"Kip," JD said, feigning calm. "I think you're overreacting just a little. One tiny mouse is not necessarily grounds for panic."

"You've *never* understood!" Kip stated, eyeing Mulden angrily. "State Health Inspectors! I asked you outside to take care of this problem discreetly! I can't even work in this office, for Chrissake! I saw it and it was everything I could do not to scream! Now look! Just look at this!" He stomped his foot on the desk, tossing his focus between Bill and Ted, both of whom were only more bewildered. "Both of them know—" Kip stated and focused on JD. "How long do you think it will be before this entire Home knows that we're infested? I should just call the Health Inspectors myself tomorrow—"

"I'll get rid of the mouse. I promise, man. Like I told you, it's nothing to get shook about. I'll take care of it," Mulden said beseechingly.

"Are you telling me...? We do have mice?" Bill asked, looking at Mulden queerly.

"I'd hardly consider one mouse a problem in a facility this big," JD mused, glancing to Kip, then to Bill. "He's overreacting."

"Why didn't you just tell me what you were doing in here?" Bill demanded, sounding confused and angry.

"Fearless up there," Mulden tossed another glance to Kip, more amused. "Asked for my discretion in light of the health codes and widespread panic." He shrugged.

Peering at Kip, annoyed but faintly amused, Bill spoke carefully, "Your mother never mentioned you suffered a phobia of rodents."

"She probably named the hairy little bastard!" Kip huffed in offhanded disgust. Warily scanning the floors around the desk, Kip spied Bill. "This doesn't change the fact that I'm taking the reins until the Will's executed!" he stated sharply. "You can either help me, and I'll let you call the state inspectors. Or I'll have you exterminated by my new—slightly inept!—security guard, and I'll place the call myself!"

How's that for chaos, Billy boy?

Bickerman needed only two seconds to realize the ramifications and inconvenience of a visit from the State Board of Health—undoubtedly, after taking the helm—unless he agreed to the terms. "By all means, buddy, you're in charge." To Ted Dorsen, he stated, "I seem to have jumped to the wrong conclusions, Mr. Dorsen. I suggest you take your orders from Mr. Patterson and your new supervisor."

With a smug grin, Kip bounced a glance off Mulden's glittering eyes at Ted. "I suggest you check Mr. Bickerman's office for rats!" He looked to Bill. "We can't be too careful with the inspectors coming," he said soberly, barely pausing. "Did you finish everything with that other grizzly business?"

"Actually, I need one of the files that ... you're standing on," Bill finished lamely.

"Oh?" Kip looked down. "Oh." He was, in fact, standing on a file. Shifting a step, Kip stooped and handed all three files to Bill, meeting his gaze at equal height. "I don't imagine I handled things as well as I should have. I do apologize if I've complicated the general routine."

"You did fine under the circumstances," Bill said in a voice reeking of fatherly praise. "Just a couple of formalities to take care of." He stepped around the desk and tugged the bottom drawer.

As Bill raided the drawer, Kip commented in concern, "Do hurry back there, Bill. Rats carry rabies, you know."

Bill cast a faintly amused, then more worried glance as he considered the implications of a rabies epidemic. "I assure you, I'm hurrying."

"You can use Carolyn's desk," Kip advised soberly, his gaze vacant. "I don't want anyone in here until JD's finished with the job he's being paid to do."

Bill nodded. He held the forms he needed, closed the drawer, and pushed to his feet. Glancing from the door across the room, to Kip, he asked, "Will you need some help to get out?"

"I'm going to remain a few moments, but thanks," Kip said gravely and glanced over the edge of the desk toward Bill's feet. "I do wish you'd hurry, Bill."

To humor him, no doubt, Bill stepped from behind the desk and addressed JD. "I apologize for the misunderstanding—JD, is it? You apparently have this situation under control. If you need anything, don't hesitate to ask."

"Will do," Mulden said with a haunting grin and coercive wink.

As Bill started toward the door, Kip threw after him, "Do shut the door, Bill. We want it contained."

Bill nodded again, flashing Mulden a glance as he clasped the door handle. "Good luck," he offered, and might have added, 'Thanks. Keep *him* contained and happy.'

The instant the door closed, Kip lost his sobriety, finding Mulden's immensely amused gaze, shrugging.

"You really have slipped a little farther off-center," JD commented.

Kip motioned for silence while asking, "You really didn't get the little bastard yet?"

"Not hardly."

Chapter 24

"Do hurry, JD," Kip said lightly while stepping silently off the desk and stooping. If he wanted to plant a listening device, he would certainly place it close to the target. With that in mind, he slid his hand beneath the center drawer along its tracking.

"A flashlight would probably make this a little easier," Mulden commented. "It's probably back in a corner. Wouldn't happen to have one handy, would you?"

"I'm sure my mother kept one in here," he said lightly. "Check that bottom drawer—left." He was closer. He opened the drawer, finding a flashlight tucked down in the front corner. "My mother hated electrical storms," he only half lied, handing the light to Mulden. Before the backup generators were installed, the Home had lost electricity periodically, or so one of the old folks had told Kip years ago. Marilyn had never admitted her phobia or told him why she insisted on keeping a flashlight in every room.

For the next twenty minutes, they continued searching around the desk, making idle comments about the little beast hiding in corners or running down a concealed hole. At the rap of knuckles on the oak door, Kip hurried two strides from the bookshelf behind the desk, stepped onto the felt mat, and sat down, Yoga style. "Enter at your own risk," he called.

Mr. Culver entered hesitantly, sizing up Kip's position on the desk, and Mulden stopped, holding the flashlight near the bookshelves. The security man hadn't changed much. If anything, he appeared slightly less plump than yesteryear with a little more frosting in his close-cropped hair. By the tension and dread sagging his face, he'd already spoken to Bill Bickerman. As he strode forward, he scanned the floor before focusing on Kip. "Mr. Bickerman mentioned you have a problem in here. I sent Ted over to the shed. We'll get some traps set in here and have the problem cleared up in no time."

"I'd certainly appreciate that, Mr. Culver. Did Bill happen to mention I hired JD as your second in command?"

"He mentioned it," Culver said heavily and continued around the desk, offering his palm to Mulden. "Glad to have you aboard, JD. Mulden, isn't it? You used to come around here a lot of years ago."

Visibly impressed, JD smiled as he shook hands. "You have one helluva memory, sir."

How could anyone forget JD, the Prince of Whistlebrook's one and only friend? Pulling from his thought, Kip pushed to his feet atop the desk. "Mr. Culver, if you're not otherwise occupied, could we—"

At a glimpse of motion, Kip halted and spied Dr. Frances paused in the open doorway. Despite his momentary curiosity directed up at Kip, heaviness announced Mrs. Lonnigan's condition far louder than words.

Damn it! This room needed to be debugged, and without the proper electronic devices, that process could take far too long. Stepping off the desk, Kip looked at Culver. "Why don't you show JD the security system, Mr. Culver? When you're finished, I'd like to speak to you." Looking to Dr. Frances, he asked, "A walk?"

"I could use a breath of air," Mark agreed.

Walking only as far as the sidewalk where the Lonnigan's sedan remained at the curb, Kip paused to light a cigarette and watched Mark tug his pile-lined collar about his neck. With his exhale, Kip anticipated, "We're losing Mrs. Lonnigan."

Within the fluorescent glow, Mark's expression dimmed. Condensed breath swam about his dark, wavy hair, whipping a tad radically as he nodded. "I'm afraid there's nothing we can do. Dr. Sheffield's treatment is in line."

Unwavering, Kip asked, "Could an outside source have triggered her decline?"

Like JD, Dr. Mark Frances wasn't slow. His focus sharpened. "Frankly, I doubt it, but you have reason to believe otherwise?"

"My mother's office is wired," he said while watching Mark's tension, no surprise in evidence. "You were aware of that. My mother spoke to you. Now tell me what you know."

"She provided you with an option to be rid of Whistlebrook. I know that you could sign over the Home and walk away."

"You could have said that much inside. Elaborate."

"If you sign it away, it becomes a state-operated facility."

"Why would my mother confide in you?" Kip interrupted.

"I assisted in negotiations," he said without pause. "Frankly, my influential family provided several shortcuts to arrange the option you are receiving." His gaze drifted with his nostalgia, returning with a faint, disheartened grin. "Ironic, even though I was thoroughly against her decision, I should be the one to assist her. I truly don't want to see you lose this Home or forfeit it."

"Why does it matter to you?" Kip asked, more curious than his tone implied. Something was wrong. The *good doctor* Frances ... lying?

Rather than answer, Mark turned halfway, scanning the front of the Home. A crosscurrent of sadness and admiration lingered on his bearded face. When he spoke again, his voice carried a quiet sincerity. "Have you any idea how unique this Home is?"

"Privately owned and operated. Yes."

"Far deeper than that, Kip. Your mother loved this Home. She loved her residents. They were as much her children as you were. And you—despite what you choose to believe—you belong here. What you have is a gift, a gift you inherited from your mother, I trust.

"The people make Whistlebrook unique," Mark continued reflectively, shrugging. Tiny laughter lines haunted the corners of his eyes, his smile thickened, still sad. "I always hoped you'd pursue a career in medicine. At thirteen, you had an incredible aptitude for geriatric medicine. You knew the illnesses and the cures. You knew as if you had a sixth sense, what each patient needed." Shaking his head, his focus held steady. "Even now, Kip, your compassion doesn't cease to amaze me. You felt more than shock at the losses tonight. And, my dear boy, you can choose to consciously ignore what you feel, but in the long run, you won't eliminate your sorrow or pain. Eventually, you'll face it."

"Nice speech," Kip said bluntly. "Explain to me, if my mother, as you said, expected me to take the reins eventually, why is Bill Bickerman slated to become administrator?"

"Bill's an administrator. He knows routine and procedure. I believe *owner* takes precedence and dictates final say. Like it or not, young Mr. Patterson, you could turn this Home into condominiums and Bill into administrator of janitorial services."

"Not a bad idea. Too bad it's a lousy place for a resort," Kip mused.

"Your mother didn't want her Will contested, Kip, not by outside sources. Whatever you decide will be final."

Mark Frances's words made too much sense. By appeasing everyone who could claim a stake in the estate, she had, in fact, eliminated any possibility of a long-term court battle, or so it would appear. "You know, she could have greatly simplified my life by picking up the goddamn telephone."

"May I ask you, now, why you asked if Mrs. Lonnigan's condition could have been accelerated?"

Turning a less blind focus onto the doctor's intense gaze, he commented, "I don't believe wholeheartedly in coincidence, doctor. The ratio of terminally ill hasn't changed drastically. To my knowledge, we've never had five deaths in less than two weeks, much less three in a three hours. I can't help but wonder if whoever's monitoring my mother's office might not have decided that you and I had talked long enough. That I was asking too many serious questions."

"You do realize, you're talking about murder."

"A grieving son, with my penchant for neurosis—crying murder in reference to terminally ill patients, could hardly rank priority in an official investigation." Kip's gaze caught on the headlights—two sets of headlights pulling into the lane. He watched them advance, oblivious to the cold against his face, pressing into his lungs. Oh, indeed, the first vehicle was a wagon turning into the back lane. Cellini's had arrived.

The second car pulled into the parking lot. A Lincoln, he identified. For as far back as he could remember, expensive cars had entered this lot. Marilyn had catered to the wealthy. His focus swept across the brightly lit parking area. Not as many large vehicles. The employee spaces were filled with economy cars. Mark's Mercedes-Benz rested in its designated slot alongside a late-model Porsche. Dr. Sheffield's chariot, no doubt. To his slight surprise, Kip watched the Lincoln roll into a space alongside the Porsche. Doubtful a clergyman, but it certainly never hurt to hope.

Across the distance, he identified the small, built man slipping from the Lincoln, remembering him through a fog of faces. Dr. Carmine. Apparently, Bill harbored serious concerns about the immediate future.

"Why do I have a feeling Greg's here to see you?" Mark asked lightly.

"Sixth sense, possibly," Kip mused and turned his focus to Frances. "How long have you known my mother's office was bugged?"

"I was never positive," Mark said, switching his thought without any trouble, his attention riveted. "But it doesn't surprise me. Your mother and I haven't spoken in that office for quite some time—at her demand. Do you have any idea of who—or possibly, why—someone would want that office bugged?"

An odd feeling crept into him. Something unsaid. Uncertain? Shaking his head absently, Kip watched Carmine advance.

For such a small-built man, the fellow mastered a confident, long stride without appearing dwarfish. He closed the distance between them in record time, his expression automated, nearly plastic behind his wind-burnt cheeks and darting eyes. "Mark. Kip. It's a little chilly to be standing around out here, isn't it?"

"Bill called you," Kip commented, watching Carmine's studied gaze. Practiced indifference.

"Would you be offended if I said he had?"

"Classic. Answer a question with a question," Kip mused. "You won't be offended if we speak out here, would you?"

"If you're more comfortable out here, I don't mind," Dr. Carmine lied badly.

"Actually, I'm not comfortable out here," Kip said honestly. The chill had begun to penetrate his fingers, as well as his toes. If he stayed much longer in this blasted climate, he'd need to invest in a pair of boots. "But we won't speak long. Do you have other business inside, Dr. Carmine?"

"I'll need to speak to Mr. Bickerman."

"Mr. Bickerman resumed his post as *assistant* administrator, doctor. Whatever business you have with him will be cleared by me, and if you intend to speak to him, I intend to be present."

"He mentioned you've assumed authority," Dr. Carmine commented.

"He and I reached an understanding, and now, you and I will reach a similar understanding," Kip held his focus steady on Carmine. "I am of legal age and sound mind to refuse your services. Mr. Bickerman, although I'm sure he means well, has no legal or moral right to summon you on my behalf. Frankly, sir, we have nothing to discuss, and as I have temporarily stepped into the administrative position, I suggest you return to your hearth and home. Should Bill contact you again—on my behalf—I suggest you consider the fact that I hold title to this facility."

"You're striking out with your anger, Kip."

"Dr. Carmine, are you prepared to wager your salary and career against my sanity?"

"Greg," Dr. Frances said quietly. "I wouldn't take that wager. I believe Bill overreacted. Mr. Patterson is neither unnaturally distressed nor suffering prolonged trauma, and I would stake my career and reputation on his sanity."

Carmine studied Mark for a moment before looking again at Kip. "If you should feel a need to speak with me, please, feel free to call, Mr. Patterson."

"Thank you, I will," Kip said simply and caught Mark's faintly amused gaze. "I'll meet you back inside, doctor." To Carmine, he commented, "It's unfortunate you had to come out on a night like this. Have a good evening."

Stepping around both doctors, excusing himself, Kip strode up the steps, vaguely aware of another set of headlights turning into the main entrance. No more games. There was a pattern to all of this, and somehow his arrival had accelerated the pace.

'The Prince is in danger. Someone's trying to destroy his castle.' *The words of a senile old man?*

Automated, Kip bypassed Angie and veered into the executive wing. He entered his mother's office in time to see Frank Culver pointing at the disassembled base of a telephone.

"The secret of catching mice is knowing where they're hiding," Culver finished saying.

Frank Culver had been on Marilyn's list. Should have talked to him sooner.

JD glanced at Kip, then Culver. "Guess you've had this problem before, huh?"

"Been known to catch one or two on occasion."

Moving alongside the desk, Kip scanned the phone base, spotting the alien object beyond Culver's wide fingernail. Oh, lovely, a receiver capable of picking up phone and voice conversations within the room. If Culver had known where to find it, why the hell was it still in operation?

Looking into abstracts, Kip tried to recall if he'd said anything of importance within this room. Not in this room, but the private suite was another matter altogether. 'Demolitions.' When had he said that word? Before or after hearing the phone tap? Before. Friday. Friday afternoon, he'd spoken to John Madison in the suite. Friday morning, upon his return, Kip placed his personal calls from the suite rather than either of the offices. Saturday morning, returning calls, he'd identified the hum and click of a wiretap while speaking to Kelly Mulden.

Mulden handed over a sheet of notepaper; his gaze held fast.

In a rapid scan of the two distinct handwritings, Kip understood. Culver hadn't bought the mouse story and had known exactly where to look for the elusive pest. Kip glanced off Culver to the receiver. On impulse, he backed away, motioning both men silent. At the door, he reached behind him, opened the oak panel, and began speaking as he snapped the door shut in his wake. "Don't tell me! You still haven't caught the little bastard!"

JD was slow on the uptake. "It takes a little time, man. You can't just call them out like a dog."

"Goddamn it!" In two quick strides, Kip reached the desk. Emphasizing his landing, he nudged and jostled the disassembled phone with his shoe, mimicking the sound of static. "How am I supposed to work in here if I can't even walk on the goddamn floor? Mr. Culver, for Chrissake! Do something!" Not awaiting Culver's words, barely glimpsing the parted, startled lips, Kip stooped. Lifting a pen from a silver holder, he wedged the point beneath the mini-receiver.

"Mr. Patterson, all due respect, we're— Culver's voice trailed, his focus intent on the pen.

His gray eyes steady, Kip locked onto Culver's critical gaze as he cried, "There it goes!" In one motion, he slammed the phone, stomped his foot, and catapulted the bug from its resting place. Catching the mini-device, he continued his cry. "Get it! For—" The telephone clattered on the floor as Kip dropped the receiver under his heel and shifted his weight to crunch the device.

Motioning for silence, Kip stepped silently off the desk, lifted the damaged device, and dropped it into one of the two coffee cups. Looking into Mr. Culver's startled gaze, Kip asked, "Could there be others?"

Frank shook his head slowly, his dark eyes doubting, his rugged face twisted into a mask of bewildered confusion. "That's the only one."

"How long have you known about it?"

"About two months," Frank answered as his gaze shifted from the cup to Kip. "Your mother came to see me over at my place."

Not with JD in the room. Looking toward Mulden, Kip caught the intensity of JD's gaze, and just for an instant, those eyes were not the eyes of the prince's only friend. Too late, Mulden's amusement returned with a more relaxed curiosity. *What were you thinking, JD? What were you looking for? A ranger ... not too good on skis? Put off by blizzards? In Aspen?*

"Pretty slick move, Kip," JD mused.

No more games. Looking at Frank, Kip decided, "If you could show JD the security system, I'd appreciate it. Possibly later, you'll join me for a cup of coffee?"

"Be glad to, sir," Mr. Culver said and gestured for Mulden to follow.

"I'll see you after a bit, JD," Kip said lightly.

Temporary assignment, JD seemed to remember. "If you need me, just break a window."

Kip mirrored his grin, watching as both men passed through the door. When the door closed, Kip began reassembling the telephone. Enough games.

Preoccupied, Kelly gazed at the television, not truly seeing the picture or hearing the words. It didn't take a rocket scientist to realize where JD had gone shortly after Bryce and Shelly had headed home. The only surprise was that he'd waited that long. In the past two days, he'd spent very little time at home, and despite what their parents might believe, Kelly doubted he was spending all his time comforting an old friend. Just what the hell was going on here?

Beside her, Richard emitted a harrumph, apparently enthralled by the Christmas program. His arm rested about her shoulder, and belatedly, he glanced over, smiling somewhat sheepishly as if embarrassed to be caught watching the set.

At least he was awake, Kelly considered and nearly cursed aloud at her silent, biting criticism. And this was ridiculous. She was sitting here, feeling like a babysitter, when she would much rather be seated with another. And this wasn't going to work. She needed to be elsewhere.

"Honey, what's wrong?" Richard asked, looking sideways down at her.

How to say this? How could she possibly say what needed to be said three days before Christmas? Damn it, she hated Christmas! She hated this feeling of being torn. As much as she liked Richard, as much as she wished she could change what she was feeling, she knew at this moment that it was impossible. She'd lost Kip once, fifteen years ago. If she let these moments slip through her fingers, now, she'd regret it, forever.

"I have something I have to do," she decided and slid from under Richard's arm, pushing off the couch. If nothing else, she needed to see Kip again. She needed to know he was all right. He had no one else. Not even JD. And a fleeting memory of him inside that dining room at the Home confirmed Kelly's thought and decision. If, as her father predicted, reality was setting in and hitting home, Kip shouldn't be alone.

"Do you want me to come along?" Richard offered as he pushed off the couch, sounding concerned. But his gaze darted to the television, verifying a commercial.

Suffering a quick, heated flash of temper, Kelly stated, "No. Enjoy your movie." Unfair, she countered as she strode toward the carpeted steps. Richard rarely gained a chance to sit and enjoy—*dang it! Doing it again! Making excuses!* Richard had chosen his profession, a worthy profession, but she was damned tired of making excuses and concessions for him!

With her decision made, Kelly strode up the second set of steps and into her old room. In mere minutes, she changed into jeans and a silk blouse, paused to glimpse herself in the mirror, and reached a single conclusion—she wasn't dressed to heat a man's blood, and that was probably the safest decision she'd made recently. Too well, she recalled how those haunted gray eyes flashed over her, undressing her too many times already. Tugging on a pair of hiking boots and her denim coat, she picked up her purse and dug for her car keys as she strode down the steps. Without pause, she strode from the house.

Only as she backed her New Yorker from the driveway did she consider what exactly she intended to do, and for the briefest instant, she thought about pulling back into the driveway. She'd likely run into JD, and she could just imagine what he'd say about this visit. Well, and to hell with him too! If she thought for one blasted minute that he was truly here to console his old friend, she might be more receptive to his advice. Until she knew exactly why JD had reported on Kip in some official capacity.

Something was going on between them, and by Kip's offbeat comments about skiing, his rapid exodus, he wasn't quite as naive as JD would like him to be. For a few crazy seconds in the living room, Kelly had sensed Kip studying JD far more critically than his smirk and musing gray eyes had indicated.

Driving on autopilot, Kelly slowed as she approached the cast-iron gates. Heartbeat quickening, she drew a breath and switched on the turning signals. The time for second thoughts had passed. One way or another, she would see Kip, and if one thing led to another, she'd deal with it. At the moment, he needed a friend whether he wanted one or not.

Chapter 25

"Is that it?" Kip asked in a monotone, his abstract focus watching a trail of smoke rising from the end of his cigarette.

"That's it," Marsh said carefully.

Automated, Kip leaned, dropped the receiver into its cradle, settled back into the leather cushion, and sorted mentally through the details. Just this once, he wished his intuition had failed him, or that Baxel's sources weren't above reproach and quite so thorough. Just this once, Kip wished he'd pursued the seminary or attended Harvard as his mother had planned. 20-20 hindsight.

Closing his eyes, he squelched the sting.

He hadn't gone to the seminary or to Harvard. He'd gone west as Horace Greeley had suggested, as far west as land mass and Greyhound would allow. With three grand in a paper bag, Kip had walked into the first brokerage house he spotted, walked up to the young man chanting figures into a telephone, and stood waiting, listening as Marshal Baxel completed his transaction and dropped the phone to its base with a string of curses.

'What can I do for you, kid?' Baxel had barked, still flushed and angry at his telephone exchange.

'I've heard you're very good at what you do,' Kip lied in a voice reserved for confessionals, soft, sincere, calculated to sound humble and repentant. 'If someone wanted to invest his life savings and preferred not to put his name on the investment, could you see to it?'

Baxel started to smile, but something in the icy gray eyes and chilled, arrogant smirk had altered his thought. 'I could, but I'm not sure I'd want to take someone's entire life savings. There's always risks—'

Kip had dropped the brown bag onto the desk without losing his focus on Baxel's inquisitive gaze. 'You're hired, sir. There's three grand in the bag.' Slipping off his watch, his class ring, and lifting the gold chain from his neck, Kip dropped those alongside the bag. 'For your knowledge only, my name's Kip Patterson. Hock the gold and apply the capital, minus your fee, of course.' Kip had rattled off several companies and the division of capital to apply to each. 'If I profit, reinvest. Leave my name off the transactions. If I lose.' He'd shrugged, glancing off the bag cynically, then tilted his abstract gaze to Baxel. *'La volonté de Dieu est faite.'*

Three years later, on a whim, Kip had searched the L.A. phone directory and found Marshal Baxel's agency listing.

'Are you old enough to drink?' Baxel had asked in a restrained voice then. 'Hell, it doesn't matter. Where are you? Hell, that doesn't matter either! Catch a cab. Meet me at the Plaza. Say in half an hour?'

'I just spent my last quarter and lost my tin cup an hour ago, sir.'

Marsh Baxel had started to chuckle, then rolled into genuine laughter. He'd laughed for the better part of two minutes before managing, 'Just get a cab, kid. I'll meet you out front and pick up the fare.'

A half-hour later, Baxel led him into a hotel clothier and told him to pick out a suit, after which, Baxel had secured a room under M. Baxel. In the rich emerald elegance of a penthouse suite, Baxel had handed Kip a cashier's check for thirty thousand dollars. 'I don't know if you put a curse or a blessing on that cash, kid, but whatever you did, it worked. That's your quarterly gain.'

"A curse," Kip uttered under his breath. *A curse, Marsh.* God's will be done.

Kip remembered wanting to learn that he'd lost every cent; the money had crashed and burned, just like everything else in his life had. *Such a fool, I was.* At twenty-one, he should have known better. He should have known that wanting or needing money was the only sure way of losing it.

At an unnatural squeak, Kip opened his eyes, not lifting his head or jolting despite the start. Halfheartedly tempted to believe in ghosts or hallucinations, he watched the brunette settle onto the arm of the chair across from him. This brunette, he certainly recognized. She'd changed clothes—her dark curls gathered about a beige sheepskin collar, cascading into the V of denim material like a second fur lining.

"Didn't mean to wake you," she said softly.

"You didn't," Kip said without moving from his lean. His abstract focus slid over her hazel eyes and strained soft smile. She truly was a beautiful young woman, but there were beautiful women everywhere in the world. This was one triangle that Kip could live without. "As much as I'm enjoying the view, Miss Mulden, if you'll retrace your steps to the lobby, I'm sure Angie would be happy to page your brother for you."

Calm and direct, her hazel eyes, searching him, carried a haunted quality, her smile a whisper on her lips. "I didn't come to talk to JD," she said quietly. "I came to see you."

Uncontrollably, his heart skipped a quick beat; unaccountable images flashed neon. Even in the bulky coat, he imagined the long, lean length of her, and several distinctive impressions soared through his mind, and halted abruptly with her brother's precarious status in his mind. Once burned, twice shy.

"I don't think that's a good idea," Kip said in a slightly chilly tone. No games. Whatever her sudden interest in him, her visit, he had only himself to blame. He'd placed that initial phone call like a fly to honey.

"I disagree," she said soberly. "And I won't apologize if I've caught you at a bad time," she said with a tiny flicker of a smile. "You look like you can use some company."

Was she tossing his line back at him, making him an offer? God help her, this was the wrong time. "No time's a good time, but this could be the worst," Kip admitted simply, holding her gaze with the same chilly indifference he adopted at the end of any negotiation. For all the wrong reasons, he might be inclined to accept this proposal. Engaged. Happily, allegedly. Although with a fleeting thought of her seated alongside her intended, he wondered. Either doctor Richard was an idiot, or there was trouble in paradise. Any man who could concentrate on a checkers board with this lady at his side was missing a few basic ingredients—

Not his business! "You shouldn't be here," he said simply.

She studied him momentarily, searching his eyes, his face. Curiosity surfaced behind her sobriety. "I can't decide if you're angry or hurt."

"Neither," he said honestly.

A sad smile touched her lips and flickered in her eyes. "You're a strange man, Mr. Patterson."

Fifteen years ago, a comment like that from a female of her caliber might have crushed him. Presently, it wasn't even mildly annoying. "Redundant, Miss Mulden."

"You look tired," she said quietly. "You sound tired."

"Looks can be deceiving," he said vacantly.

"I had an awful crush on you," she said seriously and blushed a little under the wind-chilled flush on her high cheekbones. Calm and direct, her gaze compelling, a smile quivered on her lips. "You were my first case of puppy love, and I thought I'd die of a broken heart when JD told me you were leaving. You have no idea how devastating such a traumatic experience can be to an impressionable little girl of a worldly eleven."

Faintly amused, he enjoyed the way her eyes brightened with mischief within the soft glow of the slag lamps. An impish smile quivered on her lips. Holding onto his mad, any mad, with this lady around could be a serious problem. She looked at him with such honest, open laughter, and just a touch of color to suggest the integrity underlying her teasing tone.

"Do you have any idea how hard it is for me to keep the world in proper perspective with you sitting over there—looking at me as if I've grown two heads?" She attempted to appear sober, but failed, and shook her head, bouncing a glance off the ceiling and back. "I'm sitting here, making a complete ass of myself, and you're sitting there enjoying every second of it, aren't you?"

"Frankly?" he asked.

"Please," she said curtly.

"You have my undivided attention, luv, and I'm enjoying the view," he said honestly.

"Yeah? Well. You don't hold exclusive rights," she said lightly. "The view's nice from this side, too."

"An observation like that could get you into serious trouble, Miss Mulden," he commented.

Nearly sober, she spoke carefully, her gaze intent. "I'm willing to risk it."

"One of us has far more at stake—" Only a complete fool would continue speaking as Kelly Mulden pushed off the arm of the chair. Silently, he watched her glide around the immense desk, honestly amazed, as she rested one hand on the cushion above his head and locked her hazel gaze, leaning in to brush a kiss on his lips. *Amazed. Not brain dead.* The same heated flash that startled and affected him two days ago spiraled through his mind, flashing through his system. She barely started to lift—his hand slid into the nape of her neck, twining thick silk through his fingers as he tipped her head a little more comfortably. Fantastic images danced into his mind as her lips played over his, filling his mouth and lungs with a taste of peppermint. Never had he craved a mint more than at this moment. By instinct alone, Kip drew her onto his lap, flashing erotic visions of clearing the desk and pillowing her head on her coat—

Pulling back abruptly, Kelly looked into his eyes. Her hazel eyes sparkled, alive with as much intimidation as excitement. "God," she huffed softly. "You're dangerous."

Her coat had fallen under the desk. One of his hands rested beneath her blouse at her back, his other held her hip from sliding away, but her hands were only slightly less guilty. One heated his neck under his shirt collar, the other rested under his shirttail against his waist. "Have you looked in a mirror recently, luv?" he asked softly. At close range, he admired the depth of her emerald eyes, the curve of her full lips, the soft laughter lines following the flow of her long dark lashes. "You truly are beautiful."

"I considered myself a docile, contented fish, upon a time. I even thought I wanted to be a Great White," she said carefully, looking deeply into him. "But I knew I was in big trouble the moment I saw you last week. In fact, I knew I was in trouble the moment I started packing to come home to be here for you." She hesitated, a half-smile lingering, her fingers sliding across his waist, sending rushes up his chest. "Did I happen to mention in my earlier confession? I never quite got over my first case of puppy love?"

"I'm not a nice person, Kelly," Kip said soberly, searching her hunted gaze, hoping to spot a glimmer of better judgment.

"Neither am I," she said quietly, and seemed to watch her hand slide from his neck. A single fingernail trailed across his mustache, quivering his lips, sparking an odd sensation. Her focus lifted. "You're hurt and you're vulnerable and I'm taking advantage of you." Her eyes danced despite a compelling sobriety behind her gaze. "I want to be the one you turn to," she said quietly. "I want to hold you and be held by you, and I want to be the one to make you forget the hurt in your eyes and in your voice."

How her eyes held him, enthralling him within their deep green depths—a livid green, almost too green to be real. And so few women could sound sincere while offering themselves to him. He barely started to tug her toward him—the sharp buzz halted him. His focus passed her shoulder to the telephone, where one of the in-house buttons blinked. In a single motion, he drew his hand from under her blouse, reached, lifted the receiver, and engaged the lighted button. Lifting the receiver to his ear, he barely parted his lips.

"Mr. Bickerman?" a faintly familiar voice inquired.

Before Kip could answer, Bill's voice erupted, agitated, "Yes? Go on?"

"Royce, third floor East. Mrs. Lonnigan just passed away, sir. Dr. Sheffield and Dr. Frances are both here. Her husband's still in there with her."

"When they're finished, send the family down and have her taken downstairs. Send her escort here for her paperwork."

"Yes, sir, Mr. Bickerman. Anything else?"

"There is one more thing. Did you happen to see Mr. Patterson in that wing this evening or any time at all today?"

"No, sir. Not that I can recall."

"Check with your staff, Mrs. Royce, and get back to me."

Hearing the start of a final amenity, Kip shifted the receiver and hung up as the button light flickered, disengaged. Without conscious thought, he depressed the connection for an outside line before lifting his hand to rest against Kelly's waist. What was that all about? Bill wondering about a visit to the ward? Looking into abstracts, Kip considered the first part of the conversation. Mrs. Lonnigan dead, now, too. Her file no longer rested on the desk, removed by Bill nearly an hour ago. *Three.* Three deaths in that many hours. Shaking his head, he suffered an oh-so-familiar grip in his chest as if a black hole had opened and threatened to suck him down. Three deaths. Three hours. Three days. Death always came in threes.

How far had his mother gone? How far beyond the grave could she reach? Surely this was a coincidence, but *how*, for God's sake? Or was that it? Had she made a pact with God? Negotiated a contract with Him, too? Kip imagined her bartering, promising to leave His kingdom unscathed if He helped her to secure her throne. *Dangerous.* Kelly had called him dangerous moments ago, but this thought, this *fantasy, was* even more so.

"Kip?" Kelly interrupted softly. Her palm rested against his cheek; her thumb brushed across his mustache. With a hunted concern, her eyes searched him. "What's wrong, hon?"

Wrong? What could be wrong? Another death, and he suffered grandiose delusions about his mother negotiating with God. *God—only a week!* One week and already, his sanity ebbed at light speed.

Answering an internal need for an anchor, a concrete form of reality, Kip drew Kelly forward and wrapped his arms about her tiny waist and back. Burying his face within her silky curls as her arms slid about his waist and shoulder, he drew in the scent of her strawberry shampoo, listening to the rhythmic wisps of her breath against his shoulder. Her heartbeat pulsed her breast against his chest. She was real. She was alive. Her hands held him with incredible strength.

Mourning. He'd found a cure for mourning. Holding onto a beautiful woman, anchoring himself in the living realm.

"By the time I left here, I thought I'd perfected mourning to an art," Kip uttered, holding onto Kelly as if she were a life vest to keep him afloat, to keep him thinking. Against his shoulder, within his hair, her hands, her arms offered a safety net. Internally, he trembled. His precarious grasp on reality had become a tangible force threatening to cave. Death. So much death. Now, three more. *Five.* Calfactor. His mother...? Not possible. His mother was gone, but he'd never questioned death. He'd found a means to combat the pain, learned in advance when to suffer with them, when to comfort them without lingering in stage one. The denial stage. At the edges of his mind, he sensed the long-ago mechanics threatening to engage, a safety device, fine-turned, to spare him from losing his mind behind the forces of death. When it was over, when he said his good-byes...

In a flashing instant, the immense black album appeared in his mind's eye. Gold-inlaid letters swirled in old English script. 'Family.' The letters scrolled across the cover. The image swam clearly inside his mind. Too clearly.

His fingers drew open the cover, a child's fingers—small—soft—awkward against the silky covering. Pale faded-yellow pages unfolded, broken only by the four black triangles where the corners of a photograph could be tucked in the 20s style stickers. His small fingers shrank, dwarfed against the vast yellow depth of the page. Meticulously, he slid a corner into the small black pocket—then another corner—and in his mind, his mother's face appeared on the glossy print, forever cast in the waxy image of eternal rest within the folds of emerald and white silk...

The picture aged in his stubby fingers. Emerald and pastel faded into shades of gray and black. Rather than the rigid straight edges of a modern photo, he viewed the tattered scallops, yellowed and ragged, crepe paper thin. His mother's face changed. Thickening. Aging. Confusion poured through Kip's mind.

'What are you doing in here!'

The voice, high-pitched and shrill, shot from the past, lancing terror into his frozen mind even now.

In his mind's eye, his head jerked, finding his mother's stricken young face, seeing instead the face of an old man, a decrepit old man lying within an open casket. 'Mo-omm-my?' In blinding motion, she pulled the immense book from his lap and slammed it shut. Her blue eyes blazing with rage, she grabbed his wrist in a bruising grip, yanked him off the floor, and landed him across her lap.

In her room! The photo album! The image he'd carried with him, filling it with funeral pictures inside his mind! The book was *real*!

Snapping awake to reality, Kip eased Kelly's shoulders back, looking into her moist eyes as she appeared to be searching him. Silently, Kip nudged her off his lap, pushing to his feet, clasping her hand as she parted her lips to speak. Gripping her palm, clinging to the anchor of her fingers wrapped about his hand, Kip led her from behind the desk, not fully conscious of dragging her with him to the second oak door or leading her into the carpeted hall.

Far-away voices echoed, as voices always did within the Home, blending with the sounds of metal carts wheeling gelatin and pudding from the refrigerated room off the kitchen. Automated, Kip walked past the doors on his left and right, barely pausing to open his PRIVATE door and pass through the living room.

For a long, eternally long moment, he stood in the open doorway of his mother's bedroom. Forever, he'd avoided this room, never recalling why, knowing only that it was another of those places forbidden to him.

Shivering, Kip scanned her room, sensing her image and character in every swatch of lace and delicate embroidered linen. Only in her private compact bedchamber, Marilyn Patterson buckled to the soft feminine side of her nature. But this was her, too, from the pastel, flowered wallpaper, to pink embroidered pillows and a matching ruffled bed-skirt draped at the bottom of her brass bed. In this room, Marilyn had been a woman and a little girl—a dreamer and a dancer. A magnificent dancer. His focus locked on the aged photograph hanging above her nightstand. An 8 X 10 photo enhanced within an ornate silver frame. In a costume of glitter and lace, she stood poised, arms arched above her upturned face, one long, slender leg stretched to its fullest from the tip of a toe. Her other leg folded, about to be thrust forward in a perfect kick. Magnificent. Every curve and muscle toned, her slender neck poised, accenting the countenance and beauty of her pensive expression. A prima donna.

The Wallendorf and this picture could have been cut from the same mold, and only now did he understand his attraction to that filthy treasure on a cluttered London pawnshop shelf. A long-forgotten memory of this room, this photograph, had lingered in his subconscious.

"She was beautiful," a soft voice whispered.

Startled, he glanced over, waking fully to the young woman whom he'd dragged with him on this weird journey. Absently, Kip nodded and returned the soft pressure on his palm as he cast his gaze to the single long curtain. Unconsciously, he lost his hold on the soft hand, moved past the bed, and parted the soft drape. Dark business-cut skirts and jackets, smooth, silky blouses, and dresses. His focus lifted to the narrow, slotted shelf across the top of the closet. More than twenty-odd years ago, he'd needed a chair and a dozen stacked books.

'Always kept the best books on the top shelf.'

Hugging herself, Kelly watched him while lifting one hand free to brush at the tears threatening to drip down her cheeks. Even knowing, sensing hours ago when he strode from her parents' house that he was a man on the edge, she hadn't fully prepared for this moment. For him, she trembled, remembering those seconds in the office when he'd folded his arms about her. She had felt it, something happening inside of him, something breaking. Behind his smiles, his off-the-wall comments, she suffered his pain and strange conflicts. The instant she looked into his eyes across that desk, the instant he looked at her, she'd sensed a strangeness, a chilling strangeness, and never had he seemed more like a stranger than in those first seconds. As if he'd closed a polished steel door, nothing of his thoughts had surfaced through that shine. He was dangerous. Could be dangerous.

Across the room, he stood holding a flowered drape aside, his wind-blown blond curls tipped at an angle to suggest he looked toward the ceiling, unmoving, as if startled or trapped.

Only seconds ago, when he'd looked into her eyes, she'd seen the boy—the boy she'd fallen in love with so long ago. His face had been that of a man, but his eyes were as open and vulnerable, as terrified as the first time they'd met, as if something, someone had slammed him against a wall as efficiently as the golden retriever of yesteryear. God, she was afraid for him. Never more afraid for another in her life. And there was nothing she could do, nothing but stand within this chilly empty room and watch him, wait for him.

Dancer. His mother had been a dancer. He'd mentioned that detail two days ago, although that information hadn't appeared in her obituary.

Kelly's attention trailed slowly to the framed photo on the wall, seeing, understanding the nature of that shot, likely captured on an impressive stage. Marilyn Patterson. The list of the woman's accomplishments sailed through Kelly's mind, and suddenly, she shivered more. Suddenly, all too suddenly, she felt as if she were walking in another's shoes, as if she'd stepped into the footsteps of the past ... and stared into her own future.

Chapter 26

Hands trembling, Kip lifted the thick album from its dusty corner ... *the weight of it had thrown him off balance. Beneath his feet, his Treasure Island books skidded and clamored, resounding in the windowless room, but he didn't lose his grip on the album.* How the sound of those books and his hard-soled shoes hitting the hardwood floor must have echoed through the labyrinth of empty corridors.

Trembling, he backed from the closet, reading the English script within the swirling black satin. Family Album. Like a quarter of a century ago, he sat down on rubbery legs, dragging his shoes into a semi-yoga fold, cradling the album on his calves and knees. His fingers brushed over the satin, catching a natural scent of aging paper and musty cloth, stricken by the absence of dust. In slow motion, he opened the thick cover, and a brittle, yellowed page followed halfway. A blank page. The same blank page he saw each time he tucked a photograph away inside his mind. The second page carried the meticulous English scroll with faded quill-and-ink script in a flowing, artistic hand.

'Patterson Family begun this *25th* day of *January* in this the *1887th* year of Our Lord.'

Line after line, the ledger denoted names, birth dates, death dates, notations.

His great-grandfather, Kypln Shane O'Patrick—born: 1852 – died: 1882. Murdered. His grandfather had written 'murdered' after the date. Then Ronald E. Patterson, his grandfather, born Shane K. O'Patrick—born 1870, lost his father at age twelve. At twenty-two, Shane immigrated to America with enough money to buy Whittlecreek, a boarding house. *And changed his name?*

"Kip?"

Startled, he jolted as Kelly stooped next to him, her eyes a murky olive and glistening with tears. His attention caught on the envelope she held toward him. In a split second, he recognized his mother's handwriting and his name. Looking into Kelly's soft eyes, he tried connecting thought and question.

"It—it fell out of the album," she said quietly.

Oh God. Another letter. Another clue in her grand treasure hunt? Another of Marilyn's god-blessed manipulations? Angrily, Kip slipped the envelope away and ripped the seal with far less control than he'd opened those first messages from the grave.

Hello, My Darling,

"Damn you," he uttered. "Damn you for mocking me this way!"

Have you put my photograph in this album yet, I wonder.

I doubt you remember speaking to Dr. Blake, God rest his soul, but I do. You described this album to him years ago, and though I can't pretend to know how or what you think, I can only hope that you are here now, reading my words.

How odd it feels to write to you like this. Pre-post-mortem, so to speak. I assume I'm dead or you certainly wouldn't be here—

Bulking at her words, the candid, almost angry clip to her tone with which he was so familiar. The sheet of stationery jittered. He dropped his hands, steadying the page over the open fold of the album.

—I suppose I should apologize in advance. Today, I'm not dealing well with any of this. Seems ironic. Reading our family history as I'm becoming a part of it. Note: your great-grandfather was murdered. (Your grandfather avenged his death, or so he claimed several times with his dying breaths. Probably true. I once tried tracing the O'Patricks. Wealthy Protestants, so we were.) Funny you should turn to Catholicism, in a manner of speaking. Suppose that's my fault, too. You seem destined to hold me forever responsible for the travesties in your life. Just remember, darling, I simply cannot change your past. Anymore than I could change my own. And I'm simply through apologizing to you. Thirty years is far too long to carry this burden. So frankly, my darling, I give you the

story of your birth. I just know how you love a good story. You probably inherited that from my side of the family—the O'Patricks and Pattersons were wonderful Romantics and oh, so creative. Artists, all of us.

Huh! Even now, I try to avoid the truth, believing I can protect you, and from what? Who? Your father? Or Yourself, I wonder. The Blessed Father above knows that your father would have liked nothing better than to whisk you away and publicly announce to the world that he'd fathered a son. Ah, the male heir syndrome which afflicts the socialites of my time. (As if it would make them any more manly.) My own father, God rest his soul, couldn't have been more proud of you had his own infidelity created you. A Son! After 87 years, he finally laid claim to a Son! A mystical experience. Spiritual soul jerker. And so it was, he paid to have the records fabricated in your favor.

Ahead of myself, I was never very good at telling stories—nursery rhymes were always such violent little ditties. Just consider for a moment—little Jack and Jill. What a horrific experience they had for a single pail of water!

Violence. I truly detest violence.

Where was I? Oh, your birth. Still ahead of myself. I'm not going to apologize for not telling you good stories either, Kippen James. You had more than your share of Fairy Tales told to you from early on. Frankly, I had an affair with a well-groomed, handsome—oh, tremendously handsome—young socialite. Actually, I fell in love with him despite my wisdom and superior age. He was barely twenty-eight. I was a worldly thirty-four. A widow. I'd been a widow for fifteen years. If you were forty-five, you'd have been born Robert VanAlt. Robert was a very rugged German—big-boned, blue-eyed, and blond. He swept me off my feet, literally. We were dance partners for almost a year before WW II parted us forever. After news of his death, I sank my heart and soul into dance. I played all the Clubs—from the Big Apple to Montreal—after which, I settled in Boston, where I'd grown up with my cousins. At thirty-three, I'd made a name and enough of a fortune to open a successful school. Maria Van Alt's School of Dance.

Where was I? Oh, yes, back to your birth. The details are still foggy. Things happened far too quickly in '56 and '57. Barring all good sense and better judgment, I fell in love with the father of one of my students. He was an unhappy man in a sad, socially acceptable marriage. They were—and still are—a very prominent and prestigious family in Boston. Exclusive country clubs, incredible parties. Perhaps, 'Prince of Whistlebrook' is a proper title, after all. You have royal lineage. The story. Frankly, about the time our affair bore fruit, I received news of my father's failing health. Whether I left Boston to avoid a scandal or to answer my father's call, I have no recollection now. I simply turned up here and within ten months, I gained a son and lost a father I barely knew; gained a Home and lost a lover.

Why I'm wasting my time telling you this is simply beyond me. By now, your father's undoubtedly broken the promise he made fifteen years ago. He probably ran to you in your hour of darkness and poured the story out to you himself. If I have any regrets, it's the day I called him. Without his help, I'd never have gotten you into that damned school, and though I tread on shallow ground with death knocking at my door, I loathe the day I sent you to those priests! Nothing against God, Himself, mind you. In His own way, I suppose He's looked after you. I heard later, several years ago now, that Brother Nathaniel, the one who made you so miserable, eventually left the priesthood. Seems he was having an affair throughout your stay there, but that's probably old news to you. You could always spot a discrepancy.

So, there you have it. Take it or leave it!

And now, young man, on an endnote. If you are, in fact, responsible for what's going on in this Home, I'd like you to stop it—Now! God knows, I probably haven't been able to stop you in life—not if you're reading this. If this, as it seems, is how you raid and bleed other businesses, I genuinely hope—God forgive me—someone finds a way to stop you. Personally, I love you too much to bring in the proper authorities and stop you. I wanted you to own this Home! To become the King of this Castle! But that's too much to ask of you, isn't it, darling? You're so filled with rage. I saw it. I see it every time you look at me with those cold gray blues. You were not a bitter child. Sad, possibly, but never bitter. That came later, and God help me, to this day, I don't know if you suffered a nervous breakdown before or after someone began doctoring those cocktails. God help me, Kippen, I do love you. My only wish is that I die without ever having to know for sure that you are responsible for all of this.

All my love, whether you want it or not!
Mother

"For all of what, Mother? Good God, for all of what?" Kip uttered aloud. "There's nothing—there was nothing going on here! Goddamn it!"

Couldn't she see that? With all her knowledge and experience with the aged, she couldn't see what was happening to her? The paranoia to accompany degenerative heart failure?

He'd maintained access to the fiscal reports. Watched the losses. It was never a conspiracy or raid! The only conspiracy was the one inside her mind! And the one she created!

The fabrications and stories—she'd built this entire charade, manipulated her dearest friends, and fueled the natural paranoia of the residents for what? She'd likely even tapped her own phone, and when he spoke to Frank Culver, what would that fellow say? That she ordered him to leave the taping device to keep her imaginary villain—Kip James Patterson—in the dark?'

A well of pain swept through his chest, into his spinning senses. Losing hold of the trembling pages, Kip caught his hanging head in his hands, propping his elbows at the edges of the album. "Oh God," he uttered, struggling against the lump in his constricting throat. "Oh God, she was so sssick and—and I didn't know," he spoke softly, squeezing his eyes shut against a flood of tears. "Why, damn her? Why didn't she just *talk* to me?"

Under the soft touch on his head, pain and anger collided.

In one fluid motion, Kip swept the album and letter away, sending them skidding across the floor as he rose. Still in motion, he spun, wanting, needing to break something. He needed a release from the coils of rage racing through his veins. The heel of his palm drove into the wall alongside the curtain. Delicate flowers shattered, spider-webbed, and burst. Chalky wallboard, lattice strips, and fiber-filling of old newspaper caved under the force of his strike.

"Kip!"

No! Not enough! Withdrawing his hand and spinning in a blinding flash of motion, he sent his heel into the wall. Buckling oak molding and doorframe joists screamed an earthquake cry, protesting as a section of the wall twisted, cracking, snapping, and showering ancient wall dust and splinters.

In splitting seconds, he grasped his insanity and the destruction.

Driven by a long-forgotten memory, Kip swept his eyes clear, picked up the scattered letter, and wheeled. Catching Kelly's elbow, he directed her toward the door, needing to get out of this room. *Can't be found in this room!* The noise had echoed! Trembling fiercely, he shuffled Kelly into the living room and yanked his mother's door shut as shouted voices echoed outside the PRIVATE door. Only as he looked into her stricken, blazing hazel eyes, Kip realized the futility along with lingering pain rolling through his system in violent waves.

As Kelly's lovely features washed behind a flood, Kip bowed his face, shaking his head, folding the bleary papers clumsily between his trembling hands. He wouldn't blame her for running, for screaming 'help,' and at long last, Bill had evidence of the Prince's instability. Destruction, for so long, he'd been satisfied just to watch, to enjoy some benign pleasure in destruction, a spectator. Maybe his mother was right. Perhaps they were all right. He'd suffered a nervous breakdown long ago and never recovered. His life had shattered, blasted into the stratosphere. No recovering the pieces. And Marilyn was right about that, too. The rage. Nothing ever took that away. For years, he'd restrained his rages, never striking back when the hurt or frustration took hold. Teenage years, hormones, pent-up anger. Sadness. In this Home, he'd known a great many sorrows, but never rage, not like later.

How could he blame his mother for suffering dementia brought on by a heart condition? Of course, she'd consider him a villain. Internally and externally, Kip had crushed dozens of small companies instead of directing his rage at Whistlebrook. For the pure hell of it, he'd mashed the historical building where the Marie Van Alt School of Dance had resided and turned it into a shopping mall. And she'd learned about that. Apparently, never needed to ask him.

Boston.

At the hands sliding onto his shoulders, Kip started to turn away, but the hands moved quickly, locking behind his collarbone, drawing him. Without conscious thought, he accepted the embrace, and his arms wrapped about the small waist, drawing the warmth against him, vaguely aware of the latent chills.

Poise, the word echoed faintly in the turbulence, like a fly buzzing close to a sleeping ear. His mind was deafened to the sound of a far more violent cry. His mother had died believing he hated her, thinking he hated her enough to destroy her Home—his Home—the only home he'd ever known and wanted. With every ounce of his ebbing will, he restrained a sob, heaving wisps of strawberry scent, holding onto the body against him as tremors rolled from his head to his heels.

Neither the anxious knocking nor the voice broke into his reeling mind. Not the door cracking open or Bill's started-stopped shout affected the maelstrom.

A whispered voice slipped into his consciousness, soft, lyrical, "It's okay. It's okay, honey."

Nodding within a blanket of soft silk, Kip tried to believe those words, needed to accept them, but, oh God, he'd never known either the ache of guilt or reeling confusion battering his skull. His own mother—

"Kip...? Kip, was that...? Did that crash—"

"Go a-way, Bill," Kip managed calmly, darkly. "Just go away."

"Uh...? Yes. All right. Uh ... sorry to disturb you," Bill stammered unnaturally.

An echoing voice slid through the open door. "Was that a crash in here?"

"I'm sure it was," Bill said and snapped the door shut, muffling his words.

More than any other sound or action, JD Mulden's voice started a chain reaction in Kip's mind.

'My sources tell me the Justice Department's up to its old tricks again, having called in a marker or two and pulled a DEA agent out of deep cover. Gave him a new identity as a Forestry Ranger—Justin D. Mulden. Ring any bells?'

A whole cathedral full of bells, Kip had thought to answer, his voice encased in ice as he told Marsh, 'Continue.'

'Traveled almost two thousand miles to comfort an old friend,' JD's voice echoed inside the public john. 'You aren't going to tell me... So, what do you do, now...? Didn't become a priest.'

'What difference does it make to you, JD?'

Me, personally? None. Unless it affects you.'

Anger helped. Nothing helped eradicate pain as swiftly as anger. By the time Kip eased from Kelly Mulden's embrace, his rage had resurfaced behind his abstract gaze. Swiping the last of his tears away, he concentrated on tucking the pages into his back pocket. Was Kelly a part of JD's assignment? Paranoia. Looking into her lovely, damp eyes, he donned a faint grin, willing an apology into his expression. Was she part of a contingency plan B, enlisted to stay close to him in the event the agent's friendship failed? "Did JD suggest you come here?" he asked quietly, letting his grin assure her of his approval if her brother had.

"Honestly?" she asked with a tainted smile.

"Please."

"He's going to be furious if he finds out I'm here," she said with mischief rising, dancing in her honest eyes. "I don't think he trusts either one of us." Her hand slipped through the space between them, touching tentatively on his flannel shirt. Her eyes played over his face; her smile quivered. "He knew all about my childhood fancies—or fantasies—despite how hard I tried to hide them to keep from being teased."

"He warned you to keep your distance, didn't he?" Kip asked, searching, seeing her honesty. God, she was outstanding.

"With your self-professed opinion of women, I really can't blame him for being a little worried," she teased as her hand slid up his chest, in a slow, steady path to his neck. "But it's none of his business. I'm not a love-sick eleven-year-old... And if you tell him any of this, I'll have to hurt you."

Despite all rhyme and reason, he enjoyed her impish smile and macho threat. "Sounds serious, luv." Far more serious, considering her invitation. With her fingers playing under his collar and her eyes shadowing, emitting a different shine, it occurred to him that Kelly was neither an infatuated eleven-year-old nor any part of a contingency plan. She was, in fact, a stunning young woman, and by natural instinct, he leaned into another kiss as his hands found her hips, drawing her against him. With the first throbbing pulses of excitement, he forgot about her brother. Unwittingly, his hands slid under her blouse, aware of her silky warmth under his palms, aware of his urgency growing as he drew tastes of peppermint. The couch—the bed—

The wiretap on the phone!

Recoiling abruptly, his abstract gaze held her suddenly curious eyes, his thoughts turned inward. The receiver in the office had picked up conversations. Kip's focus trailed to the phone on the end stand. Someone had bugged this room late Friday afternoon or Saturday. Why and who? His mother via Frank Culver? The Justice Department via JD?

An hour ago, while talking to Marsh, Kip had believed himself a victim of his mother's manipulation, and in her letter, she'd confirmed his belief. Her brilliant mind, as well as her anger, had wandered in highs and lows. The date. November. A month ago, her illness could have manifested and progressed to the point of dementia and paranoia.

'Nervous breakdown, before or after someone began doctoring those cocktails.' Brompton cocktails, a precise combination of drugs to combat the wicked end-of-life pain.

Doctored?

What the hell did that mean?

'Haven't stopped you in life ... love you too much to bring in the proper authorities... Without ever having to know you are responsible for all of this.'

Goddamn it, for all of what? That question remained. Whistlebrook had been losing money steadily for years, but he had certainly not lent his hand to that decline.

'Haven't stopped you in life ... bring in the proper authorities.'

Oh, Christ. The Justice Department. JD Mulden. His mother's handiwork? Brought here to monitor one Kippen James Patterson in the event of a final financial raid? Or worse? To combat a nervous breakdown?

"Want to talk about it, hon?" Kelly asked softly.

Focusing on her lovely eyes, he reached only one conclusion. He needed to be alone to think, to calm his nerves and gain perspective. Lifting his hand to the nape of her neck, he drew her against him into an embrace and whispered against her ear. "As much as I'd love to spend the next dozen hours making love to you, I don't think I'm mentally or physically up to it. Thank you for being here tonight—"

She leaned back in his arms and looked up with unmasked concern. For a moment, she considered arguing. A faint smile touched her soft features, lighting in her eyes as she whispered, "As much as I know I could regret this, I'll leave, but call me in the morning, all right?"

"Can't promise—"

"Please, Kip," she interrupted, her soft gaze compelling.

"I'll try," he said as he leaned, brushed a light kiss on her lips, and retracted his hands. "I'll walk you to the office. I seem to recall you wore a coat."

"I'm probably going to run into JD out there," she said, and with a combination of amusement and dread, she glanced down at herself and began tucking her blouse into her jeans.

Considering her words, Kip reached for the phone and pressed the appropriate code for the lobby desk. Angie's voice came through with a "Front Desk, Angela speaking."

"Miss, have Mr. Mulden and Mr. Culver returned to the executive wing?"

"Uh, yes, sir."

"Slip around the corner, will you, and have Mr. Mulden come to the phone."

"Right away, Sir! Hold Please!"

Elevator music erupted in his ear; Kip shook his head absently. Either that young woman had worked too long, or she truly was afraid of him.

Only seconds passed before JD's voice erupted, "Mulden, here."

"Did you enjoy your chat with Mr. Culver?"

"Sure did."

"Good. Do me a favor, will you? Take the back hall and check the dock exit doors. When you're finished, meet me in the office." Before JD could question or decline, Kip disengaged the button, then released it and listened to the faint static hum. Just how loyal to Marilyn Patterson was the Captain of the Guard?

"You really are a brat," Kelly mused as she came alongside him. Under his feigned innocent grin, her eyes sparkled, and she laughed softly. "And I have a funny feeling I'm not getting the sendoff over a lack of interest."

"Anything but," he said honestly, looking into her exotic hazel eyes. For the benefit of the receiver, he continued, "I do value your brother's friendship, luv." Sliding his hand into hers, squeezing her palm, he realized his honesty as he spoke. "Besides which, you have your life together, and you'd hate yourself in the morning."

"I'd be willing to risk it," she said quietly, a flash of conflict in the depths of her eyes.

"Richard's lousy at checkers, luv, but if he was willing to drive a Datsun through sleet and snow to be with you, he must love you tremendously."

His words engendered the anticipated result. Her eyes flashed hurt, even as her perspective realigned. "Brat."

"The coast should be clear by now," he decided and pushed off the arm of the recliner.

Chapter 27

Before leaving the suite, Kip returned to his mother's room, replaced the Family Album on the top shelf, and straightened the curtain to cover part of the damage. Locking both the bedroom door and the main door to the suite, he escorted Kelly to the office, not without a bit of stealth to avoid the voices echoing from Bickerman's office and the lobby. "Step into the cove," he told Kelly within the office. "I'll bring Mr. Culver in the front door. Just smile at Angie on your way out."

"Call me tomorrow," she said flatly.

Amused, he winked to her, offering no promise before ushering her into the cove and passing through the secretarial offices. Without a doubt, Bill occupied his office consoling the bereaved Lonnigans while covering the final arrangements. Frank Culver stood, sipping a cup of coffee, while Angie made small talk with another elderly couple signing out. Far too noticeably, Angie stammered as she spotted Kip, and even Frank Culver cast her a curious glance while looking from the gate monitor.

Twenty-three or twenty-four years, Kip remembered absently while motioning Frank to join him. As a young man, Frank Culver had arrived at the Home, not unlike the others within his mother's tight little fraternity. Had she needed to surround herself with young, energetic faces? Except for John Madison, her loyal friends were all at least ten years younger. Excluding Mark Frances, her present cohorts had integrated into the Home structure within four years, from 1958 to 1962.

Ushering Frank into the office, Kip wondered if his mother had strategically and systematically replaced the old regime, beginning with the inception of Edna Feeney. Three years after her arrival, Edna replaced Briggs, to a little boy's relief and gratitude, despite the tragedy surrounding that old hag's passing.

Frank Culver arrived next. Calculating the years, Kip slid into the leather chair behind the desk, motioning Frank into the nearest receiving chair. Barely in his twenties upon his arrival, Culver was barely in his mid-forties now. He slimmed down over the years, but he still posed as a rough character, enhanced by a bristle of day-stubble beard on his rugged jaw. His thick features carried shadows despite his darting eyes. Mourning shadows. In a fleeting thought, Kip remembered seeing Culver at the funeral home and funeral, but not once had Culver approached him directly.

Across the desk, Frank fumbled with something brought from his pocket. A handheld transistor radio landed on the edge of the desk. Culver's dark eyes leveled almost menacingly on Kip's abstract gaze. Anger? No. Beyond anger. Rage knotted the man's grizzled cheeks and wrinkled his temples to either side of a hostile glare.

Slightly taken aback, Kip spared a glance at the radio. Not a radio. An electronic scrambling device? Convenient and relieving though it was, Frank Culver's possession and use of the device posed several questions. "I'd imagine you've activated that device?"

"You bet I did," Frank said in a low contemptuous rumble, leaving no doubt of his attitude. The jamming device perched on the desk symbolized his entire manner. This man neither loved nor trusted the Prince of Whistlebrook. He'd loved the queen, and the queen's words, 'If you're responsible… Stop it—Now.'

Culver had stood as her Captain of the Guard, a loyal captain.

"Did you sleep with her?" Kip asked, and the dark eyes sparked with a violent shine. This once, he doubted he should have asked and nearly regretted his tactics.

Frank Culver carried a gun on his hip, the only guard on the premises, licensed and certified in its use. For several tense seconds, Kip questioned his personal safety. This man, who'd remained forever at the Queen's beck and call, was perhaps just distraught enough to defend Her Majesty's honor and memory. The only thing stopping him—for which, this once, Kip was momentarily grateful—was the man's reflection on the event in question.

What the hell was it with her? A prerequisite for employment? Possibly, the final rite of indoctrination apart from Edna Feeney? His attention wavering, Kip heard his angry, silent cry as his focus trailed to a curtained window. *Did you have to sleep with all of them, for Chrissake?* And she dared to harp on him, accusing him of sleeping with her girls, treating them like his personal harem. His single entreaty didn't hold a candle to her capriciousness. What was her beef with him? The voice of experience? *Christ, was there any man you didn't screw?*

"Happened a long time ago, boy, and it's not your business one way or the other," Culver interrupted in a warning tone.

Abstracted, Kip studied Culver's rage. "Obviously, you were in love with her," he said by way of acceptance while realizing he'd apparently inherited his insatiable libido. Obviously, one part of his inheritance he couldn't sign away. "Would you care to tell me what's going on, or should I take a stab in the dark?"

"It's your dime," Culver rumbled.

Shaking his head, more disgusted than amused despite his grin, Kip sighed and focused on Culver's hostile gaze. "You're convinced I'm behind that wiretap I disconnected this evening, and until this minute, I was convinced you were the guilty party. In fact, I intended to confront you now and have you remove its mate from my mother's personal line. Since we're obviously both wrong, why don't you tell me why you allowed that device to remain on this phone for two months, or should I bother asking?" he wondered absently, realizing. "You and my mother, apparently, assumed I was responsible. You let the device remain to throw me off track. Am I close?"

"Your mother loved you, boy, and that's what killed her," Culver growled, still prepared to slide his hand under his jacket.

His rage flowing, Kip watched Culver's hostility waver under his no longer abstract focus. The waxy luster of his gray eyes fell away, draining into the color of paper ash. "You and I will reach an understanding, Frank, or one of us won't walk out of this room," Kip said in a soft, even tone. "I am not responsible for whatever the hell you believe is happening here, and the sooner you adjust your way of thinking, the sooner we'll get to the bottom of it."

Nothing changed in Frank's eyes or mind. He'd served the queen far too long.

"In a letter I recently received, my mother suggested I speak to you," Kip continued. "I take it you are aware of my options concerning Whistlebrook."

"My position's secure, boy, you remember that if you get any notion to take over here," Frank said without masking his threat. "If you think for one minute I'll sit back and let you destroy this place, you better think again."

Annoyed and angry, Kip forced a calm through his tense muscles, shook his head, and turned his attention to finding his cigarettes. More irritated, he glimpsed Frank reaching under his jacket and heard the safety strap unsnap. Lifting his cigarette pack by index and thumb, Kip exposed the pack while holding Frank's dark, angry glare. Had his mother's love twisted to hatred fifteen years ago? Or was that a recent development?

"If you intend to shoot me," Kip spoke, exhaling a breath of smoke, his gaze leveled with deadly force. "I suggest you consider your future. I'm not armed, and the only crime I've ever committed in this Home was one of ignorance. Obviously, to my present chagrin."

"Just keep your hands where I can see them, boy."

"Mr. Culver," Kip said evenly. "You have two choices. You can either get your hand off that weapon and assist me, which I would greatly appreciate. Or you can persist on your current course, and I will be forced to promote JD to Captain of the Guard, for which he is well qualified, considering his position with the DEA. I do not have time or inclination to play games with you. In less than twenty-four hours, I will sign away the title of this establishment. If there truly is a conspiracy, which it appears my mother believed, I would like to know who's behind it."

Without missing a beat, Kip continued, "Regardless of what you believe, Mr. Culver, I loved my mother as much as she ever allowed, and if someone is responsible for sending her to an early grave, I want the bastard. Do you understand me?"

Frank sat for several long seconds, glaring across the desk as his thoughts spiraled. "Mulden's with the DEA?"

"He's on loan and frankly, that knowledge is between you and me, exclusively. If he even suspects that I've told you and compromised his position, we'll all face serious indictments." Which was likely an understatement, considering the clandestine channels Marsh Baxel had likely enlisted to gain that information. "As far as you are concerned, he's a Forestry Ranger with tactical training from an earlier career. Understood?"

"Drug Enforcement," Culver considered.

Kip nodded, waiting, watching, and considering his level of trust in his mother's Captain of the Guard.

In slow motion, Culver's hostility wavered under the weight of his thoughts.

"My mother trusted you, Mr. Culver, and she wasn't a woman easily deceived. If she—or I—have made a mistake, compromising JD and my position by trusting you... If I find out that you are in any way, part of what's destroying my birthright and taking it from me, I will find a way to prosecute you to the fullest. Is that also understood?" Kip asked quietly, watching closely, seeing Frank's understanding behind a backwash of surprise and bewilderment.

After several seconds, Frank Culver's expression transformed, becoming a complex menagerie of confusion and relief. A slow, worn-out grin dragged on his gaunt lips. "Your mom—she didn't want to believe it was you," he said finally, his gaze leveling. "Me either, boy."

"But she was starting to believe it, wasn't she, Frank?" Kip said as his chest tightened in genuine sorrow. For his mother's descent into paranoia, for this man who'd failed to grasp her dementia.

Weariness and pain spread in Frank's dark, shifting gaze as he nodded. "She didn't want to believe it," he said again. "But every time I ran into another stone wall, she started believing it." His gaze returned with a misty dampness. "The thing is, she figured you were the only one smart enough to pull this off."

"What exactly did she think I was doing, Frank?"

"I don't know all of it," he said wearily, relaxing in his chair for the first time. His gaze settled on the scrambling device. "The Home's been losing money," he said with a concentrated effort. "It's been happening for a couple of years, from what I could figure out. I'm not sure how your mom picked up on it, but for the past seven or eight months, she's had me checking the backgrounds of employees.

"Not the usual background fluff, mind you. She had me tracing histories, including previous work records, schooling, religious and social backgrounds, and birth records. Shit, even more in-depth than that. I can just about tell you what time some of our people get up in the morning and what TV shows they watch before going to bed." He shrugged, weighted by the task he'd undertaken.

Without a doubt, Frank Culver wrestled with his conscience, and considering his last statement, Kip understood. For the Queen, Frank had become a peeping Tom against his private nature. That Marilyn had gone to such lengths was Kip's surprise and sorrow. "Was your search productive, Frank?"

"Guess that depends on what you consider productive," Frank said darkly. "We weeded out a couple of rotten apples."

"Explain."

"Fella by the name of Bill Triance," Frank said, thinking. "Found out he came with a history." Uncomfortably, he shifted, his gaze heating with his memory. "The sonovabitch was manhandling patients at the state home before they caught on and dismissed him with a slap on his wrist rather than a court battle."

"Manhandling?" Kip asked carefully. Ellie Baker sprang to mind.

Frank nodded; his gaze angry. "He was an aide. Apparently, he raped one old woman. The goddamn state home could prove it, but the victim's family would have sued. Instead, they gave Billy his walking papers and a surface clean bill-of-health just to remove him quietly from their facility."

'Billy—he's a devil behind that smile. You mark my words.'

At his thought and memory of Ellie Baker's conspiratorial words, Kip's stomach knotted. Too readily, he understood Mr. Louten's and the young aide, Singer's, concern. Why burden the Prince with an old problem? "Did my mother prosecute him?"

"You bet your ass," Frank said in a voice dark with anger and not just a little pride. "That boy's sitting in the state pen for the next five years."

Not surprised, Kip nodded. "Others?"

"There was a Carl Barker. He had a history of petty theft on his juvenile record, and several residents complained about missing candy money and a transistor or two."

"Prosecuted?"

"Dismissed," Frank said with a faint smile. "Had himself four busted fingers when your mother and I saw him at the unemployment hearing. He lost, by the way. Seemed he got his fingers caught in his car door and tried suing the Home." Culver shrugged, still faintly amused. *Life's tough all over.*

"Any others?" Kip asked, mirroring Frank's amusement.

"There was a little lady with a drug problem," Frank said with honest dismay in his shrug. "It happens. It wasn't the first time medications turned up missing over the years. These girls spend all day looking at dying patients? Gets so they can't sleep for the nightmares. They start off popping a couple pills to sleep." He shrugged, appearing more tired. "Your mom understood, and she wasn't one to be vengeful."

"You didn't prosecute." Kip anticipated.

"Your Mom talked to her, helped her get into rehab. No, we didn't prosecute. The last I heard, Tracy went back to work at the mall. She's a helluva sales lady."

God Bless you, Mother! "Any others with shady backgrounds?" Kip asked.

Frank shrugged apologetically. "There are some whose moral fiber could use a scrub and others with questionable ethics, but basically, as far as I know, everyone's been pretty much cleared."

"What exactly was your focus, Frank? What sort of pattern—or crime—were you looking for?"

Frank considered a moment before answering, "Your Mom went over the information. I just collected it." He shrugged. "That's how it's always been, boy. Your mother never explained her needs."

"You simply gathered information." *Searched and snooped into the personal lives of over 120 employees, and never asked why?* "What's become of the information you've accumulated, Frank?"

"Your mom kept everything downstairs in the old fruit cellar. She converted it into a vault about ten years ago. Called it her 'archives,'" he mused fondly. "We moved the old trunks and boxes out of the attic... Anyway, we have it all down there."

Kip nodded absently, concealing his surprise and annoyance. His mother hadn't mentioned her *archives*, not to him, as if that should be any surprise.

"Your mother kept her key in the safe there, but if you, and Mulden, want to have a look, I could point you to the right cabinets and save you some time."

Kip nodded again, vacantly. His thoughts snagged momentarily on the idea of entering the basement, her archives. Even as much as fifteen years ago, he'd avoided that damned basement. He could almost smell its damp, musty scents of brick and stone. *Damn it*, he nearly uttered aloud, aware of his unnatural pause and a pulse tapping subtly at his temple. If Frank was thorough, those files probably contained enough damning evidence to ruin about a hundred lives. Doubtful that more than ten or twenty qualified for sainthood. Before he left, he'd need to visit the basement and destroy those files.

Thanks a bunch, mother. Prince my ass! Why not Keeper of the Tomb?

Aligning his thoughts, Kip glanced at the scrambling device. If Frank hadn't planted the bug...? JD? Possibly. Probably. He was one of the few outsiders who could pass through the kitchen, into the suite, and out without a need to sign in. Except that Edna would have mentioned seeing him.

A vision of a brunette flashed through his mind, a beautiful brunette wearing expensive clothes, a wedding band, and a wonderfully erotic smile. Had she found him in the shower by coincidence? Justice Department recruit? God knows, she'd presented a class act. She could have slipped into the suite while he was in the shower.

With a thought, Kip looked over to Frank. "The camera at the gate, I take it you have the tapes in-house?"

Frank nodded, "We only keep them around for a week, though."

"Excuse me?"

"We reuse the tape every seven days," Frank said carefully. "Saves a helluva lot of expense except that... Well, I plan to keep the one from Tuesday. I bought a replacement at my own expense." His sadness lingered as he wondered, "A reason you asked?"

Distracted, Kip needed a moment to remember his reason. "Yesterday." *God, it had been only yesterday!* "I'd like you to check the tape from yesterday between ten and noon and match the plate numbers against our sign-in sheet." Which could take hours. If he saw her, he would know her, and that gate camera was allegedly designed to capture faces. "On second thought, why don't we go look at that footage?" he decided and leaned forward, crushing his cigarette as he pushed to his feet.

Frank lifted his scrambler and stood up.

Kip glimpsed Frank tucking it into his jacket and met the man's critical gaze, wondering, "How many of those devices do you have, Frank?"

"A few," he answered offhandedly and brought it out as Kip rounded the desk. His concentration divided as he held it out, showing the single 'on-off' control. "It's only effective on the room receiver. Doesn't help with the phone tap. You sure the suite's bugged?"

"Reasonably," Kip answered and accepted the transistor that, for all intents and purposes, looked like an a.m. radio complete with a numbered tuning dial. He'd seen other, more compact models, and it occurred to him, "Handmade?"

Culver smiled slightly and shrugged. "I always liked tinkering with electronics."

"My mother had one of these—" In her room, on her nightstand, Kip remembered absently and looked into Frank's shaded eyes. His concentration wavered under one of those incredibly painful grips of reality—his mother was dead. *Had*—the operative word. And Kip felt suddenly as if he were merely going through the motions of a drama she'd created, humoring her, like her multitude of loyal subjects had, unwittingly, humored her.

Chapter 28

B ill's voice echoed from the lobby, and, decidedly, Kip motioned Frank toward the kitchen, preferring not to see Bill or anyone else. Passing through the shadowy kitchen, they strode silently through the narrow age-old corridor, and Kip caught the faint echo of a television voice as they passed Edna Feeney's door. He hadn't seen her at all today, and with his thought, he nearly turned around. When he'd lived in this Home, not a day passed, from the day Edna arrived to the day he departed, when he hadn't seen Mrs. Feeney. The same rule hadn't applied to Marilyn.

Following Frank into the security room, Kip remembered many of his mother's two- or three-day absences. He remembered lying in bed, trying to detect sounds from her room or the living room. He remembered once knocking at her bedroom door at 6 a.m. only to discover later that she'd been away for nearly two days.

His thoughts adrift, Kip stood aside watching as Frank brought the tapes from a metal cabinet. Within this main terminal, the system appeared efficient enough, considering the nature of the business. A series of lights on a main board designated various entrances. The exact sequence appeared on the monitor in the lobby and probably on at least three other stations within the Home. Four screens on a panel in front of Frank's desk supplied various angles of the main entrance, along with two different angles that Kip hadn't known existed. Mildly impressed, he recognized a wide-angle sweep of the front lawn and parking lot on one screen; another provided an ample view of the service lane behind the Home. How long ago had Frank added those secondary cameras? Silently, Kip watched as the front and rear angles vanished into a black screen.

"This should be it," Frank tossed over his shoulder while his hands worked the controls like a concert pianist.

This room was Frank's creation. With rising appreciation for the system and its obvious creator, Kip watched the screens. By no surprise, Franks' underlings could stand in the lobby and watch the monitor. This terminal wasn't the main terminal; however, merely an extensive duplicate of another, which probably existed in Frank's private domain, the carriage house above the garages.

"10 o'clock," Frank commented as the screens brightened. One showed a wide angle of the front lane and stone pillars; another provided a magnification of the space directly between the pillars. "Any particular car we're looking for?" Frank asked as a dark sedan turned into the lane.

Kip watched the enlargement, identifying the faces of an elderly couple through a splattering of light across the windshield. "Roll forward. Pause at every car for three seconds." Ample time to identify the brunette. "I'll tell you when to stop."

Over the next ten minutes, the screen flashed on and off on a dozen windshields as cars raced back and forth, in and out, and passed the gate along the highway. A Porsche, several Lincolns, and Dr. Frances's Mercedes. Bill drove a blue, late-model LeMans. Carolyn McAnthony arrived in a Porsche … a Porsche? Charlie apparently took good care of her.

"Stop," Kip stated simply, and the screen froze. The brunette hadn't been a mirage. Behind the steering wheel, she posed, frozen, every bit as lovely as he remembered. Her long red nails rested over the top of the wide wheel. In the secondary distance shot, he recorded the details of her car, a dark blue generic sedan. Not a Limo by any stretch of imagination, and that aligned well with his thought of government status. "What's the time on that shot, Frank?"

"12:08," he commented.

"Find her departure time," Kip commented and watched as the picture took flight at fast-forward. According to the register, Mary Smith arrived at 12:10.

"Looks like a rental," Frank commented.

Kip glanced off the back of Frank's dark, gray-streaked head with a shade of blue haze to account for his intensity on his task. An insight, perhaps, this was Frank's bailiwick and strong suit. The Captain of the Guard had spent two dozen years car watching. If Culver believed it was a rental, it was probably a rental.

"Bingo," Frank spoke as the frame halted on the back of the car. "Rental," he said bluntly, tapping the magnified screen with the end of a pencil, designating the bumper sticker. "Time—12:23." He looked up over his shoulder, waiting.

Deciding, Kip commented, "I'd like the lady's name, Frank. This one's personal. Leave JD out of it. Can it be done?"

"Give me ten minutes," Frank said confidently. "Anything else on this tape you want to see?"

A thought crossed his mind. His focus shifted to the screen, then to Frank. "Friday night. I walked in the East Wing door—" *Not undetected*, Kip realized and verified his thought. "This is a secondary terminal. You watched me enter."

Nodding slightly, Frank wore a faint apology. "Those front cameras are concealed. Your mom and I had them installed over the summer. I don't keep these monitors rolling unless I'm in the building. My assistants don't know about them, and that's the way your Mom wanted it."

Nodding absently, Kip understood. Frank truly hadn't trusted him. His gaze focused on the screen, then on Culver. "Did JD see them?"

"No, but I could bring him back—"

"Frank," Kip interrupted quietly, holding the man's gaze. "I'd rather JD not know everything we're up to," he said carefully. "I've brought him in as a precaution. I didn't know who I could and couldn't trust. I'd like to get to the bottom of this without destroying the Home or dragging it through a lengthy government inquisition," he paused, letting Culver introvert the words. A faint, odd glimmer of amusement lit behind the dark eyes. Nearly losing his train of thought to his curiosity, Kip continued absently, "Can I trust you, Frank?"

With a slow turn of his swivel chair, Frank held out his rugged palm, his gaze steady as Kip accepted his handshake. "Glad you weren't a part of this, Kip, and if you have a plan to straighten this out, count me in."

"I appreciate that, Frank. You'll find me in the office when you have information on that woman. I'd like to visit the archives if it's not too late when you're finished."

"I'll see you in the office. About ten minutes."

Kip nodded, glancing at the current screen in time to watch a car stop between the pillars. An econo car, he noted, and glanced at the sidebar. Shit! Only 10:05. Felt like three a.m.

"That's Angie leaving there," Frank commented. "She's a good kid. Comes from a shit family, but she's doing okay. She never misses a Sunday night at the desk."

"A reason?"

Frank wore another grim, reflective smile. "Your mom gives her time-and-a-half and lets her cut out early Tuesday and Thursday for night school. Poor kid's a mess worrying and..."

Grieving.

"She's flighty," Kip commented.

Frank found the comment amusing. "Seems to me, you have a way of stirring up the ladies."

Kelly Mulden? "Did JD happen to recognize any of the cars coming or going while he was in here?"

Culver considered before shaking his head, turning his gaze to the blacked-out screen. "Not that he mentioned."

Why worry about it? JD wouldn't compromise his position by starting a battle over his sister. If anything, Mulden would work on Kelly to back off, and that would satisfy all concerned. The last thing Kip needed was an affair with the sister of a DEA agent, and it was no longer a surprise that Mulden's address wasn't readily available.

His thought carried him into the lobby. Preoccupied, Kip strode to the coffeemaker, filling a cup and dumping a little too much powdered creamer on top. God, those green eyes of hers. A guy could get lost in those eyes ... and her smile. Damn it! Forget it—forget her! Tomorrow night at this time, Kip would board a plane bound for California.

Whistlebrook would be the final photo tucked into that black album; then, perhaps, he would bury the album once and for all, along with the plague of colors swirling in his isolated world.

All those faces. Absently, Kip swiveled a stir-stick through the white lumps. Faces upon faces swam through his mind, and now, at long last, he could imagine JD's face in a photograph. No more illusions. The JD Mulden that Kip had known briefly and mourned as a child was officially gone, now. Like Marilyn Patterson and the memories that went with her. Mrs. Edna Feeney. Kip would miss her, but the years had already distanced them.

Tomorrow, after the reading, he would hug her one last time, then climb into his Buick and drive away—a free man. Nothing else would he allow himself to consider. At long last, free of all the Goddamn anger and pain, free of memories and burdens, The ghosts.

One last hoorah. In his mother's memory, Kip would follow through with her little charade. What was that she'd written? 'We Pattersons are creative.' This one was a beaut, but he wasn't falling for it. Tomorrow, he'd pack his bags—maybe tonight—and put this fairytale behind him once and for all.

As he turned from the courtesy table, Kip's gaze caught on the hazel eyes across the room. This once, not even a slight smile touched Mulden's bearded lips—a beard probably only recently cut and trimmed for a Forestry Ranger image. How long was that beard and wavy hair before a week ago? Or had Mulden posed as one of those well-groomed drug-lord punks? Ironic, Mulden had accused him of acting, Kip considered as he settled sidesaddle on the cleared reception desk. "The rear doors are secure?" he asked.

JD nodded without moving from his casual pose on one of the Victorian settees. A cup balanced on his ankle, crossed over his knee. His gaze held steady. "You just missed Bickerman. Said he'd see you in the morning. My coworker—Ted whatsisname—just went to make his rounds. Angie said something about a message on the desk there for you."

Glancing sideways, Kip spotted the single sheet of stationery. Mark Frances had called from somewhere in the Home; he planned to stop at the office before leaving. Two outside calls had come for him, but the callers had neglected to leave a name or number—not surprising. Balling the note, Kip leaned and made two points in old Mrs. Conners' trash basket. Now what to do about JD?

"Think we could talk in your office?" Mulden asked.

Pushing off the desk, Kip agreed by action and fumbled in his pocket for Dorsen's key on route to the office. Forever, that sound rattled in his mind. The clink and tinkle of keys dangling from his mother's hand or jiggling in her smock or suit pockets. Crossing the room in the murky glow through the sheer curtains, Kip sidled behind the desk before igniting the reading lamp. In his back pocket, Frank's scrambling device maintained its silent vigil.

Leaning back in his mother's chair, Kip watched JD settle into the receiving chair, his vision unwavering despite his memory of Kelly perched on the arm of that same chair. Brother and sister, their eyes were alike in shape and shade, but how much more JD's eyes had seen. Within an upward glow reflecting off the desk, Mulden's eyes carried an angry shine, a surrealistic shine, true to his nature. A reflection of his occupation, no doubt, with blues and reds swirling in a mist to frame his entire image. Powerful and intense. He'd seen those colors a lifetime ago, but the shades were off now, cloaked in deceit.

"Kelly was here," JD said quietly.

By no surprise, JD knew. The time alignment coincided with his trip to the security room. Kip nodded absently, cursing the light. He would have preferred seeing Mulden's eyes without the shine.

"For old time's sake, Kip, don't play games with her," JD said carefully. "I'm not thrilled with Dr. Whitman, but he's in love with her and I think she's happy with him."

Mulden's acting abilities were impressive. He managed to mask his anger well. "Odd, I mentioned something similar, not quite so eloquently stated, before sending her home to her inadequate checkers partner."

"She's infatuated with you," Mulden said quietly; his attention shifted, returning with a subtle, wary grin. "Don't mistake this, Kip. If I thought your interest was anything more than physical, I wouldn't mind, but I've seen your moves. Women are toys, and romance is a game with you. Don't reel her in and leave her hanging."

How much did Mulden know about KJ Patterson? What had the DEA agent read in the inevitable dossier his employers, undoubtedly, compiled? Did Mulden know how much one enterprising old friend thrilled to corporate kill and how same old friend enjoyed high stakes? Did Mulden base his concern on how many unhappy mistresses and spouses had unwittingly assisted in certain conquests? Did he have any idea how difficult it was to ignore the opportunity his little sister provided and how easily he could be destroyed if revenge were a motivator?

"I just don't want her hurt, Kip," JD said carefully.

Always the Camelot—defender of Truth and Justice. *And now, Chastity?* Faintly amused behind his vacant gaze, Kip sipped his coffee before setting it aside and lifting his cigarettes from his shirt pocket.

"So, what's going on here?" Mulden asked as if forcing a subject change to offset the uncomfortable conversation. "Wiretaps and bugging devices? Double-checking security systems.? What are you worried about?"

Oh, he was good. So casual and concerned, that childhood voice of his. Exhaling smoke, Kip leveled his focus. JD had shifted. His face wore more shadows, his hazel gaze less menacing in the angled glow. "Temporary insanity," Kip commented. "And I probably should apologize for dragging you into my paranoia." Deliberately, Kip drifted his gaze over the shadowed office. "So many fucking memories," he said absently. "Too many, I think. A flood gate opened tonight, and I panicked." He admitted, truthfully, thinking about those three failing residents in the same number of hours.

A natural phenomenon, those deaths. Fr. Jordan had forewarned him over the inevitable loss only yesterday, and the causes of death this evening verified the natural decline. So much death. Likely half of the current residents would pass away within the next two or three years. They came here to die … and the big guy in the sky had probably implemented this evening's playbook to solidify a particular undertaker's course.

He looked at JD with a faintly desperate grin and a slight shrug. "Can you understand that, JD?"

Mulden nodded, appearing disheartened. "Yeah, think I can."

"Tonight's my last night here," Kip continued, looking into abstracts, rolling his focus across the felt mat. "I think I needed to step into her shoes just once, and I understand her better, now."

"You've made up your mind, huh? Not sticking around."

Without focusing, he answered, "I have a life of my own, JD. It's time I return to it."

"What kind of life, Kip? What do you do?" JD pressed concernedly.

"I'm an entrepreneur," Kip admitted in an abstracted tone. "I make a modest living in the stock exchange." He shrugged indifferently, his focus drifting. "I love the change of scenery and freedom. I always felt trapped in this Home, trapped in a crypt. Always so much death, And how I despised the scent of disinfectant." With a faint grin, he shrugged again. "Ergo, my botanical treasures, I wake up to the scent of damp soil, forest greens, and exotic flowers."

JD smirked a grin. "I'd love to see your house. Sounds wild."

"Can't see the forest for the trees," Kip mused. "It's one erotic terrarium, and I suppose I'm eccentric, but there's simply nothing like the scent of primal growth to stimulate erotica." Without more than a second's pause, he asked, "Do you have any pictures of your sons?"

In a delayed second, JD leaned, setting his coffee cup on the desk. "Matter of fact, I do," he said as he pried his wallet from a back pocket. Flipping it open, he leaned more, handing the open photo flap across the desk.

Accepting the wallet, Kip leaned back, looking down at the face. So like JD's face, the little boy smiled through a plastic case—a school photo. Eight or nine, immense hazel eyes. "Handsome boy."

"That's Justin, taken a couple months ago. PJ's on the other side."

No DEA identification in this wallet. Kip turned the flap, simultaneously glimpsing the Forestry Ranger badge behind the leather flap. His focus divided, seeing the younger child and the lovely face in the next flap. Kelly Mulden's smile drew him, sending an echo of sparks through his muscles, awakening a pulse in his groin. Her hands had electrified pulses in his chest and neck, her... *Damn it!* She was just another female. Another attractive female. But his thumb moved over the plastic cover as if he could feel the warmth of her smile and the heat of her expressive green eyes.

Impulsively, he snapped the wallet shut and tossed it across the desk as he leaned forward. Crushing the cigarette butt in the ashtray, he pushed from Marilyn's chair and moved to the window. Parting the sheer curtain, he panned his gaze over the rear parking lot within a wash of floodlights.

A reality break. Kip watched snowflakes dancing in the nearest pool of simulated light. JD Mulden had come home to evidence a government indictment. Undoubtedly, a conspiracy charge, probably concerning Amcon Co., which had crumbled like a sandcastle under a flood of the Undertaker's liquid green. Death by drowning. Formaldehyde. Five months ago, Kip remembered absently. Five months ago, Amcon had folded, and its assets liquidated. In the spring, providing the ground passed the EPA tests—which was questionable, considering the chemicals Amcon had produced on the soil—condos with a kiddie park would begin construction. Not a bad trade-off or accomplishment for a nearly year-long effort. He should have known the bastards in the Justice Department would get shook on that venture, what with the nature of Amcon's contribution to the war machine.

"Did you ever consider having kids?"

"Once," Kip answered offhandedly. "Found the possibility highly unlikely." The bastards never minded when he crunched Reibold Inc. and saved them the aggravation—and embarrassment—of admitting the German subdivision was supplying too many nuts and bolts for their fucking tanks. Maybe it was time to forfeit his loyalties and citizenship. Ireland was probably beautifully morbid this time of year. A great swell of fog over the moors. Kip remembered thinking about Misty Haven Cemetery when he last visited the home of his ancestors. With a family name O'Patrick now in his cache of knowledge, he might have more success at seeking his forefather's birthplace. Nearly a year wasted in search of a Ronald E. Patterson or Marilyn Van Alt—the names on his birth certificate.

"So many fucking lies, Mother," he muttered aloud. He'd discovered her dance career while researching the Van Alt name, and he'd visited the street where her studio stood thirty years ago. Had she nurtured the seeds of distrust he'd planted as much as eight years ago when tearing down those decrepit buildings and erecting a shopping mall in their place? Had her paranoia begun that soon? Had she believed Whistlebrook would be next? That he'd move in for the kill and erect a mall on this lovely white hillside? Randall was ripe for development. He could unload this monster and turn over a couple mil without half trying, and her fucking options were so filled with gaps they looked like cheesecloth. He could walk into Madison's office tomorrow and accept his inheritance. Before the ink dried, he could be on the phone, enlisting his attorneys to draw up proposals and begin liquidation. No one alive—or dead—could legally stop him if that were his desire.

How the hell could she have known so very little about the bastard she created?

He'd loved this goddamn relic from its catacombs to its spires, with its eccentricities from private apartments to critical care wards. If his mother hadn't sent him away, he might actually have ascended from the kitchen staff, where all new employees began, to a residency with a dozen college years behind him. Upon a time, he'd believed his course set, and if not for her divine intercession, he would have followed his heart, attended Harvard.

And the irony struck like lightning. He might have met Richard Whitman along the way. Doubtful they'd have become friends, but they might have been colleagues. With a cynical twitch in his mustached lips, Kip considered siccing Marsh on the Whitmans. North or South Carolina. Good, wholesome southern gentility. It wouldn't take much effort to discover everything he needed to know.

"Damnit," he muttered, reconsidering. Why? Why fuckup Kelly's life? Or her in-laws' lives, more precisely? If he went after them as ardently as he sought corporate takeovers, she'd likely end up married to a pauper. And for what? Jealousy? A childish tantrum? A blasted whim?

Maybe his mother was right. He was a monster.

Mulden had said something.

The knock on the office door interrupted Kip's thought more effectively. Turning, dropping the curtain, he bounced a glance off JD's critical gaze to the door. "Come in. It's open," he stated sharply. Too sharply. As if a whirlwind had begun at the edges of his mind, the tension spiraled through his muscles. He needed to get the hell out of here, once and for all. Bury the damned memories.

The door parted slowly. Frank hesitated, then continued inside, nudging the door to snap shut in his wake. He glanced off JD with a curt nod as he passed and brought a piece of paper from his jacket, handing it to Kip with a faint grin. "Sorry it took so long."

In neat block print, the name Marion Smithfield headed the paper, but Frank Culver hadn't limited his investigation to the name. Airport Hilton—12/20-12/21. Home address, street and number, Boston, Mass. Maiden name: McDaniels. As Kip read her phone number, his thoughts came to a halt. In his mind, the numbers overlapped. Denton McDaniels' phone number.

'Prince of Whistlebrook ... Kippen.'

Revelations tumbled one over another, kindling his anger. McDaniels. Kip had seen that face—one of two hundred faces within the basilica—but those gray-blue eyes had looked at him, into him, with an intensity to draw his attention for several stopped seconds with an instant spike of green and blue – powerful and caring, nurturing? He'd only begun trying to discover the meaning of those colors while haunting the halls of St. John's. For an instant, a single instant, Kip had recognized that smirked grin on the stranger's face before his search had continued for the only familiar face he'd expected to find at his commencement ceremony.

Boston, Massachusetts—home of the long-forgotten Maria Van Alt's School of Dance.

Home of a handsome married gentleman, the father of a student.

God Almighty. Alias Marion-Smithfield, who'd stood appraising him like a side of beef, then dried him off and turned him on, a half-sister?

Unconsciously, Kip stepped back, leaning against the window frame, lowering the paper that trembled in his hand. Denton McDaniels was his father. After thirty years of growing up without a father, thirty years of wondering what it would be like to have a living father and a real mother...? Shaking his head absently, Kip stared into abstracts beyond and including the paper to hover, semi-crinkled, in his fist. What did it matter? He was long past the need for familial ties. His mother was gone. His Home would be gone in the morrow, and he'd be on a flight back to his own life.

He might even spare the undoubtedly pompous southern gentry after a week of jogging on his favorite sunny beach.

"Are you all right, Mr. Patterson?" Frank intruded in a low, alarmed tone.

Mr. Patterson?

Like a match to mesquite, that address ignited the fire smoldering behind his gaze. All the deceit, the lies, the manipulations! From the late, great *Mrs.* Marilyn Patterson!

"Don't you fucking call me that," Kip said in a deep, raging tone, his gray eyes lifting with a manic, violent shine. "Don't you *ever* fucking call me that again, Frank. Call me anything—Kip—Boy—Bastard—Undertaker—Prince of *fucking* Whistlebrook. Call me a fucking moron. But don't you *ever* call me *Mister* Patterson the way you've called my mother *Missus* Patterson! Do you understand me—?"

"Kip?" JD started.

"Simmer down," Frank started.

"Get the fuck out of here," he said as he rose fully on his feet, his muscles stiffening, his adrenaline rising in a heated wave. Bouncing glances between them, he stated, "Both of you. Get the fuck out of here—" He wanted, needed to be alone. Enlightenment was not good for the soul. Enlightenment. His mother had gone to her grave, thinking him a monster, believing he'd conspired against her. Not once, but twice, if he understood that letter and her reference to fifteen years ago. Fifteen years. For fifteen years, she'd believed him lurking in the shadows, prepared to pounce and destroy her. Willing to murder to destroy her!

Mulden came off his chair and started around the desk. "Slow down, man. What's wrong? What set you—"

"What's wrong?" he asked in a descending tone, a confessional tone. "Nothing's wrong. Tomorrow I'm getting the hell out of here once and for all. If I'd salvaged any sanity over the years, I'd have taken both of my suitcases Tuesday. I could have gotten on a fucking plane and gone back to my own life. Frivolous as it is, goddamn it, I wouldn't be surrounded by death and deceit. I could have been screwing Morgan into oblivion to the scent of jasmine and hibiscus. It's my newest, most effective cure against mourning. And no, I didn't screw your sister…"

Why the hell am I telling them this?

"Goddamn it, Kip, slow down. What the hell was on that note?"

"Just one more turn of the screw, JD. My mother hated me, if you must know. She died believing I was the devil incarnate, and there's not a fucking thing I can do to change that."

"Your mother didn't hate you, boy—"

"You, sir, have no idea. She manipulated you and dragged you into her dementia. The Great Queen of Whistlebrook. She manipulated you, her attorney, doctors. Hell, probably even Edna and Carolyn with the sole intention of proving what a bastard I am."

"Slow down," JD stated. "Where's this coming from?"

For a stopped second, Kip considered the question, then knew. From fifteen years of uncertainty and growing rage, never knowing, only suspecting that his mother hated him, and never knowing why. Not why she despised the sight or sound of him, sensing she held him accountable for something. Often wondering if he'd somehow truly facilitated Mrs. Ramsey's death to be so punished. Mixed and muddled, those wicked memories, but he'd always wondered if the rumors held some grain of truth. He'd caught that wondrous old woman, cushioned her fall, and sustained a near-lethal hernia in the process. And that single moment had altered the course of his life.

Coming here had been a mistake! He should have hired his own stand-in. He lived in the actor's capitol of the world, for Chrissake, surely he could have found a look-alike to attend this affair in his stead. He could have lived his life without knowing that his mother had suspected him of murder and believed him capable of destroying her.

"Fuck it! Goodnight," Kip stated and sidestepped from between them. Avoiding JD's attempt to grab his arm, Kip spun, backstepping as he leveled his gaze on JD. "Go home or stay here. Suit yourself." Then to Frank. "Go home. Go to bed, Frank. My mother was suffering from dementia brought on by the decreased oxygen flow to her brain. There is no—and never was—a conspiracy in this Home. You. All of you who knew her, trusted her, loved her, and idolized her. She had you all under her thumb, and she used you, Frank. She drew you into her paranoia. The Home's been losing money for years. If it had suffered a serious loss, I would have known and bailed her out of the fucking hole. I'm not a *monster*, goddamn it! I was her *son*! Why the fuck couldn't she just talk to me—?" With a sting of tears threatening the edges of his eyes and his voice choking, he shook his head. "Fuck it. Goodnight," he said as he turned and yanked open the door.

Oh, Naturally! The good *Dr. Frances!*

The same fellow who'd once snowed him under for over a week to keep him from ripping his insides to shreds

In one blind instant, Kip wheeled and slammed Mark Frances in the jaw, staggering him backward into the hall. Looking into his stricken blue eyes, Kip commented, "I really fucking hate physicians, and if you even think about loading a syringe and filling me full of Thorazine again, I'll break both your fucking arms." Sidestepping past Mark as the *good doctor* Frances collected his balance and lifted a hand to his bloody lip, Kip continued down the hall. To hell with digging for keys, too. With a half turn and spin, he landed his heel alongside the PRIVATE doorknob. The door snapped open with a mighty crack of shattering oak.

Kip barely started through the doorway as the phone jolted him with a piercing ring. In one motion, he grabbed the phone base, yanked and spun, snapping the cord and catapulting the silenced instrument into the hall. As it bounced off the opposite wall, Kip closed the PRIVATE door.

At least by God, they had a damned good reason—now—to consider him insane.

The sound started as a chuckle, but by the time he lay down on the winter-colored quilt, flashing a thought of Mrs. Ramsey, sobs burned in his chest, locked behind a vault of pain. He would not cry. He'd never cried at a funeral and very seldom after.

He needed to concentrate, bring Marilyn's image to the foreground, and tuck her into the family album.

A conspiracy, Goddamn it. The only conspiracy was the one she'd created, but even as he tried tucking her photo into the black corner diamonds, his thoughts shattered.

Four months ago. He'd seen her four months ago and failed to grasp her declining health, but was that so odd, truly? Even if he'd noticed a decline, it might not have registered in his mind. The infallible Marilyn Patterson, a pillar of the community. He wouldn't have believed her failing condition even if she'd worn a black cloak from head to toe.

Why couldn't you just talk *to me, damn you, Mother! Just damn you, Queen of Whistlebrook!*

Epilogue

Nothing had changed. Not one thing had changed. Looking over the shadow world beyond the glass, she felt the weight of that single discovery running through her veins, as chilling as the frigid air whipping whirlpools on the slick parking lot outside. She stood in darkness, shivering as if the wind breached the double panes or slipped through cracks at the sill. Nothing had changed, and if she suffered any regrets about what she'd done, she could dismiss them, now. His voice, when he dropped the theatrics, was as icy as an arctic blast, as automated as the voices in the house speakers. Waiting wouldn't have helped. Letting nature take its course, letting time heal all wounds, wouldn't have helped. Bringing him home, now, had been the only way, and death—death was all he'd known in his life, here. No, no regrets, no remorse. Speeding up time had been the only way.

Marilyn Patterson had to die.

Why, then, was she fretting, she wondered absently, unconsciously, hugging her arms across her chest. Without the aid of lamps, the shadows of the night closed around her, contrasting intensely with the white glow of a dozen vapor lights lining the rear lane and loading docks. As plain as day, she'd heard the bitterness in his chilled tone, understood at last what others heard when facing him across a boardroom table. He would have destroyed Whistlebrook despite his words to the contrary, although he'd certainly sounded sincere when declaring his innocence in that regard. She knew differently, however.

He'd been such a loving child. Sad, perhaps, but naturally so with so much sorrow abounding within the halls. He'd once admitted to seeing halos ... and called them angels. The angels of death.

A shiver slid down her spine as she considered those words and the implication of those dark entities existing in the Home.

Barely four, she remembered, he'd only begun speaking again when he'd shared that secret with her. 'I know when they're ready, Momma,' he'd confided in her. 'The dark angels tell me when it's time, so I can sit with them.'

She should have whisked him away then, thrown caution to the wind, and carried him away from here. But what kind of life could she have given him? At least here, she'd protected him and kept him safe from the cruelty he would have faced, At least she believed it so. But how much worse it had become. By the time she realized the danger for him, it had nearly been too late. She'd almost lost him, mentally, physically, and if she'd kept him here, she harbored no doubts, she would have lost him. Just the thought of losing him enhanced a weight of sorrow she couldn't shake.

Sending him away hadn't helped, though. It had already been too late.

That accident with Mrs. Ramsey had become the catalyst. Or the beginning, as she'd often considered. The night he'd tried saving that dear old woman from catastrophe had triggered a series of events that no one could have predicted. And the details remained a mystery still. The only certainties were the hernia that had nearly taken his life in the wake of that accident and the deaths to follow. Sending him to a seminary school, removing him from that wicked public high school, had seemed like a sensible solution; after all, he'd lived within a controlled environment his entire life. If he were around boys his own age, away from the specter of death, she'd believed he would thrive and put the Home behind him.

And the deaths had subsided to a more natural ratio.

With that niggling thought, another chill skittered down her spine. Was it really happening again? Or could he be right? Nothing but a wicked coincidence designed by a higher power to chase him from his home?

Or something even more sinister? Did he still see the dark angels? Did he bring them with him?

Dangerous territory to believe in such things, but once the thought erupted, the image followed. Him, as a child, leading a troop of dark entities through the halls to hover around the terminally ill. And speed up the natural order on occasion? She could almost imagine him, with his empty voice bidding his minions to hasten the process, either to offer relief to one of his favorite residents. Or order the cessation of those he feared.

Too readily, she recalled at least one of the fellows in that series of deaths fifteen years ago. If Kip had truly hastened Mr. Hammond's departure by whatever means, she couldn't honestly blame him. If evil existed in human form, then Hammond qualified, a wicked man in his thriving years, a monster in his decline. Not likely anyone minded when that devil had departed. Staff, residents, one precocious little boy … even visitors weren't safe from his abuse, but kicking him out wasn't an option for Marilyn. Anyone who needed to know surely understood the concessions necessary to keep the nation safe. After all, Whistlebrook had always posed a haven, if not a safe harbor for lies and deceit.

Maudlin. She'd become maudlin in her advancing years. Or was it safer to be sidetracked than to think about the last several hours?

Residents were dying. Three in one evening, and she had the benefit of knowing this time, Kippen James Patterson wasn't guilty. A blessing and a curse, that knowledge. So many things might have been different.

She should just reach out to him. Approach him directly and let him deal with ordeal, but in the next instant, she knew. He'd destroy the Home. She had no doubts he would ruin the Home. Destruction. He made his living crushing small companies, and by his standard, Whistlebrook was small change. With a pen stroke or more likely, just a phone call, he could level the Home and walk away.

Tomorrow. Tomorrow, he would receive the option to walk away, and by his own words, that remained his intention.

A tear slid down her cheek, tickling. She brushed absently at the trail and blinked against the sting in her eyes. No regrets. Her only regret was that she hadn't thought of this sooner. If she'd brought him here five or even ten years ago? She would have been dealing with a child. He was a man now, and not one to be trifled with.

The Undertaker. She'd heard that nickname years ago, and it still traveled in some circles.

The sound interrupted, a soft, unnatural sound issuing from the console barely visible in the deep shadows across the room. A series of lighted buttons glowed within the darkness, each one designated by numbers, and the master copy remained inside her mind's eye. In a fleeting instant, she identified the placement—a device recently installed within the private suite in the administration wing. Distantly, the soft sound barely reached the receiver, but her heart ached suddenly to realize the sound came from his room, his childhood room. As much joy as sorrow touched her. A stifled breath, a started sob. A genuine emotion. He was as near to sobbing as he might ever have been. For the death of Marilyn Patterson? Against everything she'd heard over the past several days, this sound, on the heels of destruction a short time ago, offered a glimmer of hope. Perhaps, he still felt something for his mother, and by extension, the others in his trust. At least, if he left now, he wouldn't depart encased in ice. He felt. Deeply. And now, the healing could begin.

Killing Marilyn Patterson posed as the only solution. And the right decision. Maybe now, he could settle down and find a nice young woman, someone like that lovely Miss Mulden whose voice whispered like honey through the fine-tuned speakers. A pity she was engaged, although if he stayed around, undoubtedly, he could see that changed.

No. He couldn't remain. Once he departed, the danger would pass—for the residents, and for him. Whatever this specter of death to follow him—

The image blasted into her mind's eye, illuminated as if a bomb dropped from her psyche. A single dull bulb dangled from the massive oak beams at the bottom of the steep staircase. Too clearly, even in the faulty light, the black sturdy cloth appeared crumpled and rumpled in an odd heap on the cement floor. Brittle hands jutted from dull white lace at the ends of spindly arms twisted under a more spindly body. The sturdy black shoes, tipped at unnatural angles from below the skirt, and the sensible black hose barely contrasted with the cloth. Stiff gray strands shrouded the narrow face, the hairstyle befitting an old maid of another era, braided and circling the crown. With the hair pulled taut at the scalp, the natural craters that afflicted the temples and forehead smoothed the familiar gray face. Pale blue orbs wide, struck by surprise, stared upward at a twisted angle, glowing under the dull single bulb. A vivid black stain spread on the gray cement of the basement floor, shrouding Mrs. Brigg's small head.

'Mommma!'

Jolted by the child's cry from the past, she shuddered from head to heel, clasping her arms tighter at her breasts as if to thwart the whirlwind raging through her. Terror. She knew as much terror now as she'd suffered twenty-five years ago when finding the ancient woman crumpled, dead, at the base of the rickety cellar steps. Kip had been no more than five or six when that wicked old woman had met her fate. Barely six. No dark angels had shrouded that ancient. An accident. Just one of many accidents.

Thank God, he was leaving. Once and for all, he needed to leave the dying behind him. He needed to return to the sun and surf, his flighty blonds, and high finance. Whistlebrook wasn't a Home for all seasons as an old Irishman had once professed. It was a Home for mourning, and it was high time Kip Patterson closed the album and learned to live.

She had no doubts that he would board the first flight out after the Will was finally read the next day, and God's speed to him. Finally, once and for all, she could close the book on Whistlebrook, too, and perhaps learn to live as well.

In Mourning

Turn the page for a sneak peek at Book Two!

In Mourning:

Accusations From The Grave

*F*uneral!

That single word erupted in Kip Patterson's mind, resounding under an instant whirlwind of confusion. His focus cleared, his thoughts twisted as a shadowed collage of yellowed pictures, fading and peeling, came into focus in his line of sight. Images from his childhood. Alone in his windowless, childhood room, he'd cut and pasted these faces and pictures on every sallow blue wall. Directly in front of him, a magnificent white—yellowed—stallion reared against a midnight sky; its white mane thrown across the front wheel of a red bicycle; its front hooves landing upon the prow of a speedboat. The boat ran over a child's face, obliterating the soft chin. A man smiling around the butt of a cigarette rose from the bicycle's banana seat as if mounted on a wall plaque. On and on, the scenes of his childhood flowed, and the sight of a hearse near the ceiling brought him full circle.

A funeral.

His bedroom. His childhood bedroom. Not his immense bedroom with an incredible view of the Pacific Ocean through an entire wall of floor-to-ceiling windows. His home now stood on a ridge above the shore. Rather than curtains, living emerald vines rose at either side of the windows, creating an illusion of a forest. A scent of earth and hibiscus woke him, more by its absence. The crafted scent of potpourri didn't mask the musty, familiar smell filling his lungs.

Automated, Kip untangled himself from a blanket, one brought from the recliner in the next room. He still wore his jeans and flannel shirt, both disheveled. In a splotch of lamplight from the living room, he found his shoes resting neatly at the bottom of his bed, and with a lucid flash of the previous evening, he knew he hadn't removed his own shoes.

So, which kind soul had braved his insanity to remove his shoes and cover him?

At the sight of JD Mulden, just another face from the past, dozing on the recliner, a magazine lying open about to slide off his lap, Kip smirked and nearly huffed a laugh. Good old JD. A real friend, not letting the mouse out of the trap this late in the game. For the past four days, the illusion of lasting friendship had sustained them, but the game had ended with a phone call. JD, former ally and only friend of the Prince of Whistlebrook, had posed as a Colorado Forest Ranger when, in fact, he was a DEA agent in league with the Justice Department to hang a certain entrepreneur. For what exactly, Kip hadn't discovered, but he could guess with one too many government contracts under his belt.

Silently, Kip collected his garment bag, carrying it with him into the communal bathroom, and remembering to lock the door to avoid another odd encounter. Flashing a thought of a stranger, an attractive, brunette stranger holding a towel as he stood dripping outside the shower door, he shook his head, stifling a smirk. Only in Whistlebrook Nursing Home, his childhood haunt, could a fellow run headlong into a stranger while tending to his personal ministrations.

Before stepping into the shower, he glanced at his watch, verifying 9:05—hopefully 9:05 a.m., although he hadn't passed a window yet to confirm the time of day. Poised momentarily, he identified the distant hum of activity from industrial appliances to copy machines and typewriters.

Office hours had begun. A.M., then. And in another hour, Mr. Calfactor would take his final ride.

Showering and dressing quickly, Kip aligned his schedule for the day's activities. First, the funeral. Naturally. He couldn't possibly leave Whistlebrook without attending one more funeral. After which, he would return and collect his bags—along with the dancers and hats as his mother's pre-postmortem diddy had suggested.

Bullshit. He'd lived without his hat collection, and he would take only the Wallendorf figurine with him. He could take his bags to the official reading of the Will, and head for the airport from John Madison's law offices.

Passing through the broken door of his suite, he fleetingly recalled shattering the knob plate under a quick kick last evening. The old wood hadn't held up to his moment of madness, but then, he'd mastered his talent for destruction.

Already amused, Kip dropped his garment bag onto the nearest chair and caught JD's start, meeting his gaze. "Sleep well?"

"Shit, I must have conked out," Mulden said quietly, and his stark gaze intensified. "Are uh...? How you feeling today?"

"Fine. You?"

Tense, JD studied him, trying to read through his vacant grin. "What happened last night, Kip? Why did you blow?"

"Ask the sun why it shines, JD," Kip answered and glanced about the room before focusing on Mulden. "There's a closet full of hats in that room. Take them if you want them. The dancers—aside from the one under the dome—take them and give them to your sister—"

"Kip," JD interrupted soberly. "I don't think you're thinking this out—"

"On the contrary, JD. I have," he said simply. "What you don't take will become the property of the new owners as of 4 p.m. Frankly, there's a small fortune in this room, and the new administration will likely trash them." Looking into Mulden's troubled gaze, Kip commented, "Our paths shouldn't cross again, JD, but thank you for being here."

"What the hell does that mean? Shouldn't cross?"

The scrambling device rested in his pocket in the guise of a transistor radio, compliments of Frank Culver—another of the late, great Marilyn Patterson's minions. Palming the contraption in his pocket, he engaged the on switch. His gaze unwavering, his voice lowered an octave so it wouldn't be overheard through the door. "Do not cross me, JD. Accept that as sound advice from someone who does—occasionally—enjoy skiing in Aspen."

Mulden's wheels were spinning, his gaze held steady. "How long have you known?" he asked carefully.

"Long enough to appreciate your talent, my old friend," Kip answered evenly and started toward the door as JD pushed swiftly afoot. Halted, Kip studied Mulden's tense gaze. "You'll find some plastic covering the hats. Use it to wrap the dancers. I'll send someone with a box—"

"Fuck those dancers. We need to talk," JD stated.

"My dear old *friend*, there's absolutely nothing we need to discuss," Kip said simply, his focus abstract. "I've been screwed by government whores before. I just hope they're paying you handsomely for services rendered. I certainly enjoyed every second of it. Now, if you'll excuse me? I have a funeral to attend."

"What happened to you, Kip?"

"Seems to me, I could ask the same of you, JD, but frankly, it doesn't concern me. Stay out of my social circle and I'll stay out of yours."

"I didn't lie to you," Mulden said evenly. "I came here as a friend—"

"JD," Kip interrupted, looking into the tense hazel eyes. "You're fired. I'll see that Carolyn prepares your severance pay—"

"I don't want your fucking money!" Mulden snapped. "I didn't stay here because I was being paid—"

"Oh, that's right. Severance pay might look like a payoff. Too bad, really, but I suppose you'll have to settle for the hats or nothing at all for your time and trouble. Now, if you'll excuse me—"

At the start of motion, Kip's hand flew, blocking the grasp, catching Mulden's wrist. Without a conscious thought, Kip stepped and twisted, rolling Mulden over his back into the center of the floor. Not losing an instant, he followed. As startled as JD, Kip halted on Mulden's chest. Fifteen years ago, he wouldn't have stood a chance at besting JD Mulden, wrestler, weightlifter, All-Star sports material. Holding JD's neck in a firm grip between his thumb and forefinger, Kip glared into the startled hazel eyes, his own the color of ash. Mulden knew the position, knew enough to remain very still. "I didn't spend those three years in a sanitarium, JD," he said quietly. "But it was a sanctuary of a nature with few distractions, and I'm not the docile little introvert you once knew. Now, be nice and sign the register when you leave within the next thirty minutes. I don't think you'd like to explain to your superiors why you've been arrested for trespassing. Go quietly, and they need only know that your mission was a failure. Create any problems for me, and I can guarantee you'll need a new career. I can be a real bastard when I'm angry, and I am angry."

"You always—were—too—damned—fast," JD struggled with his words. His muscles had relaxed into the twisted position. "Let's talk, damn it! You're—In—Trouble. You need—my help!"

"Goodbye, JD. Be gone when I get back." In a swift, easy motion, Kip found the pressure point to short-circuit Mulden's nervous system. His hazel eyes widened for an instant and rolled back in the socket; his head lulled. Releasing his grip, Kip pushed onto his feet, muttering a curse. He really hadn't meant that end.

Stepping over JD's feet, Kip picked up his black brimmed hat, passed through the door, and closed it behind him. Kitchen clatter and business machines converged in the hall; a subtle lurch at the thought of food veered him toward the offices. He strode into the secretarial pool in time to see Angie slice her finger, utter a short breath, and pop her index finger in her mouth. A paper cut. Business as usual.

Carolyn glanced at Angie indifferently, then shifted her attention to him with a quick, worried smile. Her soft blue eyes darted down and up; her smile brightened, "Good morning, Mr. Patterson."

Angie's stricken gaze darted to Carolyn, then Kip, before she snatched her bleeding finger from her mouth and grabbed the sheet of paper from her typewriter roll.

"You spoke to Bill," Kip realized, looking to Carolyn.

She nodded with a bemused shine in her eyes. "He's informed me that we are currently under a new administration, sir. Is there anything I can do for you?"

Drop the 'sir' for starters. "Actually, yes. In about ten minutes, send a couple of boxes to my room and see that a security guard escorts JD Mulden to his car after he packs whatever he wants to take with him. Any messages?"

She glanced down, sliding three switchboard sheets from under the phone and handing them to him.

Morgan had called last evening; the block print indicated Frank Culver's handwriting. Father Jordan—8:30 a.m. M.B.—Marsh Baxel—9:15 a.m. 5:15 a.m. California time? He would return Marsh's call from a payphone. His gaze shifted to the window, half expecting to see a blizzard through the sheer curtains. Looking to Carolyn, he asked, "How are the roads?"

"Just wet. It's almost 40 degrees," she said and smiled more at his unbidden disgust. "You California boys just don't appreciate a heat wave."

"Personally, I'll take fifteen-foot waves any day," he admitted. "Tell Mrs. Feeney, I'll see her around lunch. Imagine Bill's already come and gone?"

She nodded as her eyes clouded with a thought. "I heard things got out of hand last night. Are you all right, hon?"

"Fine," he said absently, feeling strangely numb as he turned and strode into the alcove, passing into the office. He entered only as far as the coat rack, where he vaguely recalled leaving his long cashmere coat. At least he'd remembered to pack a few winter threads when hustling to catch his flight less than a week ago.

Marilyn Patterson was gone. Truly gone.

Pulling his coat on, he stood momentarily, fumbling in his coat pockets for his keys while scanning the office in the morning light. The room still felt cold. Empty. As empty as he felt as he uttered, "Goodbye, mother."

Automated, he passed through the second exit door from the office, avoiding the secretarial pool, and avoiding the kitchen a second time by cutting through the lobby.

Fifteen years later, and his body still reacted to the smells coming from the kitchen. . .

One after another, those funerals had piled up. Six of them that Kip knew of. Six of his friends. Except he hadn't considered Mr. Hammond a friend. As if cobwebs stirred in an attic, Kip remembered a distant internal battle of grief and relief when he stood at Mr. Hammond's casket. Hammond had been one mean old man in his latent prime, never missing a chance to swing his damned walking stick, and later his flat hand.

Too swiftly, Kip recalled standing at another gravesite, and it was the face of Denton McDaniels in that crowd. God, that same timeframe. One of the *away* funerals, he recalled, but no name accompanied his thought. One of the special cases. Those years, those events were too cluttered, but Kip remembered meeting the classy blond-haired man, shaking the man's hand, looking into the pale blue eyes that had appeared so stricken with grief. Not grief, but shock, Kip realized fifteen years too late for it to matter. Denton McDaniels had recognized him, had said something, asked something.

Marilyn Patterson's son?

"Damn it," Kip uttered and yanked open the car door, sliding into the driver's seat. Denton McDaniels. On two—three separate occasions, Kip corrected while flashing another memory glance of the Basilica at St. John's Academy. Denton McDaniels had stood in the shadows, in the gathering to witness his bastard's Baptism. Marilyn hadn't even bothered attempting to make the trip for that most auspicious occasion, but old Denton had flown in from Boston.

Ironic, fifteen years ago, that might have meant something to an astute, introverted teenager. Having some connection, however remote, to another living soul who'd think enough of him to make a trip, to stand in witness? One of the Brothers had stood as his Godfather. One of the nuns had stood as his Godmother. Strangers. Always strangers and stand-in relatives. Having a father would have been different. A novelty.

If his mother's third letter could be believed, McDaniels was, in part, responsible for that seminary sojourn. Must have cost him a bundle to pull that off, getting a non-denominational accepted into that holy fraternity. Kip had spent hours of private instruction, in addition to the required classes. Before the end of his sophomore year, he'd learned enough to be Christened into the Catholic faith, and Denton McDaniels had stood in witness, nearly lost in shadows toward the rear of the church, maybe hoping to be seen and recognized. More likely, hoping to see Marilyn Patterson, but that dear lady had too much on her agenda to be worried about a son's spiritual growth.

Mechanically, Kip navigated the Buick, making a three-point turn at the kitchen dock and following the lane to the highway. Always something had taken precedence—just as this alleged father seemed to hover in the shadows on at least three separate occasions. How many other times had Denton McDaniels stood in the shadows? That funeral was the beginning—that was the day Denton McDaniels had learned that his affair had borne fruit. And five weeks later, Marilyn called him. In desperation?

For the latest news and updates from
J. K. Grueber
visit:
Jkgrueber.com

"Thank you for reading!" J. K. Grueber